Dear Reader,

Every year I fall in love with a different man and I become a woman obsessed. I lie awake at night. I fantasize.

My husband has long since made peace with this state of affairs. He tolerates my affliction and pities the objects of my desire. Because even though I love them ferociously, I have no compunction putting the heroes in my novels to the test. The world I create for them is painted in darkened shades where the present is prisoner to the past, where ghosts walk with ease among the living and emotions are extravagant and grand: hate, revenge, despairing love. The villains in this universe are often brilliant and show no mercy.

I write suspense novels. I like scaring my readers and take great pains to put my characters in situations of inspired menace. But at the heart of my novels is always a love story. In writing *Windwalker*, I was attracted by the idea of two people searching for each other over the ages, but their lives never connecting—just as an amputee may feel in his nerves the ghost of a missing limb, so they know that out there is someone who can make them complete. Will they manage to defy the danger and obstacles facing them in this life in order to find one another?

Every author's ultimate aim is to draw her readers into the world she has created and to seduce them into lingering a while. So now, as authors have done over the ages, may I extend to you a simple invitation:

Follow me . . .

Windwalker

Natasha Mostert

tor romance

A TOM DOHERTY ASSOCIATES BOOK
NEW YORK

This is a work of fiction. All the characters and events portrayed in this book are either products of the author's imagination or are used fictitiously.

WINDWALKER

Editcd by Anna Genoese

website: www.natashamostert.com

A Tor Book
Published by Tom Doherty Associates, LLC
175 Fifth Avenue
New York, NY 10010

www.tor.com

Tor® is a registered trademark of Tom Doherty Associates, LLC.

ISBN 0-765-34929-9
EAN 978-0765-34929-3

First edition: April 2005

Printed in the United States of America

0 9 8 7 6 5 4 3 2 1

Acknowledgments

WINDWALKER REQUIRED SPECIALIZED KNOWLEDGE of photography and deepwater cave diving. Several people gave freely of their time and I am deeply grateful for their generous assistance. Remaining errors are, of course, my responsibility alone.

Many thanks to John Wildgoose, prince among professional photographers, who taught me to mind my f-stops and who even managed to make me understand the difference between "push" and "pull." Thank you to John Bevan, who not only critiqued my work, but also placed his library of diving books at my disposal. I am hugely indebted to two terrific guys: Clive Gardener and Duncan Price. Their input with regard to the technical aspects of the underwater sequences was crucial as was their willingness to discuss with me the risks and rewards of cave diving and the special breed of men and women who practice the sport. I was also privileged to receive assistance from Theo Schoemans, president of the Namibian Underwater Federation and veteran of more than 4,000 dives, who shared with me his formidable knowledge of Namibian geology.

Thanks to Robert Gottlieb, my agent and his associate, Scott Miller, for their hard work on my behalf. Special thanks to my editor, Anna Genoese, who possesses that finest of editing skills: a firm hand but a light touch.

A special thank you to Gaynor Rupert, who read through the manuscript with a generous heart and an eagle eye. Thanks to Chris Mostert for finding the time in the midst of a punishing exam schedule to advise me on the medical aspects of the plot. Thanks to fellow scribes Dianne Hofmeyr and Sonja Lewis for their friendship and feedback. Thanks to Catherine Gull, a good friend and talented reader.

Sadly, like most writers, I lead a dispiritingly sedentary life. My gratitude to the fantastic staff at KX Gym UK for its efforts to keep me from turning into a slug. A special thank you to Carlos Andrade, gifted kickboxer and trainer. Even though he is usually shouting at me to stop punching like a muppet, he also manages to get me focused and back on track whenever I suffer from keyboard overload!

A final word of thanks goes to my family. I firmly believe a special place in heaven is set aside for the spouses and close relatives of authors. They have to put up with our mood swings (unpredictable) and our insecurities (multitudinous). Nobody does it better than my husband, Frederick. His love gives me wings and cushions me when I fall. My mother, Hantie, is first reader, cheerleader, and an amazing source of inspiration. My brothers, Stefan and Frans, can always be relied on for words of encouragement and bracing common sense. My mother-in-law, Joan, is endlessly supportive of my work.

I have quoted from three poems in this novel: "Song" by Sir John Suckling, "Love and Sleep" by Algernon Charles

Swinburne, and "On a dark night" by the sixteenth-century Spanish poet St. John of the Cross, translation by John Frederick Nims. The prose quotation is from Jack London's Call of the Wild.

*

I dedicate this book to cave divers everywhere.
And to Frederick, my love in this life and the next.

* * *

*You may know the characters are absolutely doomed to some
fate, but the characters themselves must be allowed to hope.*
—Bruce Chatwin in conversation with
Nicholas Shakespeare

Note

WINDWALKER **IS SET IN** part in Kepler's Bay, an imaginary town wedged in between the cold Atlantic Ocean and the windswept dunes of the Namib Desert. Anyone who has ever visited Namibia will recognize in Kepler's Bay many similarities to the tiny port of Luderitzbucht and the adjacent ghost town of Kolmanskop. I have certainly drawn inspiration for my book from these two places, and have considered carefully whether I shouldn't use them as the actual setting for my story. In the end I decided to create my own town, Kepler's Bay. It is a composite of a number of typical Namibian towns: tiny, wind-scoured outposts clinging to the edge of the world.

The decision solved a number of problems. In real life, Kolmanskop and the surrounding area are sealed off and form part of the so-called Sperrgebiet, or "prohibited land." Anyone who dares cross its barren wastes is considered a potential diamond smuggler and will find himself in danger of criminal prosecution. In my book this would have posed great difficulties for my hero, who not only made his home in one of the deserted ghost towns, but wanders through the desert sands of the southern Namib at will. So in the world I've created, the artificial barriers of Diamond Area No. 1 do not exist. Still, Kepler's Bay owes much of its eerie charm to the port of Luderitzbucht and the deserted hamlet of Kolmanskop, where the ghosts walk even during the day.

Prologue

HE WAS LOOKING UP at the stars, eyes wide open and shiny. The expression on his face was ecstasy. His arms were thrown wide as though he were about to hug the sky to his chest.

His brother.

For a moment the man hesitated, wondering if he should try to close the staring eyes, smooth the pale lids over the curved eyeballs. But as he looked down at his own hands they were clenched into fists and try as he might, he was unable to open his fingers.

The grass here was wet and sweet-smelling and the fragrant wisteria with its drooping white petals looked like a bride. The shaft of a sundial gleamed palely in the moonlight. A pleasant spot, this. He had always thought so. Turning his head slowly, he looked at the house with its smooth windows. Behind the glass panes there was only dark and quiet, the rooms not empty, but their occupants asleep. The house would be silent inside except for the secret sounds of slumber. Soft breathing, maybe the ticking of a bedside clock.

He looked back at the figure in front of him. How pale the thin face with its ecstatic, frozen eyes. How still those long limbs. Only the fine hair at the hollow of the temples moved ever so slightly in the soft breeze. But the arms flung wide seemed almost carefree, stretched out in a gesture of abandon. A wristwatch gleamed gold at the edge of a snow white cuff. Dickie boy had always had expensive tastes.

Something moved at the edge of his peripheral vision and he whipped around, his heart beating wildly. He stared into the darkness. He sensed the presence of someone—something. For a moment he waited tensely, the adrenaline burning through his blood like acid. But nothing moved. No shadow detached itself from the surrounding blackness.

Nerves. And now he was aware of the cold. The knees of his pants were wet where the moisture from the grass had seeped through. His arm was suddenly on fire where he touched and even in the darkness he could see the black stain of his own blood.

He got to his feet and without a backward glance he started walking. At first he walked slowly, without any haste. But as he crossed the wide, manicured lawn he stretched his stride. By the time he reached the edge of the mile-long avenue of trees, he was hurrying.

The road stretched straight ahead for what seemed like a long, long way. The moon was directly overhead. The trunks of the beech trees on both sides of him threw slim black shadows across the path in front of his feet. For a moment he stopped and looked back over his shoulder. And the house with its tall chimney stacks, its beautiful bow-fronted windows, and the three pointed gables had never seemed to him more lovely. The stone walls glowing white in the light of the moon. The windows glittering darkly. A house serene and dreaming. A house at peace.

But as he watched, a light suddenly stabbed from an upstairs window. He waited, his blood rushing through his veins, thrumming inside his ears. And then yet another light—like a warning, an alarm—turned the darkness yellow.

He started running, his footsteps loud. The wind had sprung up and the branches of the trees danced. The wind chilled the back of his neck and the sweat in his armpits felt cold. But he had almost reached the end of the avenue and he could see the elaborately curlicued ironwork of the gate in front of him.

As he curled his fingers around one of the iron bars, he thought for a terrified moment that the gate was locked. He could feel his lips drawing away from his teeth in a snarl, and inside the cage of his chest were fist blows of rage and fear. But then—slowly, ponderously—the gate started to swing toward him.

He stepped through the narrow opening and turned around. In the distance the house was ablaze with light. Light was pouring from every window. Light was pouring through the front door. The door stood wide open and a long tongue of light licked across the stone steps.

A house in distress.

A house in a state of mortal sin.

WITH HIS BACK TO the sundial, a few steps away from the wisteria walkway, a shadow shook itself free from the darkness. For a moment the man who had stood there so motionless peered in the direction of the black wrought-iron gate. The gate was half open, but the fleeing figure of the killer was no longer visible. He had disappeared.

The watcher glanced up at the house. Light from the windows was falling onto the lawn, the yellow glow not quite reaching the dead body spread-eagled on the moist grass only a few yards away from him.

He would have liked to take a closer look, but he heard voices. He had no desire to answer questions, to describe what he had witnessed. The very idea filled him with panic. It was time to leave. But unlike the murderer, he would not be able to escape through the gate. There was no possibility of walking down the avenue of trees without being spotted.

Swiftly—the voices were drawing near—he turned in the direction of the woods, which rose tall and dark at the rear of the house. There was no clear path through the woods and the terrain among the trees was rough, but he had no choice.

He had reached the edge of the woods. Here the moonlight still silvered the leaves of the trees. A much deeper darkness awaited him inside the dense forest of moss-furred tree trunks. A dank, bitter smell rose from the earth. He shivered. His features, blanched by the white light, showed indecision.

The next moment he stepped from light into darkness and was swallowed up by the night.

One

SHE MUST HAVE TAKEN a wrong turn. She should have been there by now. Justine glanced at her watch and then at the road map on the car seat beside her. She had been making good time, but since leaving the highway, she had found herself lost in a maze of country lanes bordered by towering hedges, tiny villages with evil roundabouts, and roads without names. People living in the country didn't need road signs, of course: they knew exactly where they were. And no doubt it was considered part of the charm of life in the English countryside. But a bloody nuisance for visitors all the same. She would have to stop and ask for directions.

She found a parking space in front of a small corner shop. As she slammed the car door shut, she could see the girl behind the till watching her through a window partly obscured by flyers and multicolored stickers, her bored gaze taking in the battered, orange-colored MG, the boxes piled high on the narrow backseat. When Justine entered the shop, the girl pulled a long piece of gum from her mouth. After looking at it intently for a few seconds she skillfully reeled it back with the flick of a pink tongue.

Justine spread open the map on the countertop. "I'm looking for Paradine Park."

"Yeah?" A bubble popped slowly and the girl's thin plucked eyebrows rose only the tiniest fraction. Around her neck she wore a silver chain with the word 'Angelface' in flowing script.

"Could you direct me?"

An elaborate sigh. A shrug. Leaning forward, the girl indicated with a finger that showed a graceful half-moon of dirt under the nail. "You should have taken the turning two miles back. See, you have to drive through Ainstey and then continue for another mile and a half. It's right here." She stabbed her finger at the map.

"Thanks." Justine straightened and looked around the tiny store. In the trunk of her car she already had a box of groceries, but maybe she should take advantage of this opportunity to supplement her rations. She pulled a box of cereal from the shelves, a packet of sugar. A carton of long-life milk. A bag filled with some sickly looking pink doughnuts. For a moment she hesitated before gesturing at the shelves behind the counter. "And a bottle of Johnnie Walker."

The girl rang up the total and watched as Justine pulled her wallet from the pocket of her jeans.

"Nice shirt." For the first time there was some life in her voice.

Justine looked down at the front of her long-sleeved T-shirt. "LIFE'S A BITCH. THEN YOU DIE." The letters were faded from continued washing. She was surprised at the girl's enthusiasm. Even for the country this slogan must be pretty old. But she should probably reciprocate. So she said, "Nice chain."

The girl touched the silver-plated lettering around her neck. "Yeah. 'Angelface'—that's what my boyfriend calls me."

"Sweet." And not at all apt, Justine thought as she peeled off a twenty-pound note.

As the girl took the money she said, "No use going that way, you know."

"Which way?"

"Paradine Park. The house is empty."

"I know. I'm the new caretaker."

"Yeah?" The girl looked impressed. "Totally cool place, that."

"Oh?"

"They used to throw some wicked acid house parties down there. But they're going to turn it into a hotel now."

"Spa."

"Whatever." The girl shrugged resentfully. "Real shame, anyway." She banged the till drawer shut and stared at Justine. "So you'll be staying there by yourself?"

"Why do you ask?"

"Just curious." Her voice was sullen. "Maybe not such a brilliant idea, that's all I'm saying."

Justine waited. The girl popped a defiant bubble. "Lonely down there."

"Well, thanks for the concern. And the directions." Justine placed the plastic bag on her hip. "Cheers." As she left the shop she could feel the girl's eyes following her. Sliding behind the steering wheel, she glanced back. Angelface was watching her with a decidedly odd expression. Then, with startling abruptness, she turned her face away.

But at least her directions seemed reliable. Ainstey was small: rows of postcard-pretty sandstone cottages, a truly ancient-looking parish church with a splendid tower, a cluster of modest-looking shops. And barely a mile farther a neat sign informed her that Paradine Park lay to the right.

It was only just past five, but already the sky was acquiring a pewter sheen. There was sunshine on the green fields, still and golden, but the shadows were long. The wind bit at her cheekbones and nose. In another few weeks she'd have to put up the MG's top. Summer was coming to an end.

In the distance a dog barked once. The smell of smoke

and burning leaves hung in the air. She drove past a paddock and two horses, one gray, one black, galloped away on soundless hooves. And now a high sandstone wall was on her right, cutting off her view. She suspected that this wall formed the lower boundary of Paradine Park and indeed, the road suddenly ended and she turned the car through an impressive pair of open gates. Her breath caught in her throat at the beauty of the long avenue stretching out before her.

The road was narrow and ran straight and true for at least a mile. Beech trees stood on either side of the lane, their trunks slim and graceful, and through the branches she could see fragments of sky and racing clouds. There was a sense of both light and dark here: darkness close among the trees, sun streaking down through dry leaves and flashing bright at the edge of her peripheral vision. But it was the house that made this place seem not quite real. Small at first, growing ever larger as she drove toward it, it was set back from the avenue of trees by a blackish green splash of lawn and it seemed like something from a dream, a dream filled with wonder.

The walls were of sandstone, honey in color, soft on the eye. The regularity and symmetry of fenestration spoke vaguely of Palladian ideals. Three pointed gables, flanked by solid chimney stacks, marked the middle section of the house. The ends of the house were anchored by the fine curves of two bow-fronted windows, the sun reflecting off their glass panes with a terrible brightness. Behind the house the woods rose tall and dark.

She left the avenue of trees behind her, turning the car into the wide driveway with a sputter of gravel beneath the wheels. Another car was already parked at the front door. A tall, prematurely bald man was standing on the shallow stone steps. In his hand he held a leather briefcase. He was looking aggrieved and glanced pointedly at his watch.

The disapproving mouth and sour expression raised her hackles and compelled her to slow her movements and take her time. His impatience was unmistakable, but after killing the engine she stretched deliberately and unclipped the seat buckle without any haste. Opening her handbag she extracted a lipstick and carefully colored her lips. Then she slowly drew a comb through her hair. By the time she got out of the car, the estate agent's irritation was palpable and he looked more than ever as though he had bitten down on a lemon.

"I was just about to leave. I didn't think you would be coming anymore."

"I took a wrong turn."

He held out his hand reluctantly. "Edwards."

"Justine Callaway." His hand was bony, the fingers slack.

"Is your husband following you?"

Husband? For a moment her mind went blank, then she recovered. "He'll be along later. Something came up at work." She smiled sweetly. "He'll be out here soon."

"I hope so." His eyes lingered on her ringless hands, then turned suddenly malicious. "The owners stipulated very clearly that they preferred a couple to take care of the place."

"Of course." She held his gaze, but she was suddenly tense. She hadn't planned on having to face an interrogation this soon. When she had answered the advertisement for caretaker, she had lied easily about her marital status. And Mrs. Cavendish's references were glowing, bless her heart. Especially considering they had never met and the old lady was only doing her mother a favor. She should probably feel guilty for lying but truth to be told, she was simply relieved that there hadn't been more of a background check. It was explained to her that the previous caretaker—a single guy in his twenties—had used the house as his personal playpen. A couple was therefore considered to be more suitable for the job, a husband and wife team undaunted by the idea of living on the property itself. Not too young that they would indulge in wild parties, not too old that they couldn't reliably take care of such a big house.

She suddenly realized that Edwards was staring at her.

Following his gaze, she saw his eyes fixed on her chest. She was braless and it was chilly.

She lifted her head and drew her lips away from her teeth in a narrow smile. Keeping her eyes locked with his, she deliberately pulled the T-shirt provocatively close against her body so that it stretched taut across her breasts. As she walked past him, she made sure to pass by him so closely that he had to step aside quickly, surprised. Climbing the steps slowly, moving her hips with an exaggerated swing, she glanced back over her shoulder at his expression. She had unnerved him. He was clearly ill at ease. Good. Asshole.

At the top of the steps she paused. The porch area had not been swept in a long time and was matted over with dirt and dried leaves. Terra-cotta planters in the shape of Ali Baba pots stood on either side of two Ionic pillars. Dead geraniums drooped over the edges. The front door was tall with heavy fielded panels in vertical rows. It stood slightly ajar, and through the gap a weak ray of sunlight fell inward. The light was so pale it barely pierced the gloom, allowing her only to see that the floor was made of black-and-white marble with a finely executed pattern of squares.

But as she stood there, the sunlight at her back, the half-open door in front of her, the thought came to her mind that the house she was about to enter was weary. This was a house sorrowful at having its solitude disturbed, a place where the rooms must remain unvisited, the windows and doors locked. And she hesitated, feeling like an interloper, a trespasser.

But the next moment Edwards had brushed past her. He stretched out his arm and the door opened wide beneath the weight of his hand.

The hallway into which she stepped would have been magnificent in its day. It still had a splendor to it, despite the maimed fireplace, the graffiti on the walls, the shabbiness of the carpet on the wide steps leading upward. Neglect and vandalism had left their mark, but the ceilings were lofty, the wrought iron filigree of the staircase delicate, and deeply elegant the proportions of the room.

"How long has the house been empty."

"Almost nine years now." Edwards was looking at her warily. She must have really scared him, he was keeping well away from her. Probably afraid she'd pounce.

"That's a long time."

"We did have a caretaker living on the premises last year." Edwards rolled his eyes. "But he had to be booted out. He turned the house into a kind of dance club, even charging for admission. The property suffered considerable damage in the process." Edwards pointed to the ceiling. "We lost a chandelier. Some of the books in the library were destroyed. It finally persuaded the owner to sell. As I'm sure you know, Paradine Park is to be turned into a spa and health facility."

She did know. She also knew that the new owners, Americans, had recently become painfully aware of the muscle of English Heritage when their drawings and proposals for jacuzzis and steam rooms got bogged down in a sanity-destroying maze of permissions and planning applications. Paradine Park dated from 1720 and was listed. The process of gaining the necessary permissions promised to be laborious. In the meantime the house was standing empty; easy prey for vandals and burglars. Ergo, a caretaker was called for. Or rather, caretakers.

Well, here she was. Without the all-important husband to be sure. But maybe she'd be able to keep that knowledge to herself for a while longer. If not—well, she traveled light. It wouldn't be that much trouble to up anchors and go.

"We'll start in the drawing room." Edwards turned a drop handle on one of the two slim inner doors and pushed it open.

As in the case of the hallway, there was a formal grace to the proportions of this room. But it felt cold and held only a few pieces of furniture. An enormous sofa covered in a tea-stained fabric with a pattern of overblown roses faced the fireplace. To one side of it were two wing-backed chairs with the fabric on their arms rubbed thin and shiny. On the other side, a small leaf table, its gilt-stamped, green leather inset now faded and scarred by cigarette burns. Dirt on the windowsills. Ash in the hearth. No rugs on the floor, but a mangy-looking zebra skin with bald spots lay prostrate in front of the fireplace.

The only thing in that room that appeared fresh and without a layer of dust was the painting above the mantelpiece. A painting of a family: father, mother, teenaged girl, and two younger boys. The woman was beautiful in a languid-looking way with fair, upswept hair and almond-shaped, light blue eyes. One slender white hand rested on the shoulder of the boy who was sitting cross-legged in front of her. The resemblance between mother and son was immediate. The boy had a thin, ascetic face and the same pale eyes.

Seated next to the mother was the girl, a teenager. Compared to the wan beauty of her mother, she seemed like a tomboy, her hair cut boyishly short and the frilly blouse she was wearing quite wrong for her. She had obviously inherited her coloring from her father. Burly, with wide shoulders, he had dark hair and eyes, and sported a neat beard. He was the only one of the group standing.

But it was the last member of the group who held Justine's attention. Whereas the other figures seemed posed and rather lifeless, the artist had managed to capture the energy of the second boy, who was also sitting with legs crossed, staring directly out of the canvas. The young face was strangely hard and the wide mouth obstinate. The eyes seemed to follow you wherever you were in the room. And the eyes were remarkable. The eyes were burning.

"Who are they?" She had stopped in front of the picture and was looking up at it. But from this close, the texture of the oil paint seemed coarse and the figures flattened.

"The Buchanans. The original owners." His tone of voice was repressive as though she had no business asking the question.

"And they haven't lived here for nine years."

"No."

"What happened to them?" She could sense he found her persistence irritating.

"All I know is that they left the house very suddenly. Almost overnight." He turned away from her abruptly. "The dining room is through here."

Another large room, this one with a long oval mahogany table and chairs upholstered in Regency stripes. Against the one wall was a heavy-looking ball and claw sideboard. On top of it resided yet another hideous piece of Victoriana: a centerpiece made of tarnished brass, depicting improbable palm trees dripping with glass prisms.

The ceiling in this room was painted. She put her head back and stared up at it. A trio of plump shepherdesses with staffs clutched in dimpled fists, their expressions chocolate-box innocent, smiled down at her. They were huddled together against a fantasy backdrop of light blue sky and white, gilt-edged clouds. A large yellow stain in the middle of the ceiling told of water damage. It had spread across the face of one of the pink-cheeked girls, turning her complexion sallow.

"You're American?" Edwards's voice dropped slightly at the end of the sentence, making the question sound almost like a statement.

"No."

"The accent. I thought—"

"No."

Although it was an easy mistake to make. Her accent confounded even the London cabbies and that took a lot of doing. Her birth certificate stated that she was born in Bromley, Kent: a UK citizen. But of course it said nothing about her childhood and being dragged all over the world in

the wake of peripatetic Sam, her brilliant, exasperating father whose prim demeanor and formal manners masked the
soul of an adventurer. Copenhagen, Tokyo, Sydney, Kuwait
City, and finally New York. The American accent had proved
the most insidious and had turned her vowels slightly liquid.
But in the US they would call her accent English.

She sensed Edwards was waiting for her to volunteer more
information, but she did not feel like indulging his curiosity.

But he tried again. "So where's home?"

Where's home.

For a moment she just stared at him. Where's home. And
she felt almost light-headed all of a sudden, as though he had
struck her a glancing blow. But still, it was an innocent question. Where was home?

Home was where Jonathan was.

But Jonathan was dead.

Edwards was looking at her strangely. And suddenly she
felt immensely tired and the inside of her mouth tasted stale.
She wished he would leave.

She gestured at the door. "Let's finish this, shall we?"

His neck and back stiff and hostile, he walked out of the
room ahead of her. Turning left through a smallish doorway,
he continued down a long passageway leading to the kitchen
area at the back of the house. And now he was talking in
short clipped sentences, his voice curt, explaining about
boilers and generators and keys. She nodded and let his
words flow past her. Tomorrow would be enough time to sort
out all of that.

The kitchen was long, narrow, and primitive, as was so often the case with these grand English houses. But at least it
had a fridge and a fairly modern-looking stove. She opened
a walk-in cupboard and inside were stacks of dusty, gold-
rimmed porcelain plates and crystal glasses with fragile-
looking stems. A blackboard with a stub of chalk hanging
from a piece of string was attached to the inside wall. On it

was scribbled items for a grocery list: cream, salt, truffle oil. Someone had indulged in expensive tastes. In the far corner of the kitchen was a makeshift curtain and she had a glimpse of logs neatly stacked on top of each other and a number of old newspapers piled high.

Leading off the kitchen was a short passage with a low ceiling. At the end of the passage was a narrow door, which she assumed would give access to some kind of larder. But as Edwards opened the door, moving a dusty curtain to one side, she realized it was not the larder after all. She hesitated for a moment, but then stepped past the estate agent who was still holding the door.

This room was one of the reasons she had wanted the job. She had been assured that Paradine Park had a dedicated darkroom. One of the original family members, she was told, had dabbled in photography.

The room was very dirty and had obviously not been used in a long time, but someone had given some real thought to the design. The floor was filthy but the tiles were nonslip. The room was not large but was clearly divided into a wet and a dry zone, and there was a tap and more than enough work-table space. On the lower shelf stood three safelights. There was a clock on the back wall, its hands frozen, and next to it, she was pleased to see, an air inlet. She looked around and found the extractor fan positioned on the wall behind three grimy developing trays. What looked like an old print drum for color was pushed underneath a shelf holding an array of dusty measuring jugs. Against the wall next to the door was a notice-board with a few yellowed newspaper clippings attached to the cork surface with brightly colored tacks.

"Your bedroom is on the top floor," Edwards said impatiently. He had not stepped into the room. In fact, as he looked around him, he seemed repulsed even though there was nothing inherently distasteful about the room. Probably just a feeble attempt to put her in her place.

As they were walking back toward the entrance hall, he waved his hand in the direction of a closed door leading off to the right. "Through there is the library. It holds a valuable collection of books that has already been cataloged and sold. The collection will eventually be crated and shipped to Japan. I trust you will treat the books with care."

She bit back a retort and followed silently as he led the way up the wide central staircase. The crimson carpet underneath her feet was spotted. The wooden balustrade lacked any luster. But when they reached the top landing she stopped and turned around and for a moment she imagined what it must have been like in the days when the house was still alive: the windows sparkling, the brass fittings glowing, the clean smell of polish in the air. And a family would walk down this beautiful sweep of staircase every morning to meet for breakfast under the gaze of three merry beribboned girls floating in a sky that was always blue. A privileged existence, an elegant life lived in an elegant house. A house left to itself almost overnight. What would make one abandon such a house?

"Most of the upstairs rooms in both wings of the house are now unfurnished," Edwards's voice echoed strangely. They were walking down a long corridor past two rows of closed doors. There was no carpet up here, only a stretch of rather nasty-looking maroon linoleum and their footsteps sounded very loud. The passage itself was gloomy, but at the very end of the corridor was a tall arch-topped window and above it an oculus. In the gathering dusk the small round window sat in the wall like a white eye.

"How many rooms in the house?"

"Thirty-one." He permitted himself a small smile. "One for every day of the month. This will be your room." He opened a door and switched on the light.

From what she had seen of the rest of the house, she had expected another sad room showing the ravages of neglect. But the room was a surprise.

It was very large and airy with white painted floorboards

and ivory-colored ceilings. Wallpaper, rather charmingly faded, hugged a white paneled dado with simple moldings. The two bedsteads, the table and its chair, as well as the chest of drawers, were of plain deal and also painted white. On the one bedside table was a small bronze statuette of a cowboy on horseback. Two red honeycombed quilts made a splash of color on the beds and bright blue rugs lay scattered on the floor. The effect was fresh and winsome.

She looked at the wallpaper, the white-painted furniture. "This used to be the nursery?"

He nodded. "No bathroom en suite, you'll notice. The bathroom is at the end of the passage. There are extra blankets and fresh linen in the cupboards and you'll find a phone next to the bed. The phone bill will be forwarded to you at the end of the month."

She walked over to the window. The view from here was to the back of the house, not the front lawns and its avenue of trees. This window looked out onto a large courtyard.

"What's in there?" She pointed to the single-story detached building on the other side of the courtyard directly opposite. It was built of the same sandstone as the rest of the house but seemed to be a later addition. A trim clock tower sat squarely in the middle of the roof. In the uncertain light the clock face was merely a pale off-white disc against a slate gray sky and she was unable to make out the time.

"That building's now used mostly for storage space. The owners . . ."

His voice trailed off and she turned her head to look at him inquiringly. His eyebrows were high against his forehead and his eyes were fixed on the hand with which she had pulled the drapes to one side. She had stretched out her arm to its full length and the sleeve of her shirt had moved down to expose her wrist.

Keeping her eyes on his shocked face, she smoothed the sleeve until the cuff reached the palm of her hand. "You were saying?"

He blinked, coughed. "Storage space. Yes. Storage. Many of the original pieces of furniture are stored in those rooms." His eyes flicked down to her wrist again, but then he pulled himself together. "Speaking of storage—the closet over there and that chest of drawers are for your own use."

She followed him as he walked out the door and swiftly down the passage and stairway. In the entrance hall he picked up a manila envelope from a mahogany console table. "In here are the keys for the house. Most of them are labeled. May I remind you that the gardeners come in on Fridays." He reached inside his jacket and extracted his wallet. "My card."

He was looking at his watch now, resentfully mumbling something about traffic and the rush hour and suddenly—for a brief moment—she felt sorry for him as he stood there with his thin hair combed across a gleaming scalp, his smudged glasses perched on top of his button nose. His collar seemed limp and the suit ill-fitting. A grotty job this, and now she'd made him late for supper. She pictured a complaining wife at home, truculent teenagers camped out in front of the TV. The house filled with the smell of mince and mash.

He looked at her with weary dislike. "Any problems, have your husband call me."

Turning his back on her, he ambled awkwardly down the steps. As he walked past the MG, he gave the small car a disapproving glance. She watched as he carefully unlocked the door to his Volvo station wagon and settled himself behind the wheel. Without looking in her direction again, he turned the car around and started to drive slowly down the avenue of trees. Halfway down he switched on the headlights. The tree trunks glimmered. The taillights of the car glowed orange. And then he was gone.

*   *   *

THE BOX HOLDING HER photographic equipment was heavy and she staggered under the weight as she carried it into the house. Because she had left London in a hurry, she checked the box to make sure she hadn't inadvertently left anything behind.

After she had unpacked her clothes, she realized she was hungry. The sun had disappeared completely by this time and the house was dark. The windows at the end of the passage seemed to float in the gloom. Unable to locate the light switch in the darkness, she walked slowly down the staircase, using the balustrade to guide her.

The kitchen was truly not an inspiring place and the bare lightbulb dangling from the ceiling did not add to its charm. The cupboards were freestanding and with a new lick of paint they might acquire a cottagey charm, but at the moment they seemed merely tacky. Opening the doors, she found them stuffed to overflowing with cooking utensils, pots and pans, several different dinner services. The number of champagne glasses was quite amazing—six entire shelves filled with flutes. She rummaged around until she found a thick glass tumbler. There was no ice in the freezer and she made a mental note to herself to do something about that the next day. Rinsing the glass under the tap, she half filled it with Johnnie Walker. Doughnut in one hand, Black Label in the other, she walked out the front door and sat down on one of the stone steps.

She breathed in deeply. The darkness was soft and the air scented. Scent came from the magnolia with its polished leaves and white, aromatic goblets; perfume from the hedges of purple lavender. The house may have become blighted by slow decay, but someone was still taking pride in the gardens. She had noticed upon her arrival the sheen of the freshly trimmed grass, the abundant flower beds, the geometrically precise maze with its perfectly clipped hedges.

She looked straight ahead of her to where the wide ex-
panse of lawn was broken by an artificial lake edged by
weeping willows. Earlier today the sun had turned the water
red. Now the surface of the lake was only a bruise in the
darkness and she could barely see the outline of the trailing
boughs. And it was quiet. So quiet you could hear your
thoughts whispering inside your head.

A large cedar tree stood close to the house, its giant
branches black against the lesser blackness of the sky. From
one of the branches—motionless—hung a rope swing with a
tire. It would have supplied hours of pleasure to the children
of this house. She could hear their screams of delighted terror, see their small bodies tense with excitement as they
swung higher, ever higher. In a garden like this, life would
seem a blessing. Every apple in the orchard without blemish.
Every day an unexplored delight. The future vast, and limit-
less the choices to be made, the possibilities to be savored.

Jonathan's voice raw with anger and despair. "Why? Why
do this to yourself? This is a cop-out Justine. A cop-out." His
face crumpled with alarm. His eyes shocked as he stared at
her bandaged wrists. Her big brother who was always trying
to save her from herself.

She closed her eyes. Pushing the cuff of her sleeve up her
arm, she placed her one hand over the other wrist, feeling the
thick loathsome ridge of scar tissue underneath her fingers.

Where was home?

Home was where Jonathan was.

But Jonathan was dead.

And her head drooped and her throat muscles ached. But
her eyes were dry and she could find within her no tears to
spread their balm.

Two

THE STRANDWOLF HAD SPOTTED him. The animal stood motionless, its head hung low. The gleaming eyes stared at him unblinkingly. Then, with an indifferent toss of the head, it turned away from the human interloper and continued on its way once more, small puffs of desert dust blowing up from underneath its paws.

The man breathed deeply and pulled his hat lower over his eyes. He had followed the animal for three hours, watching as it nosed its way along the water's edge and among the sharp-fanged rocks, but without finding even a dead seagull to scavenge. The strandwolf was clearly fatigued. By this time he would have been foraging for hours, maybe even days. The animal's territory was fully two hundred square kilometers wide: an area so vast but offering so little.

After its futile search for food on the beach, the strandwolf had finally turned inland again, and it had become increasingly difficult for the man to keep up. Not that the animal was moving swiftly; it was shuffling doggedly through the thick desert sand, its paws dragging slightly: *TIP-e-tap. TIP-e-tap*. But weary as the animal was, it was still uniquely adapted to its environment, able to cover enormous distances in one day—mile upon empty mile—while he, in his thick shoes, his thigh muscles aching, strained to mount the steep curve of the dunes.

It was so quiet. He couldn't hear the sound of the ocean any longer. Sweat dripped into his eyes and blurred his vision: it was like looking through a sheet of boiling glass that had been warped and twisted by the terrific heat. *Tip-e-tap. Tip-e-tap*. The thick mane of hair at the strandwolf's neck was matted. Its jaw hung slightly open. So thin. He couldn't believe how thin the animal had become in the three weeks since he last saw it. The sides of its stomach seemed unbearably lean and attenuated.

Tip-e-tap. Tip-e-tap. A soft, rhythmic noise. A poem made of sand and sound.

At the top of the dune, the man stopped to catch his breath. He placed his hand above his eyes and looked ahead into the distance. An endless sea of wrinkled sand met his gaze. Ahead of him stretched an unbroken chain of S-shaped ripples, ranging in color from palest peach to richest red. The Namib: oldest desert in the world—with the tallest dunes—tons of sand whipped into soaring crests up to three hundred meters in height. "The land God made in anger," the San people called this vast and desolate wilderness. But he had always thought that only a god in pain could have imagined a place like this.

He started to walk again. The strandwolf had now lengthened the distance between them but he was not concerned. He had been this way before and he knew where the animal was heading. He was heading for home.

And there it was, the cluster of sunburned rocks giving access to a warren of narrow passages and deep caves. It was while he was exploring these caves that he had first stumbled upon the home of this animal and its family. And he had been fascinated ever since. He had turned into a voyeur, constantly keeping on the animal's spoor, staying close, taking note.

Some of the natives called these animals windwalkers, others referred to them as strandwolves. But in fact, this was not a wolf but a brown hyena. The sloping back, the powerful shoulders, and massive jaw were unmistakable. Still, it was true that the long thick hair gave the animal a distinctly wolflike appearance and made it seem completely different from its cousins who lived in the bush thousands of miles to the northeast.

As the man watched the animal approach the entrance to the cave, there was a movement close to the rocks and the next moment the strandwolf's mate had stepped out of the shadows and into the sun. At her side were three tiny furry cubs who barked at the sight of their father.

The man smiled. After weeks of observation he had finally given in to temptation and had christened each member of the small family. It was an act of sentimentality of which he would not have thought himself capable. The male hyena he called Dante. The bitch was Beatrice. Two of the cubs he named Virgil and Antonia. The remaining cub was the runt of the litter. Much smaller than his brother and sister, his coordination poorer, and his one paw malformed, a name from the *Divina Commedia* would be too much of a burden. So he had christened it Pint-size.

Normally brown hyenas live in communes consisting of several family members who form a well-structured support network with every member contributing food to the communal den and sharing responsibility for the care of the young. But this family lived in a territory so harsh, so sterile, that the environment could not support a proper clan of strandwolves. And therefore this family was on its own and in peril. Eking out an existence in the purgatory of the

desert, they had no fall-back position and the slightest mis-
fortune could upset the precarious balance between survival
and sudden death. It surprised him how anxious he sometimes felt when he thought of the odds that were stacked up
against the animals. He had become genuinely attached to
them; in a way they had become a surrogate family.

The young ones were sniffing at their father but today, as
was so often the case, he had no food to offer them. The
bitch lay down and the cubs fell to her side with short greedy
barks as they tugged at the teats and started to suckle. Pint-
size was slow on the uptake. As he tried to muscle his way in
between the bodies of his brother and sister, there was a
scuffle, a flash of teeth, a sharp squeal like a child in pain.
Virgil had butted his sibling hard against the head, nipping
him ferociously in the ear. The man grimaced at this display
of aggression. Love, animosity, competitiveness—a com-
plex brother to brother rivalry as old as time—instinctive
and—inevitable.

He sank to his knees and used both hands to burrow
through the hot top layer of sand until he found the deeper,
cooler sand below. Lowering himself onto his stomach, he
brought his binoculars to his eyes and settled down to watch.

Three

THE DAYS WERE SLIPPING by without Justine really being aware of their passage. She went to bed early and her sleep was dreamless, and in the mornings she would wake up late, the sun high in the sky. Out there, beyond the avenue of trees, the expansive gardens, and the sandstone wall, was a world busy and bustling, but she had no thought of it. The house held her and its quiet spaces made her lose track of time. She did not explore. Most of the rooms still stood silent, their doors closed, exactly the way she had found them on the evening of her arrival. She had not even wandered through the gardens yet. She was content to sit on the steps, hour after hour, her mind calm. Her cameras stood untouched, the books she had brought with her remained unread. Sometimes, with a start, she would look at her watch, become aware of the mug of coffee at her elbow that had long since cooled and she'd vow that tomorrow would be the day she would shake off her indolence and start afresh. But the next day would find her on the steps once again.

Until today.

To begin with, for the first time since her arrival, her sleep was troubled. Her dreams gripped her and she could not break free. She was smothering. There was no air for her to breathe. The smoke was black, attacking the lining of her lungs, and she gasped with the pain. She was pushing herself along on her stomach, moving in the direction of the door. The door seemed far away and oversized, the knob much too high for her to reach. Her eyeballs burned inside her head. She was coughing. The doorknob was hot when she touched it and she drew back in alarm. Outside was the whooshing sound of flames. And the next moment she could hear Jonathan scream, scream, scream from deep within the house; a scream of such terrible despair, it numbed her heart and she knew that nothing would ever be the same again.

She jerked awake. She was lying on her back, her arms rigid. The bedclothes were twisted tight around her legs. Sun was pouring in through the window and she could see a blue sky. It was a beautiful morning.

Her body was starting to relax, her breathing beginning to even out, but the next moment her body jerked again as the phone suddenly rang shrilly from beside her bed.

The noise seemed completely alien in that quiet house. For a moment she simply stared at the phone, where it sat on her bedside table as though she did not know how to cope with its sudden intrusion into her life. But then she lifted the receiver and brought it slowly to her ear.

"Hello."

"Justine? Is that you?"

Her mother. And as was usually the case when her mother addressed her screwed-up daughter, her voice was simultaneously sharp, accusing, and anxious.

"Hi, Mum."

"Well." She could hear her mother breathing deeply. "You might have called. I saw Mrs. Cavendish this morning and when she asked me if everything was all right at the house, I had to admit that you haven't even been in touch with me yet. I felt like a fool."

"Sorry."

"And you left so quickly, you forgot your mail. I told you to take it with you. Now you're back from Greece, you can't expect me to be your postbox any longer, you know."

"Just bin it. It's probably only junk, anyway."

Her mother sounded shocked. "I can't do that. You haven't looked at your mail for the entire three months you were away. There could be something important in there."

"Unlikely."

"And I understand you don't have an e-mail address any longer."

"I don't need one." She had always disliked e-mail, anyway. Some of her photo assignments took her to places where e-mail was not an option. People did not understand and became irritable when you did not respond immediately. But she'd better placate her mother otherwise she wasn't going to hear the end of this.

"Just put the mail aside, OK. I'll pick it up next time I see you."

"So is it what you expected? What's the house like?"

"Big."

There was an awful quiet at the end of the line. When her mother spoke again, her voice was carefully controlled. "What about food? Are there good shops nearby?"

"I'll be fine."

"Are you sure this is the right thing for you? I'm not at all convinced that you should be alone right now. Since Jonathan's—"

She tensed. "Don't."

"I merely want to say—"

"I don't want to hear it."

Her mother's voice suddenly bitter, the words edged with pain. "What makes you think you're the only one who is suffering, Justine? Has it ever occurred to you that I need to talk about my son? That I miss him? That I need to share the grief with someone?"

She lay back against the pillows and closed her eyes. "I'm sorry. I'm really sorry." Sorry. Sorry. So sorry for everything she'd done. And her mother didn't even know the half of it.

"Barry was here again last night. He knows you're back. What should I tell him?"

"I'll call him."

"You should. He's a good man, Justine."

"I know."

"Yes." Her mother's voice sounded suddenly old. "I'm sure you do."

IT WAS TIME TO face the house. Still dressed in her pajamas, she walked down the long passageway, flinging open the closed doors one by one. The rooms on the top floor were empty, or as near to empty as made no difference.

The first room she entered held only an enormous brass bed without its mattress. Sunlight streamed through the windows and the bare springs and slim brass bars at the head and foot of the bed threw crisp black shadows on the wooden floorboards.

In the next room was a bentwood chair. Its rounded back was toward the door and it faced the window directly as though someone had placed it there to make sure of a good view of the gardens outside. In the corner was a stack of yellowed newspapers and magazines.

Behind the next door, another room completely bare except for thick velvet curtains framing the windows. In the room following that, a low, obviously hand-carved dressing table, its mirror facing the wall, its shallow drawers empty. It was as though the owner of the house had found himself with only a limited number of decorative objects and pieces of furniture at his disposal and had been forced to portion them out among the numerous rooms. So he left a rug in this one. Curtains in the next. A tufted Slipper chair here, a vase with a pattern of Oriental blossoms there. But despite the emptiness, the atmosphere in the rooms felt oddly charged. It was as though the bones of the house—the walls, the floors, the ceilings, the very joists and beams—had absorbed the emotions that had existed in these previously inhabited spaces, becoming saturated with them. As though the house had trapped within it forever the laughter and the tears, the whispered words and silent dreams of its past occupants.

And there was one common denominator that linked all of these rooms. Every single room she entered had a mirror against one of the walls. Oval mirrors. Painted mirrors. Mirrors flanked by angels. Mirrors with their faces silvered by time. Large, overmantel-sized mirrors. Mirrors so small, you could hardly see your face in them. Someone had liked mirrors. The mirrors doubled and redoubled the space they reflected, making the empty rooms seem even larger and more bare. The effect was strange, deeply disconcerting. But she was beginning to feel excited.

She almost ran downstairs. Opening the box she had brought with her, she took out a Leica. She returned to the top floor and walked through the sunlit rooms once more, keeping the camera to her eye, relishing the light and the formal precision of these near-empty spaces. She clicked the shutter indiscriminately. These would only be test shots—at this stage she was merely exploring the territory. When the time came for getting down to the serious work, she would switch to her Hasselblad or Linhoff with their bellows and lens movements compensating for converging parallels. But right now, the Leica would do her fine. She was shooting without intellectualizing and for the first time in almost a year, she was actually enjoying the feel of a camera in her hands again. Maybe her creative dry spell was finally coming to an end.

Her work had always straddled two categories: photojournalism and architectural photography. She was drawn to extreme situations—war, death, social upheaval—and in Africa, the Balkans, and Chechnya had captured moments of despair. But after such a tour of duty, her mind would feel pitted and cratered and she'd consciously embark on a decompression period, immersing herself in the cool clarity of architectural spaces. By taking pictures of buildings and places, of unpopulated volume and space; by reveling in the frozen serenity of line and surface, she managed to restore equilibrium to her world.

But for the past year she had felt as though her inner eye had shut down. For her photographs to work, they had to come from within her. A photograph was not a recording; it was an interpretation, a reflection of the way she, Justine Callaway, saw the world. The instant when the camera's shutter fired was a charmed moment. It was the moment light reached the film and she knew she had captured an image colored by her emotions, to be shaped by her own unique visual vocabulary. To her, a photograph was as personal as a fingerprint.

But she had lost that ability to draw from within her. And she couldn't even blame it on Jonathan's death. The rot had started much earlier than that. She had lost her sense of wonder a long time ago. She had lost her vision. Not many people had noticed. Barry did, of course. As her editor and part-time lover, he knew her so well. But her technical expertise was such that she was able to fool her other editors and her colleagues. Every photographer has in his kit a formidable arsenal of tools and tricks, but these were devices and aids meant to play a subordinate role in the magic art of painting with light. Technique was always the handmaiden to vision. But she deliberately made technique the master and allowed it to assume center stage. She immersed herself in the mysteries of contrast and density, texture and grain.

She made sure her printing technique was flawless. But she knew she was substituting style for substance. Her pictures have lost their heart.

Even more worrying, she seemed to have lost her nerve. Whereas before she would actively seek out assignments that took her to the world's trouble spots, she now avoided them. This was one of the reasons she had come to Paradine Park. She needed to pull back, dig deep within herself. Find her lost courage in a place where no one would pressure her.

And now, as she walked in the morning sunlight from empty room to empty room, she was suddenly filled with purpose. She didn't know where it came from, this fizzing excitement, and frankly, she didn't care. She was simply grateful. She brought the camera to her eye, saying a silent prayer. And hallelujah. With an almost audible click in her mind, the camera's eye melded with her own.

She took wide-angle shots, pulling back to allow the lens to embrace the spare formality of the rooms. She moved in close, training her lens on the curl of a strip of peeling wallpaper, on the star-shaped symmetry of a cracked pane of glass. She tracked the precision of the egg-and-dart cornicing, caught the sober sparkle of an antique mirror. And as she peered through the lens into the gleaming looking glass in front of her, there she was—back to front—but still the right way up. A reflection so real, it was easy to forget it was not quite perfect.

She was focusing the camera on the tarnished brass knob of a bedroom door when she noticed the initials carved out in the doorpost. She lowered the camera and walked closer. A capital *A*, followed by what looked like a *B*. But the *A* was crossed out by two deep lines scored into the soft wood. Above and slightly to the right of the maimed *A* was the outline of the letter *R*. She ran her fingers over it. The letters had been carved with such force, the grain of the wood showed through the paint.

She looked around her. The room she had entered was very much like all the other rooms except that it was one of the few rooms with its own bathroom en suite, decorated in a rather hideous mauve and black color combination. Against the one wall of the room was a wide, freestanding wardrobe with delicate art nouveau patterning around the center panel. No doubt it was locked. She turned the handle and indeed the door stayed put, but as she ran her fingers over the top of the wardrobe, she felt the outline of a key.

The door swung silently open on its hinges. A musty smell assailed her nostrils. This closet had not been opened in a long, long time. She had half expected it to be empty, but instead it was filled with clothes: neatly folded vests and boxer shorts, a pile of laundered handkerchiefs, several pairs of socks. On the very top shelf were a number of labeled boxes stacked on top of each other. In the hanging compartment were shirts, a suit, a dark green corduroy jacket, and a pair of gray flannel pants. A long row of shoes was arranged in a straight line. The sight of the clothes was disturbing, somehow, as though the owner of the clothes might enter the room at any minute, select a scarf or handkerchief from among the contents of the closet, slide his fingers into the driving gloves that rested like two limp hands next to a pair of silver-plated cuff links. And he would look at her and wonder who this woman was and what she was doing here, snooping through his things.

She reached out and touched the corduroy jacket and as her fingers closed around the sleeve, she had the most extraordinary sensation. It felt as though she was touching something that belonged to her, a piece of clothing she valued and which she knew well. Before she could properly grasp what she was doing, she had slipped the jacket off its hanger and had draped it around her shoulders.

She turned around and stared at herself in the wall mirror. The jacket was much too big for her; it belonged to a large man. At the elbows were worn leather patches. The smell of disuse clung to the ribbed fabric.

She was still standing there, her eyes on her reflected image, now feeling puzzled and even a little impatient with herself, when she heard voices coming from outside the window down below. The next moment someone was banging the door knocker against the front door with considerable force.

The knocker was applied to the wood again as she walked swiftly down the central staircase. She opened the door to find a red-faced man with kindly eyes just about to lower a massive fist against the door once more. By his side was a lanky boy in his late teens. The family resemblance between man and boy was strong. If they were surprised to find her barefoot, dressed in pajamas and a shabby jacket at this time of the day, they did not show it.

"Sorry to disturb you ma'am." The elderly man thrust an enormous, work-coarsened hand out at her. "Mr. Edwards told me the caretakers had arrived and I thought we should stop by and introduce ourselves. I didn't want you to be alarmed when you see strange men in the garden. I'm Christopher Mason and this is my grandson, David." The boy smiled, showing a set of healthy white teeth.

The gardeners. Of course, it was Friday. She couldn't believe an entire week had already passed since her arrival. For a moment she felt resentful at this intrusion. Solitude can be a seductive drug.

"Mr. Edwards, he did warn you about us?" Mason was obviously worried by her silence.

"Yes, he did. I'm sorry. Is there anything you need?" Her eyes fell on the bunch of keys still lying on the console table where Edwards had left it. "Do you need the keys?"

"No, no. We have the key to the workroom." He patted his pocket. "We'll get started, then." He nodded at her and the two of them, their boots clattering loudly, walked down the steps together. Grandfather and grandson had the same set to their shoulders, they even had the same determined stride. She watched as they disappeared around the corner of the house and a little later the sound of a lawnmower filled the air.

She took a shower, and as the warm soapy water slid over her body, she found herself thinking of the wardrobe in the room at the end of the passage. The white T-shirts were yellowed with age and she had noticed a cobweb of great antiquity in one of the shoes. No one had made use of the contents of that closet for a long time. Why hadn't the clothes simply been packed up and taken away?

She pulled on a pair of jeans and an old denim shirt. If she was serious about her idea of photographing the house, it was high time she cleaned up the darkroom and unpacked her cameras. In the kitchen downstairs she searched for dusters and cleaning rags. Armed with Fairy Liquid and a bottle of evil-smelling disinfectant, she opened the narrow door of the darkroom and started to attack the grime and dirt of years.

After an hour of sneezing and battling her way through the dust, she stopped and returned to the kitchen to put the kettle on for tea. She hesitated for a moment and then placed an additional two mugs on the tray next to her own.

Mason was on his knees in front of a flower bed, weeding. When he saw her coming toward him he straightened and smiled at her. She held the tray for him and watched as he poured the milk and added a generous amount of sugar to both mugs. He placed two fingers into his mouth and whistled sharp and loud. From the other side of the lawn his grandson looked up and waved in acknowledgment.

Mason took a sip from his mug and glanced at her. "Lonely place this for a young lady to live."

She smiled. There was something comforting about his slow courteous voice, the kind, clear blue eyes. "I like the quiet. And besides, I'm supposed to have a husband to protect me."

"Oh, yes." He nodded gravely. "Will he be here soon?"

She looked him straight in the face. "No."

He nodded again and she could see he had it figured out. He took another sip of tea. "Everyone to his own business, that's what I always say."

For a moment it was quiet between them, then she asked, "How long have you worked here at Paradine Park?"

"Almost thirty years."

"Thirty years?"

"It's a long time," he agreed.

"So you knew the original owners, the Buchanans."

"Yes, so I did." But she had the impression that his voice had suddenly grown just the slightest bit wary.

"The little boys must miss the garden. Although, it's been nine years since the family moved out, hasn't it. By this time the boys must be just about grown."

He looked at her and his voice sounded puzzled. "Just about grown?"

"There's a painting of the family in the drawing room. The boys in that painting are nine, ten maybe."

"Oh." His face cleared in sudden understanding. "I know the painting you mean. But that was painted long ago. Just after I started working here.

"Really, that painting is thirty years old?" Somehow this information was playing havoc with her perception of time. She had pictured a young family. But those two boys must be close to forty by now.

"So, Mr. and Mrs. Buchanan. Are they still alive?"

"The governor passed away many years ago. Cancer."

"And his wife?"

Again that slight reserve in his voice. "She died nine years ago."

"She blew her brains out." David Mason's voice held the

cheerful, callous disregard for violent death of which only the young are capable. He had joined them and as he picked up his mug of tea, he nodded his thanks.

She stared at him, taken aback. His grandfather frowned a warning but the boy did not seem to notice. "Everyone says she took her own life because she couldn't stand it any more." He dropped his voice to a melodramatic whisper. "You know, the terrible knowledge that her son is a vicious murderer and all."

His grandfather spoke repressively. "You shouldn't be listening to gossip, David."

"It's not gossip. It's the truth." The young voice was defensive.

Justine looked from the one to the other. "Well, come on then. You can't leave me in suspense here. Tell me what happened."

The older Mason said, "It's an old story now. A tragedy." He was silent for a moment, then he sighed. "The two brothers never got on. Not ever. Not even as children. I watched both of them grow up—become men—and there was bad blood between them. And with Adam, there was bound to be trouble. You could tell."

"You mean the person he murdered was his *brother*?"

The old man nodded silently.

"Why?"

"No one knows. He fled after the murder. Nine years—and they haven't been able to track him down. But they know he's the one. He stabbed Richard to death and they found the weapon next to the body with his fingerprints on it. He must have panicked, to just leave it behind like that."

"How could they test for his fingerprints if he had already fled?"

Mason sighed again. "Adam had trouble with the law before. He was always hot-tempered, Adam was. Got into a fight and threw a punch. Just about broke the other fellow's jaw. That's when he was fingerprinted."

"The murder happened right there." David pointed with his finger. "You see, there, next to the sundial. Just think, to stab your own brother to death and with your family sleeping inside the house like that, yards away."

She looked in the direction he was pointing. The grass growing around the sundial was a dark shade of green and several trees of white wisteria formed a romantic walkway. Now, at the close of summer, the wisteria was faded, but at its best it must look enchanting.

"There were no witnesses?"

"No." David shook his head. "No one saw it happen."

Mason continued. "Adam killed two people that day, not just one. The whole thing broke Mrs. Buchanan's heart, it did. Richard was her favorite and he was the spitting image of his Mum. The same fair coloring. Possibly it's true what David said. She simply couldn't carry on with Richard gone."

David said ghoulishly, "They say when she shot herself the wall above the bed was splattered with blood. And that after they washed it off, the stains would appear again, sort of ghostlike. Sorry," he added quickly as his grandfather looked at him with deep disapproval.

"So if everyone is . . . gone . . . who was the owner of the house? Before it was sold to the American couple, I mean."

"That would be Miss Harriet, the sister. When old Mr. Buchanan died, Adam as the firstborn son took over. Mrs. Louisa and Richard continued to live here at Paradine Park, of course, along with Miss Harriet, but Adam was the one in charge. So with the two brothers gone—and after Mrs. Buchanan's suicide—Miss Harriet was the only one left. She lives in London now. Never married she did."

Justine remembered the youthful face of the girl sitting next to her mother in the painting. How strange to think that young woman would be well into middle age by now.

David spoke again. "She's not been back here at Paradine Park in nine years—not since it all happened. Why it took her so long to make up her mind to sell the place is a mystery. A fortune to keep it up, I'm sure."

"It's all water under the bridge now." The old man placed his mug on the tray with a determined gesture that showed he wanted the subject closed. "No use dwelling on such things." He turned around and picked up his garden shears. "They were good people, the Buchanans. And Adam—he was not an easy man, but he was straight with you. I always respected that." For a moment he hesitated, his gaze fixed in the distance. "But then, you never really know someone, do you? And even in a lovely family like that, I suppose you can have an accident waiting to happen. And there's nothing you can do to stop it."

MASON HAD SAID THE murdered brother had the same coloring as his mother. So the boy with the fair hair and pale eyes must be Richard. And he had been his mother's favorite, and the artist had captured this moment in which she had placed her hand affectionately on her son's shoulder.

And therefore Adam must be the boy whose dark eyes had been following her ever since she entered the room. Such a very young face, with such a hard obstinate mouth. An accident waiting to happen, Mason had said. She understood exactly what he meant. She knew all about bad seed.

It was late. If she wanted to get an early start tomorrow she should go to bed. At the doorway she turned around. The painted faces looked out at her and their eyes told her nothing. Except for his eyes. His eyes were burning.

She flipped the light switch and the room went dark.

Her footsteps sounded flat and strangely without echo as she walked across the marble floor of the entrance hall. For the first time since her arrival, she tested the front door to make sure it was locked. But as she turned the key, the thought came to her that maybe she should not be guarding against a threat from the outside, but a threat from within.

She was willingly locking herself up in this house with its
memories of emotions fierce and anguished—emotions so
potent, so toxic they had driven a man to murder and a
woman to madness. Maybe rage and sorrow were still clinging to the walls and sifting from the ceiling: invisible poison.

Earlier today she had walked through the house in search
of the master bedroom. Many of the rooms were roughly the
same size and without furniture to guide her, it was impossible to tell which was the one in which Louisa Buchanan had
taken her own life. No bullet marks on the wall. No ghostly
bloodstains staining the plasterwork. Just empty room after
empty room.

The house felt cold. She moved away from the front door
and as she started up the staircase she drew the dark green
corduroy jacket she was wearing close around her body.
Why she still felt compelled to wear this jacket, she did not
know. A stale smell clung to the fabric and around the collar
was the stain of old sweat. But somehow she was reluctant to
be without it. She found comfort in the long sleeves reaching
past her wrists, in the jacket's musty warmth.

She reached the top floor but continued past the door of the
nursery until she had reached the very end of the passage.
She stopped next to the large arch-topped window and
pushed her face close to the cold windowpane. From here she
had a direct view of the sundial and the wisteria walkway.

As her eyes attempted to probe the darkness, a cloud
moved away from the face of the moon and the blackness
outside became bathed in ghostly light. And now the garden
was layered with shadows: lesser shadows thrown by the
tracery of the leaves; shadows dark as ink at the base of the
dial, deeper still at the roots of the trees.

The sundial was so close to the house. Had anyone heard
as they struggled? Or maybe there had been no struggle,
only stealth and treachery, a knife in the back and wet blood
on the scented grass.

She shivered and once more she smoothed the thick folds

of the jacket against her body. And the weight of the jacket on her shoulders and the silky feel of the frayed lining against her bare arms was as comforting as a lover's embrace.

But later, as she was removing her clothes one by one, spreading the jacket across the back of the bedroom chair, a small white tab sewn into a side seam caught her eye. She picked up the jacket once more and brought it close to the light. And the embroidered letters read: *Adam W. Buchanan*.

Four

It was dark by the time he left the cave where the windwalkers lived. He had spent most of today, as he did yesterday and the day before, observing the family of strandwolves. His back was stiff and he was feeling cold.

He started to walk swiftly in the direction of the tiny twinkling lights floating in the distance. The mist was rolling in from the sea and the man could feel clammy tendrils of fog touching his cheek. During the day the sun was a blistering ball of heat. At night it was cold, and chilly, too, the early mornings when the ocean pushed inland the only moisture the desert would experience for months, even years.

He had reached the outskirts of the town of Kepler's Bay. In another five minutes he would be at the Purple Palace where his Norton was parked at the back of the bar.

The wind was blowing and the smell of sea salt was strong in the air. Kepler's Bay was situated right on top of a rocky shore. It had one of the best natural harbors along this treacherous, deadly coastline on the southwest side of the

African continent. But Kepler's Bay was isolated and difficult to reach even by the demanding standards of this vast
desert country. Stuck in the southwest corner of Namibia,
separated from the rest of the country by a sea of dunes, the
town's very survival was precarious and its population
dwindling.

Once upon a time Kepler's Bay had been a place busy and
prosperous, a place that managed to lure visitors to its burning shores with the promise of wealth, the promise of diamonds. Buried beneath its hot dunes and the underwater
gravel plains of its coast were precious stones waiting to be
mined by men undaunted by the sun and never-ending wind.

For a while Kepler's Bay had flourished. Apart from the
diamond mines, the town became home to numerous fishing
fleets and canning factories. But when even richer yields of
diamonds were discovered hundreds of miles to the south,
the exodus began. Diamond towns up and down the coast
emptied and became ghosts. Kepler's Bay managed to hang
on. Barely. Diamonds were still mined in the area, but the
days when itinerant diggers could stake their claims were
long gone. The diamond business today was tightly regulated and controlled. The small number of men still mining
the desert and the seabed hugging the shore were salaried
workers. No longer could a fabulous fortune be amassed by
any stray adventurer with dreams of glory.

Now, as the man walked into the town, blowing into his
cupped hands in an effort to warm them, he could see the
shadowy outline of his figure reflected in the vacant dark
windows of empty shops and houses. No other footsteps but
his own echoed in the narrow streets.

Still, there was a community here, mainly fishermen and
employees of the few remaining canning factories. Many of
them congregated at night at the town's most popular watering hole. He could hear laughter and the sound of a pulsing
rock anthem as he drew nearer to the substantial building,
which took up almost half the block. It was an old mansion,

built during German colonial times. Its proportions were beautiful and the onion-shaped spire contributed a touch of inspired whimsy. But up close, the place looked shabby with its plasterwork battered by a wind that rarely let up and several windows cracked and dirty.

He pushed open the door and winced at the sound level. The place was packed. He recognized some of the men who propped up the bar: big men with skin like leather and muscled shoulders and forearms. They were commercial diamond divers and for several months of the year he would join their ranks. It was a difficult, dangerous way to make a living, but the pay was not bad. During the winter months, he turned his back on the ocean. These were the months in which he subjected himself to self-imposed exile, and would not allow himself to speak to a living soul, sometimes for weeks at a stretch. He was just emerging from one such period of isolation. Winter was drawing to a close. Spring was in the air. Come summer, he would renew his contract with the company and get back to work.

One of the men at the bar had spotted him and raised a hand in languid greeting. For a moment he hesitated, wondering if he should join them. He was not really friends with them, but he had spent many evenings drinking in their company.

But it was already late. He should be on his way. He pushed through the bodies until he reached the very end of the bar where the bartender, a small wizened man with a shock of luxurious red hair, was writing into a ledger.

"Ben, I'm taking the bike."

Without looking up, the tiny man pushed his hand into a large beer mug filled with pencils and dropped a bunch of keys onto the counter. "I've filled her up for you," he said, hardly moving his lips.

"Thanks."

"Mark's been looking for you. Says a new shipment of books came in."

"Tell him I'll stop by sometime this week."

The tiny man nodded. "Will do."

The clean tang of the air outside was almost a shock after the close, smoke-filled air inside the bar. His Norton was parked against the outside wall. The bike was old, but he had rebuilt it from scratch and as he turned the key in the ignition and pumped the throttle, the engine came to life immediately with a satisfyingly deep growl.

The wind was much stronger now and he had to pull his goggles over his face to keep the sand particles from stinging his eyes. Tonight the wind would sigh and moan among the dunes, remoulding and reshaping them. *Soo-oop-wa* the Nama people called this wind and its never-ending lament. He had never gotten used to its almost constant presence, and after all these years he was still in awe of its creatively destructive power.

He turned the bike onto the dirt road leading south. The bike's headlight threw a white beam across the road, but the moonlight was so strong, he didn't really need it. On his right, the ocean gleamed. He always noticed reflective surfaces. He was repulsed and attracted to them at the same time. He never looked into a mirror if he could help it. He even shaved without the help of one.

For the first twenty minutes the road was adequate, but then it stopped abruptly, and for the rest of the way he had to push the bike through thick sand, keeping his head lowered against the force of the wind and sweating inside his leather jacket. It was another fifteen minutes before he saw the dark outlines of the abandoned houses of Kepler's Folly—sister town to Kepler's Bay—and long since deserted. He stopped for a moment to catch his breath.

Some of these double-story houses were almost a hundred years old, but no one had lived here since 1956, when the last diamond diggers had packed up and left for the stupendously rich deposits at the mouth of the Orange River. The houses were large, even grandiose, but they had been claimed by the desert. Every day "slow sand" blew in through half-open doors and windows, slumping against the inside walls in thick yellow folds.

A few kilometers to the southeast was yet another, if bigger, ghost town. In its heyday just before World War I, it had been a fabulously wealthy place, boasting a post office, a casino, and a lavish lifestyle. Caviar and white flannel pants were among the entries in the big order book, which was still lying face open on the dusty counter of the general store. The hospital had boasted the first X-ray machine in the Southern Hemisphere and opera singers were imported from France for entertainment. But as with Kepler's Folly, the discovery of richer diamond deposits had bled the life out of that town, condemning it to death.

He slowly pushed the bike past the graceful facades of the empty houses looming in the darkness. There were no streets here, only desert sand, and the houses were arranged haphazardly. A loose piece of corrugated iron suddenly rattled viciously and made him jump. But it was only the wind.

The house he had appropriated for himself stood on the very far edge of the town. From the outside it seemed derelict and he supposed it was. There was no plumbing. No electricity. During his entire first year he had squatted inside the building, not even bothering to try and cover the broken windows. He would lie in his sleeping bag, night after night, listening to the wind blowing through the open panes, bringing in the sand, slowly eroding the plaster on the walls. And he would feel lonely. So terribly lonely. At times the loneliness had been so overwhelming he thought he might go mad with the emptiness around and inside of him.

But little by little he had made the place home. He now had a proper bed and a few other pieces of furniture. He did his cooking in the hearth or on a portable gas stove. He had an outside latrine.

He opened the door and pushed the Norton ahead of him into the house. If he left it outside, the paintwork would never hold up. His fingers searched and found the box of matches and the gas lamp he always left on the windowsill just inside the door. Striking a match, he held it to the wick and blinked against the sudden white glare.

He took off his jacket and stretched tiredly. The room in which he stood was large and held only a battered leather club chair facing a black-stained fireplace, a writing table, and a massive old-fashioned medicine chest with tiny drawers. One entire wall showed makeshift shelves supporting row upon row of books. He was mildly dyslexic and as a child he had hated reading. But this was the desert's unexpected gift. Long, empty nights filled with long, empty hours and the time to discover something so precious, he was willing to struggle with letters often jumbled and out of sync. "Words are weariness," it says in *the Upanishads*, but to him words were life.

He left the room, gas lamp in hand, and walked down a passageway until he reached the kitchen. After washing his face in a large enamel bowl, he reached for the bottle of Johnnie Walker and headed back to the front room.

He placed the lamp on the writing desk and sat down in front of it. Opening the drawer, he took from it a sheet of smooth, heavily embossed writing paper. He picked up the old-fashioned nibbed pen and dipped it into the pot of ink. He always used this particular pen when he wrote these letters. Ink was not easy to come by, and he probably should settle for an ordinary ballpoint pen. But when he wrote to her he wanted to do it right.

It usually took him up to two weeks to finish a letter. Nine years he's lived here and in that time he had written a letter every fortnight. Sometimes even two or three. He had never counted them, but by this time he must have written hundreds. After finishing a letter, he would place it in an envelope, as if ready to mail. For a day it would lie on his desk, untouched, and then he'd seal it and place it in one of the tiny drawers of the medicine chest. The following day he would start on the next letter. He never read through the old letters; once they were sealed in their envelopes, that's where they stayed. Maybe after all these years he was repeating himself. He knew that some of these letters had been written while he was hallucinating. In the early days he had smoked *dagga* almost constantly and those letters probably reflected that. Mad letters. Letters incoherent with grief. Letters stained with rage and self-pity. They were all there, waiting for her.

The first letters he had written were written out of fear. It would be night, the walls smudged with moonlight and strange shadows; the silence around him thick and smothering. Never had he experienced silence like this. And his teeth would clatter with dread, his body would be shaking.

Sometimes the outlines of the room would become blurred and he'd be back in the nursery, only eight years old. On the far side of the room was Richard, his nose bloody, his eye already swelling. And the moment was filled with hate. With danger. With emotions so toxic they had turned the nursery with its cheerful wallpaper of cozy moons and smiling suns into a war zone. Two small boys staring at each other with open enmity, their hostile words like bloodied shards of glass littering the white-washed floorboards between them. And then he'd blink his eyes and the nursery would fade into the shadows and he'd be back in the desert. That's when he had started writing to her. By telling her all about it, expressing it all on paper, he had managed to cling to his sanity.

Who was she? Where was she? He did not know, but just as an amputee may still sense in his nerves the ghost of a missing arm, so he knew that out there was a woman who would make him feel complete. In her thoughts he would find himself reflected. Her mind would be his haven, her heart his refuge. He had searched for her in previous lives as

well, he knew that in his bones. Somehow their lives had
never connected, the one walking too far ahead of the other.
But in this life he would find her, he had made himself that
promise. How he would manage that, marooned here in the
desert, he did not know. But already, he was sure, his
thoughts were knocking at the door to her mind, if only she
would allow herself to listen.

He sat there in the pool of light at the table, the tiny flame
washing the immediate darkness with a yellow glow. Outside his window was a vast dark emptiness. And with eyes
half closed he sat there dreaming of a woman he might have
known, in a world where they have yet to meet.

Five

THE SKY WAS FILLED with low clouds and the wind was cool. Justine parked the MG in the shelter of the plane tree growing outside Ainstey's post office. Glancing up at the sky, she decided to put up the roof of the car. It was looking like rain and it really was quite chilly. She had picked out a sleeveless blouse this morning but she should have brought her jacket instead.

After buying some stamps and withdrawing cash at the ATM, she stopped off at the pharmacy. Unpacking her photographic equipment the day before, she had noticed that she had brought with her only three ordinary measuring jugs. They were sufficient for most purposes, but she needed greater accuracy for volumes of less than 100 milliliters. She was hoping the pharmacist could supply her with a laboratory-quality measuring cylinder.

She was in luck. The pharmacist, a gently smiling man with vague eyes, did not have a cylinder to sell, but he was willing to give her one from his own stock. She waited at the counter while he rummaged around in the dispensary, which was hidden from view.

"Heya."

The voice came from behind her. She turned around. A girl, dressed in black leggings and an orange and lime pullover, was looking at her morosely. Her face seemed familiar but it wasn't until Justine noticed the chain around her neck that she was able to place her. Angelface. It was the girl from the corner shop.

"Oh, hi."

The girl leaned past Justine and picked up a small white paper bag with a neatly printed label from a plastic tray on the counter. She shouted, "You'll put in on me mum's account then, Mr. Grimes." Turning to Justine she said almost defensively, "Me mum's pills."

"I see."

"I like your bracelets." She pointed at the two silver bracelets encircling Justine's wrists. They were thick, heavy, and fully three inches wide. They were attractive. They were also very good at hiding scars.

"Thank you."

The girl was watching her with an expression of reluctant respect. "And the tattoos. They're awesome."

Justine involuntarily touched the two small tattoos sitting high on her shoulder: lasting reminders of a long-ago episode of teenage transgression. "Oh. Well . . . thanks, again."

"Are you still living at Paradine Park?"

"Sure."

"You're there all the time then."

Justine looked at the girl carefully. "Pretty much. Why?"

The girl shrugged. "Probably dangerous all by yourself. Me boyfriend says anyone who lives there by himself must have his head not screwed on right." As she spoke she nodded her head in the direction of the open door and Justine looked past her shoulder. A youth was sitting on a motorbike outside. Black jeans. Black jacket. Black bike. He had his helmet on and she couldn't see his face properly, but the slouch to his shoulders, the way in which he thrust out his pelvis, was clearly meant to convey the message that he was cool and bad and not to be messed with. He also seemed young. There was a spindly lankiness to his figure, which appeared almost adolescent.

She looked back at Angelface. "You guys are awfully concerned for my welfare. Why is that?"

"My boyfriend says there was a murder there at the house, you know. Someone got slaughtered in the garden and all."

"You and your boyfriend must have been barely out of kindergarten at the time."

The girl looked at her belligerently. "Me boyfriend's mum still remembers. She knows a lot about murders and stuff. She reads in the paper about them and then she goes to the inquests. A real expert is me boyfriend's mum."

A real ghoul more like, Justine thought. But before she could respond, the girl was pushing the bag with pills into a grimy, macramé bag swinging from her shoulder. She gave Justine a final, unsmiling stare. "Well, cheers then. See you around."

"I suppose so."

Justine watched as the girl walked out the door. She moved awkwardly, as though she was not at ease with herself. There was something quite vulnerable about her, about the heavy breasts, chunky calves, the hair inexpertly streaked with highlights. As she got onto the back of the bike she smiled at the boy—a smile of incredible sweetness— and placed her arms tightly around his waist. As he kicked the machine to life, she leaned her head against his back.

"I hope this is what you were looking for." The pharmacist had finally finished his search and was appearing from behind a narrow door. "Yes? Well, let me wrap it for you in tissue paper."

Thanking him for his trouble, Justine picked up the package and left the tiny shop with its close-packed shelves. She did not return to her car, but walked two blocks down to a charmless brick-clad building with an orange tiled roof. The local library. She had spotted it on her way in this morning.

As she climbed the shallow steps, she noticed several bicycles chained to the link fence setting the building back from the road. But inside it was quiet. The windows were closed and covered with off-white net curtains. Beech shelves against the walls housed the library's collection of books. Propped up against a large makeshift easel were several examples of children's art: bright yellow suns, stick figures with triangular dresses and golliwog hair, lopsided houses, and curly trees. Tacked to the wall was a leaflet announcing a meeting of the local book club. Behind a long formica-topped counter sat a man, his back toward the door. It must be the librarian. He hadn't noticed her.

For a moment she hesitated, feeling slightly ashamed of herself. What was she doing here? What was she looking for?

But actually, she knew exactly what she was looking for: she was looking for a picture, a photograph. The need to know what Adam Buchanan looked like had been growing ever since she discovered the jacket in the upstairs room.

But why this morbid curiosity? Digging over old bones, dwelling on the gory details—this was unlike her. If she kept this up, she would be no better than the mother of Angelface's biker boyfriend, who went to inquests to satisfy her need to be titillated. Maybe it was simply a question of living in the house where it had all happened. It was natural that she should be interested, wasn't it? Except that "interest" was far too pallid a word.

Adam Buchanan. She was so strongly aware of his presence at Paradine Park. Once or twice she had sensed a chill in the air and had whirled around, expecting to find a man behind her, a man with dark eyes. There were times she thought she might hear the sound of his footsteps, catch a glimpse of him as he walked down the passage ahead of her. But at the moment he was keeping to the shadows. She could see the dark figure, the pale gleam of his hands. She needed to see his face. His eyes.

Still she hesitated. Something inside of her was warning her. *Step back now.* Behind her the open door and the busy high street. Ahead of her the information counter and the man who was still sitting with his back toward her, oblivious of her presence.

The compulsion was too strong. Squaring her shoulders, she placed her hand on the countertop and leaned forward.

"Excuse me," she said. "Are you the librarian? Can you help me?"

The man sitting behind the counter turned his head to look at her but made no move to get up from his chair.

She tried again. "Could you tell me the name of the local newspaper?"

"The *Dutton and Ainstey Post.*" He spoke with just the hint of a lisp.

"I would like to look at some back issues."

"What year and month?"

"I'm not sure of the month but any copies going back nine years will do."

He finally decided to get to his feet. "Nine years. It should be on microfiche. But I'll need you to fill in a visitor's card." He placed a square-shaped card in front of her. "Name, address, and occupation, please."

When she handed the card back to him, his eyes flicked over the entries.

"Paradine Park?"

"Yes." She didn't volunteer any additional information and for a moment she had the feeling he was about to say something. But he took the card without comment and placed it facedown in a tray.

Moving quietly from behind the counter, he brushed past her and walked down an aisle flanked by filing drawers. He lifted his arm to pull open one of the drawers. There was a yellow ring in the armpit of his shirt.

He took out three rolls and handed them to her. "The microfiche machines are over there." He gestured to the far corner.

She sat down on one of the hard-backed chairs and started to thread the tape through the machine. The first roll held the January to April issues. With her hand on the knob, she began scrolling her way through obscure local election battles, car accidents, and wedding announcements. No murders, although there was a piece on the theft of milk bottles.

She was substituting the second roll for the first—May to August—when she became aware of the library clerk standing behind and to the left of her. She twisted around in her seat. He was watching her expressionlessly.

"Are you looking for anything specific?" His voice was flat and uninflected except for that faintly incongruous boxer's lisp.

"Actually, yes. I'm interested in a man called Adam Buchanan. He killed his brother nine years ago."

"The Paradine Park murder."

"You know about it."

"Of course. It created a great deal of excitement around here." The colorless voice was at odds with the words.

"I don't suppose you remember what time of the year it happened?"

For a moment he was silent, looking past her. His eyelids drooped and she had the feeling he was carrying on some kind of internal communication with himself. Then he looked up and fixed his pale eyes on her face. "Winter, I think. The Christmas decorations were up. So I should say— November or December."

Way to go. She looked at him with more respect. He

caught her glance and said with the ghost of a smile, "Librarians have good memories."

"I suppose they must have." She laid the second roll to one side and looked at the third roll. "So it should be this one."

"Allow me." His movements were neat as he threaded the tape through. The film sped by in a blur. Every few seconds he'd stop and check before turning the knob again. His fingers were long and veined.

"Here." He lifted his hand off the knob and straightened.

Her eyes took in the headline, but she did not read the words that followed. Her entire attention was focused elsewhere. The photograph.

It was clearly a posed head-and-shoulders photograph. The eyes were staring straight at the camera. It looked like the kind of picture used for a passport or a driver's license. The caption read: *The Face of a Killer*.

The face of a killer. His hair was quite long, curling around his ears. The face was broad and the cheekbones prominent. The lips were pressed firmly together, as though he were keeping his emotions tightly reined, but the lower lip was full. The eyes were slightly hooded and deep set underneath strong black brows. He was an attractive man, certainly, and this was not a villainous face; the eyes weren't shifty and the mouth wasn't weak. The intelligence staring out of the eyes was evident. But still, the set expression made one feel uncomfortable; pushed you away. The burning intensity of his stare came through even on a cheap photograph like this one.

The librarian was still at her elbow, hovering. "Thank you," she said quickly. "I can take it from here." She turned in her seat, hunching her shoulder slightly. From the corner of her eye she saw him move away. She turned her attention once more to the machine.

The accompanying article was short on facts and written

in a wildly irritating, breathless style. The reporter showed great fondness for the word "dastardly" and—hard to believe—even used the words "murder most foul" without any hint of irony. As she scrolled through subsequent editions, it became clear that the tragedy had provided the paper with a rich vein to mine. The murder and suicide at Paradine Park had kept the paper's readers enthralled for months.

She pulled copies of some of the articles off the microfiche and used the library's photocopier to enlarge the photograph of Adam Buchanan by several sizes. It was not a good quality photograph to start with and the enlargement increased the graininess of the print. But the expression in the eyes did not alter.

She gathered up her handbag and walked over to the counter to pay for the copies.

"Did you find what you were looking for?" The librarian took the money from her.

"Thank you. Yes, I did."

"I'm always surprised by how many people are still interested in this murder." His tongue slipped on the *s* of "surprised." "Every now and then some reporter will write about it again. But then violent death often has sex appeal, don't you think?"

"Sex appeal?"

He smiled. "I noticed you're a photojournalist." He nodded at the card she had filled in earlier. "So you know what I'm talking about. You must have photographed incidents of violence. Of death."

She didn't answer. The guy was starting to creep her out.

"Dying is a wild night and a new road."

She looked at him blankly.

"Emily Dickinson."

"Oh, right." Creepy *and* erudite.

He reached down underneath the desk and produced a yellow and blue leaflet. "The services we provide are listed in here. As well as our opening and closing hours."

She took the leaflet from him. "Thanks."

He smiled palely. "You should go to church."

"Excuse me?"

"Church," he repeated patiently. "Reverend Wyatt, our vicar, will be able to tell you more about Paradine Park. He knew the Buchanans well."

"Oh. I see . . . Well, thank you."

"Come again."

"Not likely," she thought but nodded.

Stepping outside, she took a deep breath and looked around her. At the end of the street was the church with its imposing spire. Right at the spot where the green of the churchyard met the richly molded doorway, two small boys were throwing a beach ball at each other. As Justine started walking toward them, a gust of wind lifted the blue, white, and red ball away from the outstretched hands of one of the boys. It bumped lightly off a slanted stone marking the spot of an old grave and floated silently into the shadows of a hedge. A woman, the mother presumably, shouted something at one of the boys and stooped to pick up a blanket and a picnic basket.

Picnic in a graveyard. It was something she remembered from her own childhood as well. She and Jonathan playing among cool stone slabs. Memories of cobwebs in the grass, sun against the back of her neck, Jonathan patiently teaching her how to do handstands. Memories of summer holidays when she and Jonathan would be together. For the rest of the year they lived apart: Jonathan in the house in London with their mother and she on the road with Sam. It was part of an agreement reached by their parents at the time of their divorce. She had always wondered how the decision had been made as to which parent got teamed up with which child.

She opened the tiny black gate leading to the churchyard and walked up to the doorway. Against the one wall was a stone angel with hands folded piously, leaning forward as if in warning. She entered and the smell of old varnish and old dust was immediately familiar. It was cold in here.

Great spreading windows flanked both aisles and reached into the high vaulted roof. On the stone wall to her left was a panel with the creed and the Lord's Prayer, and high above the chancel arch were painted the Ten Commandments in flowing crimson script.

She walked slowly down the long aisle, the chill of the stone floor creeping through the soles of her shoes. Halfway down, next to a finely veined marble monument, she stopped. Two life-size alabaster figures—a man and a woman—stood side by side under a canopy. The figures stood hand in hand but their faces were without passion, the round eyeballs blind.

"Sir William and Lady Dorothea Davenant."

She turned around swiftly. Behind her was a short, portly man with a scant fringe of hair. He was smiling at her cheerfully. "I'm sorry. I've startled you."

"No . . . not really. Am I trespassing?"

"Of course not. I always welcome visitors. As I'm sure they do." He nodded at the alabaster figures. He smiled again and she noticed that his eyeteeth were small but rather pointed. It gave his smile a rather disconcerting quality. Like a cuddly little bear who suddenly reminds you he has fangs. "I'm Reverend Wyatt." He held out a pudgy hand.

"Justine Callaway. How do you do."

"Anything in particular I can help you with?" He put his head to one side and looked at her with bright eyes.

She hesitated, feeling embarrassed. She didn't want to give the appearance of sensation hunter. But before she could answer, he spoke again. 'We often have out-of-towners drifting in. The church is much admired, of course. Part of it was built not long after the Norman Conquest. That narrow window in the chancel—over there—that's the oldest part of the church. And those stone coffins in the Lady Chapel and the pillars of the nave belong to the thirteenth century."

He had placed his hand on her arm as they walked in the direction of the pulpit, an ornately carved wooden structure with tiny steps. "The pulpit is a fairly recent addition," he continued. "A gift from a parishioner just after the Great War."

She glanced around her. "The upkeep must be expensive."

"Staggeringly so." He sighed. "The church has always relied on the generosity of parish members as well as visitors. These brass plaques list the names of some of our most prominent benefactors."

They had stopped in front of a large wooden panel. The highly polished brass plaques held names and dates going back to the nineteenth century. Her eyes skimmed over some of the more recent additions: *Mr. and Mrs. Stephen James; Mrs. C. Benton; Mr. and Mrs. Michael Pickering; Mr. and Mrs. Robert Buchanan . . .*

Buchanan.

She stared at the engraved lettering.

"Anything wrong?"

She turned her head. Reverend Wyatt was watching her, a slightly surprised expression on his face.

She pointed to the plaque. "The Buchanans . . . are they— were they—the owners of Paradine Park?"

He looked at her searchingly. "Indeed, yes. Among other things, the family contributed very handsomely toward the cost of the stained glass window here." He half turned and pointed upward to a window where an emaciated Christ drooped from the arms of a stern-faced Madonna. "And Mrs. Buchanan and her son Richard are both buried here."

"I live at Paradine Park at the moment. I'm a freelance photographer and I'm very interested in photographing the house. But I'd like to know more about its early history."

For a moment an expression that was hard to fathom flitted across his face. Then he said, "You may want to talk to Harriet Buchanan, the previous owner. She was passionate about Paradine Park. At one point she had even considered writing a book about the place. Nothing came of it, though. After her mother's . . . death . . . she moved out of the house—understandably so—but she could never bring herself to sell. Until now. Anyway, she lives in London. You'll find her in the telephone directory."

"Thank you. Maybe I'll do just that."

"Paradine Park is a wonderful place." That little sharptoothed smile again. "I can certainly understand why you would find it a fascinating subject to photograph. I always looked forward to my visits there."

"Did you visit often?"

"I used to visit quite frequently; Mrs. Buchanan was very involved in parish affairs. She was one of our most gifted embroiderers. You can see her handiwork in some of the church's embroidered kneelers. And I'm a bit of a bibliophile, so the library at Paradine Park was a source of great interest to me. Richard de Bury once said, 'All the glory of the world would be buried in oblivion, unless God had provided mortals with the remedy of books.'"

She had no idea who Richard de Bury was, but his enthusiasm was infectious. She smiled at him. "If you're interested in taking a last look at the library, you should let me know. The books are about to be shipped off to Japan."

"What a shame. Maybe I will stop by one of these days— for old times' sake. I can remember spending many fruitful hours in that room. Of course, this was many years ago. Long before—" He stopped abruptly.

"Long before the murder."

He grimaced. "You've heard about it."

"Did you know them well? The two brothers?"

He bit his lower lip. She could sense the reluctance in him. She kept her face relaxed, looking at, but not quite into his eyes. It was a technique she had acquired during her years as a photojournalist. For some reason it helped gain people's trust so that they opened up to her. It had stood her in good stead more than once when she had to defuse suspicion of the camera and coax a subject into relaxing the clenched jaw, the hostile glare.

Reverend Wyatt was frowning. But then he sighed. "Yes. I did. The family were my parishioners. And you know what it's like in these small villages. Everyone knows everyone else. My mother and Mrs. Buchanan were members of the same bridge club. Of course, after finishing school Adam moved to Scotland. And even when he returned to Paradine Park after his father's death, we didn't see that much of each other. Richard I saw often. He always accompanied his mother to church." Reverend Wyatt paused. "Adam wasn't a churchgoer."

"Did you like him?"

"Adam? A fascinating man." He spoke slowly. "An unconventional thinker. I was as shocked as anyone when I heard what had happened. And that he had escaped justice. Although, *genus est mortis male vivere*."

"To live an evil life is a kind of death."

"Exactly so. I'm impressed."

"Don't be. Strictly schoolgirl Latin I assure you."

He smiled absentmindedly. Maybe it was just a trick of the light, but the eyes behind the glasses seemed suddenly as flat as pebbles. No trace of the jolly little bear left. "Adam Buchanan brought wickedness to that house. To this town."

"Wickedness. It's a word you don't often hear any more."

"It is not a word. It is a force." He spoke quite deliberately. His eyes still held that unnerving expressionless look.

"When you say Adam Buchanan brought wickedness to this town, what do you mean?"

"A crime like that doesn't happen in isolation, Ms. Callaway. It affects everything around it. The killing threw the town into a feeding frenzy. It was not pretty to see. I always think of the murder at Paradine Park as an oozing boil, contaminating the whole of the surrounding community."

It had darkened inside the church and with no sun behind it, the jewel colors of the stained glass window were muted. She looked down the long aisle and out the open doorway. Against the oblong of silver light the stone angel was a black shape. It looked as though it were about to take wing.

"I should go."

"Yes." He walked with her to the door and they shook hands. As she turned to walk away from him, he suddenly said, "Miss Callaway . . ."

She looked over her shoulder. He was hovering on the threshold. His face looked all of a sudden small and pinched.

"I remember a conversation Adam and I once had—actually, I remember it very well. In view of what happened out there at Paradine Park, it had acquired special resonance for me, you understand."

She nodded, waited.

"Adam and I were talking about morality and what constitutes evil. Adam said that evil was merely the absence of good. That evil was not an outside entity that can be fought and vanquished. I did not agree with him, of course. And neither did I subscribe to his belief in destiny."

"He believed in destiny?"

"Very much so. Not by divine decree, but by connection of cause and effect."

"So he believed in inescapable fate."

"Oh yes," Reverend Wyatt nodded. "He believed in it absolutely."

REVEREND WYATT HAD SAID that both Louisa and Richard Buchanan were buried here. Justine walked slowly through the untidy arrangement of graves. Some of the gravestones were very old, leaning forward like tired men. The pale slabs were smooth as fat and the inscriptions faded. For a brief moment she stopped at one of the graves, startled by the youthful age of the young wife buried here. *Here lyes the Corpse of Hannah Payne, Spouse to William Gardener who departed this life 14 January 1762. Aged 15 years.* As she turned her back on the rickety tombstone she wondered what had been responsible for ending the brief life of young Hannah Payne. Consumption, maybe. Or childbirth. Or perhaps it had been one of those diseases, which in this day and age sounded quaint and singular: typhoid, diphtheria, scarlet fever. Any one of these would have had the power to defeat the resilience of youth.

The newer graves appeared to be grouped toward the bottom end of the yard, sheltered by the overhanging branches of trees. These headstones were more elaborate and designed to last. No sandstone heads here—only marble and granite—unyielding, able to stand up to the assault of time. There were only a few graves and they appeared uncomfortably close together. The church was running out of space to bury its dead.

She had found what she was looking for. The two graves were side by side, the tombstones not upright, but flat against the grass. *Richard Duncan Buchanan. Beloved son of Robert and Louisa Buchanan. He leadeth me beside still waters. Psalm 23:2.* The second gravestone was almost startling in its simplicity. No "beloved wife and mother," no inspiring text from the Bible. Just the name *Louisa Mary Buchanan* and underneath it the dates of birth and death.

Suicides used to be barred from consecrated earth and buried at crossroads. But times had changed and Louisa was allowed to find a resting place next to her favorite child. Justine wondered where Robert Buchanan's grave was. Surely the wife should have been buried next to the husband, not the son?

Around the graves the russet leaves were still faintly scented with the lavish fragrance of summer. Winter's breath was in the air, but there were still bees here, humming, and flowers with brown-rimmed petals. For a few moments she stood looking down at the two partnered graves. But as she turned away from them, she wondered what she had thought to find.

She left the churchyard and started to walk back to her car. The wind was picking up. The air had a wet wild smell. At the end of the street she stopped and looked back. There were few people left on the street and she saw a woman on the top floor of a house opposite shut the window against the first fat drops of rain. Even the church doors were now closed and the spire poked into a sky the color of crushed mulberries.

She shivered. By some trick of light it seemed as though a shadow was falling from the tall spire and was racing across the narrow high street, swallowing the houses and shops. There was something not quite real about any of it, as though, were she to blink, she might wake up and find herself alone in her bed, and Ainstey—its houses and its church—a memory from a dream.

THE RAIN EASED BY nighttime, but the wind that had blown fitfully the entire day intensified. As Justine descended the staircase she could hear it crooning around the corners of the house.

She was dressed for bed. She had taken a warm bath and her skin felt pleasantly flushed as she padded down the shallow steps. In one hand she carried her portable CD player. It had traveled with her all the way from London, as well as a stack of her favorite CDs. Music was her passion. In her flat in London was a four-thousand pound Nakamichi sound system, and the portable hadn't been exactly cheap either. But music was the one thing she was unable to do without and she was willing to pay for the best. A world without music was a desert. Hell would be a place where music was lost.

She placed the CD player on top of the wide windowsill

next to the front door. With its marble floor and lack of furniture, the entrance hall's acoustics were superb. She'd be able to hear the music practically throughout the entire house.

She slipped a CD into the slot. *Dido and Aeneas*, the heart-wrenching tale of the doomed passion of the queen of Carthage. A woman desperate enough to kill herself with her lover's sword on top of a raging bonfire in the hope that he would see her funeral pyre from his ship. Certainly one of the more imaginative examples of the fury of a woman scorned. As she walked through the library door, Leontyne Price's voice followed her in all its crystalline brilliance.

The library was not her favorite room. Despite its dazzlingly high ceilings, grandeur, and size, she felt stifled in here. Every morning she opened the windows as wide as they would go, but it seemed to her as though no breeze ever managed to enter this room. The air in here was dead air and try as she might, she could not dispel the feeling of closeness. But apart from her bedroom and the dreary formal sitting room, it was the only other furnished room in the house. It had a massive, overstuffed, and very comfortable sofa. Against the window was a beautiful fragile writing desk with matching chair. It was unmistakably a woman's desk: the proportions were delicate and the small porcelain carriage clock that rested on its smooth surface had fairies and flowers peering down at the motionless gold-tipped hands. Against one wall was a big wood-burning fireplace. Earlier today she had cleaned out the black ash and cinders and had packed the cavernous hearth with the logs and old newspapers she had found stacked behind the makeshift curtain in the far corner of the kitchen. Tonight she would build a fire.

And as she stepped over the raised threshold she had to admit that the design of the room was quite lovely and as lavish and opulent as an opera set. The dark wooden bookcases reaching up to the ceiling were at least eighteen feet tall and fronted by glass. The panes were bevel-edged to such perfection they reflected even the most fugitive spark of light. Most of the books were bound in leather—hunter green, wine red, and deep mustard—and stamped in gold. The carpet was a pool of crimson, and the claret and gold drapes with their heavy fraying tassels could only be velvet.

But the most striking feature of the room was the huge twelve-foot paintings covering the length of one wall and the murals peeping from the recesses over and between the bookcases. The images had been executed with skill but somehow produced in her a flicker of distaste. As she gazed at the dramatic canvases, painted by modern-day acolytes in the style of the old masters, she wondered briefly what Reverend Wyatt had made of them on his visits to the house. Surely he must have been slightly taken aback by this strange mishmash of biblical scenes and characters from Greek mythology. Here was a double-chinned Dionysus, surrounded by overripe fruit and inanely smiling maidens. Next to him Christ, with bloodied crown of thorns and a body faintly mottled with blue, as though some dreadful disease could be glimpsed through the parchment skin. The divergent images were arranged cheek by jowl without any apparent rhyme or reason. Angels with astonished eyes. Lascivious nymphs. Haloed saints and pink-nippled goddesses. Dark shadows, buttered light. Colors as rich as polished gems.

And this room, too, had its mirror—just like all the other rooms in the house. This particular specimen was grand indeed: at least seven feet tall and obviously handcrafted. The intricate gold lattice frame was studded with tiny rosettes. She glanced into its depths and grimaced at the reflected image of herself. She was wearing a man's nightshirt and thick socks. In that opulent, theatrical room she looked faintly ridiculous with her bare knees peeping out from beneath the rounded hem and her arms sticklike within the wide sleeves.

She kneeled in front of the fireplace and slowly opened

the box of matches. Striking the match against the side of the box, she stared at the tiny flame creeping down the stick toward her thumb. At the last moment she opened her hand and the match dropped against a crumpled ball of newspaper. The fire started hesitantly before roaring to life with a furious lick of flames and she moved back from the sudden rush of heat bathing her face.

For a while she continued to sit quietly, her eyes unblinking. Considering what had happened to her and Jonathan, she ought be terrified of fire. But here she was, kneeling calmly in front of the open hearth, actually stretching out her hands to the warmth. It was practically obscene, such unconcern. And she hadn't given up smoking either, even though a burning cigarette was the reason she had woken up to flames and smoke and Jonathan screaming.

Jonathan. She could conjure up his face without even closing her eyes. The lanky figure, the silky blond hair forever tumbling over his forehead, the kind, kind eyes. She had adored him even though it would have been just as easy to resent him. He was the good son. He was lovely and sweet and liked by everyone who crossed his path. They were as unlike as brother and sister could be.

She had been a difficult child and an impossible teenager. She had shaved her head once, which did not go down well with her mother at all, and neither did the two small tattoos, which she had acquired during a summer holiday in Blackpool. Ever since she'd been stuck with the image of a snake—the top half black, the lower white—and the black head of a wolf on her shoulder. They were permanent reminders of a summer of teenage rebellion.

She had grown up into a person most people found difficult to warm to. Her father called her "willful," but 'willful' was a pretty word. A word that smacked of the exotic and slightly mischievous. A heroine in a romance novel is willful, a flirtatious Scarlett O'Hara used to getting her own way. It was not a word that applied to her. She was not will-ful; she was angry. She sometimes imagined she was born with the delicate membrane around her brain already in-fected, inflamed with self-loathing and rage. She was self-destructive. Her mother's word that; "Justine won't live to see forty. Mark my words. She's too self-destructive."

In her twenties, she had delighted in practicing sports with an edge: bungee jumping, sky diving, white-water raft-ing. Whether these pursuits had been the result of a genuine need for speed, or whether she was merely trying to annoy her parents was another question. From there she had gradu-ated to drugs, finally ending up in a hospital emergency room with a stomach pump pushed down her throat. And then there was the suicide attempt: lying in the bathtub, watching the wrinkling of the skin on her toes and finger-tips; watching her blood turn pink and thin as it mixed with the tepid water. No, she wasn't *self*-destructive. It wasn't as benign as that. She was *de*structive. Like Lord Byron: mad, bad and dangerous to know. She could be very bad for your health. Lethal in fact. If he were alive, Jonathan would be able to testify to that. If he were alive . . .

She had looked forward to spending those two weeks of holiday in Jonathan's company. She remembered that well. They had rented a house in Cornwall, a ramshackle place much too big for the two of them but all they could find at fairly short notice. The house was worn around the edges: the porch sagged and the shingles on the roof were in need of repair. The paint on the timber walls was peeling. But the front rooms had a view of the sea and flowers bloomed ex-travagantly in the front garden.

But almost from the beginning things went wrong. She had arrived at the house edgy and restless. On their first eve-ning together, after they had finished dinner, she lit a ciga-rette knowing full well it would irritate Jonathan who did not smoke. He didn't say anything. Leaning over, he simply re-moved the cigarette from her lips and stubbed it out.

She lit up again—just to spite him—not really in the mood for a cigarette, but enjoying the opportunity it would give her to pick a fight. But he decided not to play. Picking up his newspaper, he told her he was going to bed. At the threshold he paused. "You should watch out." He gestured at the pack of cigarettes and the box of matches. "Those will be the death of you."

But it wasn't the death of her. It was the death of him. Because when she had stumbled to bed a little later she had left behind—on the arm of her chair—the cigarette, still smoldering. The tired old house had gone up in flames like the box of tinder it was.

What was it that librarian had said earlier today? *A wild night and a new road*. That was what dying was all about. But sometimes you longed to walk that road even in life. Especially in life.

She shook her head sharply. *Stop it*. These were dangerous thoughts; she needed to put them from her mind. And she knew just the man who would be able to help. Mr. Johnnie Walker. Now there was a guy who rarely let her down.

She had brought a fresh bottle of whiskey only this morning and as she walked into the kitchen she could see the neck peeping out from the brown paper bag. Good. She was feeling better already. But as she extracted the bottle from the bag and twisted the top open, she thought she heard something. The sound was just sufficiently offbeat for her to lower the bottle and still her movements.

For a few moments she stood quietly, trying to identify what it was that had caught her attention. From behind her, in the entrance hall, Price was singing her heart out. Dido's lament. The trilling voice sounded far-off, muted by the passage and the thick swinging door leading to the kitchen. In here it was almost completely quiet.

The fridge made a small, shuddering noise. The window above the sink jerked sporadically against the casement. And then there was the sound of the wind.

She stood quietly. She listened.

Nothing. Her imagination was running away with her. But as she picked up the bottle once more, there it was again: a small, metallic rattle.

She walked over to the back door and slid the heavy bolt from the lock. The door opened inward and the force of the wind took her by surprise. The night was gusty and the courtyard very dark. She could barely make out the tower with the clock.

Her fingers searched for the outside light switch. There were several spotlights fixed to the walls, but when she pressed the switch, only one of the lights lit up. The others must be dead—or maybe they didn't even have bulbs. Still, the feeble light from the single bulb was better than nothing.

She had no shoes on, only her socks, and the gravel underneath her feet cut into her soles. She walked forward hesitantly, straining her ears. And there it was-the same flat, metallic rattle that had first alerted her. Her eyes darted to the left.

A beer can. That's all it was. She could see it clearly in the yellow light. With each new gust of wind, it skittered across the cement walkway. She stooped and picked it up.

Where had it come from? As she turned the aluminum can over in her hand, she heard a door bang and her head snapped up.

The noise came from the direction of the storage rooms on the far side of the quadrangle. Her heart was suddenly racing. She stared at the long freestanding building with its row of closed locked doors.

Except one of the doors was slightly ajar. As she watched, the force of the wind pulled the door open briefly and then slammed it shut once again with a muffled thud.

She started to walk slowly across the empty courtyard, her eyes fixed on the door, which was continuing to open and close with each breath of wind. Every time the door swung inward, she was able to see only a deeper darkness than the blackness of the night that surrounded her.

She placed her hand against the splintered wooden surface of the door and took a deep, steadying breath.

Here goes.

With a swift, determined gesture, she pushed the door open and it crashed loudly against the inside wall.

Nothing. There was no one there.

But there had been—and recently. The light falling over her shoulder was just strong enough for her to see a thin filthy mattress and two pillows. In the corner was a six-pack of beer, with two of the plastic rings empty. It was easy to guess where the beer can she had picked up outside had come from.

A greasy little nest of candy wrappers and empty bags of potato chips was sitting beside one of the pillows. Spread open at the bottom of the mattress was a magazine. She sat down on her heels beside it and grimaced at the cover: a topless woman with a gravity-defying bosom and a come-hither pout.

Two people had made use of this room, not just one. On top of the seat of a chair were two glasses and a half-empty bottle of cane spirits. Pink panties hung jauntily from the back of a broken chair.

Mattress, panties, porn, alcohol . . . a love nest?

Not a very romantic place for an erotic tryst, she had to admit. The cement floor was filthy and there was only one tiny window high up against the one wall. But if it was privacy you wanted, this would certainly qualify. Anyway, whatever this was all about, she would have to put a stop to it. She dusted her hands and got to her feet.

As she stepped out the door, she made sure to close it tightly behind her, so that the wind would not be able to blow it open once again. For a few moments she stood looking around her, her eyes traveling around the courtyard, the walkway, the arch opening to the gravel driveway and the avenue of trees beyond. But she could see no one.

She started to walk back toward the house where a bright yellow wedge of light sliced through the open kitchen door into the darkness. Mason and his grandson would be coming in to tend to the gardens tomorrow. She would ask them to clean out the room and put a lock on the door. And to replace the dead bulbs in the wall-mounted spotlights, while they were at it. It was high time she took her duties as a caretaker more seriously. She entered the kitchen and dead bolted the door behind her.

Six

THE WATCHER LIKED HER name. Justine. He liked her eyes. In fact, he had liked everything about her from the first moment he saw her. Such an uneventful morning, the church dead quiet, the pews empty, and then suddenly there she was like the answer to a dark prayer.

Small, heart-shaped face. Cigarette-thin arms. Fragile wrists that looked as though they might break from the weight of the thick silver bracelets clamped around them. Her eyelashes were long, the tips pale. The curve of her upper lip was naturally exaggerated. But despite the pretty cupid's bow of her mouth, there was a wildness about her. It marked her person like a birthmark. It was evident in the set of her jaw, the tone of her voice. It thrilled him deeply.

Justine. A good name: feminine, but it had that connotation of justice, and justice was a masculine concept, despite the ubiquitous blindfolded lady and her balancing scales. And her eyes. He really liked her eyes. She spoke of Adam Buchanan and there was a tiny tick at the corner of one eyelid. The expression on her face almost rapt. When he saw that expression and recognized her deep fascination with the man, he had felt his pulse quicken.

The Buchanans. Fair-haired Richard and his mother, the lovely Louisa. Richard Buchanan had charm, there was true artistry in the way he seduced those with whom he came into contact. Such cunning was always fascinating. The mother, too, was a seductive personality. But it was the older, brooding heir who was truly worthy of attention.

In his own life he had experienced two life-changing events. The first one had been his father's death. It was the reason he had chosen to become a priest. The second was the murder at Paradine Park. It was the reason he became the Watcher.

On the night of the murder he had found himself, quite by chance, in the gardens of Paradine Park. Except that it probably wasn't chance that had led his footsteps there on that lovely spring evening. Everything in life had purpose. Nothing was random. It was destined that he witness Adam Buchanan's fall from grace. He had never before visited Paradine Park so late in the day, but on that evening he had felt restless and had decided to go for a walk. When he set out, he did not consciously have Paradine Park as his destination in mind. Nevertheless, he had walked there without hesitation and had arrived just in time to witness the argument between the two brothers. The struggle.

Death.

Why had he not tried to intervene? If he had stepped out of the shadows, the situation would have been diffused immediately. Richard Buchanan would still be alive. His brother would be master of Paradine Park instead of a fugitive.

And why had he not tried to stop Adam from getting away? In the years to come he would relive the moment over and over again. Adam on his knees next to Richard's still body. The sheen of sweat on Adam's forehead. His features dramatized by the light of the moon, the hollows of his eyes, the angles and planes of his face stark as a theater mask. And for one breathtaking moment Adam had looked straight at him. He was convinced the man would see him. But then he turned away.

Of course, he was no match for Adam physically and would probably not have been able to overpower him. But he could have raised the alarm. Or followed Adam to find out where he was going. But he did not. He watched.

His failure to act was not because of shock or fear. It was a deliberate choice on his part to let Adam go on his way un-hindered. Without Buchanan even knowing about it, the course of his future was being determined by a watcher in the shadows. What power. What heady power to impact so strongly on another man's destiny. The fascination of that moment would stay with him for the rest of his life.

Madness and passion. Violence and death. The Paradine Park murder was the Book made flesh. Fratricide was the original sin as far as he was concerned. Tasting the fruit from the tree of good and evil was an act of disobedience— the first instance when man realized his potential for free will. But Cain's murder of his brother was an act evil by its very nature. The Paradine Park murder had suddenly laid bare the mechanisms of the process. Up till that day he had pondered the human capacity for succumbing to evil in an abstract intellectual way. His religious studies were dry as dust. But Richard Buchanan's death was like tearing away the skin, prying open the rib cage, and watching the bloody heart pumping. He had always been a watcher at heart. But the murder was the one single event that had propelled him into action. It was only after watching Adam Buchanan kill his brother that he had started playing the game. And what a game it was.

The game was of his own making and he set the rules. Of course, like all the best games, it needed two to play even though the second player was rarely aware of the game. But the second player was key. And that was why the Watcher did not invite just anyone to play.

He had to be intrigued first. Something about the subject needed to engage him and engage him powerfully. Interesting players were few and far between. As parish priest he was constantly reminded that the majority of people led deeply mundane lives; possessed deeply mundane minds. But every now and then he got lucky.

Sometimes he chose a man. More often than not his choice was a woman. Women were more furtive—they had more secret places in their minds. He knew that better than anyone. Exploring the most private thoughts of his parishioners was part of his job description. For fifteen years now he had been the recipient of confidences and secrets.

But those confidences still didn't bring him close enough. Even when confessing to their spiritual adviser people presented masks. He needed to get behind the mask and strip the skin to the bone. The game enabled him to do that.

The word "game" was probably not the correct word to use. "Study" was more like it. A complicated study. Samuel Beckett said: "All men are born mad. Some remain so." The Watcher was interested in madness. Henry David Thoreau believed most men to lead lives of quiet desperation. The Watcher was interested in desperation. And so he observed. Closely. And became a shadow attached to the footsteps of his subjects.

He would enter their homes when they were away and go through their most private possessions. Diaries, drawers, household waste. It was amazing how much you could learn about people's lives just by going through their trash. Sometimes he would even dare to stay inside the house when his subject was at home. In one instance he had managed to get into the ceiling of the house. That had been a superb experience. For months he was able to look down on the occupant through strategically placed holes. With his last subject he was so bold as to sit in a chair in her darkened room and watch her while she was asleep only an arm's length away. The low-level light from outside allowed him to see the white slash of her underarm, which was folded back on the pillow beside her. His senses sharpened with every moment ticking by. Every now and then her lips would make a soft sighing sound as though she were deeply tired. The taste of cigarettes on her breath. He knew he was leaving traces of himself behind as well. The smell of his body seeping into the fabric of the chair. A stray hair clinging to the headrest . . .

He was not a stalker. The impulses driving the stalker were crude and he was not a crude man. Simply terrorizing someone held no appeal to him. The game was far more elegant than that. He was engaged in a research project and he was disciplined in his approach. And so he made notes of his observations and even cataloged them in neatly labeled folders. Every one of his subjects had their own file filled with the details of their daily lives.

The game lasted until he became bored, his observations stale. He would then move on and the subjects he had watched would be little the wiser—largely oblivious of the presence, which had shadowed their footsteps for months, even years. True, they may have sensed something—a premonition, a slight chill in the air—but he was extraordinarily proficient at being invisible. This was one of the challenges of the game, to walk through someone's life leaving no trace behind. And he was very skillful. He was caught only once. A real pity, the way that had turned out . . .

The Watcher knew he had a gift. People never really noticed him. He fulfilled a certain role in the community and his work as a man of the cloth meant that he knew most of the residents in Ainstey and most of them knew him. As Reverend Wyatt he was a familiar figure among the parishioners of this village. But he never truly registered with them. They might remember his words, but they did not remember *him*, the man behind the words. He was just the keeper of the Book.

Take Justine Callaway. Doubtless, when they meet again, she'd nod her head in his direction and smile. She might even stop to talk to him, but just as with all the others he will make no real imprint on her consciousness. Fortuitous, really. It was this strange anonymity that allowed him to change from Reverend Wyatt into Watcher.

When he had looked into Justine's eyes, he had felt his breath catch. In that instant he knew he had once again found someone worthy of the game. And when he recognized her fascination with Adam Buchanan, he knew fate had brought her to him.

The Watcher was feeling tremendously energized. The first goal, of course, would be to gain access to the property. It shouldn't be difficult. Paradine Park could hardly be considered a fortress. His visits would be furtive, but at the end of the day he would know the rhythm of her days. And the fragmented landscape of her mind.

The game was about to start. Observe the observable. The imprint of her lips on the rim of a cup. A passage marked in a book. The crescent of a stray eyelash on a pillowcase. The slope of her shoulders as she sits at her desk. The sound of her breathing as she sleeps.

The shape of her dreams.

Seven

HIS MOTHER WAS PROBABLY the most beautiful woman Adam had ever known. Louisa Buchanan's coloring was that of milk and ice: creamy white skin, ash blond hair, and eyes of a blue so pale, they appeared transparent. Slim and long limbed, she walked with grace and every gesture was elegant. But there was something about her that was almost unbearably languid. Just the way she lifted her hand or turned her head made it seem as though she was always in the grip of lassitude. She never raised her voice. She never laughed out loud. And when she touched you, her skin felt cool.

But she was lovely and throughout the house were mirrors that reflected her beauty as she walked from room to room. There were photographs of the family scattered throughout the house—adorning side tables, bookshelves, the piano— but remarkably few pictures of Louisa herself. It was as though her beauty could not be adequately captured on film and was better served by the shiny, reflective surfaces hanging from the walls—to be copied again and again—endless variations on the same beautiful theme. His mother and mirrors: in his mind they became inextricably linked. Often Adam would enter a room, which she had vacated only a moment before, and he would look at the gleaming piece of glass on the wall as though he expected to still find within it a glimpse of her moving form.

She had dutifully christened her firstborn, Adam, after his grandfather. Dark haired and dark eyed, the child did not resemble the mother. Her second son was born only a year later and this time she had felt free to indulge herself and choose a name she liked: Richard. It was a name she associated with chivalry and virtue, she always said. It had that ring to it. It was a romantic name, a name that would suit a knight, or a king. Just think of Richard the Lionheart—leaving behind his kingdom to endure the horrors of a bloody crusade and save the Holy Land from the heathens. And she'd smile gently and from across the room her fair-haired son, whose long-lidded eyes mimicked the shape of those of his mother, would smile back. And then he'd turn his head and look at his brother who was watching this silent interplay carefully and his smile would deepen into something approaching contempt.

The library was Louisa's favorite room. She had her desk there, her papers, her footstool with the seat hand-embroidered by herself. Richard could often be found sprawled on the sofa nearby, although on that day he had been standing behind his mother, reading something that was lying open on the desk in front of her.

They hadn't noticed him when he entered the room. Adam did not like the library—in those days his reading problem had made him feel inadequate in the presence of all those volumes packed with erudition and knowledge. And the opulence of the room was smothering. For his mother and Richard, though, it was the perfect setting. His mother was wearing a low-cut, plum-colored jacket that was as rich in color as the velvety petals of the roses drooping from the crystal vase on her writing table. His brother was wearing one of his fancy waistcoats of paisley silk.

As he stood there watching them, they seemed like characters created by an artist's brush, characters who had decided to step down briefly from one of the large canvases behind them. Richard's one hand was gripping the back of the ornately carved eighteenth-century chair; the other hand rested lightly on his mother's shoulder, the long white fingers barely touching her collarbone. His mother was exclaiming softly, pointing at the book in front of her, and Richard leaned forward and murmured something. She laughed, a low chuckle, turning her head to look up at her son. And then they saw him.

He would never forget that moment. The two sets of pale blue eyes. His mother's face limpid and tranquil; Richard's gaze intent, diamond hard. And the message in his eyes was clear: you are an outsider here, it said. This is a circle of two. No intruders allowed.

". . . an intruder. Don't you agree?"

"What?" Adam glanced at his friend, suddenly jerked back to the present and to this small room with its linoleum floor and shiny, lime-green walls from which hung, a black-framed medical diploma, an off-white eye-examining chart, and a faded poster warning against the dangers of unprotected sex. In one corner of the room was a narrow examining bed, half hidden by a flowery curtain, and next to it a glass-fronted cabinet displaying the tools of the medic's trade.

Mark Botha was sitting behind a veneer wooden desk. Tall and thin, he had soft, slightly bulging brown eyes and a noticeably protruding Adam's apple, which he could move up and down like a ping-pong ball. He was able to do so at will and joked that this came in handy when he had to examine his youngest patients. Mesmerized by this unusual sight, they'd forget their tears and their nervousness of the white-coated figure. As an added bonus, he was also able to wiggle his ears.

He was now looking at Adam expectantly, obviously waiting for a reply to his last question.

"I'm sorry." Adam shook his head. "I spaced out. What was it you were saying?"

"Yuri Grachikov. The man is a menace. He has no call to be there. He's an intruder."

Adam shrugged. The feud between Mark and Yuri Grachikov had been simmering just below boiling point for months now. Grachikov was Russian, a relative newcomer to Kepler's Bay. After Namibia became independent in 1990, the South African administrators left the country, and the new Namibian government had imported a large number of Norwegians and Russians to run many of the country's fishing plants. Grachikov was one of the new immigrants. He had started out as a laborer, but had worked himself up to the position where he had taken over management of one of the canning factories. A big bearlike man, he struck an imposing figure.

Adam did not like Grachikov—there was a coarseness about him, a savage quality that inspired caution. As for Mark, he detested Yuri Grachikov. And his initial animosity had grown to monumental proportions after the Russian decided to try his hand at being an entrepreneur: Grachikov had plans to build a hotel on Pennington's Island.

Pennington's had once been home to a roving band of guano gatherers, but for the past twenty years or so, no one had lived in the tiny cement houses except for a clan of jack-ass penguins. But Grachikov had ambitious ideas for the place—envisaging a hotel that would cater to tourists who might find the idea of staying on an island off the main coast rather exotic, and who would regard the short boat trip from the island to the town not as an inconvenience, but as a picturesque attraction.

Personally, Adam thought the hotel was a pipe dream and one that would cost Grachikov dearly. Others before him had tried to develop Kepler's Bay into a more welcoming destination for tourists, but the fact of the matter was that the town was simply too isolated. It was hundreds of miles away from the port of Walfish Bay and the sleepy resort town of Swakopmund. There was only one road leading into town and it was often impassable. The dunes in this part of the Namib were "walking dunes" and every now and then residents would wake up to find the road connecting them to the outside world blocked by a massive mound of sand. The hotel would ultimately be a failure; it was simply a matter of time.

Mark, however, was appalled by the very idea of Grachikov's hotel. Pennington's Island was home to a wide variety of marine life, which would suffer dreadfully if the place was developed. The penguins were already endangered; of the three thousand original breeding pairs only a hundred and thirty were left. Mark had even confronted Yuri Grachikov in the street, and if a passerby hadn't intervened, the situation would have turned ugly.

But Mark refused to be intimidated. Never one to do things by halves, he had started a campaign to stop Grachikov in his tracks—even going so far as to travel to the capital—Windhoek—and seek support there. His persistence had paid off. A commission of inquiry was to be launched into the matter and until such time, Grachikov was not allowed to continue building his hotel. The foundations of the hotel were already in place, but for the past month, no further activity had taken place on the island.

Still, the matter was far from settled. Mark had won the first battle, but there was no guarantee he would win the war. The town needed all the economic help it could get and the commission could very well decide that the loss of biodiversity might be a necessary price to pay for new job opportunities.

"And I would like to know where Grachikov gets the money for his grandiose schemes." Mark frowned. "He can't have made it just by harvesting seals and running the factory. You know what they say . . ."

Adam nodded. He did know. There was a rumor going around that Grachikov was in the diamond smuggling business. If so, the man was incredibly lucky not to have been caught yet, or extraordinarily cunning. Probably a mixture of both.

"You shouldn't obsess, Mark. What will be, will be."

"I don't understand how you can be so blasé about this." Mark frowned again and the corners of his mouth turned down. "If we lose those species they are lost forever. Doesn't it bother you at all—what's about to happen there?"

Adam smiled slightly. "Many things bother me."

"Well, for goodness' sake. We can't just sit around. We should organize among the people here, show them that the hotel is an experiment bound to fail and that we'll be robbing our children of something precious. Let's do something."

"Certain things are a waste of energy. Do I think Grachikov is a pig? Yes, I do. Do I think that in the long run he'll be stopped? No, I don't. And I think you're playing with fire. He's dangerous."

"If your precious strandwolves were at risk, you wouldn't be so sanguine."

"You give me too much credit. What do you think I'd do? Sock him one?"

Mark leaned back in his chair, clearly exasperated. "Sometimes you're pretty hard to take you know. I wonder why I even try."

Adam looked at his friend with affection. Mark Botha was the one man in the world he felt he could trust. The two had met eight years ago, after Adam had returned from a trip to the Etosha in the far north of the country. There, in that silver-white wilderness, he had contracted malaria. Shivering with fever, his veins cold as ice, his brain burning up, he had staggered—barely conscious—into Mark's consulting room. He had been very ill indeed; delirious and hallucinating. And he must have cut a strange figure: a man with wild eyes, matted hair brushing his shoulders, and a voice hoarse from disuse. A man with no home, no friends, no ties. But Namibia was a country tolerant of drifters and Mark had nursed Adam back to health without asking any questions.

Mark was the first person with whom Adam had engaged after a year of self-imposed isolation. There was something about the lanky, white-clad figure with the slightly protruding eyes and gentle voice that inspired trust. For the first time in months, Adam had allowed himself to lower his guard—just slightly. And slowly, very slowly, the relationship had progressed from doctor and patient, to a meeting of minds.

They became friends, close friends. Mark Botha was the only person here who knew what had happened nine years ago at Paradine Park. And it was because of Mark that Adam had managed to start earning a living. As one of only two doctors in Kepler's Bay, Mark was a person of stature in the small community. Life in this wind-smothered town was hard and the services of a good doctor were recognized as a blessing. Mark's personal recommendation carried weight and his friendship with Adam opened doors to Adam that might otherwise have remained closed. It also kept at bay intrusive questions.

A further bond between the two men was their passion for diving. Kepler's Bay had a large community of divers and Mark was a talented sports diver. Adam worked as a professional diamond diver and his hobby was cave diving. If there was one thing that revealed the strengths and weaknesses of a man to the full, it was his behavior within the dangerous environment of deep water. In the cold, murky depths, friendship and trust could be destroyed—or taken to a new level.

This did not mean that the two men didn't at times argue

quite fiercely. Underneath that meek exterior, the soft-spoken doctor hid a fiery temper. And if he felt passionately about something—as he most certainly did about his quest to save the island—he would embrace it with the fervor of an Old Testament zealot. Obviously, he now found Adam's indifference irritating beyond measure.

Adam looked at the cross expression on Mark's face and smiled again. "I'm a hopeless case, my friend. Why not accept that."

"You can't live your life always keeping a distance. You know what it says in the Bible. Those who are neither hot nor cold will be spewed from the mouth of God."

"God is a pretty intolerant fellow all round."

"Watch what you're saying." Mark was frowning quite dangerously now. He was a devout Christian. Adam often thought their friendship was based in part on the fact that Mark considered him merely another challenging cause, someone whose soul must be retrieved before his number came up and he was plucked screaming into a fiery hereafter.

Adam lifted an eyebrow. "You know I'm right, though. We're talking about the same guy who made Abraham think he'd have to set his son on fire. Who sent his chosen people on a hellish forty-year merry-go-round in the desert. Not to mention the fact that the blueprint for creation is based on the premise that the death of one must provide bread for the other."

"They're tests, Adam. God sends us tests every day."

"You don't say. Well, excuse me if I don't see these tests in quite the benign light you do. I've always considered the morality of God rather suspect."

"How can you not believe!"

"I never said I didn't believe in God. I just don't find him very inspiring."

There was a terrible silence. Mark had compressed his lips and his nostrils were quivering. "You make me think of that tribe in central Africa who shoots arrows at rainbows," he said. "Apparently it is their way of communicating with their maker."

"A rather hostile way of communicating."

"Exactly. That's my point."

Adam smiled. "Mark, give it up."

"Is there anything in this world that makes sense to you? Anything you truly believe in, which you can talk about without being flippant?"

Adam didn't answer. Turning his head sideways, he looked out the window. A rusted bedpost, several split tires, and a petrol drum with the bung turned outward leaned against a fence made of open, diamond-shaped wire netting. On the other side, the desert. The idea of wire netting keeping the immense sea of sand at bay seemed utterly bizarre.

"Adam?"

He brought his eyes back to the room. For a moment, with his eyes still adjusted to the outside glare, Mark was reduced to a dark outline behind his desk.

"Oh." Mark's voice had changed. He sounded faintly mocking now. "Of course, how could I have forgotten. Your mystery woman. The one whose ultimate destiny is intertwined with yours. Now do tell me again, how do you know she even exists?"

"I just do."

"You just do. And you're saying the two of you have pursued each other—oh, for centuries now. But somehow you've never managed to meet. You're still searching."

"We're all of us searching."

"You're saying everyone has a soul mate?" Mark's eyebrows lifted.

"That's what I'm saying, yes."

"And if people get tired of searching? If they stop looking?"

"They don't. The yearning is too strong. The longing too powerful."

"So you think we're all destined to meet up with the one who is meant for us."

"Only when the time is right."

"Oh, Adam. You can't truly believe any of this."

He sat quietly, not responding to Mark's tone of voice. And he thought to himself that, yes—it must sound insane. The idea of separated lovers traveling through the ages hoping that their time has come, that this will be the life in which they will finally meet up with one another. Ridiculous, really.

Except, he knew he was right. Somewhere out there was a woman who was prey to the same hunger he was; to the same tremendous longing. When they were ever going to meet up with one another, however, was the question.

He sighed. "How about we talk about something else. I'm going diving tomorrow. Care to come along?"

Mark shook his head. "Sorry, I can't. Tomorrow I'm off on a two-day trip into the interior. Vaccinations. Where were you planning to go?"

"I want to continue exploring the caves at Giant's Castle."

"That's a dangerous dive to do by yourself. You know what I always say: If you dive alone, you die alone."

"We all die alone, anyway." Adam smiled but he could understand Mark's caution. Although Mark was becoming experienced at cave diving, he came from a tradition of scuba diving where divers paired up for a dive for their own safety. Paradoxically, because of the extreme danger of cave diving, cave divers often preferred to dive solo, because it freed them from having to take responsibility for another diver's safety.

He glanced at his watch. "I should go. By the way, I hooked the sidecar up to my motorcycle today. Ben told me the books have arrived?"

"Yes. They're in that box over there." Mark pointed to the cardboard box, which sat on the second chair. Every now and then Adam would use Mark's computer to order books and specialty magazines. As his house was not exactly a stop on the postman's rounds, the double package would be delivered to Mark's house.

"How much do I owe you?"

"Four ninety."

Adam opened his wallet and peeled off the notes. He hefted the box into his arms. "Thanks. So long then. I'll see you next week."

"Yes. Thursday."

Adam sketched a brief salute and turned to leave. As he got to the door, Mark's voice stopped him.

"Adam . . ."

He turned around slightly and waited.

"You really do believe she's out there, don't you."

"Yes."

"And somehow she'll be struck by a blinding insight and come searching for you."

"You don't understand." Adam's lips twitched into a crooked smile. "We'll search for each other."

THROUGH HIS WINDOW MARK Botha watched the tall, heavy-shouldered figure of Adam Buchanan—or rather Adam Williams, as he was now known—walk to his Norton and place the books inside the sidecar. Despite their argument, he was pleased that Adam had stopped by. It was good seeing Adam again. He hadn't had more than a few glimpses of his friend during the winter months and he had missed his company. But around this time of the year was when Adam usually came out of hibernation and they were able to resume the friendship where they had left off.

Mark was fascinated by Adam. Even after all these years of friendship, Adam was still an enigma to Mark and in many respects as much of a stranger as when he had entered the hospital all those years ago.

Mark had been startled by the filthy, unkempt figure with

the burning eyes who had walked in out of the desert like a
mad prophet. The man was hallucinating with fever, and
from his lips—cracked by the sun—tumbled wild, incoherent descriptions: images of moss-draped forests dripping
with rain, glittering frost-rimmed windows, orchards filled
with red-cheeked apples and circling bees drunk with
pollen. Images that sounded unbearably exotic and completely alien to the wasteland of shifting sands and endless
sun that lay outside the hospital's dusty windows.

Their friendship was still a surprise to Mark, as was his
decision to protect this man: a killer, a man who had taken
his brother's life. If Adam had expressed remorse for what
had happened, Mark would have better understood his own
resolve to keep Adam's secret. But the fact of the matter is
that he had never once heard Adam voice a plea for forgiveness at what had transpired nine years ago. It troubled Mark.

But that this was a man plagued by demons was certain. A
few, a very few times, Adam had let his guard down and
Mark had caught a glimpse of a despair so profound it had
left him feeling shaken. And he also realized that Adam was
subjecting himself to a kind of self-imposed purgatory.
From what Mark could gather, Adam had lived a normal existence in England and had certainly not shown any hermit-
like inclinations. He had been a talented athlete and a man
who had liked the company of women. But here in the
desert, Adam chose to live in that wreck of a house even
though he earned good money as a part-time diamond diver
and could certainly afford something more comfortable in
town. And then there were those few months in the year
when Adam virtually disappeared from sight and did not allow himself to speak to anyone. In this country of endless
horizons that could be a very dangerous thing to do. Mark
knew, as did anyone who had spent time alone in the desert,
what that kind of loneliness entails. It is a loneliness that can
burn holes in your soul. The never-ending wind. A sky too

vast to comprehend. And the crushing silence of infinite spaces.

All those years ago, when Adam had turned up at the hospital, Mark had noticed for the first time the tattoo marks on the inside of Adam's wrist. A black and white snake swallowing its own tail and the stylized head of a wolf. But it would be years later before Adam would explain to him the significance of these images. These were marks of destiny, Adam had told him. A destiny that was to be shared ultimately by another person: a woman. They had never met, but they had been searching for each other through many lives.

Samsara, "the wheel of rebirth" and the curse of successive lives. The idea of reincarnation was completely foreign to Mark's sense of the world and his understanding of life on the other side of death. But he was not a man who shut himself off from ideas simply because they did not fit in with his perception of things. Mark wanted to understand his friend better and because of that, he had made a study of the subject of reincarnation. He acquainted himself with *The Desatir*, written in 500 BC, and with the Hindu texts of the *Bhagavad Gita* and the *Upanishads*. He studied the Buddhist *Pali* canon, as well as the incantations for rebirth in the Egyptian *Book of the Dead*.

His research taught him that reincarnation was known to the ancient Persians prior to the arrival of Islam, and Mark found it interesting that there were Christians who had believed in reincarnation as well. The Gnostics, according to ancient Coptic records, believed they had more than one life to live and this belief survived into the Middle Ages among the Cathars and Albigenses, the Knights Templar, Rosicrucians, and alchemists.

But by far the most fascinating concept he had unearthed in his studies, was the conviction held by a certain school of Kabbalists who saw in reincarnation the punishment for

Cain's slaying of his brother, Abel. Mark wondered if Adam was aware of this concept—he had never discussed it with his friend.

As for the idea of soul mates, surely that was just a romantic obsession. And it was completely at odds with what he had learned of Adam's character. Adam was not a sentimental man. He had an uncompromising way of looking at life. His situation as a fugitive had, understandably, instilled in him a wariness, a disinclination to get involved, but Mark wasn't sure if Adam's ability to distance himself mentally from what was going on around him was a product of circumstance or seeded in Adam's very nature. How amazing, then, that this man believed fervently in finding his soul mate, an idea that wasn't just romantic but extraordinarily hopeful.

Mark glanced at his watch. He should quit daydreaming. Within the next hour, the waiting room outside was going to fill up with patients. And tomorrow he would get into his jeep and drive two hundred kilometers into the desert to administer polio shots to the members of a small tribe of roaming nomads. Polio was unheard of farther to the north, but here in the south it was becoming a problem. Namibia was one of the most sparsely populated places on earth—a country with only a million and a half inhabitants—but distances were vast and reaching patients in the more remote parts of his catchment area was often a logistical nightmare. Pulling his desk calendar toward him, Mark Botha proceeded to put Adam Buchanan out of his mind.

But that evening as he was sitting at the table of his kitchen, waiting for Rita to serve him his dinner, he found his thoughts turning once more to the taciturn man he now called his friend.

"Adam stopped by this morning," he said as his wife placed a bowl of chicken soup and dumplings in front of him.

"I saw." She nodded and sat down in the chair opposite him. "How is he?"

"Fine . . . I suppose."

She nodded again. He had never told her the real story, but Rita was not a stupid woman and he knew she was aware that something was off kilter. She had asked him about it once, but had accepted without demur his explanation that he would be violating the confidences of a friend if he told her.

The night insects thrummed against the steel mesh mosquito screens at the windows. The lamplight shone on his wife's hair. She was his conscience, his anchor. When he had married her almost two decades ago, she had been slim and willowy and had fire in her eyes. Over the years her waist had thickened and the fire in her eyes had dimmed. It made him feel guilty even though he knew she did not blame him for the life he had imposed on her. In the eighteen years they had been together, he had seen her break down only once: the day they had placed their thirteen-year-old son on the train to continue his education at a boarding school hundreds of miles to the south. But apart from that one dark moment, she had given him her unconditional support.

But he knew this was not the life she had imagined she would be living. Many years ago, as a young resident, Mark had been the star student in a class filled with other bright minds also intent on probing the mysteries of medicine. His professors had high hopes for him and his friends were convinced that he was destined for great things. "South Africa's next Christian Barnard" was a phrase used quite often.

Instead he had chosen to exile himself and his pretty young wife to an isolated country in the southwestern corner of Africa and to work among the people who lived in this tiny town wedged in between the desert and the cold Atlantic Ocean. He was a deeply religious man and he regarded his work as a calling, inseparable from his faith in a benevolent God.

It was a hard life. Namibia had always been a country that tested the resolve of even resolute men. Its history told of hardship and deprivation: thirst, drought, and death. Deep in the hinterland lived tribes like the Herero, Ovambo, Damara, Nama, Kavango, and Caprivian. The inaccessible Kaokoveld was home to the beautiful Himba. But the coast of Namibia had always been a place so inhospitable, so barren, that even the nomadic Khoi San avoided it.

The Phoenician explorers were probably the first to sail past this deadly shore. Those intrepid seafarers, the Portuguese, followed in 1486 and erected stone crosses to mark their passage. The Portuguese had a rough time of it, their skills tested to the limit by the savagery of a coast more treacherous than anything they had encountered before. They were followed by other European expeditions, often ill-fated. The coastline became a graveyard of wrecked ships and the bleached bones of those who had sailed in them, earning itself the name Skeleton Coast.

But there was wealth buried underneath the sands of this barren country and even today Namibia was still dependent for its existence on diamond mining. Here in Kepler's Bay, however, the prosperity of the diamond boom was long gone. Life was mostly a struggle for those who lived in the town's modest houses. The diving community aside, Mark's patients were poor and for the most part, uneducated. Still, he found it a fulfilling life and he admired the hardy people who were his patients. He could see himself living here until the day of his death. But it wasn't always easy for Rita.

She looked up from her plate at him and smiled. Returning her smile, he placed his hand on hers, feeling the roughness of her skin, the wedding band he had placed on her finger almost two decades ago and which, over the years, had become enfolded by flesh. He looked into her patient eyes and he wondered, was this his soul mate? The one he had pursued and would pursue for all eternity? Was theirs the stuff of poetry and dreams and magic?

No. There was no high drama here; no immortal passion. But deep affection, yes, and boundless trust. Above all, gratitude.

And that, after all, had a poetry all its own.

Eight

JUSTINE HADN'T SLEPT WELL. The discovery the night before of the tawdry love nest in the storage building had upset her more than she would have imagined. The idea that people might be walking around the property at night without her knowledge was disturbing.

This morning, first thing, she had asked the caretaker and his grandson to clean out the back room and throw out the spotty mattress and porn magazines. They had also placed a massive padlock on the door, barring all possible entry, and every spotlight in the courtyard was now in working order. So at least that was taken care of. But she still felt unsettled.

Maybe the day would improve once she started developing the film she had taken of the house. She was curious to see the outcome of her exploratory shots.

She walked down the narrow passageway leading off the kitchen and opened the door to the darkroom. The walls were painted matte black. Against the frame of the door was taped a heavy-duty draft excluder. A light trapping brush pinned to the bottom edge of the door further minimized the possibility of light seepage. There were black blinds in the encasements and when she pulled the heavy folds of the blackout curtain across the door, it was so dark she could not see her hand as she brought it up to her face.

For a few minutes she stood without moving, aware of the beating of her heart. She had always suffered from claustrophobia—a real drawback for someone who had to spend many hours in tiny, cramped rooms. The first few minutes in a darkroom were always especially problematic. This was the moment when she felt as though the darkness would enter her lungs with every breath she took and slowly fill her veins with blackness.

She took a deep breath and moved carefully toward the countertop where she had placed her film. Once she focused on her work, she would be able to push the thoughts of panic to the outer reaches of her mind. And indeed, as she started the familiar routine of processing film and developing prints, she could feel herself relaxing. By the time she switched on the safe light to start the development process, her concentration was absolute.

It was about to happen: a piece of blank paper transforming itself into an image. She gently slid the print into the open tray of developing solution, making sure that it was emulsion-side up to avoid trapping bubbles against the paper's surface. Placing her hands firmly on the edges, she started to rock the tray.

And there it was, slowly swimming up through the liquid, an image as ethereal as a fragment from a dream—fragile, insubstantial—as though, if she were to reach for it, it would be sure to disappear. But then the outlines hardened into the shape of a door, a window, a long empty corridor.

She smiled. Magic.

* * *

But an hour later she wasn't smiling any more. She was frustrated and puzzled. Leaning forward, she examined once more the sheets of contact prints, the result of her labors. There was no getting away from the truth. A large number of the black-and-white prints were flawed.

The pictures she had taken had been of empty rooms, but the prints in front of her showed something different. There was something else in those pictures—something alive. She stared at the contacts, her eyes aching. Surely this can't be. But yes, just about every third print showed the dark shape of an animal positioned somewhere in the picture. An animal with a narrow head, strong shoulders, a sloping back. A dog?

In most of the pictures, the dog was massively underexposed and reduced to a mere silhouette, a stark black shape. In one of the prints the dog seemed to be running directly across the lens's field of view. The outline of the animal was blurred, indicating movement. If this had been a real photo shoot, she would have used a much faster shutter speed to arrest the motion, but this seemed for all the world as though she had accidentally captured the animal in full flight as it had burst out of nowhere.

In only two of the pictures was the image sharper, less two-dimensional. But unfortunately, in these pictures the dog was also at farthest point from the camera. In one, the animal was standing sideways at the very end of the long passage. In the other, it had turned its back to the camera. But in both cases the animal had an appearance of roundness and solidity that was missing from the other prints, which gave no impression of depth.

But was this a dog? She narrowed her eyes. She couldn't put her finger on it—maybe it was just the way it held its head, or the furtiveness of its posture—but there was something about the animal that seemed wild somehow.

She stepped back, baffled. She knew that photographers will sometimes come across "wild images" during the course of their career, images appearing in their pictures for which there seemed to be no logical explanation. It had never happened to her, but she had read about it. She had always thought that these images were probably the result of careless printing. Stale paper, staining splashes from one tray into another, contamination from tongs or fingers. There could be any number of reasons. But how on earth to explain what had happened here?

She should check the negatives. Maybe they would provide a clue as to what went wrong.

She placed the negatives on the light box and carefully looked at each frame through the magnifying loop. The enlarged, perfectly focused images were easy to check. What she needed to do now was to cross reference the negatives with the frame numbers on the contacts in which the animal appeared.

This was bizarre. The negatives were clear. Not one of the negatives showed anything else than empty rooms devoid of life. No dark shape. No blurred movement.

For a moment she stood thinking. Maybe she should simply do another run? Feeling slightly irritated and, for some reason, apprehensive, she selected a slice of paper and placed the strips of cut film on its surface. After covering the negatives with glass, she flashed them with the darkroom white light. Removing the glass, she placed the contact sheet into the "soup."

Whatever was going to show up on these prints would not be the result of sloppy printing. She had used fresh developer and she had checked the fixer and the paper. She was keeping a close eye on the thermometer. And as she worked she tried hard to keep her mind calm and to merely accept—not evaluate—the images that were rushing up through the developing liquid.

But it was difficult to stay unaffected. By the time she had finished producing the new sheet of contacts, she felt almost a chill. The palms of her hands were damp.

The animal was still there. Except the pictures were different now. It was as though—in the time it had taken her to print the new batch—the animal had moved from one side of the room to the other side. From behind the chair to in front of the chair. From the end of the corridor to right inside the doorway.

The print that had showed the animal running now showed an empty room. But as she brought the loop to her eye, there it was. Captured in the large oval mirror against the wall was the reflection of a retreating form, as though the animal had sprinted from the room and was now slinking away into the shadowy passage beyond.

And then there was the picture she had taken of the staircase in the hallway. The detail was clear, the contrast pin-sharp. Light was streaming through the tall windows and the filigree patterning of the wrought-iron balusters threw shadows onto the marble floor. The wall behind the staircase was splashed with graffiti, the outline of the words clearly defined against the white backdrop. It was an interesting shot: the grace and beauty of the staircase, so reminiscent of a more gracious age, juxtaposed with this angry expression of modern angst. But she had no time to admire the composition. As she peered through the loop, her eye was fixed on the dark shape that dominated the frame. In the first sheet of contact prints the staircase had been empty. No longer.

At the top of the stairs was the animal. It was looking straight at the camera. The light from the windows reached even the back of the staircase and she could see the animal clearly. Watchful eyes, the ears pricked at full alert, even the hint of a fang.

Not a dog—she could see that now.

A wolf.

Nine

THE WATCHER WAS EXCITED. It would be his first foray into the house, although certainly not the last. Not that he was greedy. He always restricted himself to one incursion only every seven days. It was one of the rules of the game. If he didn't stick to it, he became obsessive and when he was obsessive, he became careless. That was the way he was caught the first time around. Even the most oblivious of subjects will sense if someone walks through their house every night.

He had prepared carefully. By this time he knew her routine. When she was at home the gates were open. But if she were going to be absent from Paradine Park she always shut the gates. He couldn't quite understand why she even bothered. There was no lock to keep out intruders, just a bolt. But it certainly made things easier for him. It was as if she were posting a sign. *Hello. I'm not here. But come on in.*

This morning the gates were closed.

He walked quickly up the avenue of trees, keeping to the shadows. But he took care not to seem furtive. And there was

no need. No one would find it alarming if they saw Reverend
Wyatt on his way to paying a welcome visit to the new resident in the village. Once he entered the house, though, it
would be different. At that point he would make the transi-
tion from priest to watcher.

He reached the top of the driveway and stopped. Her car
was nowhere to be seen, so she was definitely gone. And
every window was shut tight.

Cautiously he walked around the house. He had discovered an outside coal cellar with a chute on one of his previous visits when he was scouting the lay of the land. And
there might just be an internal door in that cellar. And that
door would open into the house.

For a moment he hesitated, grimacing. The chute was
black with grime. He had put on a new pair of trousers this
morning for the ladies' prayer meeting. He should have
changed into his garden clothes before coming to Paradine
Park. Well, it couldn't be helped. He eased himself gingerly
over the edge and slid down the chute on his stomach.

The cellar was very dark and the ceiling low. He shuffled
forward inch by inch. Something brushed against his face
and he slapped the air wildly with his hand. And now he had
reached the door. Just a wooden door, nothing out of the ordinary. He turned the black knob, which rattled loosely underneath his hand. And what do you know, the door wasn't
locked. He smiled.

The door opened into a passageway. On the one side was
the kitchen; he could see the stove and the edge of a kitchen
table. On the other side was a closed door. He opened it,
peeked inside. A darkroom. Cameras, measuring jugs, and
trays. There was a strange smell in the air. Chemicals.

The cameras were expensive. Nikon. Leica. Haselblad.
He picked one up, squinted through the lens. Over the past
ten days he had immersed himself in the topic of photography, reading everything he could possibly find. He always

made a study of his subjects' passions and interests. It was the most obvious route into their psyches.

He had underlined a passage in one of his new photography books: "The virtue of the camera is not the power it has to transform the photographer into an artist, but the impulse it gives him to keep on looking." The words had spoken to him powerfully. What thrilled him more than anything was that he had discovered a kindred spirit. She was a watcher, just like him. That compulsion to look, to record, to catalog—oh, he knew it well. He and Justine shared a magnificent obsession. And they both dealt in minute observations.

Life passes people by in giant strides. When they look back at their lives, they notice the landmarks but lose track of the details. But he is the keeper of details. He hoards them. His office at home was filled with folders holding notes on his fellow players: all those easily forgotten details, or details that weren't even consciously noted. The worn-out bra strap peeping out from underneath the party dress. The shadow at the corner of the mouth. The yeasty smell of unwashed armpits. The huskiness of a voice in the aftermath of making love. The anemone flaring of the pupil in a startled eye.

Justine, too, dealt in details. Fleeting, fugitive images, which would disappear forever if she did not capture them in a flash of light.

He replaced the camera on the shelf, his fingers lingering on the shutter. He was very much aware of her presence in this room. He would have liked to spend more time here, but he needed to move on. Time was wasting and he did not know how long she would be away for.

He left the room and as he pulled the door shut, he noticed his hand leaving five black fingerprints on the wood. That was no good. He'd better wash his hands first. He stepped into the kitchen and after rinsing his hands, dried them on paper towels. Then he rubbed off the fingerprints. He squashed the towels into a tight wad and pulled out the trash bin from underneath the kitchen sink.

The bin was free of household waste, which was disappointing. He was fascinated by trash. It revealed a great deal about people. But inside this bin there was nothing except a used tea bag. He dropped the paper towel inside and shoved the bin back into place. Next time, when he came back, he would check again and this time he might be luckier.

As he pushed past the swinging door leading into the entrance hall, he had a bad moment. On the opposite wall was a full-length mirror and for a second he thought there was someone else in the house. By the time he realized the figure with the black stained face and white eyes was himself, his heart was racing.

He'd better get a grip and make no mistakes. But he felt as though there were eyes watching him. The Watcher being watched. For the first time he felt uneasy. And then he realized what it was. The mirrors. He couldn't get away from himself. Everywhere he turned, there he was, looking ridiculous with his black face. It was almost painful to watch himself in these big mirrors, which reflected not just his face but his whole body—the whole pathetic mess from head to toe. All these mirrors. Why the fuck would anyone have so many mirrors?

The profanity popped into his mind without warning and shocked him. Calm down. He placed the palms of both hands against his heart. Calm down. Keep playing the game. Observe the observable. That was the rule. The thing to do now was to turn his focus back to where it belonged. Justine. Focus on Justine. Her bedroom: that was what he should be looking for. Her most intimate place.

He climbed the tall, wide staircase, his heart hammering. Down the long passage, past the empty rooms with their big, shiny windows. This part of the house was unfamiliar to him. Years ago, when he had visited the house as Louisa

Buchanan's guest, his visits had been confined to the library and the dining room. This was all new.

The house so quiet. His footsteps so loud.

But here it was. The door was half closed, but he spotted a bed with a red quilt through the opening. He pushed the door fully open and stepped into the room.

There were two twin beds and one wasn't made up. The quilt was dragged all the way down to the foot of the bed and the sheets were twisted.

So that's where she slept. He was feeling better. He picked up the pillow and brought it close to his face. Oh, yes. This was more like it. He could smell her. He could definitely smell her.

He dropped the pillow back on the crumpled sheets and turned toward the other bed. This one was covered with copies of newspaper clippings. He moved in to take a closer look. *Face of a Killer*.

For a long moment he stared at the picture. This man's life had touched his own with the impact of a meteor and even though they would never meet again, the two of them were linked. He had read once that certain African tribes believed that if you save someone's life, he belongs to you forever. He may not have saved Adam Buchanan from a literal death, but by choosing to let him go, Buchanan was in his debt as surely as any survivor was to his rescuer.

Nothing in life was random. As priest he believed in destiny. As Watcher he believed in the interconnectedness of things. If Adam Buchanan hadn't turned his hand to murder, the Watcher and Justine would never have met. If not for a killing nine years ago, she would never have entered his church. It was all meant to be.

Unlike the other residents of Ainstey, with their avid lip-smacking inquisitiveness, their prurient curiosity, the Watcher was able to appreciate the awful aesthetics of Adam Buchanan's crime. In one split second Buchanan's reptilian brain had taken over and had caused him to lift his hand with deadly consequences. A devastating impulse cutting cleanly through all the restraints of intelligence and upbringing. How does it happen? What was it like to experience emotions so devastatingly passionate?

The Watcher's own life was blancmange: smooth, uncratered. His feelings were flattened and his emotions tepid. He recognized that his compulsion to be a watcher was not only rooted in his quest to study the seeds of madness but was also a longing to live vicariously through the lives of others. By observing closely, by acquainting himself with the smallest detail of the lives of those he chose to play with, he *became* them. Their passions became his passions. Their desires sparked something in his own fallow heart. Watch them with great attention, observe the observable and it will give you access to the jagged rhythm of their thoughts.

Justine was obviously fascinated by Buchanan. Against one wall she had taped up a picture of the man. It was enlarged, big and rather blurred. Imagine going to sleep with the picture of a murderer in your room. Did Justine fantasize about this man? Did she dream of that moment when Adam Buchanan sliced a blade into his brother's chest? Women found violence erotic. Go to any wrestling or boxing match and it was the women who were screaming with pleasure. Murderers on death row received marriage proposals from women who knew nothing about them except for their bloody crimes. The entire book of Genesis revolved around a woman's attraction to evil. Justine's interest in this man was completely understandable.

The tall, white-painted chest underneath the picture looked promising. He walked over and pulled open the top drawer. As the drawer slid open, he got a whiff of flowery scent and he smiled at the contents. Panties. Blue and pink and girly. And they were excellent quality. He picked up a white one with lace all over the crotch and couldn't believe how silky it felt. He would write about it in his notes tonight.

As he replaced the panties, he felt the outline of something hard underneath his fingers. It was a blister pack, several rows of tiny pills covered by plastic bubbles. Underneath every pill was an abbreviation for the day of the week. Birth control pills. So she was not living the life of a nun, was she? Well, considering the kind of work she did, traipsing around the globe all the time, he supposed he shouldn't be surprised. She has probably had her fair share of men. And these men would be explorers out there in the real world, not stuck in a church trying to breathe life into the dead words of a book thousands of years old. He slammed the drawer shut.

A small washbasin with a tap was set in the corner of the room. Next to the tap was a glass with a tube of toothpaste and a toothbrush. In the mornings this was where she'd wash her face. He touched the hand towel hanging from the rail and was disappointed to find it dry.

He looked at the toothbrush; he liked the translucent green color. He picked it up and stared intently at the bristles. They were slightly worn out. Time to replace your toothbrush, Justine.

He always liked to leave something of himself behind. Something for his subject to remember him by, so to speak. But of course the rule of the game was that his subject should not be aware of the Watcher coming and going. So he had to be very subtle. He brought the toothbrush up to his face. Slowly he rubbed the bristles across his tongue. Back and forth. Back and forth.

He dropped the toothbrush back into the glass. He should probably be on his way.

But he was back in the game. The unease that had gripped him earlier was gone. Observe the observable. Play the game. If you stick to the rules, you stay in control.

But as he descended the staircase and walked into the entrance hall, his eye was caught by a door standing slightly ajar. Through the opening he glimpsed a dark bookcase filled with handsome volumes. The library.

He smiled. It would be good to visit it again. He hadn't been inside for many years. He pushed the door wide open.

And stopped, surprised.

There were photographs all over the place. On the sofa, the writing table, propped up on the mantelpiece, layering the floor. Pictures everywhere. Black-and-white images, which made no sense at all.

He touched one of the photographs. The surface was glossy, liquidlike; he almost thought it might stick to his fingers. It showed a large room with a big vase on the mantelpiece. In the middle of the room was an animal. A wolf.

For a few seconds he simply stared at the image, dumbfounded. The wolf stared back, the unblinking eyes utterly feral.

With difficulty he tore his gaze away. But everywhere he looked there were more photographs. They appeared to have been scattered all over the room with a kind of mad abandon. In some of the pictures the wolf was out of focus, a mere silhouette, but as his eyes wandered from picture to picture, there was no doubt in his mind he was looking at the same animal.

And the house. He felt the hair on the back of his neck rise. He recognized the house. The staircase, the tall windows, the entrance hall with its black and white tiles.

A wolf was walking through the rooms of Paradine Park.

Trick photography. It had to be. Photographic sleight of hand. But the vibe coming off these pictures was strange, really strange.

But also wonderful. Even though he dealt in details and details were often mundane—the cracked heel in the pretty sandal, the vein at the back of the knee, the Q-tip stained with makeup and facial oil—he believed in enchantment. Underneath the placid rivers of ordinary reality lurked secrets touched by magic. Miracles. The Bible was full of them.

And wasn't magic what being a watcher was all about? The art of being a watcher was to tune in to the mental resonance of his subjects' thoughts. He was fully aware that by watching his subjects he was trying to pursue some darker unexplored part of his own psyche. Only by observing others was he able to he connect with his own inner life. Their energy enhanced his own. And if this process wasn't miraculous in itself, then he didn't know what was.

He touched the picture hesitantly once more. Trick photography. Surely it couldn't be anything else. It had to be. But born of a highly creative mind. These pictures told him a lot about her. She was hankering after something wild and luxuriant and passionate. Something she had lost along the way, maybe.

There were so many pictures. If he took this one, she probably wouldn't even know. He got to his feet, holding the picture carefully so as not to smudge it.

He had been inside the house for almost an hour. Time to get going. No use pushing his luck.

But at the door he stopped. He looked back over his shoulder and silently made himself a promise.

Ten

THE SEA THIS MORNING was white. The sun had not yet penetrated the dense shroud of mist, which was rolling in toward
the ivory-colored coastal dunes. Within a few hours, the
bank of fog would start to dissipate, disintegrating under the
onslaught of the sun. But this early the sky had the glimmer
of mother-of-pearl and Adam could feel the skin on his face
tightening from the chill of the fog that pressed moistly
against him. He was wearing not only a dry suit, but an insu-
lating layer of underclothes as well; still, as he pushed the
boat from the white sand into the milky waves, he shuddered
from the shock of the icy water biting into the exposed skin
of his hands. The water here was always cold—the Benguela
current that flowed along this coast had its origin in subpolar
latitudes. Grabbing on to the edge of the boat, he swung his
body over the side. With strong, rhythmic strokes he started
to row away from the shore toward the calmer water behind
the break line.

The gulls were flying close to land, their wings skimming

the glittery surface. The swell was strong and he could feel his muscles straining with effort. After rowing for fifteen minutes, he lifted the oars and sat back.

On his left was Pennington's Island, Mark's latest mission in life. The island used to be covered with birds, but after Grachikov sent in the mechanical diggers to start digging the foundations of his hotel, they had left their nests in alarm. From where Adam sat in the boat, he could see the bulky outlines of the heavy equipment, transported by Grachikov at great cost and with enormous effort. Their mechanical jaws were eerily silent and still. They looked like stranded dinosaurs.

He turned away from the island and glanced back over his shoulder. From here he had a long, long view of the fog-shrouded coastline. As always the sight of the pale undulating dunes made him think of the bleached bones that lay smothered underneath those mounds of sand. Whales, boats, and the skeletons of desperate men were buried there, shipwrecked seafarers who had approached this evil shore with a prayer in their hearts. Scurvy ridden, in dire need of fresh water, their ships destroyed by storms—the sight of land must have seemed to these men a blessing from heaven. Until they went ashore and found a land with no life, only wind.

One group of sailors had seen "people" in the distance and had started to walk toward them. But after stumbling through the sunburned sand for hours, the travelers had discovered that what had seemed like humans from afar, were in fact, not people but bobbing seals, chattering and screaming.

Adam wondered what had gone through their minds as the men had turned back, desperately searching for a source of fresh water that did not exist. He had once got lost in the desert himself and he would never forget the raging, agonizing thirst that had taken possession of him as the sun drained his body of precious moisture and the concentration of salt increased tremendously in the mucous membranes of his mouth. He was lucky. He had managed to find his way back to civilization in time to reverse the calamitous loss of moisture. But from the moment those sailors had set foot on land, they were beyond hope. They had escaped from being swallowed by the ocean, only to find themselves drowning in the desert. Hallucinating, their body temperature rocketing, their brains disintegrating absolutely under the stupendous stress of heatstroke, they had perished among those windswept dunes, their parched, wide-open mouths filling with sand, their dry eyes staring.

With a sharp shrug of his shoulders, Adam started rowing again. If he wanted to finish his dive today as planned, he certainly did not have time for morbid daydreaming. Not that he had far to go. As the crow flies, Giant's Castle was only a mile away. But he needed the boat; there was no other way for him to transport his diving equipment. No road existed that could take him there and even a four-wheeler would have difficulty braving this terrain as the coastline became ever more inhospitable and the soft, white sand gradually gave way to jagged outcrops of rock.

Giant's Castle was itself an enormous rock formation jutting out into the sea. From afar it did actually give the appearance of a fortress crenellated with towers and sturdy battlements. Even from a distance, Adam could see the waves breaking against the rock face in a fanlike spray of white foam. For centuries a battle has raged here between rock and water, the fury of the sea carving deep fissures into the stone, sculpting it into bizarre shapes, wrinkling it as though it were mere paper.

The Castle was home to a large colony of birds—cormorants, Cape cormorants, and gannets—as well as a sizable population of seals, which used this barren strip of coastline as a breeding ground. The two colonies lived side by side, usually in harmony, although it sometimes happened that the heavy seals would slide down the rock face without much regard for their winged neighbors, leaving behind them a trail of squashed, dead birds. The last time he had visited the Castle, the female seals had been heavy with the burden of their unborn young. But as he approached the rock, the air was filled with the cries of hundreds of newborn pups. In the past month the Castle had, in effect, become a giant crèche for a new generation of baby seals. The sound of their thin, sharp squeals, mingling with the baritone barks of their parents, was deafening.

But the seals were not what interested him. Giving the breaking waves a wide berth and rowing hard against the current, he headed for the far side of the Castle. Here a small, sheltered bay had formed, the inlet deepening to create a natural lagoon of calmer water. The lagoon was the gateway to a labyrinth of underwater caves, which he and Mark had been exploring over the past few months. It still amazed him that Africa—continent of plains and deserts— had some of the biggest underwater lakes and cave systems in the world. The network of caves he and Mark were discovering section by section, was vast, covering miles of water-filled tunnels and chambers. What made exploration of these caves time-consuming, not to mention dangerous, was that it required some deepwater diving—beyond 130 feet—which was usually considered the extreme limit for recreational diving.

He was not just a recreational diver, of course; he was a professional. For several months of the year he was involved in marine diamond mining, using an eight-inch suction hose to remove gravel from the shore bed. But this was not the kind of diving that fired his imagination. His passion was cave diving.

No glory awaited those who explored underwater caves, no public acclaim for feats of daring and skill. And unlike wreck diving there were also no trophies to collect. But cave divers were a breed apart. They dived for the love of the art and explored for exploration's sake.

The caves drew him. He was enthralled by these water-filled caverns; sometimes when he entered their tremendous

silence he almost had a feeling of déjà vu, a tremulous sense
of recognition. They were a place of secrecy and the water
moving through the twisting tunnels seemed like primeval
water; ancient amniotic fluid. Within the quiet of these caves
he could sense the heartbeat of the earth. It was an ancient,
ancient place formed during the last ice age and subse-
quently flooded. Some of the rocks to be found in this part
of the world were more than a 1,100 million years old, the
product of gigantic tectonic movements and the eruptions of
submarine volcanoes. A time of cataclysm: so extreme were
the forces at work in the inner earth that some of the deposits of the former sea floor had melted; the rocks—even
today—showing the veins and spots of billion-year old ana-
textite. Not far from here a massive crack had developed in
the earth's crust. This crack would eventually extend
through the entire continent, leading to the break-up of the
great Gondwana landmass 120 million years in the past
when the continents of Africa and South America had
drifted apart like lovers torn asunder.

He had reached the lagoon and was now paddling into its
shallows. The smell of rotting kelp was strong in his nose.
The looming rock face above him was white with the drop-
pings of thousands of birds. He looked up at the mass of
seething birds, as always slightly overwhelmed by the presence of so many beaks and wings and eyes. The land was
barren, but the ocean was teeming with life, able to support
the birds as well as the colony of seals, which seemed to him
as though it had just about doubled in size since his last visit.

For a moment he thought of his family of strandwolves
eking out an existence in the sterility of the desert. Not for
the first time he thought: Why could they not share in this
bounty? Why did their life have to be one of such bleak and
never-ending struggle? The odds against the three wolf cubs
even reaching maturity were staggering, whereas the seals
and the birds were breeding strongly; the teeming life on the

rock a testament to their fecundity and the powerful cycle of life.

Thinking of the strandwolves made him frown. He was worried about Dante. The male wolf had disappeared. He had been keeping an eye out for him, but without any luck. If the animal didn't return to the cave soon, the family of windwalkers was going to find itself in serious trouble. He sighed. Not that there would be anything he could do about it.

Jumping out, he pulled the boat behind him and dragged it as far above the high watermark as he could. The last time he had visited, a massive bull seal had taken a fancy to the boat in his absence and it had taken a harrowing twenty minutes of flapping his arms and making aggressive honking noises before the bull could be persuaded to leave.

After stowing the boat, he started to kit up to get ready for diving. Preparing for this part of the diving expedition was a painstaking process. Deepwater diving required gear that weighed more than 200 pounds. By the time he had finished kitting-up, he not only had tanks on his back but extra bottles hanging from underneath his arms as well. The weight was severe and even though he was a well-built man, he grunted from the effort as he started walking. Fins splaying his feet in a bizarre approximation of a balletic movement, he inched carefully backward until he reached the water's edge.

But once he entered the water, weightlessness set in and with it that incredible feeling of liberation and euphoria. This was the feeling he had craved ever since he was introduced to diving as a teenager and water had become his solace. By the age of sixteen he had obtained his BSAC certification. By the time he left school, he had been trained in cave as well as cold-water wreck diving. His father had envisaged Oxford or Cambridge for his eldest son, and was outraged by his decision to pursue a career as a commercial diver.

For seven years he had lived away from home, working mostly off the coast of Scotland but visiting Paradine Park whenever he could. He was passionate about the place of his birth and it broke his heart to leave, but he could not bring himself to live under the same roof as his brother.

Richard, with his knowing, pointed smile, so adept at finding his older brother's weaknesses. Richard, so handsome, so charming, so utterly manipulative. As a child he hadn't stood a chance and as he and his brother entered adulthood he had continued to find himself at a disadvantage.

But then his father died unexpectedly, and overnight he found himself the master of Paradine Park. His mother, Richard, and Harriet would have the right to live in the house for as long as they wished and share equally in the financial assets, but the property itself was his. He was the firstborn son and his father was a conservative man. The only provision was that he would not be allowed to spend more than sixty days in the year away from the house. If he could not see his way open to living at Paradine Park, the property would go to the next in line.

He was stunned by the sudden turn of events, even considered refusing his inheritance. But if he did not accept his father's gift, his brother would, and that was something he could not bring himself to contemplate.

Paradine Park. If he hadn't returned home to claim what was his, things might have worked out so differently . . .

He was now swimming parallel to the lagoon's surface. In order to conserve as much of his air supply as possible, he was using a snorkel for this, the first part of the swim. He took care to stay out of the way of the seals that glided through the water at fantastic speed. The lagoon was shallow, but at its landward edge was a long, narrowish gap opening up between outcrops of jutting rock. This was the entrance to the cave system. A submerged tree barred the entrance with its spreading branches.

He swam past the sunken tree and carefully tied off a

white nylon guideline to one of the large branches. This thin line would ultimately lead him out of the warren of caves he was about to enter. Like Hansel and Gretel following crumbs of bread, he would, at the end of his dive, follow the line back to safety. As he hovered outside the entrance, he methodically ran the final checks of his equipment: cylinder pressure gauges: check; valves open: check; spare regulators: check.

Within the lagoon the darkness was not complete. The rays of the sun formed shafts of light penetrating the water. But the black stillness beyond the entrance gap promised a much deeper darkness. He hesitated, his mind preparing itself for the gloom. Then, with a powerful flip of his leg, he dropped into the enfolding blackness, the water pierced only by the beam of his primary diving light.

The chamber in which he found himself was big and wide, and to reach the tunnel that led from this cavern into the rest of the main cave system, he would have to descend yet another twenty-five feet. He and Mark had christened this first underwater chamber the Waiting Room because this was the place where they usually completed the final decompression stops on the way out. Once he left the cavern he would find himself in a magical maze of tunnels and chambers, the rocks sculpted into weird and wonderful shapes. It was a beautiful, eerie kingdom, a mad man's underwater palace filled with cavern upon cavern, some vast and cathedral-like, others tiny with low ceilings where the least clumsy movement of a fin could stir up a curtain of blinding silt. And it seemed to be never-ending, the water-filled passageways long and often changing direction with unexpected suddenness. He and Mark had explored this network jointly for two months now and still the cave continued.

As he looked around him, he realized that many people would find it difficult to understand the attraction of cave diving. Down here there was no color, no life. This was a sterile place. The winding tunnel and hollow cave through which he was finning were empty. The picture most people had in their minds of underwater diving—bulging-eyed, colorful fish, waving anemones and jewel-like coral—did not apply to the environment in which he now found himself. In fact, some of these tunnels were so silted up you were practically blind, anyway. The allure of the caves was more subtle than visual gratification. Cave diving was a supremely dangerous sport and claimed far more lives than mountain climbing or sky diving. But that was part of the addiction. There was no topping the rush of pushing the envelope and of swimming through waters, which had known few, if any other, human visitors.

He glanced at the dive computer strapped to his forearm, which had automatically sensed the start of his dive. He was at a depth of thirty feet. This was where he was going to leave his staged decompression tanks. The air in these tanks would be used on the way back. Leaving them here, clipped to the line, freed him from the extra cumbersomeness of having to take all the tanks with him and would give him the freedom to squeeze through narrower openings.

With a feeling of elation he started to fin his way into the narrow entrance of a tunnel branching steeply off to the left.

TIME, AS ALWAYS, WAS the enemy. You entered the water and you carried time with you as though it were thickly spooled around a fisherman's reel. At the beginning of the dive time feels plentiful, but as the dive continues, precious time starts to unravel like thread, uncoiling with ever increasing swiftness. And the longer you stayed deep, the longer you needed to decompress on the way up to the surface. Decompression time was usually much, much longer than the time spent on the dive down. And the longer you decompressed, the more air you needed.

He glanced at the dive computer. He was at a depth of 165 feet and he had been down below for half an hour. He could feel the buzz of nitrogen narcosis. The martini effect, divers called it, a lighthearted name for a condition that is anything but amusing. Underwater, nitrogen is forced from the lungs into the blood and from there into the tissues, including the brain. The effect on the diver is very much like alcohol intoxication. For every fifty feet of depth, a diver breathing compressed air would experience the equivalent of downing one martini on an empty stomach. Adam knew that at the moment he was at least three martinis down. Although he felt fine, he was aware that his hand-eye coordination might already be affected. But he was fortunate: his tolerance for nitrogen narcosis was good. He had never suffered from the intense paranoia or hallucinations that have even caused some divers to forget the limited quantity of air in their tank—with disastrous consequences. But he was never complacent. If the buzz got too severe he'd immediately turn back.

At any rate, he had reached the end of his bottom time. He should start making his way back to the entrance. But he was frustrated. He was hovering above a passageway that angled down to unknown depths. The passageway seemed quite restrictive, and with his bulky tanks it would be a tight fit. He longed to know where this shaft led, but he was already facing over an hour of decompression time and if he didn't leave soon, he would not have enough air left. Besides, he had no idea how deep this tunnel went. He would probably need to have his tanks filled with mixed gas, not compressed air, in order to explore it. But maybe he could venture in for just a little. He gave the enticing passageway a longing glance. Just another few minutes perhaps.

No. There was no sign of the passage leveling off—he could not chance it. He had seen what can happen if a diver runs out of air or if he skips decompression stops. Many years ago one of his best friends had surfaced after a deep dive to over 200 feet without decompressing on the way up. Malfunctioning equipment had confronted his friend with an impossible choice: stay underwater and drown, or surface and risk going through the hellish nightmare of getting bent. His friend had chosen to surface.

What had happened next was something Adam would never forget. His friend had died in torment. Once at the surface, nitrogen bubbles overwhelmed his blood, cutting off the flow of oxygen to his body parts. The pain in his joints and muscles made him scream in agony. He became paralyzed, lost control of his bladder and bowels. A massive heart attack finally ended his life. The pathologist later told Adam that when they opened the heart, it had been filled not with blood, but only a curious, rose-tinted froth.

No, it was definitely time to make the ascent and to begin the process of decompression. After tying off the line to a suitable rock projection and cutting free his reel, Adam turned his back on the dark tunnel. Fortunately, the profile of the cave was such that he could decompress partially as he made his way back to the entrance. At thirty feet he retrieved the stashed cylinders he had dropped on the way in. With ample supplies of air ensured, he slowly ascended to his next stop at twenty feet for an hour's wait.

The sound of his breathing as he drew air from his regulator and then exhaled was rhythmic, hypnotic. He found himself watching the floating silver bubbles with profound concentration. Decompression was time consuming, but usually he relished the sensory deprivation of floating in the dark for hours. The cave was a soothing insulator from the world outside. Still, with nothing to do but wait in the water, there was no escaping your thoughts. With your body still, your mind took over. Memories crowded in on you and sometimes these memories were dangerous: they could drive you mad. You could suddenly find yourself in the dark of night, in another time, where two brothers were fighting each other, their hearts filled with hate. And behind them a house loomed gracefully in the darkness, the house, which had brought them to this moment.

Paradine Park. A gift, but also a curse. The house left to him by his father had turned out to be poisoned chalice. It hadn't taken him long to bring himself up to date with his father's financial affairs and to discover just how precarious the position of the family was. The upkeep of the estate was shatteringly expensive and his mother and Richard were spending money like water. Richard, especially.

The ensuing battles over money between him and his brother were bitterly fought, but he was fighting a battle he could not win. Richard had a devastating trump card. Louisa Buchanan would never deny her youngest son even his slightest wish. Nothing Adam might say could sway her. She would listen to him pleading with her; warning that if they weren't careful, they would have no choice but to open the house to the public and have gawking sightseers traipse through their private rooms, they could even end up losing the house altogether. Nodding her head, she'd agree that they needed to be more frugal, that it was time to get serious about the financial situation. But her eyes would slide free from his gaze whenever he mentioned Richard and his extravagances. Even though he was nominally the master of Paradine Park, Adam found himself becoming irrelevant, if not shut out by a physical wall, then by a psychological divide far more formidable than any built of brick and mortar.

The situation came to a head one warm summer night. He was working late at his desk when he discovered yet another staggering bill. He could still remember the sense of hopelessness descending on him, followed swiftly by blinding anger. Storming out of the office, he decided to have it out with Richard once and for all.

He finally tracked Richard down to where he was smoking in the garden. The sight of his brother made him shake. His tongue felt clumsy, his mouth awash with saliva. And Richard looking like a blond angel, completely calm. He didn't say a word. He continued smoking, his slender body relaxed, listening quietly to his brother's stammering, trembling voice.

And then he smiled.

A smile. That was all. Just a smile. But a smile filled with contempt and triumph. A smile that said, No matter what you say, I will prevail. No matter what you do, you will always be the outsider looking in. And in that moment, memories of the slights, the insults, the tiny cruelties of years collided in Adam's mind with an almost physical blow.

Rage. He had never felt such rage. It triggered in him an impulse to violence that was utterly devastating. A red mist sifted over his mind. He rushed at Richard and his shoulder hit his brother's body with sickening ferocity. The force was such that he lost his own balance and sent both of them sprawling onto the grass.

He could see the white of Richard's eyes and the gleam of his teeth. He could smell his own sweat and that of his brother's. They were struggling together in near perfect silence, an unspoken pact between them not to wake the inhabitants of the dark sleeping house. And the scent of the grass was strong and the snowy blooms of the wisteria made it look like a ghostly bride.

And then Richard's outstretched fingers found the garden shears, the pair his mother had used only that very morning to prune the roses. Why it had been left behind, Adam did not know. An oversight on her part, a twist of coincidence. The curved blades ripped across his arm and even in the darkness his own blood was easy to see. But he managed to twist Richard's hand holding the shears away from him.

Had Richard said something? Had he, at last, cried out? Adam could never remember. All he recalled was the feel of the shears in his own fist, the dull gleam of the blades. Was he fighting for his life at that moment? He was stronger, more powerfully built than his brother. Surely there was that one split second when he could have stayed his hand? But his only memory was of anger.

Anger. His alter ego, the shadow at his elbow. Free-floating anger, poisonous, destructive but also—perversely—

empowering. Anger was passion. Passion made you feel alive. Ever since he was a child, he had cultivated his anger assiduously and this may have been his greatest crime. Instead of fighting it, he had allowed it to grow. The violence of that night had been years in the making. The fights over money, the battles over the survival of Paradine Park—these were merely symptoms of a festering rage with its roots many years in the past. And even now, after all this time, there was within him the fear that anger might one day cause him to lash out in violence once again. There was no greater fear than this: the fear that you cannot trust yourself.

You can change, Mark once told him. Everyone has within him the possibility to change. He had watched his friend's earnest face, had looked into the kind eyes and he had wanted to believe, but he could not. Was it really possible to change yourself fundamentally? Past experiences were hidden tripwires lying dormant within you, ready to sabotage actions still in the future, ready to circumvent any attempt at reinvention. Character is destiny, and thus fate is set.

Except for love. Love was the wild card. Love—not the power of will—could cut the shackles of conditioning and stop the past from intruding on the present. The woman in his dreams, the woman whose essence he sensed whenever he sat down to write his letters—in her presence he might find grace. The day she places her hand in his will be the day he finds himself at peace. He needed to find her. She was the healing rib in his aching side.

And suddenly, just thinking about her, his mind felt calm and completely clear. His blue rose. At once a symbol of the impossible and a way out of the labyrinth. She was waiting for him, somewhere, holding the key to freedom.

But did he deserve freedom? Did he deserve happiness? He had killed his brother and though he regretted what had happened with all his heart, he had never been able to find within himself the desperate desire for forgiveness his crime demanded. Would this disqualify him from finding his soul mate? From finding the woman who could make him feel whole?

He placed his one hand over his wrist and in his mind's eye he saw the tattoos marking the soft skin on the inside of his arm: the head of a wolf, and a black and white serpent swallowing its tail. The snake, *Ouroboros*, was a water element and a mythical, ambivalent creature. A splendidly destructive force but also a regenerative source of birth, rebirth, and immortality connected with the Wheel of Life. Maybe, like the serpent, he would be allowed to shed his skin, attain a second chance. Maybe . . .

Ssssh went the sound of his breathing as he inhaled. *Ble, ble, ble* and the bubbles left his mouthpiece in blobs of blurry noise as he pushed the air from his lungs. He was starting to feel the cold now, it crept through the seals in his suit. Finning slowly upward, he ascended to his last decompression stop. Turning his arm, he glanced at the dive computer.

Another thirty-three minutes to go.

BREAKING THE SURFACE AFTER a long dive was a disorienting experience. Within the honey-tinted water, shapes were soft-edged, and suddenly emerging in a world of colored light and sharply delineated objects never failed to produce in him a light shock. But today the feeling of disorientation was even worse than usual.

The noise. The noise was wrong. Slipping off his face mask, he blinked his eyes against the sun that was now beating down from a cloudless sky. He pulled back his hood and there it was again: voices. The sound of human voices intermingling with the shrieks of the birds and the high-pitched, panicked bellows of seals in distress. They came from the shore behind him. He turned around, bobbing in the water, and the sight that met his eyes was such that his brain had difficulty processing the image.

In the hour and a half since he had entered the water, the

bay had been turned into a place of slaughter. The rocky beach was littered with the corpses of baby seals. Men, dressed in gaily colored anoraks, moved between the heaving mass of fur, shouting and prodding the mature seals with poles ending in long, curved hooks. A big motorized boat with the name *Andrea* stenciled on the side was moving gently on the swell, only yards away from him. Above his head, high in the sky, birds wheeled and cried at one another in warning.

The sealers were so focused on their task that they did not notice him as he emerged, dripping from the water. A few steps away, a giant of a man, tall with a broad back, was leaning forward. His eyes were on a baby seal that was screaming, its tiny flippers scrabbling furiously against the rocky surface. As Adam watched, the big man drew back his arm lazily and brought the club in his hand crashing down. The impact of the club as it splintered the animal's skull was strangely muffled. The baby seal made a sick sound and its eyes died.

The man slowly straightened. He must have caught sight of Adam in his peripheral vision because he turned his head and smiled. His teeth were even and very white. His skin had a reddish tint and even his scalp where it showed through the fine, flaxen hair was pink. His eyes were startlingly blue and his lashes so fair they seemed almost nonexistent. Yuri Grachikov.

Intruder. As their eyes met, Mark's description of the man flashed through Adam's mind. It was an apt word. Standing there with the bloodied club in his massive fist, his skin showing the effects of a sun far stronger than ever shone in his native land, Grachikov seemed out of place, like a dangerous, transplanted form of animal life about to wreak untold havoc on his new habitat.

Grachikov smiled again. "Mr. Williams, yes?" His accent was strong, making his words sound as though they had been dipped in grease.

Adam nodded slightly. He lifted his one foot up on a ledge to unfasten the weights around his ankle and pull off his fin. He wanted to get away from here. The stench of fear and blood made his stomach turn. The harvesting of seals was perfectly legal, but it was a sickening business. There were some activists—Mark, of course, was one of them— who had tried to get the practice banned from Giant's Castle; so far without success. But this was not his fight. He should be on his way.

"I recognize you. We meet at the Purple Palace. You are the friend of Doctor Botha?"

Adam paused. Straightening slowly, he looked at the grinning man opposite him. He nodded again, warily.

"Good, yes. I know you. Maybe you can give your doctor friend a message?"

"Message?"

"I try to speak to him but he does not speak to me." Grachikov pulled up his shoulders in a gesture of mock surprise.

"Maybe you should try again." He had to stop himself from mimicking the man's accent. And he'd better watch out; it wouldn't do to underestimate Grachikov. Just because the Russian talked with an accent didn't mean he thought with one. Adam removed his second fin and started to walk toward his boat, dragging his gear behind him. This conversation, as far as he was concerned, was over.

But Grachikov was following him. "No, Mr. Williams you must help me. You must talk to the doctor."

He sighed. He was obviously not going to get away this easily. Perhaps he should let the man have his say. It was probably the quickest way to get rid of him. He carefully placed the cylinders in the boat before turning around. "So what is the message?"

"A man has to make a living, yes?"

"I suppose so."

"A new hotel. It will be good for business. It will bring much work for the people here."

Adam did not respond, waited. He found himself suddenly fascinated by the scar that ran across Grachikov's chin, ending just underneath the jawbone. The wound had healed untidily and the flesh appeared as though it had been folded over and then stitched together by a clumsy hand.

"Dr. Botha. He is making things difficult. It will cost me much money if I am not allowed to finish my hotel. You see what I say?"

"No doubt you'll have the opportunity to state your case when the inquiry gets underway, Mr. Grachikov."

"We have to wait a long time for that, yes? And the machines, they rust. And soon I must start paying back money I borrow. You must talk to your friend. Tell him, he is making trouble for me."

"I'm sure he knows that." This was a ludicrous conversation. He'd had enough. He started to turn toward the boat.

"Tell him, he does not want me making trouble for him."

Adam stopped and turned back slowly to face Grachikov once again. He suddenly registered the cold animosity in those heavy eyes. Grachikov was swinging his club gently to and fro, to and fro. Sunlight flashed off the two diamond rings he wore on his pinky and middle finger.

Adam felt his own eyes narrowing and a deep, icy rage settled in the pit of his stomach.

"That sounds like a threat."

Grachikov held up his hands, showing the palms. "Not to understand me wrong. But a man's gotta do what a man's gotta do." The American colloquialism sounded ridiculous coming from his lips.

"It still sounds like a threat."

For a moment they simply stared at each other. It was as though they were alone, far removed from the noise of the dying seals, the curious glances of the other men moving around them, aware only of each other, their eyes locked in a strange battle of wills.

Then Grachikov drew back his head and laughed, his lips pulling up above very pink gums. "We are like children now. This is not good. We are men, not children. We forget about this, yes?"

Adam realized he had been holding his breath. He exhaled and consciously tried to let go of the tension inside of him. He felt slightly nauseous. The swiftness of his anger had been an unpleasant surprise. He should leave. Now.

But as he started to turn away again, Grachikov said, "Mr. Williams."

He glanced over his shoulder. Grachikov was holding out his hand. "Friends, yes? Maybe one day we go diving together, look for buried treasure?" He laughed again.

Adam hesitated, but then stretched out his own hand. Grachikov's hand was cool and the palms strangely smooth. His grip was firm but not crushing.

Grachikov nodded. "Good. Goodbye Mr. Williams."

Eleven

As Adam pushed the boat into the water, Grachikov watched him thoughtfully, the club still swinging from his hand. The Russian's gaze took in Adam's muscular figure, the strong back and legs, the set of Adam's head on his shoulders.

Trouble. Adam Williams was trouble and an unexpected complication. He had plans for Mark Botha and he did not need the friend interfering. The doctor was vulnerable: he had a wife, he had patients he cared for. There were any number of ways pressure could be applied. But Adam was the joker that had suddenly popped up in the middle of his deck of cards.

Grachikov let his mind go over what he knew of this man. A lone wolf, that much was clear. A man who kept very much to himself. A man with only one friend as far as he knew: the doctor. So he may just be someone who has something to hide. Not that this made him unusual in a country where drifters with secret pasts were not only tolerated but even welcomed. *He* certainly didn't hold it against the man; his own past would not stand up to much scrutiny either.

But he had the feeling that he should tread warily. For one moment there he had seen something in Adam Williams's eyes that had given him pause. This was a man not to be taken lightly.

The boat had reached the open sea. He saw Williams look back over his shoulder at the shore. He lifted his hand and waved merrily at the figure in the boat. Williams did not wave back.

Grachikov dropped his hand to his face and touched his fingers to the ridge of scar tissue on his chin. He did not like the way Adam Williams made him feel. He sensed that this man could become a serious obstacle to his plans and that was unacceptable. Things usually went the way he intended. Only once in his life had his luck deserted him. He touched the scar on his chin again.

But on the whole he had led a charmed life. He had grown up the son of a well-placed Communist official and had enjoyed the privileges his father's position entailed. When perestroika came to the USSR, his father managed to switch his allegiance to Mikhail Gorbachev fairly effortlessly and the family continued to prosper. After high school, Grachikov joined the navy—a patriotic gesture expected of the son of a prominent member of government—and was trained as a navy diver. Diving satisfied his sense of adventure, but the miserable conditions under which he had to live did not appeal in the least. After four years, he returned to Moscow and found a city that had become a dangerous but exciting place for anyone with guts, cunning, and the instinct for criminal enterprise. It was a place tailor-made for a man like himself.

For ten years he lived well. And then he made a mistake. A stupid mistake that almost cost him his life. He had been over-confident, convinced he could muscle in on the territory of Fyodor Voznesensky, and his arrogance had cost him dearly. Not only did he have to flee his beloved city, but he also had to leave behind Susanna, his half-sister. Susanna Georgievna with her black hair and eyes and her ready laugh. Susanna who played the violin with a passion that could bring tears to your eyes.

He had gone on the run, fleeing first to St. Petersburg, then to Volgograd. But Fyodor's tentacles stretched everywhere. He needed a new place to start over, somewhere he had no history and where Fyodor would never think to look for him. But where?

And then his friend Valery told him about an opportunity that existed on a different continent, in a country thousands of miles to the south. A place where a wealth of precious stones were buried beneath shifting sands.

He remembered the two of them sitting in Valery's tiny apartment on Gorki Street. It was already dark and there was a steady drizzle. Even so, it was possible for him to see clearly into the apartment on the opposite side of the garbage-strewn back alley that separated the buildings. He was so close he could make out the gold and crimson flocked wallpaper, the peeling paint on the steel bed frame. Even with the windows closed, he thought he could smell cabbage and potato coming from the pot on the stove, which was being stirred by a scrawny man with a bald pate. Over the shoulder of the man, on the far side of the apartment, was another narrow window and through that window, Grachikov could see into yet another apartment. And no doubt, at the back of that apartment was a window looking straight into another living room. Tiny box upon tiny box. And here was Valery talking about a vast land with almost no people. A place where the sun always shines. Sitting in that mean, cramped little room, the rain outside the window turning to snow, it had seemed like the perfect escape. He could start fresh in such a place and maybe, after he had built up his fortune again, he could bring Susanna and little Valka to live with him. His future beckoned. It would be a dream come true.

What he found was no dream. Namibia was situated on tropical latitudes, but this was no paradise with balmy palm-strewn beaches and shimmering oases. Of course, he knew even before he arrived that Namibia was a desert country, but this knowledge had in no way prepared him for the desolation, the dreadful horror, of endless dunes of sand and a wind that blew without mercy.

He detested this country. He had come to hate the sun. The air was so dry, he never found himself sweating, but his skin blistered easily and even now the flesh around his watch strap was raw and pink. Often, when he went to bed, he would step into a recurring nightmare in which he was being sucked into an ocean of sand, the particles filling his mouth, clinging to his palate and the soft tissue at the back of his throat, creeping up his nose, coating the inside of his eyelids. No, this was no place for Susanna. How could he ever expect her or her child to follow him here?

Only one thing made it bearable—and essential—for him to live in this country. Diamonds. He had always loved diamonds—their fire and brilliance—and the two rings with their enormous marquise diamonds, which adorned his pinky and middle finger, had been bought in Russia, when he was still one of the princes of Moscow. Grachikov knew his appreciation of the stones was almost feminine. Diamonds did not just represent financial gain. They satisfied inside him something deeply sensual.

But it wasn't easy to get a foothold in the smuggling business. The diamonds mined in this country were not conflict diamonds, but mined by legal and tremendously powerful diamond companies. Security was stupendously tight and if you were caught, they threw away the key. Almost half of Namibia's budget came from the 65 percent taxes on the diamond industry and it was in the government's best interest to have tough legislation in place. Still, there is always a way. It only takes planning and perseverance. Besides which, he had found this to be the perfect base from which to handle traffic of blood diamonds coming in from Angola.

He had proceeded cautiously. Over a period of three years he had worked his way up in the diamond-smuggling ring operating from Kepler's Bay. He was smart and resourceful. He still had friends abroad. He was now the driving force within the ring and under his leadership, their network of contacts had expanded, stretching all the way into South Africa and even as far as the Congo and Liberia. The canning factory was providing him with a good cover and he had also branched out into other legal but lucrative activities such as sealing.

But for a while now he had been hankering after something else. It embarrassed him to acknowledge it, but what he yearned for, was—of all things—a memorial. He wanted to build something of value. Something durable. The hotel he envisaged for Pennington's Island would be the culmination of this desire. He did not plan on living in Namibia for the rest of his life, but he would like to know that when he did leave, the hotel would still stand as a beautiful, lasting testament to the drive and energy of one Yuri Konstantin Grachikov.

He was surprised by how passionate he felt about his project. He experienced such pride whenever he studied the architect's drawings. In his mind's eye he would wander through the cool tiled entrance hall with its vaulted roof, past the wood-paneled registration area and into the cocktail lounge with its picture windows and view of the ocean. The decor would be tasteful and minimalist. Each hotel suite would have its own tiny plunge pool. It was perfect.

Or it would be, if it weren't for Dr. Mark Botha. He still couldn't believe his plans were in imminent danger of collapse because of the efforts of a mild-mannered, soft-spoken but intensely obstinate man with an irritating obsession for preserving marine life. Fish and birds—who gave a damn?

This backward place was barely clinging to life. His hotel would serve as a lifeline to the people living in Kepler's Bay. They should be grateful for his ideas to rejuvenate the place. But instead of thanks, what did he get? Nothing but grief and suspicion.

The truly worrying thing was that he had overextended himself, borrowing heavily not only from legitimate financial institutions, but also from some rather unsympathetic characters who would show little understanding if he went belly-up. And the longer it took for him to start work on the hotel, the more that prospect seemed likely.

But he must not even allow himself to think such defeatist thoughts. Ultimately, he would prevail. He had underestimated Mark Botha, but he could still change the good doctor's mind for him. Offering him money didn't work, so maybe the time had come to take off the gloves.

The face of Adam Williams suddenly came into his mind again and he frowned. This was a dangerous man.

But even dangerous men had their weaknesses. Grachikov smiled grimly. He would make it his business to find out what Adam Williams's might be.

Twelve

THE ANIMAL WAS TROTTING down the long avenue of trees, the play of moonlight and shadow drawing fugitive patterns on the broad chest and thick pelted back. He was a large male. His tongue was lolling. Once he stopped and lifted his nose as though to scent the air, but then he continued his journey, moving effortlessly.

He had reached the house. Trotting through the wide-open front door, he started up the shallow steps of the curved staircase. And now he was moving on silent feet down the moonlit hallway. His paws barely brushed against the slippery linoleum and he threw no shadow against the moon-washed walls. On and on he went down that long passage with its row of smooth closed doors. On and on he went, toward that one room at the end of the passage with its door open.

He was at the threshold. He crouched down till his belly touched the ground; his senses locked on the soft breathing

of the sleeping figure in the bed beneath the window. The
window was open. A breeze pushed against the white net
curtains like a ghostly hand and gently lifted a few tendrils
of hair at the softveined temples of the sleeper in the bed.
The woman stirred and sighed.

The animal delicately stretched out one paw and moved
his body stealthily forward. The muscles in his massive
shoulders bunched. His eyes were phosphorescent blue and
glowed like coals inside his head.

And then he entered the room.

Justine jerked awake. In a terrified daze she bolted upright
and groped, panic-stricken for the switch of the bedside
lamp. Heart hammering erratically inside her throat, she
pulled the bedclothes up to her chin like a frightened child
and sat with her knees drawn up to her chest, eyes blinking
in the sudden light.

This was the fourth night in a row that she had woken up
in terror. Every night she went to bed and a phantom shape
glided silently through her dreams. And every night he got
closer. During the previous night visits, he had stopped at
the threshold, had hovered just outside her door. But tonight
he had entered the room.

Still clutching the sheets with one hand, she leaned sideways and opened the drawer of the bedside table. She desperately needed a cigarette. Her fingers found the packet of
Dunhills and her lighter. The feel of a cigarette between her
lips and the familiar rasping sound of the lighter was comforting and she leaned back against the bedpost and sensed
her heart slowly calming itself.

For a while she sat quietly smoking. It was dead quiet.
The night sky outside the window was black as pitch. The
light from the bedside table was soft and the corners of the
room were in shadow, but as she let her eyes wander through
the room, there was more than enough light for her to see.
The green corduroy jacket hanging from the back of the

chair. A cup and saucer with coffee stains. A dead tulip in a glass of water.

And pictures. Many, many pictures. Dozens of black-and-white prints—not only contact sheets, but many enlargements, as well. Pictures taped against the walls, spread out on the bare floorboards and stacked in glossy piles on every available surface. Pictures of empty rooms and empty passages; of twilit gardens and quiet walkways. Images shot and developed with obsessive fervor. The pictures were everywhere and downstairs in the library there were even more.

What was happening to her? Was she losing her mind? Ever since her photo spree last week, she had been gripped by an overwhelming desire to find the wolf-like animal in her pictures once again. Her desire was shot through with feelings of dread, but the need to find the animal was all encompassing.

Her quest had been unsuccessful. She had fully expected to discover the wolf once more, but the new prints had turned out completely unremarkable. The images captured on film were empty of life and showed nothing out of the ordinary. No ghostly shape lurking behind doorways. No animal staring out at her with glowing eyes.

So she thought she might have better luck shooting pictures in other parts of the house, in rooms as yet undiscovered. Camera in hand, she had worked her way all through this big, empty house.

She had walked through rooms where the dust settled quietly. She had discovered an attic, shiny with cobwebs. She had searched through the storage rooms on the other side of the courtyard, pushing her way through taped up cardboard boxes, and chairs and tables swaddled in plastic wrap. She had wandered down the avenue with its whispering trees, had lingered at the well and the wisteria walkway. She had shot roll upon roll of film, but in her pictures she did not find even a glimpse of the animal she was seeking. No dark shape, no moving shadow. It was gone. If she didn't have the original contact sheets and developed pictures as proof, she would have thought the whole thing was the product of a drunken fantasy. As she developed each new roll of film, her hands would shake with anticipation, an anticipation that would dissolve into part relief, part frustration when she pulled the paper from the tray of liquid and found no trace of the phantom animal that haunted her mind.

Only in her dreams did they meet. But her dreams terrified her.

And there was something else. She couldn't shake the sense that some connection existed between the elusive wolf who lived only in her photographs and the man who had left the house a fugitive almost a decade before. They were linked. How, she didn't know, but the feeling was too strong to ignore. She had even taped up a print of the wolf right next to Adam Buchanan's picture against her wall, in the vague hope that it might help her make sense of the jumble of feelings and impressions plaguing her thoughts.

Drawing deeply on the cigarette, her eyes settled on the grainy photocopy of his face. The strong jaw, the hard mouth, and uncompromising stare. He was not easy company to have in the room. The eyes were so unflinching. More than once she had considered removing him from her wall, but each time she held back. There was a connection between this man and the wolf. If she looked hard enough, surely she would find it . . .

To hell with it. This was insane. Clearly she needed help. She glanced at the alarm clock; the hands stood at ten to three. Stubbing out the cigarette in the ashtray, she picked up the phone and, without hesitation, dialed Barry's number.

Barry Winthrop. A good man, her mother had called him and she certainly could not fault this description. He was a man who would go the distance. He had stuck by her through it all. Drugs. Anorexia. Her suicide attempt. He was the one who first discovered her after she had sawed away at her wrists. Scooping her out of the bath, he had placed her in the backseat of his car where she had sagged against the door, sick and confused. She had only the vaguest recollection of what had happened next as he drove the car to its limits. All she remembered was the squeal of tires, traffic lights throwing nightmarish smears on the gleaming blacktop, white tiled walls and bright lights inside the hospital. His face was the first face she saw when she came out of surgery. And afterward he had sat with her hour after hour, he and Jonathan taking turns, the two men who had taken it upon themselves to look out for her.

Barry was kind and wise and he had a wry sense of humor, which could be piercingly insightful. He cared for her deeply and the truth of it was that she treated him abominably. They were lovers, but she was not faithful to him. Whenever she was in England, they would spend their time together quite happily for a few weeks, even months. But then she'd get restless and push her "art photography" to one side and accept an assignment that would take her away to cover some or other bloody conflict at the edge of the world. And during these periods of absence she would share her bed with other men—journalists, fellow photographers—like herself, members of a motley band drawn to turmoil and death like flies to meat.

Barry was aware of her infidelities and they caused him pain, but whenever she turned up on his doorstep, he always accepted her back. He had asked her several times to marry him and each time she had said no. But she had also made sure to keep the possibility alive, allowing him to think there was hope. She knew she was being selfish. She knew she was being cruel. But she did not want to lose him, even though she refused to share her life with him. The idea of giving him up was unthinkable. He was a rock. He was her safe harbor in a mad world.

The phone kept on ringing in her ear. Was he away? She hadn't seen or spoken to him since Jonathan's funeral more than three months ago when she had taken off, hiding out in a friend's house in Greece. But then there was a click and his voice, hoarse and groggy with sleep, answered.

"Hello?"

She took a deep breath. "I'm driving into town tomorrow. I need your help. Can I see you?"

There was a long silence. Then he said, "I was wondering if you were ever going to call. I'll be here."

HE OPENED THE DOOR almost at once after she had rung the bell and when she saw his face it was so immediately familiar it felt as if she had never been away. She walked into the apartment and here, too, everything was just as she remembered it: cramped and cozy with a shabby velvet sofa, fringed lamps, and the walls covered with gilt-framed oils and watercolors.

But a lot had happened in the time they'd spent apart and for a moment, as they stood in the middle of the room, there was an awkward silence. It suddenly felt to her as though they had run out of things to say to each other before they'd even properly started a conversation.

But then he leaned forward and placed his hands on her shoulders. "Justine. I've missed you."

Placing her arms around his waist, she drew closer and rested her head on his chest. The jersey underneath her cheek was scratchy and she could smell the scent of his aftershave. Feeling his warmth, hearing the thud of his heart underneath her ear reminded her how very fond she was of him. The tension brought about by the previous night's dream was starting to disappear.

"Tea?" He pushed her gently away.

"Coffee."

"Of course. I won't be a minute." He smiled and disappeared into the tiny kitchen. She heard a cupboard open then the clink of spoons and cups.

She had met Barry almost seven years ago and his magazine had bought many of her pictures over the years. He had first called her in for an interview after she had sent him some photographs of a Somalian warlord and his soldiers.

She was very proud of those pictures. There was something brutally beautiful in the elongated oval faces, in the khat-hazed eyes. The thin elegant limbs, the long fingers cradling the AK-47s so casually were splendid images. They radiated a kind of evil allure which repulsed, but also attracted.

Barry had studied the photographs without saying a word, scrutinizing the images intently. She stood by, slightly alarmed at his silence and the intensity with which he was examining the pictures spread out before him.

Finally he straightened. "These are good."

"But?"

"But I find them deeply offensive."

She flushed. "The business of death is always offensive."

"No. That's not what I mean. The way you treat the subject matter. The style you've given them. You're glamorizing evil."

She was outraged, but afterward in the solitude of her bedroom, she had found the courage to admit to herself that he may be right. Still, despite the criticism, he had accepted the pictures. This, in turn, had brought her new work. Barry was her most demanding critic, but also her biggest supporter. Over the years he had acted not only as an editor, but also as a kind of agent, constantly on the look-out for new opportunities that might further her career.

"I'm sorry," Barry was emerging from the kitchen, a tray in his hands. "I've had to use instant—as you haven't been around, I didn't think to stock up on the good stuff."

"Instant's fine."

For a while they were quiet as they sat opposite each other

at the dining table, sipping the hot liquid. Then he placed his cup carefully inside the saucer and looked her full in the face. "So what's wrong?"

She leaned forward and opened her camera bag, extracting the folder with the enlargements she had made. Without saying a word she slid it across the tabletop toward him.

He opened the folder and took out the pictures one by one. She watched his face; the way his expression changed from casual interest to frowning concentration.

He looked up. "What's going on here?"

"I wish I knew."

"I take it these images have not been manipulated."

She shook her head. "Absolutely not. And I can tell you now that when I shot these pics I was alone. But when I did the developing, there it was. A wolf in my house."

He picked up the photograph, which showed the animal poised on the staircase. "Damn odd-looking wolf this." He squinted. "If it is a wolf."

"Well whatever it is, it damn well wasn't there when I took this picture. You believe me, right?"

"I do, of course." He lowered the photograph in his hand and leaned back in his chair. "Suppose you tell me exactly what happened. First of all, where is this place exactly? Paradine Park? Tell me about it."

He kept his eyes on her face while she talked, pressing his thumb against his lower lip the way she had seen him do a hundred times before. It was always a sign that he was troubled.

When she stopped talking, feeling suddenly spent, he said quietly, "It sounds like a bad place, Justine."

"It's an unhappy house, yes."

"Maybe you should think about moving out."

"Why?" Her voice was sharp. "Afraid I'm losing my mind?"

"Of course not. But why would you want to go on living

there? Putting these pics aside for the moment, it still sounds like a desperately creepy place. You should leave."

She shook her head vehemently. "I can't do that."

"Why not?"

"It's just . . . I don't know. I just can't. And besides, my flat's on a long let. I won't be able to go back for another six months. Plus I can't face London yet. I need more time."

"You're fascinated by him, aren't you," he said suddenly.

"By whom?"

"This man—this killer—Adam Buchanan. You kept repeating his name."

She shrugged, feeling unexpectedly embarrassed. What would Barry think if he knew she even had the guy's face taped against her wall? And really, what did she do that for? Why force herself to look into the eyes of a murderer every day? She couldn't even begin to answer this question, except for that nagging, persistent feeling that man and wolf were somehow connected.

Barry was watching her, frowning. She shrugged again. "Well, this guy is the star performer in the whole sad story, you will agree."

"Maybe." His gaze was puzzled.

She looked away. "All of which still doesn't explain this." She gestured at the pictures in front of them.

"No." He sighed. "It doesn't, does it." He suddenly frowned. "You know . . ."

"What?"

"I remember reading something about ghost photography once."

"*Ghost* photography."

He nodded, his eyes alert. "As far as I can remember, the article was about this woman who had taken a picture of her garden, I think it was. There was no one but herself in the garden, but when she made the print, she discovered the outline of a male figure standing underneath one of the trees.

She developed the same negative again, and this time the figure was standing next to the garden gate. When she repeated the process for the third time, the figure had moved yet again, and was approaching the front door. She was never able to explain it and when the newspaper asked her to replicate the whole thing, she was unsuccessful."

"Do you remember where you read this? Do you still have the article by any chance?"

He shook his head regretfully. "Sorry. It was some time ago. And quite frankly, I didn't set much store by the whole story. It simply sounded too weird to be true. What I do remember is that it turned out badly for her in the end, though."

"What do you mean?"

"Well, she died shortly after. In a climbing accident. The reporter had played up that part of it, of course. You know, death coming to her door to claim her and so on."

Justine shivered. "Pretty spooky."

"So is this." He nodded at the photographs.

She smiled wryly. "Well, I have a soft spot for wolves, you know." She tapped her shoulder. "I even carry one permanently around with me." She thought for a moment. "Perhaps I could go to the library and look up anything they have on ghost photography. That would be a start."

"I suppose so." He watched her, his eyes concerned. "Or you could forget about all of this and come home."

"Barry . . ."

"Please, Justine." He reached across the table and took her hand. "Forget about your flat. You still have things here. I've kept your room as it was, haven't touched it. You can simply move in. And I promise you, I'll give you the space you need."

She looked into his kind, trusting face and tears pricked her eyes. "It's not the right time."

"It never is," he said sadly.

"Maybe some day . . ."

He didn't answer. She shuffled the photographs together and placed them in the camera bag. In silence he helped her with her jacket and adjusted the strap of her bag so that it fit easier onto her shoulder.

But as they walked down the passage toward the front door, he suddenly said, "I forgot to tell you, that feature article about you—the one for *Polkadot*—it was finally published."

"I thought they'd decided against it."

"So did I. But apparently they reconsidered. Wait. I'll get you a copy." He turned around and disappeared into his workroom.

Polkadot was a fairly new and very prestigious publication aimed at amateur and professional photographers alike. Every edition was devoted to the work of only one photographer. To have your pictures showcased in its pages was excellent exposure. The magazine had interviewed her for the article nearly a year ago, and when nothing happened afterward she assumed they had cooled to the idea of profiling her work. But apparently not.

"Here," he said as he returned. "Page thirty-seven."

She took the magazine from him. On the cover was an arresting picture: the inside of the domed library of a beautiful house in the Kashmir region of India, which she had visited years ago during a trip to this strife-torn province. Suspended from the library's elaborately honeycombed ceiling were old handmade brass spheres representing the heavenly bodies: Venus, Jupiter, Saturn with its lovely rings. They were works of art, these brass spheres, examples of craftsmanship and beauty, and her host had explained to her that they were more than a hundred years old. This particular picture was one of her favorites. She had used Kodalith paper and the result was everything she could have wished for. The colors were mink and parchment and the slight graininess gave the image texture and depth. Below the picture were printed the words: *The Universe of Justine Callaway*.

"They did a good job," Barry said. "But they also focused quite heavily on your personal life. There's even some stuff in there about Jonathan's death, I'm sorry to say."

"Probably the reason why they decided to run the article after all. Nothing like a little tragedy to add some spice." She flipped open the flap of her camera bag and pushed the magazine angrily inside. "When did this come out?"

"Last month already. Your Mum was actually the one who first noticed it."

"You've spoken to her?"

"She calls me regularly, you know. She's lonely." His voice was slightly reproving. "Are you going to stop by and visit her today?"

"I think not, thank you."

"She talked about some mail waiting for you—some letters. You should go pick them up."

"It'll keep."

He sighed but didn't insist. As he opened the door for her, he said, "Call me. Don't disappear on me again, OK?"

"You're a lovely man, Barry. I don't know why you put up with me."

"Just promise to keep in touch. Say you will."

She touched her lips to his cheek. "I promise."

She left her car in the parking bay outside Barry's apartment—the resident's parking permit on her windshield was still valid—and took the tube from the South Kensington station to the British Library in St. Pancras. The library in Ainstey would almost certainly not be up to the job. However, she should be able to find something in the British Library's massive treasure trove of books that could shed more information on her phantom pictures. Fortunately she had renewed her reader's pass at the beginning of the year.

Even though the new library was efficient and streamlined, she missed the old reading room in the British Museum with its wonderful light and exquisite proportions. Despite the enormous open-volume entrance hall, the St. Pancras library was oddly tomblike. The stark modernity was chilling. She entered, aware of the marble floors giving a faint echo to every tiny sound. Leaving her jacket and bag at the check-in as required, she took with her only her wallet, a pencil, and her file of pictures in the transparent plastic bag provided for the purpose.

As she rode up the escalator, she stared at the old, beautifully tooled leather-bound volumes that faced her behind a sheet of protective glass. They seemed out of place in their see-through coffin. They belonged in a room with wooden paneling, scratched desks, and scuffed floors. These books should be encased in a room that bears the invisible imprint of generations of eager minds, a place that had soaked up the whispers and thoughts of those who had come seeking information and enlightenment. This library with its bright lights and smooth clean surfaces would never be able to absorb the silent conversations in the heads of those who linger here in their search for knowledge.

There were surprisingly few people in the reading room. Slipping behind a terminal, she scoured the data base but found only two books, which appeared to address the topic of ghost photography. She gave the information to the bored-looking librarian and returned to her seat to wait for the call back.

It was quiet. The only sound was the tapping of keys and the barely audible hum of the computers. While waiting, she took out the folder with the photographs once more. She had studied these pictures so many times, she knew every detail, every shadow. But as always she was gripped by that same feeling of excited, if fearful, anticipation.

She stared at the images longingly, as though by concentrating hard enough she could transport herself into their depths and find herself walking down those shallow stairs, one hand resting on the balustrade, the other intertwined in the animal's thick coat. The fur scratching her fingers, the pelt rough, not soft. The skin underneath her fingertips exuding warmth. And now she was kneeling down, and its breath was on her face. She placed her hand on the deep chest, felt a ripple of muscle. The musky animal smell. The sandpaper tongue as it touched her wrist. The eyes stared at her unblinkingly—yellow eyes ringed with black—and she was unable to look away . . .

The light above her desk was flashing. She snapped out of her reverie and looked across to the checkout counter where the librarian was watching her with exasperation. As their eyes met, he made urgent gestures to the effect that she should collect her books.

She slammed the folder with the photographs shut, aware of her heart beating in her throat. The room seemed overly bright. Walking slowly to the counter, she put one foot carefully in front of the other as though her balance might be affected.

When she returned to her desk with the two books, she did not open them immediately. She tried to steady the nausea that was gripping her. So real. The image of the wolf had been so real.

Oh, hell. So now she needn't even wait for nighttime, her dreams were catching up with her even during the day. Way to go, Justine. You've finally lost it. Stupid, stupid, and oh, shit. She stared hopelessly at the two books in front of her. She was afraid of what she might discover.

But there was nothing the slightest bit unsettling within the pages of the first book. The author was writing from a skeptic's point of view and his style of writing was deliberately dry. The book was little more than a history of photographic deception, starting in 1862 with the "spirit photographs" of a certain William H. Mumler. Using double exposure, the author explained disapprovingly, the intrepid Mr. Mumler succeeded in creating eerie images of misty figures hovering ghostlike in the background. A host of imitators followed and the sale of "ghost" pictures to grief-

stricken relatives became a profitable sideline for many un-
scrupulous photographers. After discussing some of the
more well-known hoaxes—fairy pictures and the like—the
book ended with a chapter on photographic retouching and
the digital magic of the computer. *The idea that the camera
never lies, is no longer true.* The digital images on these
pages were in the typical chic-freak mode: long-necked
fashion models morphing into animals; the breast of a beautiful woman unraveling like a peeled apple; a powerful male
figure kicking off the head of a slightly built opponent, the
head exploding in a mosaic of violet and rose fragments.
Still, for all their overt shock value, the images were too
stylized, too perfect—too carefully thought out—to be truly
disturbing.

And it was not what she was looking for. Disappointed,
she pushed the book to one side and picked up the second
volume. *Thoughtography* was the title and as the book fell
open in her hand, she could feel her skin starting to prickle.

The page showed three black-and-white photographs of
the same woman—the same picture, in fact—but increasingly distorted. The first picture was unremarkable: a head
and shoulder shot of a sad-eyed, middle-aged blond, hair
pulled back from her face to reveal a jawline no longer
smooth. In the second picture the color quality of the photograph had deteriorated to assume a sepia hue and the face
seemed to be overlaid with the outlines of another face, a
face very similar in shape to the original face. Even though
the impression was slight, the effect was startling: the personality of the sitter had been subtly altered. The eyes
seemed more alive, the expression less placid. In the third
and final picture the outlines of the second face had hardened and now the effect was rather horrible: it was as though
some malevolent being had gleefully taken up residence
within the sitter, staring out from her eyes, pulling up the
corners of her mouth in a knowing smile. The impression of
vicious amusement was unnerving. The text at the bottom of

the page intensified the sense of disquiet. *The above pictures are of Mrs. Beth Edmunston of Columbus, Ohio. She was strangled by her husband three weeks after he had taken these pictures. They were developed after his arrest by police technicians and had not been retouched in any way.*

On the next page, another picture—a polaroid this time—of a rain-smeared landscape superimposed by the ghostly figure of a young man. The young face was eerily dispassionate. It seemed the young man—the photographer's younger brother—was killed by a car a few days later as he stood in the exact same pose as the figure in the picture.

The remaining images contained within the book were also deeply haunting. A baby with what looked like a rose growing from its cheek. A stone angel with animated eyes. A girl, her face blank and moodless, her garments on fire. But unlike the digitally manipulated images of the first book, these pictures were messy, flawed. In the world of digital manipulation, detail is king and images invariably sharp with clean edges. The pictures beneath her hand seemed somewhat blurred, almost amateurish. And there was something about them, something indefinable, that chilled her mind.

Most photographs which claim to belong to the realm of the unexplained will not stand up to vigorous scrutiny and are the products of trickery. Still there are those rare pictures, which do indeed defy understanding.

Also known as "ghost" or "spirit" photography, we have termed these pictures "thoughtographs," as it appears that the photographer is the key. It seems to be the photographer's ability to affect unexposed film—consciously or unconsciously—which creates these startling visual images.

The most well-known thoughtographer was Ted Serios who worked as a Chicago bellhop in the sixties. Mr. Serios, who was able to project mental images on to photographic film, often did so with the lens cap of the camera still in

*place or by using a camera without a lens. The images cre-
ated by him were often of recognizable buildings such as the
Chicago Hilton, but the images were distorted as if they
were the product of faulty memory or imagination. Mr. Serios's talent was researched by several investigators without
their ever being able to furnish an explanation for the pictures created by his mind.*

*Thoughtographs can be premonitions and often either the
photographer or the person photographed will face traumatic events shortly after.*

She leaned back in her chair, her mind trying to come to
terms with the words on the page. It was difficult. She did
not believe in mysticism or the supernatural. Her photographs were of real people engaged in real conflict. Her architectural photographs were of buildings that have
weathered time and the elements. Durable, solid. She did not
think there had ever in the past been anything in her photography that hinted that she might have a talent for thoughtography. But how to explain her pictures of the wolf? What did
the wolf represent?

*Thougthographs appear to be projections of the photogra-
pher's thoughts, desires, and fantasies—unedited, at times
disturbing. Maybe these pictures are indeed instances where
the camera does not lie. They are visual reflections of a dark
longing.*

A dark longing. Justine stared at the words for a long time.
When she looked up again, she saw the light outside the window had failed. The sky was black.

She emerged from the South Ken tube station to find the
streets wet and the rain sifting down, thin as gauze. She
stopped next to her car and searched for her keys. As she
opened the door, she glanced up at Barry's apartment. The
curtains were open and there was light in the window, yellow

and warm. She could see the gleam of the mirror above the mantelpiece and the shadow of a potted palm against the cream wall. For a moment, as she stood there in the darkness, the raindrops furring her jacket with silver, she experienced a fierce desire for the calm and comfort of the world glimpsed behind the tall window. Maybe she should spend the night. It would be good to enter the apartment, flop down in the easy chair next to the gas fireplace and put her feet up on the ratty old Ottoman. Barry would pour her a drink and there would be something beautiful playing on the old-fashioned stereo.

The picture was so appealing that she hesitated. But then, in her mind came the image of Paradine Park: the sandstone walls silvered by moonlight, the glittering windows staring out at the deserted, immaculate gardens. An unhappy house, but a house she could not bring herself to leave. The place gripped her, its hold on her imagination was too strong. And even more compelling, deep within her was the growing conviction that at this moment in her life, she was exactly where she should be.

The thought brought her up short. She was a rambler, always had been. As a child she had had no option but to follow her father whenever he made one of his frequent decisions to move on. Later she had adopted this lifestyle by choice. Drifting from one place to another, never really putting down roots—one can develop a taste for it, an addiction. But now, despite the fact that Paradine Park filled her with misgivings and deep unease, she did not wish to spend even one night away from its echoing passages and empty rooms.

She turned her back on the brightly lit window. Sliding behind the wheel, she turned the key in the ignition.

TRAFFIC OUT OF LONDON was heavy and it was another two hours before she spotted the church spire in Ainstey. The main street was deserted and so, too, the untarred road stretching past dark paddocks and fields and leading to the wrought-iron gates of Paradine Park.

The gates were open.

Her brain registered this fact almost as soon as she noticed the motorcycle parked off the road, next to the weathered stone wall. She frowned. She had closed the black gates herself this morning. She was sure of this because at the time she had debated with herself whether she should go through the trouble. In the end, because she knew she might be away for the entire day, she had in fact stopped the car and she remembered how dusty her hands were after she had slipped the long black bolt into position. But now the gates were open—not wide open, but definitely ajar, as though someone had pushed them apart just far enough in order to step through. And the motorcycle had not been there this morning, either.

She brought the car to a standstill. Keeping the engine running, she got out and pushed the gates all the way back so that she could drive through. The gates made a thin, screeching sound, which set her teeth on edge. She looked up the long avenue with its tall trees. The headlights of the car played against the tree trunks, blotting out the shadows close to where she stood, but fading away further on where the avenue stretched ahead into deeper darkness.

She shivered. The wind was chilly. Drawing her jacket close to her body, she got back into the car and started driving toward the house, which sat in ink-black silhouette against the sky. She drove slowly, keeping the growl of the MG's engine at bay. As she reached the driveway she switched off the headlights and stopped the car with only a whisper of gravel.

For a while she sat without moving, giving her eyes time to adjust to the darkness. The windows of the house were black, but then, she hadn't switched on any lights before she'd set out this morning. Stupid of her, really. She should have at least left the porch light on. The front door was shut. Apart from the wind in the trees, there was no other movement.

She got out of the MG and closed the car door gently. There was no one around at the front of the house, but that did not mean that someone might not be lurking somewhere else on the estate. She thought of the black motorbike parked at the wall. The bike must have an owner. Perhaps she should go inside and call the police, tell them that she suspected there was an intruder on the premises. She hesitated, feeling apprehensive and foolish at the same time. Maybe she should just take a quick look around the courtyard.

The scream that suddenly pierced the air was completely unexpected. Her blood went cold. She started running toward the back of the house, her feet slipping on the heavy gravel. She turned the corner and her hand scrambled against the wall for the outside light switch. The blackness gave way to blinding light. Mason and his grandson had replaced every single outside bulb with high-voltage spotlights. The courtyard was flooded with light bright as day.

A few yards away two figures were staring at her. They were not moving, as if the light had somehow frozen them to the spot. The man had his hand uplifted, the gesture was menacing, and the girl in front of him had her hand clutched to her cheek. Then the girl gave a kind of sob and gave a step backward. The man slowly lowered his arm. He turned to face Justine fully.

He was young, he couldn't have been more than eighteen. His face was pasty-looking and there were pimples on his forehead. The wrists sticking out from his leather jacket were thin and his fingernails were painted black. His chin was soft-looking, but there was a glint in his eyes that made her watch him warily. That and the red mark on the girl's face.

But they couldn't just go on staring at each other. She used her most authoritative voice. "What's going on here? Who are you?"

He sneered at her. His body was as taut as an unsprung

trap. She could sense the aggression and violence lurking just beneath the surface.

The girl was watching her with wide frightened eyes. And now Justine recognized her, the streaked hair, the pancake makeup, the silver chain with the looped script: *Angelface*. The girl from the corner shop. And her Prince Charming—the black-clad knight on his iron horse. The one with the mother who followed murder cases as a hobby. Everything suddenly made sense. The pink panties, the six-pack of beer, the dirty mattress—she now knew whom they belonged to. Obviously these two had hoped to continue using their hideout, only to find their plans thwarted by a new shiny lock on the door.

The mark on the girl's face was fading, but her lip was split at the corner and blood welled through the cut.

"Are you all right?" She spoke to the girl but kept her eyes on the boy.

"None of your business, bitch." His voice was raspy, but almost comically high-pitched. He probably was given hell in high school because of it.

"Please, Timmy. It's all right. Let's go." The girl placed a tentative, placating hand on his shoulder.

But Timmy was not to be so placated. "Shut up," he snarled. "Shut up."

"You should listen to her." Justine spoke carefully. "This is private property."

"Private property," he mimicked. "Maybe I like private property."

"Maybe you do. But if you don't leave now I'm calling the police. So be a good boy . . . Timmy."

His face turned red. A vein swelled in his temple. He gave a threatening step forward, but the girl—a new note of urgency in her voice—grabbed his arm tightly. "Come on, love. We don't need the trouble. Let's go."

He moved his shoulder violently and tore free from her

grip. Hand knotted into a tight fist, he struck the girl savagely against the side of her face. She screamed and fell to her knees, her arms held protectively over her head.

This had gone far enough. Justine lunged forward. His arms were away from his body and his stomach was exposed. It was almost too easy. Without hesitation she rammed her fist into his diaphragm. When he snapped forward, she brought up her knee. There—take that. She heard the deep gasp of pain. "Cunt," he shrieked. "Cunt."

Still bent over, he swung his arm wildly and grabbed her by the collar of her jacket. He was surprisingly strong. She tried to twist free, but he jerked her toward him with such force that her blouse cut painfully into her neck. His face was next to hers and she could smell alcohol. "You'll fucking pay for this. See if you don't. You'll—"

Without hesitation she grabbed his free hand with both her hands and pulled his little finger viciously in the wrong direction, away from his palm. The howl of pain that left his mouth was truly harrowing. He let go of her and staggered to the side, his hand to his mouth. "My finger. You broke my finger, you fuck, you. My finger. You broke it." He made a gurgling noise deep inside his throat.

"Get out. I'm calling the police, right now. Get out."

He gave her a sick look, didn't move.

"I mean it. Get out."

He started walking, stumbling slightly, his hand clutched underneath his armpit. She stepped back as he passed by her, but the fight seemed to be out of him. Giving her a final wretched look, he rounded the corner and she heard his footsteps on the gravel pathway. She waited a few moments, her body tense, but when he did not reappear, she walked quickly to the archway and looked out. He had reached the trees and was limping dejectedly down the long avenue in the direction of the gates. His head was bowed.

She looked back at the girl who was watching her with horrified eyes. "You shouldn'a done that."

"What?" Justine stared.

"He'll get even, you'll see."

"No, he won't. We're going into the house right now and we're calling the police. You can tell them everything. Get him charged with assault."

"No!" She jumped to her feet, her mouth working. "You mustn't do that. Please you mustn't. Promise you won't. Promise."

The girl was obviously simple-minded, and it was rather galling that she wasn't showing any signs of gratitude either.

"Are you crazy? You should take a look at your face. You're going to have a black eye tomorrow. What's wrong with you? You should report him. Of course you should."

"No. You mustn't. Please. Please. Please don't." Her voice was rising hysterically and she was actually wringing her hands.

This was ridiculous. She felt like shaking the girl. "Look," she stopped. It probably wasn't going to help if she shouted. "Look," she said again in a milder tone. "Your boyfriend is abusive. He should be stopped. Helped." Yeah, right. With a cricket bat cracked over his head if possible. "If you don't report him, this will happen again. You don't want that, do you?"

"He loves me. He does."

"He has a crappy way of showing it."

"No, really. He loves me. He's good to me, but I made him angry tonight. It wasn't his fault, see."

"No, I don't see."

"I'll tell the coppers, you're lying. I'll tell them it's all a mistake. If I don't press charges, they won't care."

Which was probably true. And suddenly Justine realized she was exhausted. Her head throbbed and her neck felt sore where the fabric of her blouse had cut into the flesh. Now that the adrenaline was drying up, she felt cold and shivery and her overwhelming wish was to get rid of this girl with her chalk-white face who had started weeping, streaks of mascara running down her cheeks.

Feeling helpless now and irritated beyond belief she stared at the girl who was breathing noisily, wiping her nose with the back of her hand. Her eyes were swimming.

Oh, to hell with it. She's had enough. "OK. You win. Let's go to my car and I'll run you into town."

"I'm all right. If I go now quickly, I can catch up with him."

"Wait."

The girl stopped, one foot in front of the other, poised for flight. She looked apprehensive, as if afraid Justine might have changed her mind about the police again.

"This room." Justine gestured at the door with its brand new padlock. "You two—you used this room, didn't you."

The girl's voice was flat. "We have no other place to go, see. Timmy, he still lives at home. And me mum, she doesn't like Timmy."

At least stupidity didn't run in the family. "Well, tell Timmy not to come around again. If I see him anywhere near this place, I will report him to the police at once, is that understood?"

The girl's face was set now and the tears had drained back into their ducts. "Can I go now?"

Justine sighed. "I don't even know your name."

The girl stared. Then she said softly, "It's not your business now, is it?"

She turned around and ran down the walkway and through the arch.

ON THE FAR SIDE of the quadrangle, on the opposite side of the arch, the Watcher was looking on. His heart was pounding with excitement. His palms were wet.

He had witnessed the confrontation between Justine and Tim March in its entirety and his blood was pumping through his veins joyously. He felt *alive*. It was the most spectacular stroke of luck that he had decided to visit Paradine Park this evening. He hadn't planned on coming until the next day, but Mrs. Denton, the organist, had a sore throat and choir practice was canceled. Not for anything would he have missed this. Not for the world. The scene he had just witnessed confirmed everything he believed about Justine. The wildness he had sensed within her was not just his imagination.

If there was one thing all his years as watcher—and priest—had taught him, it was that courage was in scarce supply. Aggression was common, but a warrior heart was rare. Justine hadn't backed down an inch. She was a magnificent Judith.

And it could have gotten ugly. March had something of a reputation in Ainstey. Small stuff, mainly—joy riding, vandalism—but there was also a rumor going around that he and some friends had beat up one of Mrs. McEvoy's lodgers after an argument in a pub. The man had ended up in the hospital. Actually, come to think of it, Justine should watch out. Tim March is just the kind of vicious bully-boy who would seek retribution for tonight's events. It would take him a while to get his courage up again, but Justine had humiliated him in front of his girlfriend, a dangerous thing to do. March would want revenge. As for the pudgy little girlfriend, the Watcher rather thought her name was Holly. He hardly ever came in contact with the girl, but he knew the mother. The girl was running now, her fat legs flailing. Stupid little cow.

He looked back to where Justine was still standing. In the harsh overhead light she looked utterly drained. Her face was white and her eyes black shadows. He saw her open her handbag and remove her keys. She walked to the back door and fitted the key to the lock. The door opened inward.

Just as he thought she was about to enter, she suddenly swung around. She seemed to be looking straight at him. For a long moment she stared in his direction, her eyes probing the darkness. He tensed, he hardly breathed. He was half hidden behind a pillar but he couldn't take the chance of trying to move completely out of her sight. The slightest movement and she'd see him. For just a moment he remembered another night, nine years ago, when he had also watched from the shadows and Adam Buchanan had looked up and in the darkness their eyes had met. Buchanan's unseeing; his own filled with panicked excitement.

Justine didn't move. Did she sense he was out here? Contrary to popular belief, it was very difficult to observe someone without their knowledge. That indefinable feeling of knowing that you're being watched was man's true sixth sense. He had seen it over and over in his years of playing the game. The subjects could be completely relaxed, their antennae in sleep mode, but if he watched them for too long, they'd sense it. And after what happened tonight, Justine's senses were already in high alert. There was a line of tension stretching taut between the two of them.

She knew he was out here.

On the one hand there was nothing more thrilling than a subject sensing her watcher. A connection was established. But if she saw him now, it would be the end. That was the rule. The game ended if the other player saw his face. But it was too soon, much too soon. The game was just starting . . .

A telephone rang inside the house. Her head moved to the side. The line between watcher and subject slackened. She turned around and walked through the door, closing it behind her. A light went on inside the kitchen.

The relief was almost unbearable. He should be leaving now but he felt himself quite, quite unable to even place one foot in front of the other. And so he stood there in the darkness without moving, completely rigid. He stared at the yellow window half-face from behind the pillar, one eye wide open.

Thirteen

THE PAW PRINTS WERE large. Even in the moonlight they were easy to see. Adam stopped and sank to his knee to examine the dark row of prints. He felt a huge wave of relief washing over him.

The prints belonged to a strandwolf and judging from their size, they belonged to an animal that was bigger and more powerful than Beatrice. So these prints could only belong to Dante. He had finally tracked the animal down.

For two weeks there had been no trace of it. Not at the cave and not at any of the animal's usual haunts. He had begun to despair of ever finding the strandwolf alive again. And he was deeply concerned for Beatrice and the cubs. The situation had become so desperate that Beatrice had been forced to leave the cubs on their own more and more often, while she went foraging for food on her own. Without their mother close by, the cubs were vulnerable in the extreme. Without a male protector, the future for the little family was in serious doubt, anyway. If Dante had perished somewhere in the desert, things looked bleak.

But here it was, evidence that a windwalker had passed this way. The prints beautifully formed, a pattern of shadows against the smooth moonlit slip face of the dune. Delicate, impossibly fine, as ephemeral as a memory conceived in a dream. Later tonight the wind would blow, sweeping the sand into smoking crests, and these prints would disappear as though they had never been. But for now they were tangible proof of life.

He got to his feet. The joy that swept through him made him smile into the darkness and throw his arms wide.

THE FEELING OF ELATION lingered until late into the evening. As he sat down in his battered armchair, a glass of Johnnie Walker at his elbow, he was feeling tired but relaxed and looking forward to opening the box of books he had collected from Mark earlier in the week.

His pocket knife sliced cleanly through the masking tape and he pushed back the flaps of the box. Apart from the four books he had ordered, it also contained a half a dozen or so magazines.

The cover of one of the magazines caught his eye. It was a stunning picture of a domed ceiling from which dangled what appeared to be brass spheres representing the heavenly planets. Something about the picture was deeply haunting. It was as if this beautifully conceived image was, in fact, not a reflection of an actual place in real life, but only an approximation of it. As though the photographer had drawn from memory and had somehow, magically, created a unique, faintly surreal image shaped by her mind, not the camera's mechanical eye.

And there was something else. He knew he had never seen this picture before— he was convinced of it—but something about it triggered a powerful sense of recognition and a response that was almost physical. He touched the glossy paper with throbbing fingertips. *The Universe of Justine Callaway.*

It was a photography magazine. He hadn't ordered it so it must belong to Mark and had somehow found its way into his own batch of books by mistake. He opened the magazine to the contents page and worked his finger down the row of entries. *Page 37. Justine Callaway: A Different Perspective.*

He did not immediately read the printed text. He was too captivated by the black-and-white photographs, which filled the pages. They had the same eerie, otherworldly quality that permeated the image on the cover. Enthralled, he turned from one page to the next. What made these pictures so unsettling was that they all had this strange, dreamlike feel to them even though some of the pictures were horrifying images of real violence.

Earthquake survivors staring into the camera, their faces stupid with shock. Victims of the Ebola virus with eyes drowning in blood. A village covered in a white shroud of volcanic ash. Pictures of crumpled, rag-doll bodies decomposing in the Rwandan sun or wet with snow in icy Chechnya. Brutal street dramas in places where sanity was lost. Pictures of man turning against man; nature turning against man; man turning against nature.

But oddly enough, the sense of alienation was strongest in her pictures of unpopulated buildings and empty spaces. Beautifully proportioned rooms. Fine architectural details. Space, volume, light. And a sense of loss so profound he felt his heart contract. A troubled eye, a bruised mind had conceived these. A mind precisely tuned to pain.

A mind . . . *A mind, like his own.*

The thought brought him up sharp. For a moment he sat quietly, almost afraid to breathe; afraid of losing this feeling—tantalizing, insubstantial.

There was a picture of her. *Photograph of the photogra-*

pher at work by Barry Winthrop. It filled half a page and was the only color picture among the other cool black-and-white images. It showed her about to shoot a still-life of a spray of flowers drooping from a striking asymmetrical vase. She was leaning forward. In her one hand, hefted to shoulder height, was the camera. The other hand was stretched out, touching one of the crimson blossoms, probably arranging it to best effect. Her fingers were broad tipped, the palms narrow. Around both wrists were clamped broad, chunky silver bracelets with turquoise beaded clasps.

Her face was in three-quarter profile. She was concentrating intently and the expression on her face was one of purpose. Thin, fastidious nose. Generous mouth. Short, fair hair sticking out from her head like a halo. The color of her eyes uncertain—blue? She was wearing a white tank top and her arms were thin but strongly corded with muscles.

He turned his attention to the opening paragraph, aware that his heart was beating quickly.

Justine Ann Callaway. Freelance photographer. Born in Britain; educated in Sweden, Japan, Kuwait, Australia, and the US. Now based in London. Parents divorced. Father a financial consultant. Mother a homemaker. Older brother, Jonathan, a gifted musician, had died a few months before in a house fire.

He paused. The tone of the article was becoming arch, hinting at scandal. Brother and sister on holiday in Cornwall. A rented cottage. A smoldering cigarette. A fire in which one sibling perished, the other to blame.

His eyes traveled to her picture once again. When was this photograph taken? Before or after her dead brother's shadow had attached itself to her footsteps? He touched his finger softly to her face.

The article continued with a discussion of her work, citing the opinions of peers and critics. Several paragraphs followed that were devoted to a demanding technical description of her photographic techniques. His read the sentences in frustration. He was searching for something else, something personal. Her own words. A glimpse into her thoughts.

And unexpectedly, there it was. The writer had wrapped up the piece with a cryptic question-and-answer interview. The interview started out innocuously enough, but as he continued to read he could feel his breathing becoming strained; as though he was underwater with his air about to give out. Toward the end of the interview her responses to the questions were careful, deliberate hammer blows hitting him between the eyes.

Which photographers do you most admire?
Eve Arnold: first woman to have joined the Magnum Agency. And Lee Miller: savage shutterbabe.
Do you have a motto in life? If so, what is it?
A line I borrowed from Tori Amos: 'My fear is greater than my faith but I walk.'
What makes you happy?
Music.
What do you wish for yourself?
A willing heart.
What is your biggest fear?
That much of my work makes me so preoccupied with death that I'm blind to life.
What is the most irrational feeling you have ever experienced?
The feeling that I am missing someone I've never met.
What do you think is the source of goodness?
Joy.
Of evil?
Anger. Like a fire covered with smoke, a mirror with dust, an embryo with its sac—it is everywhere. A sick passion.
If you could be granted one wish, what would it be?
A second chance.

The words were receding and expanding before his eyes. His chest felt constricted. He got up from the chair and his sudden movement sent the glass of whiskey flying through the air in an amber arc, smashing against the floor in a shower of crystal. He walked to the makeshift bookshelves against the wall, and as he had done so many times over the past years, he pulled out a thin green paperback from among the many volumes.

The Bhagavad Gita. It fell open in his hand at the page he had read a thousand times before, the spine broken from being opened at this exact page so often.

So what is it that drives a man to commit evil, Varshneya, even against his will but as if compelled to it by force?
It is desire, it is anger, produced from the seed of passion, all-consuming, all-injuring; understand that this is the enemy here.
As a fire is covered by smoke and a mirror by dust; as an embryo is covered by its sac, this world is enveloped by that.

He lowered the book and turned away from the shelves. Opening the drawer of his desk, he urgently searched through the loose pens, pencils, and sheets of paper, until his fingers closed around the magnifying glass. He placed the magazine on top of the table and smoothed his palm lightly across the surface of the page. Bringing his face close to the picture, he trained the magnifying glass on her sinewy arm, the finely muscled shoulder with its two tattoos. He had noticed the tattoos immediately, but they were small and he had to be absolutely sure.

The two tiny marks swelled in size. He was able to see them clearly now.

A wolf. A serpent swallowing its tail.

He straightened slowly, the blood rushing in his ears. He was clutching at the inside of his arm and as he looked down, he could see the outline of his fingertips where they had pressed into the flesh and into the black-and-white images needled into his skin.

He felt as stunned as a sleepwalker. He stepped out the front door and into the night. The wind had come up and he felt the sting of infinitely fine grains of sand blowing against his face, settling between his lashes and into the hollows underneath his eyes. He suddenly had a fierce desire to see the ocean, to be close to water.

He started to walk and the derelict houses around him filled the darkness like mournful ghosts. The houses were groaning in the wind, their empty rooms filled with noise. A loose shutter banging against a wall. A door weeping on its hinges. The scarred oak floors creaking, as though they were registering the passage of ghostly feet.

He passed by the hospital where the wind moaned down the long passages and the rusted skeletons of metal beds lined the wards. He passed by the school building and through the broken windows he glimpsed old tip-up school benches, row upon row. Close by was the children's playground. He could make out the shape of the slide. Its bottom lip was covered by a mound of sand. In the distance, the rust-covered hump of a desalination plant.

When at last he stopped he had reached the ocean. It was high tide and the roar of the waves was tremendous. The sand on the long stretch of beach seemed white as powder in the light of the moon but the moon itself was blue, a weathered coin in the wine-dark sky. He stretched his hand toward it as though he might roll it into his palm and fold his fingers around its worn edges.

He had found her.

Impossible as it seemed, he had found her. He knew that absolutely; there was no hesitation in his heart and his mind was clear. He had found the woman he had searched for not just in this present life but in other lives as well.

The knowledge of it was overwhelming, so enormous that it blocked out emotion. He did not feel joy. He did not feel apprehension. She was thousands of miles away and he was a fugitive and just how they would ever manage to find themselves face to face was a mystery. But for now the act of knowing was enough. It was everything.

He sat there for hours watching the dark water swirling, the waves capped with foam. Above his head the stars were scattered crazily across a windblown sky. His clothes became clammy and the mist chilled his skin. But he could not bring himself to leave.

There was the merest glint of pink against the horizon when he finally returned to his house. And as he laid himself down to sleep, he immediately sank into deep and total oblivion. He slept as soundly as he had ever slept, his body hardly moving, his breathing slow.

But inside the palms of his hands were maps of time and place. Behind his eyelids pulsed a knowledge of many lives and deep in his unconscious he sensed ancient forces at work. The massive shifting of tectonic plates. Mountains forming, oceans expanding. Erosion, flood, and searing wind. Forces at work a billion years ago; forces that will be at work a billion years hence. Birth, rebirth. A never-ending cycle.

Fourteen

THE ROOM IN WHICH Justine found herself was conventional in the extreme. Glazed chintz sofas, doilies on the armrests, old-fashioned lace curtains, a small tidy pile of magazines and a china figurine of a dancing shepherdess on the coffee table. No books, only a leather-bound Bible on one of the side tables. The walls were covered with pink and pistachio striped wallpaper.

The only extraordinary piece of furniture in that room was the mirror hanging above the fireplace. It was enormous: a confection of silver, ivory, and mother-of-pearl with two fat angels carved from wood arranged on either side and holding garlands of flowers and fruit in their chubby fists. The mirror was old. Chemical decay had attacked its face. From where she sat she could see a slightly distorted reflection of herself and of the room captured in its depths. The diffuse sheen of the mirror's surface gave the pedestrian room a luxurious gleam it did not possess in real life.

She brought her eyes back to the woman sitting opposite

her. Harriet Buchanan, older sister of Adam Buchanan and the previous owner of Paradine Park. Reverend Wyatt had told her that Harriet was living in London and in the end it had not been at all difficult to track her down.

The girl in the painting at Paradine Park had been young and slightly tomboyish in appearance. The woman facing her was stodgy. Dressed in a lavender twinset and beige shoes she looked every inch the matron. Her gray hair was fastened in a tight roll behind her head. She had seed pearls in her earlobes and resting against an ample breast was a small watch-face hanging upside down from a gold-plated ribbon. Her face was unlined—round as a digestive biscuit—but there was something about the set of the tiny mouth that hinted at an inflexible personality and her eyes were without warmth.

Justine smiled at her and took a sip of tea. "These are lovely cups," she said as she placed the thin, gold-rimmed porcelain cup back in its saucer. "Are they antique?"

Harriet Buchanan nodded. "My great grandmother received the set as a wedding gift. And I've been fortunate. There have been remarkably few breakages. I still have twenty-eight cups left from a set of thirty-two." She somehow made it sound as though this extraordinary circumstance had been brought about by strength of character alone.

"You brought these with you from Paradine Park?"

"Yes." A sigh. "I did not bring many things with me. They would hardly fit the cottage. A few bits and pieces. This mirror, of course."

"I've been admiring it. It's beautiful."

"It was my mother's favorite possession." For a moment something flickered behind her eyes. "It used to hang above her bed. It looked wonderful in that room, the proportions were right for it. In here it looks a little out of place, but I could not bring myself to part with it."

Justine fiddled with the spoon in her cup. "With the house empty, it's difficult to know which of the rooms is the master bedroom . . ."

"Third bedroom on the right to the front," came the immediate answer. "But you're right, the rooms are all so evenly sized, any one could have filled the purpose."

Third bedroom on the right to the front. It was the room with the large Chinese vase on the mantelpiece and the bathroom with the taps sculpted like fish. She had walked into that room several times. She had taken pictures of it, sensing nothing amiss. But a woman had taken her own life in that room. Had placed a shotgun against her face and had shot her head off. This mirror, hanging above the bed, had probably reflected the entire bloody scene. She glanced at it, shivered.

Harriet Buchanan leaned back in her chair. "So, you would like to photograph the house for a book."

"Yes. I know that you've sold the house recently, but as it's been in your family for such a long time, I thought it would only be right if I checked with you first. But I hope you won't have any objections. It's an extremely photogenic house. A lovely place."

"It is that." A tinge of nostalgia softened the tiny mouth. "I photographed it myself when I was younger. I had plans to write a history of the house. But I never got that far. I only took the pictures."

"I'm actually using your old darkroom at the moment."

"You are?" She smiled, genuine pleasure lighting her eyes for the first time. "I spent many happy hours there. Of course," she smoothed the fabric of her skirt across her knee, "that was many years ago."

Justine hesitated. "When you took pictures of the house, did you . . . have you . . . was there anything unusual about them?"

"Such as?" Raised eyebrows.

"Oh, you know. Anything. Any strange pictures, wild images?"

"Wild images?" The tone of her voice suggested that she found the idea incomprehensible if not positively distasteful. "I don't know what you mean."

"Never mind." Justine made a self-deprecating gesture with her hand. "It was a stupid idea on my part. It's just that since I started photographing the house, I seem to have more flawed pictures than normal. Almost as if there's a jinx." She laughed but received not a glimmer of a smile in return. She continued lamely, "But I haven't worked for a few months so it's probably just a matter of getting my eye in again."

"Well, I can assure you I never had any problems. As a matter of fact, if you're interested I can show you my photographs."

"Please." Justine nodded. "I'd love to see them."

The photographs were excruciatingly self-conscious. Weird angles, odd close-ups. And despite the deliberate attempts at creativity, the pictures were devoid of imagination.

There were many of them. An entire box full. Still, it was interesting to see what the place had looked like furnished. In contrast to her daughter's bland taste, Louisa Buchanan's taste had run to the exotic. Lots of velvet, gilt, and tasseled cushions. And, of course, the mirrors. Even in these pictures there was no escaping their presence. She had hoped to catch a glimpse of the occupants of the house—of *him*—but no such luck. These pictures were "arty" and obviously not meant for the family album.

As Harriet extracted yet another pile of photographs from the yellow box, she suddenly made an annoyed, clicking noise with her tongue. The reason for her irritation seemed to be a snapshot, a head and shoulder picture of a woman.

"I don't know where this came from." She placed it on the coffee table and pushed it away from her quite vehemently.

"What a lovely face." Justine picked up the photograph.

The woman in the picture had wide green eyes and long red hair. Her smile was wistful. "Who is she?"

"That's Pascaline. My brother's wife."

Justine felt her heart miss a beat. He was married? For a moment she felt as though she couldn't breathe.

She strove to keep her voice normal. "Pascaline. It's an unusual name."

"She's French." Harriet's voice was grim. "Richard met her in Paris."

Richard. Pascaline had been married to Richard. Not Adam. Richard. Of course, the newspaper clippings had mentioned a widow. She felt almost lightheaded with relief. But why? Why the hell should she care?

Something must have shown in her face because Harriet suddenly slammed the lid of the box shut. She turned to face Justine directly, her eyes cold. "Are you a reporter?"

"What?"

"A reporter. Is that what this is about? You people. You just can't leave it alone, can you. It's been nine years for God's sake."

Justine made a time-out gesture with her hand. "Please, Miss Buchanan, I assure you I am not a reporter. Yes, I'm a photojournalist, but not this kind of thing, please believe me. But I have, of course, heard of the tragedy. Reverend Wyatt told me."

"Reverend Wyatt?"

"Yes." Which was stretching the truth a little, but she didn't think it would go down well if she told Harriet Buchanan she had gossiped with her former gardener and his grandson. And indeed, the good reverend's name worked like a charm. As she mentioned his name, she could see the woman visibly relax.

"I'm sorry." Harriet touched her lips with a handkerchief. "But it is still so upsetting. You have no idea how people talked. Socially it's been a nightmare."

"I'm sure it must have been." A social nightmare. Not a word about grief and loss. But she shouldn't judge the woman this easily. Who knows what her thoughts are in the midnight hour?

Harriet pushed the handkerchief into the sleeve of her suit. "Reverend Wyatt was wonderful. A real support. I could talk my heart out to him." She suddenly placed her hand on Justine's. It was so totally unexpected that Justine had difficulty stopping herself from pulling away. "People say terrible things, Ms. Callaway, but I'm sure Reverend Wyatt told you we were a good family."

"Of course." The hand on hers was clammy and cold. She felt embarrassed and suddenly the only thing she wanted to do was to get away from this woman who was now leaning toward her, bringing her face too close to her own. Something in Harriet's eyes told her she was about to share a confidence. But even though she had traveled here today with the express purpose of finding out everything she could, she suddenly didn't want to hear any more. But the grip on her hand tightened.

"A good family, Ms. Callaway. But one bad apple. You know how it is. It was my brother Adam, you see. He was the thorn in our side. His jealousy destroyed us."

"Jealousy?"

"He knew he could not compete with my brother Richard. Richard was a wonderful man, Ms. Callaway." The tone of her voice almost shockingly flirtatious. "So handsome, too. I wish you could have known him. And he was close to his family. He and my mother—it was a delight to watch them together."

Justine watched in fascination as the tip of a pink tongue—quick as a snake's—darted across her lower lip. "You cannot believe how different two brothers can be. Even as a child Adam was a troublemaker. He got into fights at school, you know. He was always getting into fights." The tongue darted out again. "After the funerals I burned all his pictures. I did not keep even one. He was a blight on the family. I wanted nothing around that could remind me of him."

"And this one," she gestured with her hand to the photograph of Pascaline. "She should never have married Richard. She wasn't worth his old shoes. She could not even be bothered to attend his funeral. The witch." The words exploded like bullets. The ferocity on her face was frightening.

Justine found her voice. "Have you kept in touch? Did she go back to France?"

A snort. "Oh, no. Madame now lives in Knightsbridge, no less. Where did she get the money, that's what I want to know. And she kept Richard's name, heaven knows why."

For a few moments it was quiet. Then Harriet picked up the photograph and tapped it against the side of the coffee table. The sound was tiny but vicious. "She and Adam." Tap, tap. "I always thought there was something there." Tap, tap.

She turned her round eyes to Justine. "I couldn't be sure, but I sensed it. I'm never wrong about these things and it would be just like Adam. He probably would have enjoyed cheating with his brother's wife. Oh, yes indeed. That is just the kind of thing he would enjoy."

WHEN JUSTINE FINALLY MANAGED to leave the cottage it felt to her as though the clammy imprint of Harriet Buchanan's hand was still on her wrist. She gulped the fresh air into her lungs. Her head was aching.

There was a telephone box right across the street and she could see a battered telephone directory dangling from a chain. She crossed the street and entered, her noise wrinkling at the smell of old urine. The directory was two years old, but that probably would not matter. She was right. Here it was: *Buchanan, P. 27 Pelham Close. SW7.*

For a few moments she hesitated, debating whether to call. What would she say? Pascaline Buchanan would probably just hang up on her. The chance of actually getting to talk to the woman might be greater if she gave her no advance warning. So maybe the best solution would be to simply pitch up on her doorstep.

But as she got behind the steering wheel Justine suddenly wondered what on earth she was doing. Why was she so obsessed with a man she had never met—a killer at that—and a simply pain-in-the-ass kind of person from all she could gather?

She sighed and looked at her watch. Knightsbridge. That meant at least another thirty minutes of driving and the Brompton Road in rush hour. Well, it couldn't be helped. She was probably going to get a door slammed in her face, but what the heck. She could only try.

BUT THE DOOR WAS not slammed in her face. In fact, quite the opposite. From the moment Pascaline Buchanan opened the front door of her house and the two women looked at each other, there was a connection. And for someone who was probably striving to put the events of a terrible time behind her, Pascaline was astoundingly forthcoming. She accepted without censure Justine's interest as though it was the most natural thing in the world to discuss a personal tragedy with a woman she had never met before. The idea was disconcerting but it was almost, Justine thought, as though she was expected.

Pascaline's face was still recognizably the same face as the one in the snapshot. Her hair was as red and there was about her that same air of fragility and wistfulness. But there were deep lines running across her forehead and a web of tiny lines at the corners of her eyes. She spoke fluent English, but her words carried a strong, albeit very appealing, French inflection.

She was now talking about Louisa Buchanan.

"Louisa was extraordinarily vain. She did not give that impression, but her beauty was everything to her."

"She was blond."

"Yes, very fair. Like Richard. I still find it amazing to think that she had placed a gun in her mouth and had blown her lovely face apart. Poison, yes, that I would have been able to understand. So she could die looking beautiful, like *La Dame aux Camélias*."

"Richard looked a lot like her?"

"Oh yes. And they were two of a kind. They shared the same kind of self-love." Pascaline's voice was calm but there was a trace of bitterness in her eyes.

"Everyone I've spoken to says Richard was a charming man."

"Charming?" A very Gallic shrug. "Yes. He could be if he so chose."

"But?"

"But he was vain and shallow. And cruel."

"Cruel. Cruel how?"

"Cruel in every sense of the word. He was good at manipulating people; finding their soft spot—their most shameful secret—and exploiting it. It gave him a sense of power. And he beat me."

Her voice was flat, without emotion. For a moment Justine thought she had heard incorrectly.

"He beat you? You mean he was physically abusive?"

"But of course."

It was quiet. The only sound was the twitter of two white budgies in a wrought-iron cage hanging from the conservatory ceiling. Justine looked at the face of the woman in front of her. Pascaline was smiling ruefully.

"I'm so sorry."

"*Tant pis.*" Pascaline leaned forward suddenly, keeping her eyes locked with Justine's. "But you're not here because of Richard, are you. You want to know about Adam."

Justine hesitated. "Yes. Yes, I do."

"Adam was not cruel, no. He was easily angered, certainly, and he was too quick to use his fists—but never cruel. And he was not calculating enough to defeat Richard at his own game. Richard knew exactly what to do to make Adam lose his temper. He hated Adam and he knew which buttons to push. Even as children. You know what he did once? He told me, he was laughing about it. Adam had these pets—rabbits—when he was a child. With these rabbits, the males need to be kept apart or they'll kill each other. So Richard thought it would be fun to throw them together to see what happened. The next morning, Adam found the animals with their stomachs ripped apart. Nice, yes?"

"Delightful."

"It was bad between them as children. And with Louisa so obviously preferring Richard to Adam. Well, you can imagine." She made a gesture with her hand.

Justine looked her full in the face. "I want to ask you something very personal. If you don't want to answer, I will understand. And I apologize in advance."

Pascaline turned her head quizzically to the side. "Yes?"

"Harriet Buchanan said that you and Adam had had an affair. Is that true?"

"Poor Harriet." Pascaline smiled sadly. "She adored Richard. And then something happened that made her think Adam and I were involved. You see, Adam knew Richard was beating me. He had to take me to the emergency room once. Adam drove me to the hospital and then he went back and it was bad for Richard. Adam is a strong man, Richard did not stand a chance. Harriet was horrified by what had happened and jumped to all the wrong conclusions. But to answer your question: no. Adam and I never had an affair, Justine. Did I care for him? Yes. Like you would for a friend. And I was grateful to him. After he beat Richard up, things became easier for me. Richard backed off. My life was better."

"Forgive me, but . . . why did you stay with Richard?"

"I still ask myself that question every day. Was I still in love with him? The truthful answer is that I don't know. I had enough money of my own. I could have left him at any time, but I didn't. And even after all these years I still don't know why. It doesn't make me feel good about myself, that I can tell you."

"Did Louisa know about the abuse?"

She smiled wryly. "If Louisa knew, she never let on. Richard was careful—he usually stayed away from my face. If I hadn't broken my rib that night, Adam wouldn't have known, either. But I did talk to the priest once and he might have raised the issue with Louisa. Those two were close."

"The priest? Reverend Wyatt? Did he help you?"

Pascaline gave a half-shouldered shrug. "There wasn't much he could do, I suppose. But he was a very good listener, I remember that. Very good, indeed."

"What about Harriet?"

"Harriet knew, but Harriet didn't have much sympathy for me. Probably thought I deserved it. She thinks I'm a witch, you know."

"That's rich, coming from her."

"No, you don't understand. She really thinks I'm a witch. The broomstick and pointed hat kind."

"You can't be serious."

"Oh, I am. The thing is, she may be right." Pascaline suddenly laughed. "Don't look so alarmed. It's just that I do sometimes have a very strong feeling about people and I can sometimes sense things that are about to happen."

"Visions?"

"Not really. It is difficult to explain. Let's just say that at the time of the Inquisition I would probably have ended up on a stake."

She suddenly took Justine's hand and enfolded it with both her own. "I have such a strong feeling about you, Justine. I had it from the moment I saw you. I can't describe it, but I know it was meant that you came here today."

It was time to ask the one question that mattered. Justine took a deep breath. "Why did he kill him?"

Pascaline sighed. "It would be so much easier if there was a clear-cut motive, wouldn't it? Or some dreadful traumatic event that tipped Adam into insanity. A neat pat explanation?"

She didn't answer, but of course that was exactly what she wanted to hear.

Pascaline sighed again. "Who knows what really happened that night? Me—I think it was a matter of hate building up between them. A long, slow process and then, one day, it reached breaking point."

"But it was not premeditated."

"I don't think so, no. The weapon, you know, makes it seem unlikely. Even the police said that. But the problem is, Adam had threatened Richard once before in front of witnesses. Had threatened to kill him in fact. They had some stupid argument again and Adam's temper got the better of him. At the time, no one paid any attention—we all say irresponsible things when we are angry—and those two had been at each other's throats in public before. But when Richard was killed, of course everyone remembered those words. Louisa killed herself soon afterward." Pascaline suddenly pressed her fingers against her forehead.

Justine reached out her hand. "Pascaline, I'm sorry. I shouldn't make you go through this."

"No. Don't worry. I'm all right." She shook her head. "You said you wanted to show me something. What is it?"

Justine opened her bag and extracted the picture of the wolf on the staircase. She placed it carefully on Pascaline's lap. "Do you understand this? Can you explain this to me? I don't know why, but I feel that this wolf is connected to Adam Buchanan somehow. I know it sounds completely crazy but—"

Pascaline stared at the picture. "Adam has a tattoo—a wolf—right here." She touched the inside of her wrist.

"A tattoo? Are you sure?"

"*Bien sur.* Why?"

"A tattoo like this?" Justine was on her feet now, frantically trying to rid herself of her jacket. "Like this?" she asked again and pushed up the short sleeve of her blouse as far as it would go.

A sharp intake of breath. "Yes. Like that. *Exactement.* And the snake, too."

"What?"

"Yes, *Wepwawet.* And *Ouroboros.*"

"What's that?"

"You don't know what they mean? But you have them on your shoulder?"

"I had these done years ago. I just liked the way they looked, that's all. It was one of those stupid teenager things. I had wanted an eagle and a Union Jack, but then I spotted these on the chart in the tattoo parlor and changed my mind."

"Wepwawet." Pascaline's voice sounded almost dreamy. "The Egyptian wolf god. Adam chose it because he is the opener of doors." Her fingertips were cool as she touched her fingers to Justine's shoulder. "And the snake— Ouroboros. A Gnostic symbol this one. A sign of rebirth."

The clouds were moving across the sun and the pretty feminine room with its fresh colors and white wicker furniture was suddenly in shadow. Pascaline's face seemed pallid, the red hair a bright slash in the gloom. When she spoke again her voice was very gentle. "You must be tired, Justine."

"Tired?"

"This immense longing you have inside of you. This yearning for something you cannot express. I wonder what it must be like to feel such hunger. You're sickening of it, aren't you?"

Tears were pricking Justine's eyelids. She never cried, had not even wept after Jonathan's death. Depression, yes. She knew all about depression. Every day it perched on her shoulder like a dusky owl. But no tears. Now they were leaving the corners of her eyes and when she placed her hand against her cheek, her palm was wet.

And she was scared. She didn't understand any of this.

"I should go." She looked at Pascaline almost fearfully.

Pascaline did not try to stop her from leaving. But as they reached the front door, she placed her hand on Justine's arm.

"Adam believed we all have a soul mate. That each of us is traveling through many lives with a map of time clutched in our hands, waiting for that one moment when our time line will intersect with the path of the lover we're destined to meet." She paused. "I have the strongest feeling that you will not fail in your search, Justine."

"I'm not looking for him."

"Are you sure?"

Justine shook her head. She couldn't remember the last time she had felt this exhausted. "Thank you. Thank you for talking to me."

"I hope it was of help to you." Pascaline's lips brushed her cheek. "Stay in touch, my new friend. And when you find him, tell him I think of him fondly."

Fifteen

THE WATCHER CLOSED THE book he was reading with a sense of disgust. The book had been a complete waste of his time.

He loved books. They had always provided inspiration. By drawing on the creativity of great minds, he was able to spark a little heat in his own soul. The thoughts of others helped him make sense of the world. Disraeli once said: "Life is too short to be little." He agreed. And that was why he extended his horizons by borrowing the thoughts and lives of others.

He looked again at the book in front of him and grimaced. He prided himself on his exquisite taste in literature. Not that he was above reading a good commercial suspense novel every now and then. It helped him relax. But these days your average thriller seemed to be only about the author's ability to think up ever more bizarre ways of making people meet their death. The book he had just finished had a dead body on every second page. Flagellated bodies. Flayed bodies. Bodies impaled upside down. Eyeballs pickled in jars. Victims devoured by rats while still alive. You could almost feel the writer straining to stretch his mind to come up with ever more innovative and twisted ways to die.

His study into the topic of insanity had required him to do research on serial killers and he knew that thrill deaths were rare. Murder was certainly common, as was indiscriminate killing, but for every Jeffrey Dahmer who decided to stock his fridge with human steaks, there were thousands of ordinary people walking around like ticking time bombs. People frustrated, greedy, despairing, drunk. Good people who simply snap. The harassed father who suddenly decides to shoot the employer who had fired him. The abused wife who harbors ideas of poison. The drug addict who turns savage in order to feed his habit.

The man who succumbs to anger and kills his brother . . .

Surely the possibility that the person sitting opposite you at the breakfast table might one day simply plunge into madness was a far more terrifying prospect than the unlikely event of ever confronting a monster? When his own father had tried to shoot him, his mother, and his sister one ordinary weekday morning just as he was about to leave for school, there had been no warning. One moment he stood opposite a man he loved and admired. And the next he looked into eyes rinsed of all sanity. Only afterward, after his father had taken his own life, had they learned about the disastrous financial investments. But he always knew that the explanation was not as simple as that. And it would be fair to say that his father's descent into insanity had triggered his own interest in madness and its connection to evil. It was the reason he chose to become a priest.

Relatives used to say he handled the trauma well. Only nine at the time, he was a placid little boy who never mentioned what had happened. But that morning was a turning point. The pitying glances from his schoolmates made him cringe. The constant attention from teachers and relatives was terrifying. His mother became cold and distant. In his own mind he struggled with the knowledge that he might have been able to prevent his father's suicide. He was convinced there must have been a sign. If only he had paid more attention. If only he had observed his father more closely. If his watcher's skills had been developed in those days, he might have sensed the fault lines originating deep within his parent's troubled subconscious.

And it was as though the experience of that day had caused something inside of him to break, evening out all his emotions. He experienced no highs and no lows. He moved through life and left no hint of turbulence in his wake. If he wanted to feel passion, excitement, lust for life, he had to find it elsewhere. In someone else's life. He started to live vicariously.

Sometimes he'd walk down the placid streets of Ainstey and look at the people passing him on the street and for one split second it would be as though the tops of their heads had been sliced off and he could see right into the dark wormy hollows of their brains. Mrs. Chapman eating her clotted cream scones at Duke's Tea-room; young Peter Smith on his paper rounds; Mr. Bishop leaning over the counter of his hardware shop: all of them carrying inside the gray-white grooves of their brains that devastating ability to lash out. Deep in the amygdala flowed dark currents that could turn into a swirling vortex of violence in the blink of a startled eye.

He was not without guilt himself. He had lifted his own hand once with deadly intent. But there had been an irrefutable logic to the act. It was not born out of sick passion. His survival had been at stake. And survival was the primal imperative. Survival had nothing to do with insanity.

He pushed the book away from him and stretched. He glanced at his watch. It was approaching nine o'clock. Still early.

Maybe he should go for a drive. Get some fresh air.

Maybe he should go to Paradine Park.

He knew he was breaking one of the rules of the game. A single visit every seven days. That was all he allowed himself. Otherwise observation would turn into obsession and in that direction lay disaster. He had visited Paradine Park only four days ago, so he wasn't permitted another visit until Sunday. But he really, really wanted to see her again.

As he pondered the dilemma he drummed his fingers on the table. Then he came to a decision. Life was short. Sometimes an indulgence—a treat—was a positive thing. He wouldn't stay long. He promised.

SHE PROBABLY SHOULD HAVE stayed in London overnight rather than drive back to Paradine Park in this state of near exhaustion. Her visits with Harriet and Pascaline Buchanan had left her drained. Traffic was predictably heavy and it seemed to take forever before she managed to leave London behind. By the time she drove through the gates at Paradine Park and turned the MG's nose up the avenue of beech trees, night had long fallen.

The first thing she did was to build a fire in the library. The second was to pour herself a glass of whiskey. Only after emptying the glass did she go upstairs to run a bath.

As she undressed she caught sight of herself in the mirror. For a moment she hesitated. Then she turned sideways and tightened her fist so that the skin of her upper arm tautened.

Wepwawet and Ouroboros. She remembered the day she had the tattoos done. She had just turned fifteen.

She walked into the parlor scared but determined. Her friend Caroline was looking on, wide-eyed. In her hand she had a soft-serve ice-cream cone. A pink one. Strange how she was able to remember that detail still.

At first she had considered having at least one of the designs needled into her cheekbone, but the tattoo artist—a surprisingly ascetic looking man with long David Copperfield type fingers—had lost his nerve and had, thank God, persuaded her to have them done somewhere where they would not be as conspicuous. The whole thing had been an exercise in defiance, one of a long list of things she had thought of to irritate her parents. She certainly had never given any thought as to what the two symbols might mean.

Somewhere out there was a man who was carrying the exact same images on his own arm.

It was coincidence. That was all it was. It would be ridiculous to try and attach any deeper significance to what was only a freakish twist of chance. But as she turned away from the mirror and climbed into the tub, she found herself clasping her fingers to her shoulder protectively.

God, she was tired. She lay in the hot water, her eyes fixed unseeingly on the ceiling. She was deliberately trying to keep her mind blank, but the images of the day kept crowding in on her. Harriet Buchanan's dimpled fist and clammy hand. *A good family, Ms. Callaway. I'm sure Reverend Wyatt told you that. But one bad apple. You know how it is*. The sweet smell of flowers in Pascaline's house and the stains of lily pollen on the tablecloth. *I wonder what it must be like to feel such hunger. You're sickening of it, aren't you?*

She must have drifted off. As her eyes snapped open, she noticed immediately that the water had turned from hot to lukewarm. How long had she been lying here? For a few more moments she listened, trying to pinpoint what it was that had woken her.

"Hello?"

Silence.

She hoisted herself out of the tub and padded to the bathroom door. The passage outside was dark. She poked her head out the door. The passage stretched out empty ahead of her.

There was nothing there. She was being ridiculous. She was over tired and should get herself to bed. But maybe she should go downstairs and pour herself one last drink. Just to help her relax. She toweled herself dry and slipped into a long-sleeved nightshirt.

The Johnnie Walker was in the library. As she entered the room, the fire was crackling and spitting and a smell of resin hovered in the air. She filled her glass and drank deeply.

Glass in hand, she approached the bookshelves lining the wall. The light of the flames had created a shadow for her, which floated across the crimson carpet and followed closely in her footsteps. Her eyes wandered across the titles without much interest. *Further Wanderings Mainly in Argyll* by one M. E. M Donaldson. Next to it *De Granville's Travels to St. Petersburgh Volumes I and II.* Three massive red tomes carrying the title *The Chiefs of Grant. Wright's Universal Pronunciation Dictionary* and shelf after shelf of bluish gray volumes telling *The Story of the Nations*.

Pushed in between *The Hunting and Harriers* by H. H. Bryden and *The Queen's Hounds*, written by someone carrying the faintly comical name of Lord Ribblesdale, was a book not bound in leather or cloth. It was a large coffee table–sized book with a glossy paper cover and the title on the spine read: *Namibia. Portrait of a Desert Country*.

The first thing she noticed as she opened it was the signature in the top left-hand corner of the title page. *Adam Buchanan.* The second thing she noticed was that her breathing was suddenly quick and shallow. And there was this sense that she was holding in her hands something of significance. It was the same heart-stopping feeling that had gripped her when she had discovered the green corduroy jacket in the upstairs wardrobe.

The signature was black and strong: the capital *B* towering over the rest of the letters. She placed her fingers on top of the boldly written name and the sensation that swept through her was so strong, so overwhelming, that she snatched her hand away. She felt as though she were on the threshold of making a long sought-after discovery, if only she had a brave enough heart and an unflinching mind.

Hardly breathing, she turned the first page.

It was a book featuring a series of stunning desertscapes. These were images of a land punished by the sun. Dead mountains with rocks the color of fire. Sand dunes glimmering with light. Glittering gypsum plains and eerie fog-wrapped beaches. A forest of petrified tree trunks, which, according to the sparse text printed below the picture, was 200 million years old.

It was beautiful. Every image was exquisite. But it was also dreadful. These were scenes of aching desolation, of an emptiness so vast and so barren it chilled the heart and numbed the brain. Many of the pictures exhibited an almost feverish quality. The red-rimmed dunes, the cobalt sky—they seemed alien, as though they were not of this planet. And the names were magical as well: Khorixas, Omaruru, Mukarob, Ai-Ais, Skeleton Coast.

Toward the middle of the book were pictures of derelict houses facing an empty horizon. The lines of the houses were graceful, the walls thick and sturdy. But desert sand showed through the broken panes. There was sand outside and sand inside. The desert was stealthily, insidiously, claiming these houses as its own.

Something was written in the margin. She turned the book sideways and saw that the handwriting was the same as on the title page. He had written these words himself. They were in pencil and very faint, but she was still able to read them: *Is this redemption?*

For a few minutes she simply sat there, staring at the words. It was very quiet. The heavy drapes across the windows shut out all sound. Only the fire hissed.

Redemption. To make amends. To atone. To buy back freedom and a release from captivity and bondage. He had pored over this book, his hands had turned these very pages, had touched these images forever captured in pristine silence. And something about their awful beauty had spoken to him and had held the promise of redemption.

He had written these words not after but before he had taken his brother's life. He must have. Mason had told her he had fled on the very night of the murder. So did he know in his heart that he would one day make a journey that would require atonement? Adam Buchanan believed in destiny, Reverend Wyatt had said. He believed in it absolutely. So maybe he had sensed that he was walking down a road that was drawing him inexorably toward a certain fate.

There were more images in the book to explore, but as her hands moved to turn the page, she suddenly stilled their movement.

She looked over her shoulder at the doorway. It was empty. Windows? No, the windows were shut and curtained. So what was it then? Why did she suddenly have this disconcerting feeling that she was being watched?

The murals. Of course, that must be it. She was surrounded by paintings from which limpid eyed, slyly smiling figures were watching her quizzically. And it was stifling in here. For one dizzying moment it felt as though the tall bookcases might actually topple over and come crashing down.

She slammed the volume shut. She needed to get away from this room with its smothering colors and avid eyes. But as she left the library she still felt as though the house with its empty spaces and inky corners was closing in on her. She was feeling severely claustrophobic. Why?

Opening the heavy front door, she walked into the darkness outside. The night was cold and chilled her body through the flannel nightshirt. But she did not stop walking until she reached the long avenue of trees.

She turned around. The sky was so clouded that the outline of the house was only slightly darker than the surrounding blackness. The heavy velvet curtains in the library did not allow the escape of even a chink of light.

For the longest time she simply stood there, aware of her

heart beating in her throat. The clouds thinned and the moon broke through. And still she waited, staring up at those unlit windows as blank as empty eyes.

FROM INSIDE THE HOUSE, upstairs, the Watcher could barely make out the slight figure standing so motionless outside in the dark. Even with the moon glowing through the wispy clouds, she was just another black shadow in a garden filled with blacker shadows. He could hardly see her and he knew she wouldn't be able to see him—not at that angle and without any light behind him.

Finally. She was starting to walk back toward the house.

He pressed his head against the cold glass pane and stared down at her. He had given up trying to fathom what she was doing out there. But he did find it quietly exhilarating that they had changed roles: he looking out, she looking in.

His breath was condensing on the glass pane. He lifted his finger and wrote in the gray-white cloud one word only:

Hello.

Sixteen

"HOW CAN YOU BE sure?"

"It's her. I found her. I know it."

Mark looked at the photography magazine lying open on the coffee table between him and Adam. "You know it's your soul mate because she has two tattoos on her arm and knows a quotation from a 2,000-year-old religious text."

Adam leaned forward. He spread his fingers open and placed his hand on top of the page. "I know it's her when I look at her photographs. I know it from the planes of her face and the shape of her mouth. I know her."

Mark pushed his chair back from the table as though to put distance between himself and the picture covered by Adam's hand. "For God's sake, Adam. You don't know her. You've never met her."

For a moment it was quiet between the two men. From the kitchen where Rita was doing the laundry came the sound of the radio tuned to a request program. "The next request is from Lydia for her darling Simon on their wedding anniversary. Love you lots, pumpkin. Thank you for eight wonderful years . . ."

Adam spoke slowly. "Why are you so uncomfortable with this? I don't understand. I would have thought you'd be happy for me."

Mark grimaced, looked away. The truth of the matter was he was indeed uncomfortable with this development. It was totally outside his frame of comprehension. But more than that, he was apprehensive, concerned for Adam. His friend was setting himself up for one almighty fall. What woman would accept a murderer on the run into her life?

"Adam . . ." Mark made a helpless gesture with his hand toward the magazine. "It's wishful thinking."

"It's faith. You should know all about that."

"So what are you going to do now? She's on the other side of the world."

Adam smiled. "There is actually something called a telephone you know."

"What?" Mark's voice rose sharply. "You're going to call her?"

"I called international inquiries from the post office this morning. She's not listed. But I got her number through the magazine. Told them I'm with a news magazine and I want to commission her for a feature piece. They gave the number to me no questions asked."

"Have you lost your mind? What are you going to tell her?"

"The truth."

"The truth? Oh, OK. Let's see. 'Ms. Callaway—or may I call you Justine? You don't know me, but I'm your soul mate and have been searching for you through the ages. Oh, and by the way, I just happened to kill my brother ten years ago. But let's not allow that to keep us from our destiny, shall we.' "

"Something like that."

"You're insane."

"I need to use your phone. The post office isn't private enough."

"You're really serious."

"I've never been more serious about anything in my life."

Mark looked into the dark eyes. They were burning, the gaze too intense to hold with his own.

He looked away. "Take it in the study. You know where it is."

"Thanks." Adam got to his feet. "Mark . . ."

"What?"

Adam smiled and for a moment he seemed to Mark heart-breakingly defenseless. "This is the first time I'll hear her voice."

THE WOMAN'S VOICE ON the phone was screechy and so unpleasant it took Adam completely aback. For a moment he even had difficulty speaking.

"Hello?" The woman said again impatiently. "Who is this?" Her voice was sharp edged and the underlying irritation made it worse.

He took a deep breath. "Justine Callaway?"

"No. I'm her tenant. She doesn't live here any longer."

Thank God. He felt tremendously relieved. "Do you have a new phone number where I can reach her?"

"I think she's abroad or something." In the background a baby started crying. "Denise," she suddenly roared, "get that bottle away from him for Christ's sake."

He held the receiver away from his ear. "Abroad?"

"Yes. Look, I can't help you, I'm sorry."

He persisted. "As her tenant you must be able to get in touch with her somehow."

The woman sighed with exaggerated impatience. It sounded like a valve blowing off steam. "You could try her mother. Patricia Callaway. She lives in St. John's Wood.

She's in the book." Without giving him a chance to respond, she hung up and he was left with a long dead tone in his ear.

Abroad. Abroad where? She could be in the middle of a war zone for all he knew. His only hope now was the mother. Fortunately, the razor-voiced one had spoken the truth. Patricia Callaway was indeed listed and he managed to get her phone number from international inquiries without any problems.

He dialed the number and listened as the phone started ringing. As he waited his eye fell on a framed poster against the wall. It was a print by Magritte of a man staring into a mirror and seeing only the back of his own head. Adam looked away.

"Patricia Callaway." The voice was that of an elderly woman—soft-spoken, cultivated.

"Mrs. Callaway, my name is Adam Williams. I wonder if you can help me. I would like to get in touch with your daughter."

"What about?" The tone was suddenly distinctly frosty. It made him pause.

"I'm a friend of Justine's, but we've lost touch. I thought it might be good for us to catch up again."

This time Patricia Callaway's response was even chillier. "If you give me your phone number, I'll ask her to call you, Mr. Williams."

"I understand she's abroad."

"She's back. So, if you'll give me your phone number?"

He thought quickly, remembering the article in the magazine. "I'm sorry I wasn't able to attend Jonathan's funeral, Mrs. Callaway."

"You knew Jonathan?" A definite crack in the armor.

"Yes." He decided to improvise. "I'm a musician as well. I was a great admirer of your son's work."

"Thank you. Yes, he was very talented." Her voice was suddenly heavy with tears and it made him feel like a heel.

But it couldn't be helped. He had to discover Justine's whereabouts and this woman held the key. If he had to resort to this kind of underhanded tactic to make her tell him where her daughter was, so be it.

But even though her tone was now much warmer, the mother still wouldn't budge. "It's for Justine's own good, Mr. Williams. Please don't take this personally, but some of Justine's friends . . . Well, let's just call them overnight friends. And the next day it would be very difficult to get rid of them. I've made it an absolute policy not to give out contact information over the phone. It would be much better if she called you. I promise to deliver the message."

It was no use. He was going to have to face the fact that she was not going to help him out with a phone number. And he certainly wasn't going to give her Mark's number. He couldn't drag his friend into this. But perhaps she'd be willing to give him an address.

"I'm actually going abroad myself. It might be best if I write to her. I also have some photographs I want to pass on to her. If you could give me her address . . ."

But even this was not going to fly. Patricia Callaway was having none of it. "Why don't you just send the letter to my home, Mr. Williams. I'll be sure to pass it on to Justine."

He sighed, defeated. "All right. Where shall I send it to?"

She spelled out the name of the street meticulously. At the end she said, "Have a good trip, Mr. Williams. And I'll give Justine her mail. You have my word."

He felt like banging his head against the wall, but he managed to keep his voice even. "Thank you. I'll be writing soon, then."

He hung up the receiver and turned around to find Mark staring at him.

"You're going to write to her?"

"Maybe it's for the best. I've been writing her letters for the past nine years, after all. So I'll simply write her another one. And this one I'll send."

"Adam . . . What if she takes the letter to the police?"

"She won't."

"You don't know that."

"It's a chance I'll have to take."

"Faint heart never won fair lady." Mark's voice dripped with sarcasm.

"Exactly." Adam was imperturbable.

"At least don't tell her everything. Don't tell her about Richard's death. Don't give her your real name. That's putting yourself in needless danger. If she takes the letter to the police, they'll be able to trace it."

"She won't take it to the police."

Mark opened his mouth to protest again, but the next moment Rita had entered the room. She looked from one man to the other, and Mark knew his wife had sensed the tension between them. She smiled hesitantly. "Adam, are you staying for dinner? Bubble and squeak only I'm afraid."

"You know I love your bubble and squeak, but I have to go." Mark watched as Adam leaned over and kissed the top of his wife's head. He was always slightly startled to see how gentle Adam could be. He was such a large man, he made the room feel small and he towered over Rita. But his hands with their long fingers and broad knuckles rested on Rita's shoulders with the delicacy of a moth.

"Let me see you out." Mark nodded at Adam.

The two men walked in silence to the front door. As Adam took his leather jacket from the hook on the wall, his eye fell on a long sheet of paper covered with signatures, which was lying on the entrance table next to a bowl of potpourri.

"What's this?"

"A petition. To stop Yuri Grachikov for good from building his hotel on Pennington's Island. I'm circulating it among my patients. The more signatures I can collect before the commission sits, the better."

"Grachikov won't like it."

"I don't care what he likes or doesn't like."

"Don't play with him, Mark."

"I'm not playing, Adam. He needs to be shut down. He's a cancer."

Adam pulled the jacket over his shoulders. "I had a rather disturbing conversation with him the other day. I bumped into him at Giant's Castle and he wanted me to give you a message. He says you're making trouble for him."

Mark pushed out his chin pugnaciously. "I sincerely hope so."

"He also said that you don't want him to make trouble for you."

"Oh, please. First he offers me money and now he's threatening me? It just confirms my belief that this man needs to be stopped."

Adam sighed. "Just be careful, all right? Even the loss of an entire marine terrace isn't worth getting hurt for."

Outside the day was dying in a streak of scarlet and gold. Mark and Adam stepped through the door into a lukewarm dusk. Rita's attempt at a garden was not very successful—a tiny patch of dusty grass flanked the front door, the borders struggling against the encroaching sand. Mark paused and watched as Adam and his shadow—all broad shoulders and long spidery legs—moved quietly toward the front gate.

Suddenly Adam stopped. "Look." He lowered himself to his heels.

Close to his shoe, caught in the yellow light spilling out of the hallway, was a black tenebrionid beetle. Called *tok-tokkies* because of the sound the female of the species makes when she taps the back end of her tiny body against the ground, these beetles were hardy little survivors. The male sometimes traveled for miles in his quest for a mate, following the tapping sound like a siren's call. Farther south, tok-tokkies were common, but out here this particular type of tenebrionid beetle was something of a rarity.

Adam touched the black beetle lightly with his fingertip. It scurried off into the growing darkness. Adam looked up at Mark and smiled with delight. "It's a sign, don't you think? Don't you think it's a good omen?"

Seventeen

"GOOD GRIEF. WHAT A weird room."

Justine looked up. Her mother was standing in front of one of the murals in the library—Leda and a very lascivious swan—the expression on her face outraged. She pursed her lips. "Really, it's positively grotesque."

Justine shrugged. "De gustibus . . ."

"Nonsense. There is such a thing as good taste and this is not it."

She shrugged again. She actually agreed with her mother, but she certainly wasn't going to say so.

Her mother turned away from the offending mural to look at her daughter. Her expression didn't change noticeably as far as Justine could see.

"You're too thin, Justine. Are you eating properly?"

She didn't answer, merely opened the drawer of the writing desk where she knew she had left a packet of Dunhills. Her mother's lips tightened as she watched her light the cigarette but she said nothing.

She drew the cigarette smoke deep into her lungs. God, that felt good. Exhaling, she watched her mother through a cloud of smoke.

Patricia Callaway was impeccably dressed, as usual. A beige and russet-colored cashmere two-piece. Tasteful, expensive. In her hands she held a pair of suede gloves, which matched the suede uppers of her high-heeled pumps. Underneath one arm was clasped a Ferragamo clutch bag, the leather as soft as butter. Her mother was plump but her legs were still shapely. Her face was smooth and rosy, and her hair a stylish cap of silver. But ever since Jonathan's death, sharp lines bracketed her mouth. Justine looked away.

It would be fair to say that she and her mother had always disappointed each other. Her mother did not approve of her lifestyle or her choice of career. And when Justine was a teenager, the battles between them had been epic in scale. For the greater part of the year she had lived with her father, of course, but for six weeks every summer she and her mother would share the same roof and the atmosphere would be toxic. It was only Jonathan who had been able to keep an uneasy peace between them.

On one level she knew she resented her mother for allowing her father to take her away after the divorce. Even though, if asked, there was no question that she would have chosen to roam the world with Sam rather than be cooped up in her mother's house in St. John's Wood. She preferred her father's company by far, but it still hadn't made her feel any less abandoned. Her mother should have put up a fight, for God's sake. And so, ever since she could remember, she had delighted in tormenting her parent. Everything her mother wanted her to do, she would do the exact opposite. It was a compulsion. A childish compulsion, to be sure, but one she could not seem to break. Not that she tried very hard.

The only thing she and her mother had ever had in common was their adoration for Jonathan. Now he was gone.

She knew her mother blamed her for his death. And of course, her mother was right. She *was* to blame. And so guilt had been added to the witches' brew of resentment, damaged trust, and failed expectations that made up this particular mother-daughter relationship.

Her mother stroked her gloves. "I understand you saw Barry, recently?"

"I saw him two weeks ago, yes."

"And?"

"He looks well."

"He won't wait around forever, Justine."

"I'm not expecting him to." She stubbed out the cigarette into a tea-stained saucer. "So, what's up? Any particular reason you came out here?" She didn't actually add the words "except to spy on me," but she hoped her tone of voice was clear enough.

Patricia Callaway extracted her handbag from underneath her arm and opened it. "I brought you your mail."

"You shouldn't have bothered. I told you to bin everything."

"That's an extremely irresponsible way to react, Justine."

She could feel her face flush and her teeth were suddenly on edge. But before she could respond, her mother continued: "For goodness' sake, why on earth wouldn't you want to check your mail?"

"There is actually a reason why I'm shut away here in the country, mother. It's called 'getting away from it all.' "

"But you don't have e-mail. And what about bills, business letters—"

"Everything is on direct debit. If you're worried that you'll have to bail me out of jail, you can put the thought out of your head." She viciously pulled out the drawer of the table as far as the stop and shook out another cigarette from the pack. Her mother could have forwarded the letters. The mail was just an excuse to check up on her. A very transparent excuse at that.

"People have been calling for you."

Justine looked up from the cigarette she was just about to light. "People?"

Her mother made a vague gesture with her hand. "Friends. I don't want to give out your new number—"

"No, please don't."

"—so I've asked them to write. Which is another reason you really should go through your mail."

"OK, fine. Just leave the letters here on the desk."

Her mother glanced at her wristwatch. "I should go. I'm meeting the ladies for bridge at six."

As they walked toward the car, her mother asked casually, "Have you heard from your father at all?"

"He's in Antigua the last I heard."

"With that other girl? What's her name again?"

"Deborah. She seems to make him happy."

Her mother sniffed. "We'll see for how long. Your father is not exactly a long-distance runner when it comes to relationships."

Which was true, Justine thought. And like father, like daughter. Short stamina and a low threshold for boredom were traits she seemed to have inherited from him. Along with his blue eyes and a tendency to burn in strong sun.

At the car, her mother turned around and pecked her on the cheek. "Take care of yourself. When do you think you'll be ready to return to London? Any time soon?"

"I don't think so." Justine opened the car door and watched her mother get in behind the wheel, pulling her legs into the car with one contained, ladylike movement. "I'll let you know."

"You do that." Her mother started the engine and gave her a hard, tight smile. She pulled the door shut and reversed slowly. Giving a brief wave of her hand, she accelerated the car down the avenue of trees.

Justine turned around and walked back into the house.

From the hallway she was able to see through the open door-way of the library to where the stack of mail was waiting. Within those letters her life was waiting for her. Friends, colleagues. New opportunities for work.

Reluctantly she walked over to the writing desk. Her mother had fastened the letters together with a thick elastic band. She picked up the stack of letters and riffled through the edges. There were quite a few letters from abroad; she recognized an American stamp, a German chancellor, and a couple of stamps of unknown origin. She had a good idea who had sent them. They must be from foreign magazines, offering her assignments. But she was not up for it. She had lost her nerve. Sad, but true.

She stared at the stack of letters irresolutely, slapping it against her palm. "Irresponsible" her mother had called her behavior. Well, probably. But it was her own damn business how she wanted to behave. She simply couldn't face any of this.

Letters in hand, she walked into the kitchen. She opened the door underneath the sink and pulled out the garbage bin.

Without a further thought, she dropped the letters into the bin and closed the lid.

HER MOTHER'S VISIT HAD upset her. She felt restless. On a sudden impulse she decided to go into Ainstey even though it was already late afternoon. On one of her previous visits she had noticed a nice looking little restaurant just opposite the church. It had tablecloths and candles and the flowers on the tables seemed fresh. Maybe she should treat herself to a decent meal.

And maybe she should get some exercise while she was at it. Rain was predicted for tomorrow, but today was one of those lovely mild autumn days with blue skies and not a breath of wind. Instead of taking the MG, she would make her way to the village using the bicycle she had spotted hanging from a beam in one of the storage rooms.

And here it was, an old Raleigh bicycle with the black paint flaking off its steel frame. The frigging thing was massively heavy. And the wheels were flat. By the time she managed to inflate the wheels and maneuver her way through boxes and trunks thick with dust, she had snagged her ankle on a broken wicker basket, her arms were tired, and her enthusiasm for the adventure was waning.

But it would be utterly wimpish to give up now. She wiped her hand across her forehead and eased herself cautiously onto the scuffed leather saddle. It creaked lamentally but it felt not too bad. She might even end up enjoying it.

Enjoy was probably too strong a word, though. By the time she managed to pedal into Ainstey, her calf muscles were aching and her bum was decidedly the worse for wear. But what a sense of accomplishment. Now to find a place to leave the Raleigh.

The church. The link fence setting the church back from the street had several bicycles chained to it already. She glanced at the open church doors and debated on whether to go inside and do the right thing. She should probably ask Reverend Wyatt if he'd mind if she made use of his fence as well.

Oh, what the heck. Why should he mind? She stopped and leaned the Raleigh against one of the poles. She did not have a chain and lock but she could hardly imagine that anyone would be interested in stealing this vintage model. And what could be safer than a church.

The restaurant looked as though it was going to live up to her expectations. Even though it was only five o'clock, they agreed to serve her dinner—that is, if madam wouldn't mind a small delay; the kitchen was not quite ready yet. She shook her head. Madam wouldn't mind at all.

She ordered the cassoulet and a glass of chardonnay. She

was given a table at the window and a newspaper. It was all very pleasant. For the first time since her meeting with Pascaline Buchanan she was starting to relax.

By the time she had finished her leisurely dinner, which included a double cream raspberry compote, she was feeling so mellow that she actually regretted the argument with her mother.

She left the restaurant feeling lazy after her meal. But she still had the trip back to Paradine Park to make. Her bicycle was the only one left and the church itself seemed deserted, the doors shut tight. As she pushed the bicycle onto the road, all the street lamps suddenly switched on.

She looked at her watch. It was already half past six. The proprietor of the hardware shop was still behind his counter, she noticed, but most of the other shops had closed for the day.

Whereas the trip into Ainstey was mostly uphill, once she left the main road it would be mostly downhill back to Paradine Park. And it would be much quieter as well. At the moment she was cautiously pedaling at the very edge of the road, wincing when cars passed her by with only inches to spare. But the off-road was coming up. She could see the sign for Paradine Park gleaming white in the dusk. The wheels of the bicycle sang as she turned into the dirt road.

It was a lovely evening. A silver sickle of a moon was hooked into the velvet sky. She pedaled across a stone bridge and the water flowing silently beneath the bridge glimmered as though the heat of the day had entered the watery darkness and was now glowing from deep down below. A night bird chirred exuberantly and was answered by its mate. In the air was the smell of gently rotting fruit.

But suddenly the bicycle swerved violently underneath her hands. She was taken by surprise and unable to control the movement. The front wheel skidded and she tumbled from the saddle, scraping her knee painfully in the process.

Shit. She ran her hands over the wheel. The tube was completely free from the rim. The Raleigh had spent too much time in the storage room.

She straightened and brushed the dirt off her hands. She was just about exactly halfway between Ainstey and Paradine Park. She could still see the spire of Reverend Wyatt's church in the gathering dusk. She probably had another fifteen minutes or so to go.

She started walking, pushing the bicycle along next to her. Her knee burned. The air, which had seemed so mild only a moment before, suddenly felt decidedly chilly. The birds were quiet.

After walking for about ten minutes she stopped and glanced over her shoulder. It wasn't that she had seen or heard anything—it was just a feeling, a suggestion of a shadow passing just outside the grasp of her consciousness. Her eyes traveled from the black patches underneath the trees to the other side of the track. She could see no one.

She increased her pace. The bicycle dragged beside her. Her knee felt wobbly, like it was filled with something jellyish.

Thank God. Paradine Park's boundary wall loomed in the darkness. And there were the gates. Not long now and she'd be inside the house. Safe.

On some level she knew she was being irrational, but the night air suddenly seemed full of noise. A twig cracking. Someone breathing hard?

Unease was turning to outright fear. She needed to get out of the dark. She needed to get inside the house. Dropping the bicycle, she left it where it fell and started running up the avenue of trees. Her hair was plastered against her forehead and despite the coolness of the night, her shirt clung to her body with sweat.

The porch light was on. She stumbled up the steps, her fingers groping frantically inside her handbag for the keys. She could feel her shoulder blades hunching, her back becoming stiff with tension, but she did not look around to see what was behind her. She did not look around. She did not want to see what was coming toward her from the darkness.

The door opened and she stumbled inside and slammed it shut. With trembling fingers she turned the key.

She pushed back the thick drapes covering the windows next to the door and stared out into the garden.

Everything was peaceful. The lawns were empty, the hedges motionless. The well-lit steps outside the door held nothing but a few dry leaves. Nothing stirred.

It had all been her imagination.

But then she heard the noise. Not outside the house, though.

Inside.

It came from the kitchen. Or did it?

Fear spread through her thoughts like a bloodstain in water. She kicked off her shoes and walked on tiptoes to the swinging door.

She placed her hand on the door and pushed it open softly. At the same time her hand reached for the light switch. Click.

The kitchen looked exactly the way she had left it. Breadcrumbs on the table. A few unwashed cups and saucers in the sink. The logs and stacks of old newspaper peeping out from behind the green and white striped curtain. The tap dripping as usual. From where she stood she could see the back door was dead bolted.

Her heart was still hammering in her chest, but the fear was now mixed with anger. Anger at her own timidity. For God's sake, she had braved war zones in Rwanda and Iraq. Once she had even endured a night in a prison cell in Guatemala. And now, here she was, scared of her own shadow, flinching at noises that did not exist. Stupid idiot. What the hell was wrong with her? Where was her nerve? But she knew very well where her nerve had gone. It had left her during a night of fire and death. She was a hollow woman.

The kitchen was empty. For good measure she pulled to one side the green and white curtain, half expecting to find someone hiding behind it. But of course, there was no one. And the dark room was empty as well. But her heart was still racing and in the back of her mind was still the memory of the noise she had heard as she entered the house.

Oh, for heaven's sake. This was stupid. She grabbed a knife from the butcher's block. It had a satisfying heft to it. The blade actually gleamed.

It took her a full thirty minutes to check every room in the house. Every time she opened a closet, her throat closed. Every time she looked behind a door, she held the knife at the ready. But she opened every door and looked inside every closet. She checked under the beds in her room. She pulled away the shower curtain. As she marched from room to room, her heels striking angrily at the floor, she continued to switch on the lights. By the time she ended back in the kitchen again, every light in every room was burning and the house was lit up like Canary Wharf.

As she stood there, slightly breathless and not quite sure what to do next, she noticed that the cupboard door underneath the sink was ajar. This was odd only because she always made sure to close it tightly because of the garbage bin. She was concerned about odors. One of the little paranoias of the single woman.

She walked over and pulled out the bin. It was half-filled with waste. An empty Kellog's Special K box. An empty can of tuna. A milk carton. Coffee grounds. Orange rinds. An empty whiskey bottle, of course. Several tea bags. As she stared at the odd assortment of rubbish, something in her mind was nudging at her. She was missing something. What was it?

The letters. The letters were gone.

She looked again, actually reached in with her hand and rummaged through the assorted articles. No letters.

They had to be in there. She pulled the bin all the way out and upended the garbage onto the floor. Nice. The oil from the tuna can splattered the tiles and there must have been more milk left in the carton than she had thought because it left a sour-smelling trail of white. The place was going to reek if she didn't clean it immediately. She felt stupid and scared sitting on her heels, surrounded by trash.

What should she do now, call the police? And tell them what? Someone had stolen her garbage? That would work. And how did the intruder get in? Or, for that matter, leave? Every window was closed. All the doors were locked. There was no sign of a break-in anywhere.

Oh God. Maybe she was a madwoman after all. What the hell had she done with those letters? She could swear she had dropped them in the bin.

She got to her feet and looked out the window. With the light behind her, her face formed a pale outline against the glass pane. She blinked at her reflection, a woman staring at herself clutching a butcher's knife in her hand. She suddenly felt like weeping.

You should leave this place.

The words popped into her mind as clearly as if they were spoken out loud. For a while she stared at the ghostly image caught in the glass frame. Blurry eyes, mouth turned sadly down.

She leaned forward and placed her fingertips against the cold glass. "I can't," she told the face in the window. "I can't leave this place. I have to find a wolf first."

Eighteen

THE HANDWRITING WAS DECISIVE. Adam Buchanan had used a fountain pen—the Watcher could see where a few stray drops of ink had spattered across the page, as though the man had needed to shake the pen impatiently to get the ink flowing.

Dear Justine. You don't know me, although maybe your heart already does . . .

The Watcher felt nauseous. This wasn't possible.

During his visit to Paradine Park he had checked her bin as usual, not really anticipating anything of interest. The stack of letters was an unexpected treasure. He had been delighted. Until he opened the letter he now held in his hands.

The letter seemed to burn through the skin of his fingers. His forehead felt feverish. His tongue was dry as paper. He had read the letter through so many times he knew it by heart. He was trying to come to terms with the reality of the contents but his mind slipped every time it attempted to grasp the fact that Adam Buchanan had written to the woman who was now occupying his own mind almost to the exclusion of anything else.

The Watcher felt disoriented. It was as though he had looked through a keyhole to discover that the world around him was a virtual world and that another, fantastical world was hidden behind a charmed door. A world where synchronicity and fate were conspiring to create a different reality, darkly wonderful, infinitely mysterious. A black-hued fairy tale in which two figures were desperately searching for each other.

What a wonderful place to explore.

The only problem was, he was standing on the outside of the door and to him, the door was locked. He was stuck in the mundane world. Strange how that hurt. He didn't think he had it in him to feel this strongly. He tried to identify the feeling he felt toward Adam Buchanan. Jealousy? An unfamiliar emotion.

He fingered the letter. What was he going to do about this? Once again, he held the fate of this man in his hands.

As far as he could see, he had two choices. One: send an anonymous tip to the police. He now knew where the fugitive was hiding out. The address was written at the top of the page, bold as you please. So let the police take care of Adam Buchanan.

There was a downside to this scenario. If they caught Buchanan, there would be a media frenzy. He could imagine the news coverage something like this was likely to get. Justine might flee from the press hounding Paradine Park. Once Buchanan was caught, there would be nothing keeping her here. She'd simply leave. That was the last thing he wanted.

Two: he could send the letter back to her. This was quite a delicious idea, actually. It should be intensely fascinating to observe. What would her reaction be?

And what a heady rush knowing he had the power to impact so powerfully on these two people's lives. A man who had fascinated him for almost a decade. And the woman who intrigued him as no other person ever had. His decision could change their very existence.

He looked at the letter again. The urge to send it back to her was strong. It would be truly enthralling to observe how she handled something as weirdly wonderful as this in her life. Would she embrace it? Or shrink from it?

But what if the letter caused her to leave Paradine Park and go look for Adam Buchanan? Come to think of it, she probably would. If he ever received a letter like this—so passionate, so filled with need—he certainly wouldn't hang around. Not that something like this was ever likely to happen to him, of course.

No doubt about it, she'd go looking for the man.

He was suddenly consumed with a ridiculous feeling of dread. This letter must never, ever reach her. In fact, it would be best if he destroyed it.

He opened the drawer of his desk and took out his cigarette lighter. He had given up smoking years ago as an example to his parishioners but had kept the lighter. It was a gift from his mother and she was not a generous gift giver. He could exactly name the gifts he had received from her over the years. There weren't that many.

He snapped the lighter and held the letter to the tiny flame. The paper curled and singed, those passionate, vibrant words fading into a brown haze. He held the letter close to the flame until the page disintegrated and fluttered to the surface of the desk in black flakes. Now that it was done, he felt an enormous sense of relief.

He got up from his chair and walked to the window. It was late and Ainstey's streets were empty. He opened the window and leaned out. The lemon verbena growing in the garden outside scented the air. As he stared out at the night sky there was a brief exploding streak of light on the horison. A shooting star.

He placed both hands on his chest and with all his heart he made a wish.

Nineteen

THE PURPLE PALACE WAS packed with bodies. It was the end of the month and everyone with a paycheck to spend had congregated underneath its roof. Cigarette smoke hung white in the air. At the bar, men with sun-wrinkled faces and calloused palms stood shoulder to shoulder. There was not a single chair available at any of the rickety tables. Above the deafening noise of voices shouting, arguing, laughing, pulsed a Springsteen anthem. The Boss proclaiming his heritage. Born in the USA.

Most of the customers were male, but as Adam's eyes scanned the room, he could see that many of Kepler's Bay's ladies of the night were present as well. One of the prostitutes, a redhead with a fresh smile, slid her arm around his waist. "Adam. I haven't seen you forever. Why have you abandoned me?"

He brought her hand to his lips. "I yearn from afar, fair lady."

"Like a freaking knight in armor." She giggled tipsily.

He smiled at her. "I'm looking for Mark. Have you seen him?"

"Sure. He's over there." She pointed to a table in the far corner squashed in between a coatrack and a pillar from which drooped a grimy Jolly Roger. "He's on to his second bottle already."

"Thanks." Adam started to push his way through the throng of bodies, the smell of sweat, dust, and alcohol filling his nose. On his way, he grabbed a miraculously vacant chair and held it above his head as he moved through the crowd to where Mark was sitting at a tiny table, staring at the glass in his hand with a beatific smile.

"Hey." Adam lowered himself onto his chair.

"Hey." Mark stared at him hazily. "Have some," he said, picking up the bottle of whiskey with the clear intention of pouring the liquid into Adam's nonexistent glass.

"OK. Wait, steady there." Adam removed the bottle from Mark's fist. "I see you started without me."

"Well, you were late," Mark said, sounding perfectly reasonable. His speech was clear and only the constant smile and cloudy gaze showed that he was, in fact, terrifically drunk. Adam watched him take another swig, eyes half-closed, mouth just a little slack so that the liquid dribbled in a thin stream down his chin. He was always amused and bemused by this monthly ritual of his friend. Mark, the most sober-minded man of his acquaintance, a man who lived a life so exemplary and commendable, had one vice. Once every four weeks he went on a binge. A massive binge. An epic drinking spree that usually ended in a sad epilogue of vomit, shaking hands, and a shuddering headache. Rita had long since made peace with this state of affairs.

Mark squinted at him. "You look like shit."

"Thanks. So do you."

"It's because she hasn't replied, isn't it, oh friend of mine. I told you. Didn't I tell you she wouldn't respond." Mark paused and picked up a soggy fry dripping with oily cheese from a small basket in front of him. He popped it into his mouth and after munching noisily, continued. "She thinks you're a sicko. A madman. A madman. A me-me-mad me-me-man." Mark repeated the syllables, seemingly fascinated by the alliteration.

"Maybe this isn't the place to talk about it, what do you say."

"What do I say? I say she thinks you're cuckoo. Cuckoo. Cu—"

"Yes. OK, I get it. And I think it's time for you to head back home. Come on, I'll walk you."

"No." Mark pushed out his lower lip petulantly. "Don't want to. Besides, I love this song. Love it."

"This song?" *It's the end of the world as we know it. And I feel fine.*

"And I feel fine," Mark reiterated, singing along with gusto.

"Mark, come on. Enough's enough." Adam placed his hand on Mark's wrist, but Mark shook it off with a sudden shake of the arm, in the process knocking over the basket of fries as well as his glass onto Adam's lap.

"Shit." Adam looked down. A large wet patch was spreading across his thigh. Yellow cheese streaks stained his crotch. He looked up at Mark who had started to laugh, mirth nearly closing his eyes. "I'm pleased you're amused. Now, I'm going to the bathroom to take care of this. You sit here and wait for me, OK? And then I'm taking you home. No arguments."

He got to his feet. After bumming a bottle of soda water from the barman, he walked to the men's toilets at the end of a dimly lit passage next to the kitchen.

The walls of the restroom were scribbled over with graffiti. As the place hadn't been painted in decades, some of the slogans were of great antiquity. A lady by the name of Tina—obviously a flame that had burned with some brilliance—was remembered fondly and figured prominently among the various inscriptions.

He poured the soda water over the stain, rubbing at it with his handkerchief. The dark patch was now even bigger. No doubt when he left the restroom, people outside were going to think he's had an embarrassing accident, but what the hell.

He looked up and into the mirror that was set into the wall above the dirty washbasin. It was a shock to see his own face. He avoided mirrors. He had even become expert at wielding a razor without a mirror to assist him. It wasn't that he had forgotten what he looked like, but it was as though, in some deeper sense, he didn't have a memory of himself any longer.

For a long moment he stared into his own eyes. They looked back at him, inscrutable. He couldn't read their expression. He turned his head slowly, first to one side, then to the other, keeping his eye on the mirror. There was a line running across his forehead. He never even knew it was there. His skin, grazed by the wind and darkened by the sun, seemed yellow in the blue light coming from the stuttering strip of fluorescent tubing attached to the ceiling. He couldn't remember his hair being this dark.

The face of a killer. Or a madman. That's what Mark had said. She thought he was a madman. When she had read his letter, had that been her first reaction? Did she believe she was reading a letter produced by a deranged mind? It was a letter in which white-hot longing and hopeless yearning burned through every word. A terrifying letter, perhaps. Yes, that was it. She was afraid. He had scared her. The letter had been too desperate; too desperate by far.

Five weeks since he had written to her and not a word from her in return. Every day he came into town and checked his mailbox at the post office and every day the box was empty. He knew he had taken a tremendous risk writing to her, signing it with his real name, giving away the location where he had found refuge from the law. But the highest reward required the highest commitment.

Maybe she had found the letter funny, something to dine out on. He could picture it. Sitting in some chichi restaurant in London, showing the letter to her friends. "You won't believe what's happened . . ." And all of them speculating and laughing and picking out phrases they found particularly amusing.

God, how could he have been so naive. But he had so believed that she would *know*. That her heart was tired with his constant presence shadowing her thoughts so that his words would make immediate sense; provide sudden balm to the incessant irritation of an inexplicable longing. 'I recognize you,' she'd say. 'You're the one I've been waiting for.'

Behind him the door suddenly flew open and a man dressed in cut-off jeans and a T-shirt emblazoned with the words "Mamma's Boy" staggered in. Adam recognized him: Dirk Pottas, a crayfisher. He looked decidedly the worse for wear. With a sigh of relief, Pottas unzipped his pants and with eyes blissfully closed, commenced to relieve himself in the urinal.

After a few moments he opened his eyes and focused on Adam who had finished washing his hands and was now trying to dry them on his handkerchief.

"Maybe time for you to go back in there, Adam." He jerked his head toward the door.

Adam looked at Dirk. "What do you mean?"

"The doctor. I think he's in trouble."

"Oh hell. Has he started throwing up?"

Dirk Pottas stepped back and zipped up his pants. "No. But by the time Yuri Grachikov's finished with him, he may feel like it."

"Oh, Christ." Adam turned around and opened the door violently. As he walked quickly down the passage toward the front room, he realized how quiet it suddenly was. The noise of voices had died down. And someone had killed the music.

Mark was sitting where he had left him, hands clutching the edge of the table. The expression on his face showed drunken outrage and the beginnings of real fear. Sitting next to him on the chair vacated by Adam was Grachikov. He was smiling. One massive forearm rested on the table. Behind him stood five men whom Adam recognized as Grachikov's constant companions. They were watching Mark with expressions of contemptuous amusement. The other people in the room looked uneasy, but it was also clear that no one felt like getting involved in this particular showdown.

"A doctor's hands are important, yes?" Grachikov reached out and touched Mark's clenched fingers. "You should take care of them, my friend. Accidents, they happen very easy."

"Are you threatening me?" Mark's voice was high.

"Threaten a doctor? A healer of the people?" Grachikov shook his head sadly. "Of course not. I'm just saying. It is good to take care, yes? I've seen it happen before. One stupid move and *pfft*—you lose a finger. A hand is crushed. It happens."

Mark tried to speak, but his voice seemed to fail him. The tip of his nose was glowing. His eyes were watery.

"What's going on here?"

Grachikov turned around in his chair and for one moment a look of pure annoyance swept across his face. But the next moment he was smiling again. "Mr. Williams. I did not see you here before. How are you?"

Adam walked over to Grachikov slowly. When he reached the table, he stopped and placed his hands palms down on the surface. He leaned over and brought his face close to Grachikov's, as close as if they were about to kiss.

He could see the sheen of sweat on the man's cheekbones, the pores on his nose. He could smell him—the sweetish odor of his skin, the oiliness of his scalp. Grachikov didn't move, but his lips pulled away from his teeth, just slightly.

"My friend does not like you." Adam paused. "*I* do not like you."

Silence. It was quiet enough in the room that you could hear a pin drop.

He leaned in even closer. "Do not talk to him. Do not talk to me. Ever."

Grachikov pushed his chair away from the table with a violent screech. He got to his feet, his body coiled, the tension in his shoulders unmistakable.

"No." Adam spoke succinctly. "Walk. Away."

Grachikov flushed. The two men kept their eyes locked, the moment dragging on and on. Someone laughed nervously.

A flick of an eyelid. Grachikov looked away.

"Adam." Mark's voice was desperate. "I feel sick. I need to get home."

Adam felt his breath leave his body with an explosive gasp. He looked down at Mark. His friend was deathly white and his lips appeared almost blue. As Mark tried to get to his feet, he stumbled. Adam stepped forward quickly, propping him up.

And suddenly, as though someone had flipped a switch, people were drifting back to their tables and the sound of voices in conversation filled the air. From the speakers came the voice of Shania Twain saying, "Let's go girls." No one even seemed to be discussing what had just happened. It was eerie, as though what had taken place had left no dent in the memories of those who had witnessed the scene.

Adam looked back at Grachikov. The man had stepped back and was talking to one of his friends, his voice low. But Adam knew he was watching from the corner of his eye.

He placed his arm firmly around Mark's waist. "Come on," he said. "Let's get out of here."

*   *   *

AFTER HE HAD DROPPED Mark off at the house, depositing him into Rita's waiting arms, Adam collected his bike from their backyard and headed for home. He had a throbbing headache and the confrontation with Grachikov had left him with a bad taste in his mouth.

The wind was exceptionally strong tonight, forcing him to drive slowly, his head pulled into his shoulders, the desert sand blinding against his goggles. The wind sighed, moaned, crept into the ridges and hollows. It was a relief when the first of the deserted houses loomed up from behind a dune of sand, the sweep of the roof black against the windy sky.

The sudden quiet as he closed the door of his house behind him was almost disconcerting. For a moment he stood in the darkness, sensing the pupils of his eyes widening and adapting to the gloom. As always there was that odd moment of hesitation when he experienced a reluctance to banish the darkness by striking a match. He sometimes thought that darkness was his true habitat. In the ocean, when he swam away from the sun, he accepted the watery darkness as something natural, not to be feared. And he preferred to explore the desert at night, as did most desert creatures. Even the windwalkers kept to their cave during the day, usually venturing forth when the sun slid down the sky and got sucked into the ocean. Life was a voyage between dark and dark. Nighttime, which brought with it sleep and dreams, was the time he was most true to himself. This was the time he could descend down the spiral staircase of his unconscious, access memories of a previous lifetime, walk hand in hand with his love through a shadowed dreamscape filled with landmarks and places known to them alone.

His eyes could now make out the outlines of the furniture in the room. He walked toward the fireplace and sank to his knees. The logs and paper were already stacked into a pile and it only needed the flick of a match to set it alight.

The glow of the fire gave the room a golden tint. He got to his feet and walked to the desk. He had copied her picture on

Mark's photocopier, blowing it up to four times the original size.

How focused she looked as she worked. How filled with purpose. Her face was set in an expression of stern serenity. There is beauty in concentration, in a mind fixed with scalpel-like precision. His thumb stroked lightly down the line of her jaw. She had a lovely neck. Her hands were quite large.

He sat down at the desk, opened the drawer and took out a blank piece of paper. He unscrewed the top of the pot of ink, dipped the nib of his pen into the oily depths.

Dear Justine,

You never responded to my first letter. It was not my intention to scare you. He lifted the nib off the paper. For a moment he sat motionless, trying to find within him the words that would cause her to catch her breath, lift her hand to her throat.

Every night I dream of you. You come to me, driven by a knowledge of what might have been, charmed by a sense of what is yet to be. If only I could wake inside my dream come true. Your breath on my cheek. Your heart underneath my hand.

He closed his eyes, suddenly swept by a feeling of such hopelessness he thought his body might shut down from the awful despair, the blood at once frozen in his veins, the beat of his heart suddenly stilled.

He looked down at what he had written. His fist closed on the sheet of paper, crushing it between his fingers so violently that the paper cut into his palm, leaving a thin line of blood welling through the broken skin.

In the corner of the room was the tall medicine chest with its many drawers. Inside that chest were hundreds of letters he had written to her during so many empty nights, through so many empty years. They were all still sealed in their envelopes, waiting for her to read them.

He got up from his chair and pulled open one of the tiny drawers. Removing the top letter, he ripped open the envelope and looked at the date. He had written this letter fully six years ago. His eyes moved over the closely spaced lines:

I am troubled by the sense that somehow, in my mind, I have divorced myself from the act of murder. I feel myself to be the snail, not the disgusting smear he left behind . . . but at the same time I am fully aware that only a snail can leave a trail of slime in its wake.

If only I could talk to you. If only you could come to me . . .

His vision was blurred and he felt nauseous. He rammed the letter back into the envelope. He was a fool. Of course, she wouldn't come to him. Even though it was meant to be, he had destroyed any chance they might have at being together in this life. He had killed his brother. He did not deserve to find her. And she would not want him. Why would she wish to walk side by side with a murderer?

His eye fell on a large cardboard box that was shoved up against the wall. He pulled open the drawers of the medicine chest haphazardly, grabbing letters and dropping them into the empty box. With the box balanced in his arms, he unhooked the front door and walked into the night.

The box was large and awkward to carry, and the wind was very strong, but he did not stop until he found himself surrounded by dunes and night sky, his house vanished from his sight, around him only emptiness. The wind raced across the sand, plucked at his shirt, narrowed his eyes. There was a full moon tonight and the lunar light seemed chaste and cold.

He put the box down and kicked it on its side. The white envelopes spilled out and were immediately swept up by the wind. Like a swarm of pale butterflies they fluttered away into the dunes; his words—thousands and thousands of words—scattered into the wind-filled darkness.

Twenty

THE ENTRANCE TO THE cave was right ahead. Yuri Grachikov stopped and wiped his hand across his forehead. His breathing was ragged from the effort it took to walk through the thick sand, all the while pitting himself against the force of the wind. His teeth felt gritty. There was even sand underneath his collar.

About a half an hour ago, he had thought he'd lost his way for sure. He had been this way before, the two times he had followed Adam Williams, but in the darkness everything seemed suddenly strange. And it wasn't as if this landscape stayed the same. The wind changed the face of the desert every day.

What a hell hole of a place. Kepler's Bay itself was like a terminally ill patient and he sometimes thought the people who lived here were the walking dead. The lethargy of the inhabitants made him crazy. They had no drive, no initiative. They had given up: there was no urgency in their step or spark of enthusiasm in their eyes. Here he was about to help them inject some economic prosperity into their miserable lives, but instead of recognizing the advantages his hotel would bring, these people were signing petitions left and right, following the saintly Dr. Mark Botha like sheep.

For a moment he felt intensely melancholy. He missed home. In his mind's eye he was back in Moscow, watching the lamp light gleaming on Susanna's thick black hair. His sister's fingers delicately clasping the violin's bow, her eyes closed as she followed the lead of his cello. Borodin's Second String Quartet—it had always been their favorite, especially the third movement nocturne with its sublimely romantic melody. How many times had they played thus— brother and sister, shoulder to shoulder—the cello playing first, the violin following in close imitation. The room bathed in light, the smell of his cigar burning in the ashtray and the feeling that all was at peace in the world.

But when was the last time he had played the cello? He couldn't even remember. Music belonged to a different time in his life, a sweeter time, he thought, suddenly filled with self-pity.

He started walking again, keeping his head low. He didn't like being out here in the darkness, but he didn't really have a choice. Windwalkers walked at night. The best time to find the cubs alone and defenseless, would be when their parents were out hunting. And he needed to do this while the rage still burned coldly inside his blood.

He thought back to the confrontation with Adam Williams earlier that evening. It had been a battle of wills and he was the one who had blinked first. The others may not have noticed, but he knew. And Adam Williams knew. He felt the bile rise in his throat.

And that was why he found himself here, at the cave where the strandwolves lived. He had followed Adam Williams to the lair twice in the past month, part of his plan to find out as much as he could about the man. He was puzzled by Williams's obvious fascination for these scavengers.

Williams would spend hours on his stomach, binoculars against his eyes, simply watching. He obviously admired the animals, had a real affection for them. But then, there was a decidedly lupine quality to Williams himself. It had struck him afresh earlier tonight—something in the man's eyes was feral. Very few men indeed had the power to make him hesitate, but Adam Williams was one. The man made him lose his cool every time. He sensed a rage in Williams. It was reigned in, banked down. But if let loose, it could probably equal in ferocity anything he, Grachikov, could come up with—and more.

Which is why he had decided on this course of action. The time was not yet right for a full-scale war, but he needed to decompress and take care of his frustrated anger. He had side-stepped a physical confrontation. Now he needed to assuage the startling sense of inferiority he had experienced earlier tonight.

He felt with his hand against the side of the cave. The last time he had watched the cubs, they had been sunning themselves just outside the cave entrance. But tonight they were nowhere to be seen. They must be in one of the inner chambers.

It was a relief to enter the first chamber and escape the wind. He switched on his flashlight and the yellow beam played across the weathered rock. There was a powerful scent of musk and urine in the air. He moved cautiously. If one or both of the parents were in the cave, he was in serious trouble. The cubs were now big enough that they did not need constant supervision, but the mother could very well be lurking inside the cave as well. He touched the large hunting knife in his waistband.

But the cubs were alone. As he entered the second chamber, the three pairs of eyes gleamed in the artificial flashlight. They were watching him without any fear at all. They had probably never seen a human being before. One of the cubs, a little runt with a gamy foot, was even hobbling toward him curiously.

He propped the flashlight against a ledge in the cave wall. Stooping down, he grabbed the cub by the scruff. It was a cute little thing, really, with its long hair and soft ears. He slid the hunting knife from his belt. Placing his thumb against the softest part of the animal's neck, he sliced cleanly through the pulsing throat muscles.

He dropped the small lifeless body into the cool sand and reached for the second cub. This one squealed like crazy, a high-pitched scream, which agitated the other one as well. He grabbed the cub by the loose skin at his neck. The animal was barking, snapping at his wrist, already displaying the power of what was destined to become one of the strongest jaws in the animal kingdom. A full-grown strandwolf could snap your hand right off your arm with a single bite. But this one was still several months away from adulthood and his knife was large and the blade sharp.

Maybe he should spare the life of the last one? He stood considering, looking down at the snarling animal. Then, calmly, he reached down and picked it up. A female this one. For a moment he and the animal were face to face. He imagined he could see a tiny picture of himself in the gleam of her eyes.

A sweep of the blade against the throbbing throat. The blood spurting warm and sticky onto his hands, running down his wrists and forearms. Without another glance at the three bodies, he turned away. He felt suddenly tremendously energized; it was almost as though he could feel power surging through his body.

As he stepped out of the darkness of the cave into the starry blackness of the night, he threw his head back and screamed into the wind. He unbuttoned his trousers and urinated against the rock wall, the yellow liquid steaming and pungent.

His scent. His territory.

Twenty-one

WINTER HAD COME TO Paradine Park. One morning the day was still tepid with autumn sun and the next Justine woke up to find a thin haze of white covering the lawns and the black-skinned trees.

And as though the advent of cold and mist was a signal, she withdrew behind the walls of Paradine Park even more decisively than before. She stocked up on food and rarely went into the village now. And when Mason and his grandson told her that during the winter months they tended the gardens only once every three weeks, it felt right.

Every now and then she would make a call to Barry and to her mother—not from a sense of duty but because she knew a protracted silence would alarm them. It might even compel them to drive over from London and that she could not allow. She did not understand where it came from, this sense that now, more than ever, she must keep the place undisturbed. Paradine Park should remain inviolate. The drawbridge up, the walls fast.

Outside her window the landscape was wreathed in mist. Every sound deadened. The sky opaque. She would wake up and find the fog pressed up against the panes so closely that she could not even see the wrought-iron gate guarding the entrance to the avenue of trees. But inside the house the light appeared strangely translucent. The days in here passed one after the other as cold, hard, as clear as marbles made of glass.

Day following empty day. Her cameras lay untouched. She hadn't entered the darkroom in weeks. She had given up trying to capture the wolf within the camera's snare of light. She was searching for him in the world of sleep now, but he had even disappeared from her dreams.

She covered herself with the green jacket. She slept with her mind wide open. She waited for his footprints to impress themselves on the dusty floor of her dreamscape. But her sleeping world had become a desert. Empty. Lonely. So terribly, terribly lonely.

Wepwawet. Opener of the ways. Man, wolf. They were connected. Her heart knew, her mind was accepting. If she found the one, she would find the other.

She opened the book with its burning pictures of a thirsty land and her fingers traced the outline of his signature. *Adam W. Buchanan.* By this time she knew it as well as her own. The towering *B*. The two strong lines of the *W* and the extravagant loop of the *h*. A strong hand had written these. She studied the photocopy of his face. Not even the graininess of the poor quality photograph could blunt the intensity of that gaze. *The face of a killer.* Fratricide. The very word sounded malevolent. She should be repulsed, outraged by his crime. But she touched his face, her hand lingering against his mouth.

Where was he? Where had he found a hollow for his foot? Some of the newspapers told of sightings in Australia and the United States. Was he hiding out in the anonymity of a big city, or had he slipped into an unremarkable life in a fea-

tureless suburb? White picket fence, children, a wife unaware of the mental darkness of the man with whom she
shared her bed?

Or maybe he had died. Justine felt suddenly cold. Maybe
he had died far from home and no one to care or be curious
enough to find out who he really was. Just another drifter dying in a cheap motel. The terror of the image paralyzed her
mind. Her thoughts were ragged, like peeling wallpaper in a
derelict room.

She wondered if she had a fever. She wondered if she
were insane. She was in love with a ghost. Sometimes she
felt as though she were a ghost herself. She'd say her name
out loud. "Justine. Justine." As if the mere sound of vowels
and consonants would prove she did exist. She looked into
the mirror not expecting a reflection. But there she was: pale
face and hungry eyes. The face of a greedy woman. A
woman whose heart was a dark hollow, her longing a luminous, bright-edged, all-devouring thing.

She spent hours in the bathroom. Scented foam, perfumed
water, brushing her hair, creaming her body. A body that had
not been seen by anyone but herself for a long time.

Waiting. Waiting. Like a princess languishing in a tower.
Waiting for a knight whose heart was brave and true. *Why so
pale and wan, fond lover?* Banner streaming, pennant pinned
to his chest. A white horse with wild eyes and flying, blood-
soaked mane. A rider fresh from battle, the smells of car-
nage still clinging to his hands. *Why so dull and mute, young
sinner?*

The day she found the toy airplane. A small biwinged
plane made of balsa wood. A young boy's plaything,
brightly-colored, the word *Valiant* written on the side in a
childish hand. Her heart beating with such excitement she
thought it might burst. She threw the plane into the air, but it
hardly took flight. It fell down and when she picked it up the
wing was broken.

Sitting cross-legged on the floor, drawing on a piece of

paper. The tip of her tongue sticking out of her mouth in concentration. The pencil scratching busily against the paper's surface. A heart. She was drawing a heart. A big luscious heart impaled with an arrow from which dripped fat drops of blood. In one corner of the heart the letter *J*. In the other a lopsided *A*.

She stared at the banal image, suddenly ashamed. How inane. How pathetic.

THE SKY WAS DEEPENING in color from gentian to bullet gray. Gusts of wind hinted at turbulent weather to come. But it wasn't until after nightfall that the storm that had threatened all day finally broke loose. Justine slammed shut the window to her bedroom just as the heavens opened and drops of rain spattered viciously against the glass panes. At that very moment, all the lights in the house went dead.

The darkness was all but complete. With her fingertips lightly trailing against the side of the wall, she felt her way downstairs, intent on retrieving the flashlight in the kitchen. But when she found it where she had left it on the windowsill, she was disappointed. The batteries were dead.

She remembered seeing candles in the larder. She shuffled over and opened the door. It was pitch-black in here and she suddenly felt severely claustrophobic. Her groping fingers grazed the smooth surfaces of bottles, touched the metal edges of cans and tins. Something fell over and a sticky substance covered her palm. But then her hand closed around an oblong package and she could feel through the waxy paper the unmistakable shape of candles. And sitting neatly next to the package of candles, a box of matches.

She struck a match, but it took several tries before the candle started to burn. Holding the candle upside down, she dripped wax into a coffee cup and planted the candle firmly inside.

The switchboard was situated underneath the stairs. She

flipped the master switch on and off a couple of times, but the lights stayed dead. She picked up the phone and called the electricity help line. A taped message clicked in immediately. Storm damage. Downed lines. Vague assurances of remedial action.

After a supper of bread and cheese, she decided to go to bed. There really was nothing else to do.

She creamed her face and brushed her teeth in the light of the candle gleaming off the tiny mirror in the corner of her room. Her face seemed strangely mottled in the uncertain light, like that of a drowned woman. As she dropped the toothbrush back in its glass she noticed how worn the bristles were at the outer edges. She should remember to buy a new one.

For the past few days she had started sleeping in different parts of the house. She harbored the forlorn hope that she would have more success enticing the wolf back into her dreams if she explored the entire house. So every night she dragged her mattress and blanket into a new room—rooms that had not been used in years. Stretched out on the floor, the smell of old dust in her nose, she'd watch as the moving clouds drifted past the window.

Tonight she had chosen a tiny room at the very end of the wing that held the nursery. In years past, it had probably been the room of a maidservant or a governess; it had that make-do feel to it. It was only half the size of the other rooms and the wainscoting was humble pine.

For a while she lay on her back, watching the candle's shadows dancing against the walls. Then, pushing herself to her elbow, she blew out the tiny flame very carefully and pinched the wick between her fingers. Her thoughts dimmed, her eyelids closed. Turning on her side, her legs drawn up close to her body, she went to sleep.

* * *

THE WATCHER EASED HIMSELF through the door of the coal cellar and stepped into the corridor leading off the kitchen. He stooped and took off his shoes. He didn't want to leave wet footprints everywhere.

It was late. By this time she would be asleep. And she'd have drunk a few glasses of her favorite Johnnie Walker, now wouldn't she? So a deep sleep for his Justine. And it was storming something fierce outside, so she wouldn't be able to hear much, anyway.

Softly he walked into the entrance hall. The sound of the wind was loud. The tree outside the window was swaying back and forth like a giant black hand. The windowpanes seemed almost white. He turned toward the staircase, taking the shallow steps two by two, his hand hooding the tiny beam from his penlight. Not that he really needed the light, by this time he knew his way around.

When he reached the landing upstairs, he stopped. He needed to calm his breathing. His heart was beating so hard.

More than a week had passed since his last visit. And the day after tomorrow he would be taking his mother away on their annual vacation. Usually he looked forward to their going away together, but this time he wanted desperately to stay. But there was no way he could duck his filial duty. For the next two weeks he'd be playing backgammon and taking brief, bracing walks with his Mum at their usual place near Fort William. Scotland in winter was always daunting, but his Mum liked the snow.

Before leaving for Scotland he had decided to give himself a special treat. Up till now he had been very careful not to get too close to Justine whenever he visited the house. They had never been inside the same room at the same time. But tonight, for the first time since the game started, he would go right up to her bed. Touch her hair, maybe. He was scared but excited all at once. There was too much saliva in his mouth. He couldn't stop swallowing.

It was a risk. If she woke up and saw him, that would be it. Game over. But he needed to actually touch her. The one part of his brain was dead set against it. He still remembered what had happened the previous time he had given in to his compulsion to make physical contact. But the other part of his brain was already sensing her breathing against his hand, imagining the silkiness of the hair at the nape of her neck . . .

This was it, her room. The door was wide open.

She wasn't there.

For a moment he stood rooted to the spot, his head moving from side to side; his eyes following the beam of the penlight as it probed the corners of the room. But there was no sign of her. The one bed was all made up. The other one was empty with not even a mattress.

It was such an anticlimax, he could feel his body go soft. He left the room and walked down the passage, peeking into a few rooms leading off the corridor. They were empty.

Her car was in the driveway. She *had* to be in the house.

Where was she?

WHEN SHE WOKE UP, her mind was as alert as though she had never gone to sleep at all.

Something must have woken her up. For a few moments she lay quietly, trying to identify what it was that had pressed the warning button deep within her unconscious. But it was still storming outside and the onslaught of rain against the windows was so strong, she could hear little else. Moving carefully, she got to her feet and flicked on the light switch. The power was still out.

She fumbled with the matches. The first match she struck died immediately. The second burned all the way to her fingertips before the wick took to the flame, trailing black smoke and an acrid smell.

Cupping her hand around the uncertain flame, she stepped out into the hallway.

SHE APPEARED SO SUDDENLY at the end of the passage he almost lost it. One moment nothing and then she was standing there. Like a ghost. It took him by such surprise, his nerves were suddenly gone. Any moment now and she'd look up and see him and her eyes would widen in recognition. And then she'd scream . . .

She walked by him as though he wasn't even there.

She passed by so closely, if he stretched out his hand he could touch her wrist. But she never looked up. She kept her eyes on the candle, her hand around the flame.

It was so disconcerting, he felt utterly stupefied. Several moments passed before he was able to move.

He was relieved, of course, that she hadn't noticed him, but mixed in with the relief was a tiny but disquieting flame of anger. It was as if he didn't even exist. She had glided past him as though he were part of the furniture. But that was what he wanted, wasn't it? This was how you played the game. You mimicked invisibility. It was the only way to remain a watcher. So why was he feeling angry?

He was following her down the staircase. He was only steps away. He realized she couldn't hear him. The sound of the storm was loud; it blotted out any other noise. But surely she must sense his presence?

The glow of the flame threw her shadow against the wall. Her shadow—and his. Two shadows walking one behind the other. The larger one drawing ever closer . . . She was bound to see it.

She didn't. She was oblivious.

And now she was leaning forward, candle in one hand, the other hand checking to see if the door was locked. She rattled the knob.

If she looked around now, she would see him. He realized, shockingly, that that was exactly what he wanted. He wanted her to look into his eyes. He desperately wanted her to recognize him, to acknowledge him.

He was sweating like a pig. The hollows underneath his arms were wet. Keeping his moist palms pressed against the wall behind him, he waited.

THE DOOR WAS LOCKED. Of course it was. She had turned the key herself earlier that evening.

She pulled the velvet curtains away from the window flanking the door and stared out into the blackness. It was hopeless. She couldn't see a thing through the driving sheet of rain.

She let the heavy drape fall back into place. The candle was sputtering, the wick drowning in dirty wax. She hoped it wasn't going to die on her. There was a strange smell in the air; she had only just noticed. It was very faint, but it caused her nose to wrinkle in distaste. Sweetish, slightly sour. Body odor?

She turned around. The hall was empty. The black and white squares of the marble floor seemed to float in the flickering light, her shadow a lone queen on a giant chessboard.

She was imagining things. And it wasn't the first time. A few days ago she had opened the door to the nursery and had heard the echo of children's voices and feet clattering. And what about that one afternoon when she had nodded off in the library, her head resting on the hard surface of the writing desk? She had woken up to find the air redolent with perfume. She remembered thinking that the perfume could only belong to a woman confident enough to wear such a heavy, personalized scent. A beautiful woman with fair hair and pale blue eyes.

Hallucinations. By-products of loneliness. She was beginning to scare herself. It was time she took stock. Reclusiveness exacted too high a price: the mind becomes fractured and you could lose yourself in the silence. The house had held her in its spell, but it was time she shook herself free from its tyranny.

What had she hoped to accomplish, anyway? She was turning into a bad joke, trekking through this enormous house with her blankets and her mattress like some pathetic homeless woman. And for what? Because somehow the ridiculous notion had lodged in her brain that she should prepare herself to meet the one person in the world who could make her feel she wasn't an intruder in her own life. *Each of us is traveling through many lives with a map of time clutched in our hands . . . At some point the time lines of all separated lovers will cross.* Well, this was obviously not her time.

It was enough. Tomorrow she'd call Barry. Return to the world.

THE WATCHER FELT SICK. He had come close to ruining everything. What had he been thinking of back there?

Three years ago the same thing had happened. The girl would never have known of his presence if he hadn't forced her to look at him. She had red hair and a beautiful smile. For one moment he experienced the gratification of having her acknowledge him, truly see him. But then followed the shame and along with it the fear of what would happen if she exposed him. Police, the press, cameras, greedy eyes watching him constantly.

Even as her eyes widened, he struck her. Her head slapped against the wall with a surprisingly loud noise.

Carrying the limp body in his arms, he took her into the bathroom and filled the tub with water. When he placed her inside, some of it slopped onto the floor. He would dream of that moment for years to come. Her hair spreading around her head like red seaweed. Her face a moon underwater. The long string of oxygen bubbles breaking the surface like translucent pearls.

He didn't want that to happen to Justine. It was a blessing he would be forced to go away for a fortnight. They needed the break from each other.

If only he could keep the game going without ever having to worry that he might lose control and force her to look at him. He realized how weak he was. The next time around he might not be able to restrain himself. How to stop that from happening?

Imagine if he could walk through her life without fear of being observed. Wouldn't it be wonderful to be in the same room, to look into each other's eyes but without her seeing him?

Maybe this could actually happen. At the back of his mind stirred an idea. A genuinely brilliant idea. It needed some thought, some planning, but it might just work.

The Watcher's favorite movie was *Magnificent Obsession* with Rock Hudson and Jane Wyman. He had watched that movie more times than he can remember. Lovely Jane Wyman, accidentally blinded by playboy Hudson, falls in love with a stranger who enters her life and takes care of her in her disabled state, little knowing that the caring stranger is the remorseful Hudson, the same man who was responsible for her losing her sight. The Watcher never tired of the story. There was something tremendously appealing about it. Beauty and the Beast . . . and Beast never in danger of being recognized by Beauty . . .

Imagine if he were able to come up close. Imagine if he could be in the same room and she'd look at him with eyes that did not see. Midnight eyes.

Eyes that were blind . . .

Twenty-two

THE WEATHER THIS MORNING was miserable. Gray cotton wool clouds and a steady drizzle of rain that chilled to the bone. Justine pulled up her collar and adjusted the scarf around her neck. She had used the train this morning, switching to the tube for the last part of the journey. It would be a relief to get off. The train was packed and she was tired from the effort it took to keep her claustrophobia in check in the midst of the crushing press of bodies.

Oxford Street was filled with pale-faced people shuffling sullenly to their different destinations. A large van passed by too close to the curb and its front wheels threw up a spray of dirty water against her coat.

Shit. She looked down. The bottom part of her coat was soaked. This was all she bloody well needed. After her night of broken sleep chasing phantom intruders through the house, she had woken up tired and with a headache. And now this. Thoroughly out of temper, she trudged through the wide entrance of Borders bookshop, her bag almost knocking over a display of the newest bestseller, the cover showing a mad-eyed figure with a dripping knife: *He made them beg! He made them scream! Their pain was his joy!*

Barry was already waiting in the coffee bar. When he saw her step off the escalator, he raised his hand in greeting.

"You look like you need something hot to drink," he said as she plonked herself into the chair opposite him. "Cappuccino?"

She nodded, leaned over for a kiss on the cheek. "You look good."

"Thanks." He smiled. He *did* look good, she thought as she watched him walk to the counter. He was wearing a moss green sweater, which brought out the color of his eyes. He was not a handsome man in the traditional sense of the word, but his intelligence and innate kindness showed on his face. No wonder women always warmed to him immediately.

She shrugged out of her coat, accidentally bumping the arm of the young man sitting at the table next to her. He and his girlfriend were poring over some snapshots. As she jogged his shoulder, some of the pictures fell to the floor.

"Sorry."

She leaned over to scoop up the photographs. Obviously holiday pictures. She caught a glimpse of a young woman in a black bikini on a deserted beach with very white sand. And another one of a huge multicolored air balloon with smiling passengers clutching a bottle of champagne.

She straightened. The young man was glaring at her. As though she had done it on purpose, she thought irritably, pushing the pictures into his outstretched hand.

Barry placed a froth-capped cup of coffee in front of her. "Here you go."

"Thanks." She picked up the spoon and scooped the chocolate sprinkles into her mouth.

"I like your hair like this." He was looking at her appraisingly.

"Thanks. I just haven't had the chance to have it cut recently."

"It suits you."

"Maybe I should keep it this way, then." She looked away, took a sip of her coffee.

"You also look tired."

"I haven't been sleeping all that well, that's all."

"Anything wrong?"

"Not really." She picked up the spoon again, twirled it around in her fingers before replacing it in the saucer once more. She looked up at him. "I think I'm ready to return to London."

His face lit up. "When exactly?"

"Well, I'll have to give notice, I suppose. I'll call the estate agent when I get back, find out what needs to be done."

"I can't tell you how pleased I am. I was worrying myself sick about you out there on your own. And then that spooky stuff with the photographs . . ."

"Yes, well. Let's just say it's been an experience."

She looked over at the table next to them. The young man and his girlfriend had just about worked their way through the stack of snapshots. The glossy pictures with their slick surfaces were piled precariously on top of each other. If he wasn't careful the pictures would land up on the floor again. Some were starting to slide out from underneath the others . . .

She blinked. She suddenly felt as though she couldn't breathe properly. The hum of voices around her was all at once muted, as though her ears were stopped with water.

"Justine." She turned her head slowly toward Barry. He was watching her frowningly. His mouth opened again and he said something, but she couldn't grasp his words. It was as though her brain had shut down.

She looked back at the pile of snapshots. Her hand reached out as if of its own volition and she grabbed the pictures with clumsy fingers.

"Oy!" The young man was staring at her, his mouth an outraged *O*, his face distorted with anger and what could be alarm. The girl, eyebrows lifted, looked as startled as if she'd been slapped.

"Where was this? Tell me, where was this?" Justine thrust one of the pictures into the young man's face, grabbed his arm so hard that she saw him wince.

"Are you mad?" He swiped her hand off his elbow.

"Justine. What is it? What's wrong?" Barry's face was a mask of concern.

She tried to speak, but her voice was suddenly gone. She could only point at the picture clutched between her fingers.

He leaned forward. "What?"

"Look." Her voice was high and shaky.

He took the picture from her. She saw his expression sharpen.

"What the hell's wrong with you people?" The young man was now red in the face and had pushed himself to his feet. "You have no right. Give me back—"

"Sir, I'm sorry." Barry spoke softly, but something in his voice caused the young man to sink back into his seat slowly. "Our apologies," Barry continued, "but please, we need to know where this photograph was taken." He placed the picture on the table between them.

The girl spoke for the first time. "We took these during our honeymoon."

"Where?"

"Did a wilderness tour of Namibia, didn't we?"

Namibia. Justine closed her eyes briefly. "They have wolves like this over there?" She touched the picture with the very tip of her finger.

"It's not a wolf." The young man was still looking at her warily, but the outright alarm in his eyes had faded. "It's called a strandwolf, but it's really a brown hyena. They're very rare. We were lucky to see one. We were exploring this old ghost town and there it was."

"Ghost town."

"Yes. We have some pictures of it." He picked up the photographs and thumbed through the stack. "See."

The picture he was holding out at her was an inexpertly taken snapshot, but she recognized it instantly. Derelict houses with broken windows and mounds of sand creeping into the empty rooms. The picture was taken from exactly the same vantage point as one of the pictures in the book she had discovered in the library at Paradine Park.

"This isn't the only ghost town around there," the girl said. "This one has become a bit of a tourist attraction— there's a museum there and everything—but apparently there are others as well that are completely unspoiled. We didn't have the time to look for them, but I'd love to go back there one day and explore properly."

Justine stared at the picture blankly. In her mind's eye she saw words written in a strong hand, words that had haunted her ever since she first discovered them, secreted in a margin next to this image of total desolation.

Is this redemption?

"Please. May I have these?" She picked up the snapshots of the strandwolf and the house. "I'll pay for them. Anything. But please, I need these."

The young man and the girl looked at each other. Then the girl shrugged. "They're yours. We don't want anything. We have the negatives." She reached into her bag and took out a pen. "Here. This is the name of the nearest town." She turned the picture over and scribbled something on the back.

"Kepler's Bay." Justine said the words tentatively.

"It's in the southwestern corner of the Namib. Difficult to get there." The girl got to her feet and looked at the boy. "We should get going, what do you think?"

"Sure." He picked up the remaining pictures and dropped them into his satchel. For a moment he stood looking at her awkwardly. "OK, then."

"Thank you." Justine's voice was thick with emotion. "Thank you so much."

He bobbed his head, embarrassed. "Sure. Glad we could be of help." He took the girl's arm and they moved away. At the top of the escalator they looked back over their shoulders, their faces still puzzled.

"He's in Namibia. Here, at this place. Kepler's Bay." Justine tapped with her finger on the picture.

"He?"

"Adam Buchanan."

"What on earth are you talking about?"

"There is a connection between the wolf and this man."

"This man. The guy who killed his brother?"

"Yes."

"Do you know how crazy that sounds?"

"I know. But I've never been more certain of anything in my life."

"Well . . ." He stopped, looking lost. "Well, let's say for argument's sake you're right. So what?"

"So what?" She made an irritable gesture with her hand. "I have to go there. I have to find him."

He stared at her and it was clear that words had failed him.

She spoke rapidly, her thoughts racing. "Do you think they have nonstop flights to Namibia? I should have asked those people. Does BA fly there? I still have some frequent fliers. Although if you want to use them you have to book at least two weeks in advance, don't you. That's too long. I need to go now. And to hell with giving notice."

He found his voice. "You're serious."

"I'm deadly serious."

"Why the hell would you want to go chasing after a killer for God's sake. Have you lost your mind?"

The sudden fury in his voice brought her up short. "Barry." She paused. There was something in his eyes she had never seen before. It made her feel insecure, as though the world around her had all at once become very fragile. "I don't know how to explain this to you. I feel it here." She touched her hand to her breast. "He and I . . . we are linked. I know it. I will never be at peace unless I find him. This is the man I've been waiting for my entire life."

Silence. His lips were tight, his face paper white. The expression in his eyes was one of confusion and anger. Hurt.

"He's a murderer."

"I know."

"A man without conscience. A man without compassion." He paused. "This is sick."

She didn't answer. Couldn't really. What was there to say?

"I can't wait for you forever, Justine. Even the most death-less love needs oxygen."

"I'm sorry." She placed her hand on his.

He took her hand and quite deliberately removed it from his wrist.

"Don't be like this, please." Her eyes were wet.

For another moment he stared at her stonily, then his face seemed to sag. He passed a hand across his mouth.

"I'm so sorry," she said again. She sniffed, gulped.

"Don't cry." His voice was muffled. "I can't bear it."

For a while they sat in silence, simply looking at each other. The coffee bar had filled up. A sour-faced woman and her teenaged daughter were edging steadily closer, looking pointedly at the empty coffee cups in front of them.

"Maybe we should leave."

He got to his feet. He moved stiffly.

The weather had changed from miserable to foul. Outside it was pelting rain, large icy drops chasing pedestrians into the shelter of shop entrances and restaurants.

"Do you have an umbrella?" Barry's voice was formal, polite.

She opened her handbag and extracted a small fold-up Tote.

"Good." A pause. "So you'll be leaving the country right away, then."

She nodded wordlessly. He bit his lip and it looked as though he were about to say something.

But then he gave an odd, half shrug and the next moment he had plunged into the rain, walking away from her with long strides. His shoulders were set, his hair plastered wet against his head. He did not look back once.

Twenty-three

"LOOK."

Mark lifted his head and his eyes followed to where Adam was pointing. An oryx antelope. It stood completely motionless. One moment the horizon was empty and the next minute the oryx had appeared like a mirage. The sweeping horns etched like pencil strokes against the trembling sky. The head and body so still the animal seemed like a posed prop, lifeless, something merely conjured up by his brain to fill the emptiness.

He looked back at Adam. Adam was still staring at the antelope, his eyes creased against the glare of the sun. Mark knew Adam was fascinated by oryxes. The "ultimate survivors" Adam called these mammals whose unique cooling systems enabled them to survive body temperatures of more than forty-five degrees Celsius. Unlike strandwolves, which could withdraw into caves, the oryx was forever at the mercy of the sun. But by a countercurrent heat exchange of cool venous blood from its sinuses and hot arterial blood from the carotid artery, the oryx managed to keep its brain safe from irrevocable collapse. It was a tenuous survival mechanism but it allowed the oryx to wander deep, deep into the sea of sand.

"Miraculous," Adam murmured, his eyes still fixed on the distant shape.

Mark nodded. "It is that."

"By all the laws of nature, it's not supposed to work, you know. That animal is cheating its way through life. Cheating death."

"Hmm." Mark stooped and picked up his diving kit and dropped it into the rear of the Land Rover. "We should get going. Why don't you drive?"

"Sure." Adam turned away reluctantly. He caught the keys Mark tossed at him. "Let's go."

On their way to the boat, Mark watched Adam from the corner of his eye. Adam's body seemed relaxed, his hands clasping the wheel lightly, one elbow resting on the open window ledge. But his mouth was taut and the expression on his face seemed remote. The shutters were back in place. Every day Adam seemed more like the man he had met all those years ago, the man who had shut out the world, clutching to him the terrible bonds of self-imposed isolation.

It all started when they discovered the dead cubs in the cave. The parents had deserted the den. Inside were only three tiny bodies covered with buzzing flies; the lips of the one cub drawn away from its teeth in a petrified smile. There were boot prints in the dust. The perpetrator hadn't even bothered to try and cover his tracks. Mark knew Adam suspected Grachikov, but he was not so sure himself. Certainly he hated Grachikov, but he also believed that Grachikov was a practical man and not someone who would engage in a sick little orgy simply for the hell of it. If there was profit involved, yes—the man would be capable of anything. But Mark thought it more likely that this was the handiwork of an illegal hunter, a member of the fraternity of poachers who

sometimes moved through the wilderness like lethal vandals—shooting and maiming anything that moved.

Adam had wept that day in the cave. And as they walked
away from that place of death, Mark looked into Adam's
eyes to find a stranger staring out at him. The voice was still
friendly, the manner easy. But the walls were up.

Still, it wasn't only the cubs. There was another reason for
the change in his friend. And it was time the whole thing was
brought out into the open.

"Adam . . ."

Adam flicked a glance across at him. "What?"

"We should talk."

"What about?"

"About her. We should talk about her. About the two of
you." Mark held his breath. He knew he was trespassing.
Adam had made it clear on the previous occasions he had
tried to raise the subject that he did not want to discuss Justine Callaway. He was on dangerous ground.

But to his utter surprise, Adam nodded. "You're right. We
should." He paused. "There's something I've been meaning
to tell you. But let's do the dive first. I don't want us to be
distracted while we're down there."

"Of course." Mark gave a sigh of relief. "After the dive,
then. We'll talk after."

THE DIVE WENT WELL. They were only searching for spiny rock
lobsters today and the dive was unexacting, no dangerous
depths or disorienting caves. Usually rock lobsters were captured by rectangular traps and ringnets, but you could also
nab them at depths of seventy meters on rocky bottoms.
Mark had a license and was allowed a catch of six.

After the dive they did not head back to the mainland immediately as usual. They dumped the lobsters in the boat,
stripped off their fins, and made their way to a smooth slab
of rock. Here they took off their suits and stretched them-

selves out in the sun, staring up at the sky, the sunbaked rock hot against their exposed backs.

After a while Mark said, "Next time, let's head for Giant's Castle again. It's been too long."

Adam was silent.

"Adam—did you hear what I said?"

"Yes. It will have to wait."

"Wait? Why?"

"Because I won't be doing any diving for a while."

Mark tilted his head, perplexed. "You have to start working shifts again in a weeks' time. You told me so."

"I didn't renew my contract. I told them I'll be sitting this summer out."

"I don't understand."

Adam turned his face away, his eyes fixed on a spot somewhere in the ocean.

Mark stared at him. "Oh, no. Tell me it's not what I'm thinking."

"I have to find her, Mark. And it's not going to happen while I'm trapped in this place."

"Adam . . . You can't go back. It's too dangerous. You're a fugitive. You can't just breeze into the UK." Mark stopped. His voice had become unpleasantly high pitched. "They'll catch you," he continued in a more moderate tone. "Nine years is not that long. They'll be waiting for you."

"I'm leaving for Windhoek tomorrow." Adam continued as though Mark hadn't spoken. "I have an appointment to see Van Horn. He's helping me out again with papers and a passport. It's costing me, but it can't be helped."

"You're crazy. It's one thing to have papers forged for this place, but for the UK? It won't work."

"It will work. It's already done. Van Horn has a contact in the home office in Pretoria. That's what I'm paying for. And if they check, I have a life here. An employment record. A return ticket. Hide in plain sight—that's the best way."

Mark sat quietly. Around his chest was a steel band

squeezing his heart. He suddenly realized how extremely fond he's become of this man who was watching him with a strange, resigned little smile.

"Don't worry, Mark. I'll be back."

"I'm afraid for you."

"I know."

"And if you find her? What then?"

"I don't know. It will take care of itself." Adam smiled again. "You're the one who's always complaining that I'm hanging around the outskirts of things; that it's time I committed myself to a leap of faith. Well, this is it."

"I've never advocated foolishness."

"Everything in life comes down to a few crucial moments, Mark. Most of the time we have no control and circumstances make the decisions for us. And these decisions ultimately determine the lives we lead. But some moves we get to make ourselves. This is one of those steps that's up to me, not fate. The most important step of my life."

Mark leaned forward. He spoke urgently. "If it's really written in the stars that the two of you are soul mates, then it *is* set—determined—*not* up to you. Have you thought of that? In this case a decision *not* to go would be an expression of free will, not the other way around."

"You should wish me luck."

Mark sighed, defeated. "My friend, I wish you all the luck in the world."

HIS TRIP WAS CIRCUITOUS. He had flown from Windhoek to Cape Town and from there to Athens. Athens was the easiest point of entry into the EU, Van Horn had assured him. And as he was in transito, he wouldn't require a Greek visa either.

Adam paged through the green backed passport. He was now a South African citizen. Born in Johannesburg forty years ago. Employed in Namibia. The document seemed startlingly authentic. "It *is* authentic," Van Horn had assured him. "That's why you pay the big bucks, hey. This isn't some scuzzy second-rate forgery. With this baby you can travel the world and no worries."

And so far, it was working out. He hadn't been that concerned about flying into Cape Town; many Namibians worked in South Africa and vice versa and South Africans accepted the desert country on their border almost as an extension of their own. But at the Athens airport he had thought the immigrations official would be sure to pick up on his thundering heartbeat and the phony smile, which try as he would he could not remove from his face. However, after taking a look at his London-bound ticket, the man had merely riffled briefly through the pages of the passport and, without a second glance, had waved him through.

But now they were about to touch down at Heathrow. For the past twenty minutes the plane had been in a holding pattern. With every minute that passed, he felt the tension increase. His head was pounding. His stomach had turned to acid. He had wondered how he would react to his first sight of home. But he was in an aisle seat and the passenger next to him was looking out the window, blocking the view. He had no sense that he was back in England.

When he finally stepped out of the plane into the walkway, he felt a brief, welcome blast of cold air. It was a tremendous relief to get out of the cabin. He hadn't been in close proximity to so many people in many, many years. His shirt clung clammily to his back; he was perspiring heavily. He looked down at the passport clasped in his hand and was horrified to see a sweaty imprint of his five fingers on the mock leather. He rubbed the passport frantically against his jacket. He was going to be fine. But not if he started oozing sweaty guilt from every pore.

That distinctive airport smell. Disinfectant and nylon carpets. Everything decorated in gray and blue. Had it been the same when he had left here ten years ago? His blurred gaze took in the large advertisements lining the walls. The names,

even the products made little sense to him. Eidos. Tomb
Raider. He had no idea what that was. Was someone watching him? He looked over his shoulder. Behind him was a
gaunt-looking woman in a knitted dress. The woman's lipstick, a bright crimson, had rubbed off on her teeth and
when she smiled at Adam it looked as though she were suffering from bleeding gums.

He looked back in front of him. They were approaching
the immigration hall. EU citizens were processed at the very
end of the hall by a young woman sitting on a high stool behind a counter. The passengers were passing the counter,
hardly breaking step. They had their passports open at the
page with their photograph and the young woman would simply place her hand on the page as if bestowing a benediction.

Not for him. He had to cue in the long line of non-EU
residents.

He counted the number of passengers in front of him and
looked at the row of immigration officials, trying to calculate
which one of the uniformed officials would be the one processing him. The elderly woman at counter six had a moth-
erly expression, but her line was moving the slowest. Not
good. So maybe he should hope for the young man with the
widow's peak. He looked new to his job, slightly awkward.

He shuffled forward. He was second from the front. A
woman in a white robe and then him. The objects around
him were swelling in size with every thump of his heart.
Number six. He was going to get number six.

The white robed woman was gesticulating at an immigration official with a pencil-thin mustache. He looked at her
impassively, then said something and turned around to wink
at someone behind him. Another man in uniform walked up
to the passenger and led her to a nearby desk. The immigration official looked over at Adam and signaled to him.

His eyeballs felt like stones in his head, his hand was
shaking.

But as he walked forward, his mind suddenly emptied.

The fear was gone. His journey could not end here, not without seeing her. Justine, Justine. They were destined to meet. He approached the desk without a tremor. Sliding the passport onto the counter, he smiled easily.

It wasn't until thirty minutes later when he slid into the seat of the cab taking him to London that the trembling returned. He looked down at his hand; it was jumping where it lay against his thigh and try as he might he was unable to stop it.

THE FIRST TWO DAYS in London passed in a daze. He was in shock, his mind numb from the assault on his senses. Too many colors, too many different odors, too much noise. The air he breathed into his lungs had a taste to it. A taste of the city. It coated his mouth, the inside of his nose. His eyes felt scratchy. And there was no relief inside his room in the tiny hotel just off King's Cross. He wasn't used to central heating any more and it made him feel headachy, the air unbearably thick and oxygen deprived.

People. Too many people: he could not get away from them. No escape. Even in his hotel room with the door closed tightly, he felt jostled by bodies. He'd sit on his bed and hear the sound of bodies moving above him, in the rooms next to him, on the sidewalks on the other side of the glazed window. When he ventured outside, he walked gingerly, taking elaborate care not to bump into anyone. He felt clumsy, as though he took up too much room. A teenager on in-line skates whizzed past him and he drew back in alarm.

The unexpected shock of rain. He couldn't remember the last time he had seen the sky pouring rain. He should have been delighted at the feel of the wet drops on his skin but he shrank from it. It was alien, suspect.

Black garbage bags hemorrhaging smells outside shop entrances. The odor of wet coats and unwashed bodies. Constant, constant noise. His mind becoming bruised from it; from crashing endlessly against a wall of aggressive, pounding sound. The sights around him surreal. He found himself staring at the window of a Chinese restaurant, mesmerized by the long necks of a row of dead ducks hanging from greasy butcher's hooks. He suddenly became aware that he wasn't able to see a horizon. The realization bothered him more than he would have thought possible.

He was tired but he couldn't sleep. He lay in bed and the light from the flashing neon sign on the other side of the street pulsed through the thin curtains and painted the inside of his eyelids. Yellow, black. Yellow, black.

On THE THIRD DAY he went to the house in St. John's Wood. He had shaved meticulously and had dressed with great care. The day before he had bought a suit, a conservative navy blue tie, half-brogues. "Overnight friends"—that was the word Patricia Callaway had used to describe some of her daughter's casual acquaintances, her voice filled with contempt. So it was essential that he projected an image of staid respectability if he wanted her to open up to him. An old friend of Jonathan's, a fellow musician. Someone who merely wanted to touch base with his former friend's sister. A courtesy call, really. No urgency, no desperation. Just friendly interest. Nothing that could set off an alarm bell in the mother's mind.

As he walked through the lobby of the hotel, he caught a glimpse of himself in the ceiling-to-floor mirror. Clothes maketh the man. The charcoal gray suit and crisp blue shirt had changed a desperado into a gentleman. He would now be able to pass as an ordinary productive member of society. There was only one wrong note. His skin was very dark from the sun. It was quite startling compared to the pallor of those around him. But it couldn't be helped.

Giving a last look at the stranger in the mirror, he walked through the sliding glass doors and into the pale sunlight.

THE HOUSE WAS BIG and freestanding with a front garden, which was probably lovely in summer. But the neat flower beds were grayed by the chill of winter. The only splash of color was a tub of blue and pink chrysanthemums at the front door.

He placed his finger on the brightly polished doorbell and heard it tone deep inside the house. The door opened so quickly and suddenly, it took him by surprise.

A young woman dressed in jeans and a smock looked at him inquiringly. She had a dust cloth in her hand. The cleaning lady. In the hallway behind her, he could see the handle of an upright vacuum cleaner.

"I wish to speak to Mrs. Patricia Callaway, please. If you could tell her Adam Williams is here to see her."

"Sorry. I can't do that."

He stepped back, looked again at the number of the house soldered into the wall. "She does live here?"

"Yes. But she's away. She's in Paris."

He felt as though a bucket of cold water had been thrown at him. "When do you expect her back?"

The woman was looking at him thoughtfully. Something must have shown in his face and he knew his body language probably spoke of tension. He tried to relax. The last thing he needed was to scare her and have her shut the door in his face.

He smiled. "I'm an old friend of the children. Jonathan and Justine."

"Oh." She looked stricken. "You do know that Mr. Jonathan . . ." Her voice trailed off.

"Yes. Yes, of course I do and that's why I'm here. I wish to convey my condolences to Patricia and Justine. Is Justine around by any chance?" He waited, hardly breathing.

But the woman shook her head. "No, sorry. I don't know where she is. She doesn't live here. Do you want to leave a number where Mrs. Callaway can reach you?"

He hesitated. The telephone in the hallway suddenly started to ring. She looked over her shoulder and then back at him. "If you'll excuse me . . ."

He gestured with his hand, stepped back. "That's all right. I'll stop by again on Monday." Before she could ask anything else, he had turned around and was walking swiftly in the direction of the front gate. He heard her close the door behind him.

Three more days. He felt paralyzed. He had psyched himself up for this meeting to such an extent that the anticlimax was too much. Suddenly at a complete loss as to what to do next, he stood on the corner of the street, blinking. He realized he was shivering. An icy wind was blowing and he felt chilled to the bone.

His eye fell on a tiny café on the other side of the street. He entered and the air inside was so close and overheated, he recoiled. It was so hot in here that the plate glass window had steamed up and he could hardly see anything in the street outside. But he sat down on one of the uncomfortable steel chairs and ordered coffee from a glum-looking waitress.

Some of the coffee slopped into the saucer when she plonked it down in front of him and the liquid was only lukewarm. But he placed both hands around the cup and drank greedily. He hadn't realized how thirsty he was.

Three more days. Three more days of juggling tedium and tension. Three more days of staring at the walls of his hotel room, of walking through streets he had no wish to see. The thought of it was a gray veil settling over his brain.

And then, unbidden, came to his mind the image of green rainwashed fields, of dark woods, and a house with honey-colored walls. The driveway matted over by falling leaves, the barks of the shadowy trees covered in moss. A landscape with the subdued richness of a canvas by Corot.

No. That door was closed forever. The man who had been master of the spacious rooms and elegant gardens was gone, and the man in his place had forfeited the right to return. There was no going back. And what a cliché it would be, the murderer returning to the scene of his crime. The idea of it was ridiculous. The mere thought of it was madness.

Madness. It wasn't even to be contemplated.

HE DECIDED TO CATCH the five o'clock train. He had no wish to arrive at the Ainstey train station in broad daylight. Nine years was a long time, but maybe not long enough. He might still be recognized.

But the station was deserted and apart from a couple walking their dog, the streets were empty. The windows of the houses were closed, the lights shining from behind the flowery curtains a butterscotch yellow. Even the church was dark. He looked at the thick stone walls, the silvered stained-glass windows. His mother had visited this place so often. It had been her second home. Her and Richard's. But he had never considered it a refuge.

He passed quietly by the village pub. The sign with its gilt lettering and colorful design swayed in the wind. The Slug and Pudding. It was just as he remembered it. From behind the closed doors came the sound of voices and laughter and he glimpsed the dark shapes of moving figures on the other side of the tiny windows with their leaded panes.

The evening was clear but it was bitterly cold. He had bought a wool coat this afternoon before setting out, but he had no gloves on him. He pushed his fists deep into his pockets.

Stars peeping through wisps of rapidly moving clouds. The moon luminous in a blue-black sky. His footsteps mak-

ing little sound, not even when he crossed the wooden foot-
bridge spanning the narrow, darkly flowing river. For a moment he stopped and gripped the railing with both hands,
looking down at the water, listening to its icy whisper.
Somewhere underneath him, in the shadow of the bridge,
was a large boulder with sensuous curves. He couldn't see it
in the darkness, but as a boy he had paused at this exact spot
every time he had to cross. It had been his own private ritual:
throwing pebbles at the boulder, watching as they spun off
and hit the rapidly flowing water like bullets. Two pebbles
only; never more than two. The first for safe passage. The
second for luck.

He left the bridge and started to walk down the narrow
lane which would eventually lead him to the gates of Paradine Park. The gravel track seemed frosted in the strong
moonlight and he could see hawkweed flourishing at the
edges. He passed by MacGregor's Stud Farm and he smelled
the horses and saw in the gloom the white poles of the paddocks. And now the high sandstone wall that marked the
outer boundary of Paradine Park was on his right. It was tall,
the height of two men, and formed a formidable barrier. But
the wall was in need of repair. He saw gaps between the
stones and the coping was crumbling.

The gates loomed up in front of him. The moonlight was
strong and the graceful filigree pattern of the gates stood out
clearly. They were shut and for a moment he wondered if his
way would be barred and he would have to turn back after
all, but when he slipped his hand between the icy spokes, the
bolt slid easily out of its lock. He stepped through and on either side of him the pale limbs of the beeches rose tall and
lovely in the darkness.

He stood; his heart weak, his mind softening with remem-
brance. The track, ribbed with shadows, stretched ahead of
him like something from a dream, like a ribbon of endless
longing, exactly as he wished it, more perfect than he recalled.

He found that he had moved, without realizing he had done so. On his left, on the other side of the row of beeches, he glimpsed the dark hump of the maze and farther back the sheen of the man-made lake, its water still and glassy. An owl called softly. The tentative sound hovered in the air, causing him to glance over his shoulder. His eyes probed the latticework of branches, but he could not find it, and after a moment he pressed onward once again.

At the very edge of the avenue he stopped, his body in shadow. In front of him was the house, as secretive, as mysterious as a storybook castle. Its windows were black, showing not a gleam of light. There was no sign of life, no cars in the driveway, no sound of a door slamming, or a dog barking or music or voices. No windows left slightly ajar.

He had no idea if the house had been sold. Maybe Harriet was still living here. But the house gave the strong impression of being deserted. Abandoned. His feet scrunched through the loose gravel. Walking hesitantly up the front steps, he peered through the windows flanking the front door. He imagined he could make out the sweeping curve of the balustrade, the gaping hole of the fireplace, but the shadows in the entrance hall were too deep for him to be sure.

The drapes were drawn across most of the windows on the ground floor, but as he walked down the length of the house, he noticed one set of windows with the curtains open. The music room. Cupping his hands, he pressed his face close to the glass pane.

The room was empty. He strained his eyes, but he could see no pictures on the wall, no furniture. A piano used to occupy the space right beside this window, a Steinway with real ivory keys and a mellow voice. And on its walnut surface had stood a bowl of flowers and photographs in gilt frames. Pictures of his mother and Harriet arm in arm; Richard in his cricket whites; his father seated in his study, an old-fashioned pince-nez clasped to his nose. He remembered that there had been a picture of himself, as well, to complete the array of family snapshots, but as he stared into the empty darkness, he found he could not recall what the picture had looked like.

The house was deserted then. He turned away from the window. To the left of him was the giant cedar tree, its leaves moving sleepily in the wind, the rope swing with the tire swaying gently. The bushes in the rose garden were a tangle of thorns. The wisteria walkway was without blooms. The tough stems made a vault above his head as he entered, but they were naked, stripped even of leaves. And there, pale in the moonlight, was the sundial. *Time that Was. Time that Is. Time that is Yet to Be.* He rested his hand on the dusty surface and waited.

Nothing. No echo of the past came to him as he stood there on the springy grass, the smell of rotting wood bitter in the air. If he were to find ghosts, surely this was where they would be, here where hate and rage and death had come together one summer's night when the grass was fragrant and the drooping sprays of wisteria had looked like a bride.

The owl hooted again from deep within the avenue of trees. A night bird answered hesitantly. The sound floated on the cold night air like a call to prayer.

There was nothing here. He had been foolish to come. Paradine Park had been abandoned even by the ghosts. And what had he thought to find? Catharsis, a sense of forgiveness even?

He turned his back on the walkway and walked toward the front of the house, intent now only on leaving this place behind. But as he stepped onto the gravel driveway, he stopped. A car was approaching fast, the lights two glowing eyes in the darkness. It was already more than halfway down the avenue and he wondered that he hadn't heard the engine earlier. Quietly he stepped back into the shadows, finding shelter behind a thick leafed magnolia bush.

A door slammed. Quick, light footsteps. The footsteps of a woman. He drew back into the shadows even farther. She was now standing in front of the door, he could hear her fidgeting with the keys. The door swung open with a protesting creak and then a wash of light suddenly spilled out into the night.

He peered cautiously around the bush. He caught a glimpse of a slight figure, a long black coat and red scarf. The next moment she had closed the door. But the light in the entrance hall was on and he could see through one of the long slim windows adjacent to the front door. She was pulling off her coat, her back toward him. But then she turned around and her delicately boned face was in the light.

His breath caught. His thoughts seemed to thicken. He stared at the figure framed in the window and his heart shouted, Oh! Oh! Oh!

SHE WAS TIRED BUT filled with a sense of accomplishment. Her bags were packed. Her passport, ticket, and a pocket-sized travel atlas were stacked on top of each other next to her bed. The ticket was open-ended; she had no idea how long she would be out there for. All that was left was for her to drop off her winter clothes, her cameras, and the MG with her long-suffering friend Caroline. She'd do that tomorrow on her way to the airport and take a taxi from Caroline's flat in Guildford out to Heathrow. Usually she would have stashed her stuff with Barry, but after their scene in the coffee bar, she did not feel she had the right anymore. And she certainly did not wish to ask a favor of her mother.

She could hardly believe that she was almost on her way. In another eighteen hours she would be in the air on her way to a country thousands of miles to the south, like a migrating bird attracted to warmer weather. She had decided to simply leave without saying anything to anyone. She felt a little ashamed to abandon ship like this, but the managing agents of Paradine Park would be sure to insist on a reasonable notice period. And the story about her fictitious husband could come out and the resulting unpleasantness might slow her up even more.

She stretched. Maybe she should take a shower to get rid of the city grime. She had spent the day in London arranging the visa and buying cotton slacks, T-shirts, and a hat. She had summer clothing at her mother's place, but she had no wish to go there. She did not want another verbal run-in with her irate parent.

She undressed and dropped her clothes on the foot end of the bed. She found herself shivering slightly as she walked down the hall to the bathroom. The heating in her bedroom was adequate, but the long passage was drafty. The soles of her feet were freezing and the chill in the air made her clasp her hands to her bare shoulders.

She turned on the shower and waited for the water to turn from tepid to hot. It always took some time.

After a few minutes the bathroom started to fill up with steam. She slipped into the cubicle with its old-fashioned bottle-glass doors.

The hot water felt like a blessing. She shampooed her hair and soaped her body using the expensive body wash she had bought that morning in a sudden burst of extravagance. It was a waste of money, really—she would have to leave it behind. But the gesture had suited her mood. Now that she was actually about to leave, her thoughts were light as air and she felt playful. She squeezed the bubbles between her fingers, enjoying the woody scent. She was happy. Certainly, there were some doubts, apprehension even, but she hadn't allowed herself to think too much about what exactly she would do once she arrived on the other side of the world. The important thing now was to get there.

She stepped out of the shower and draped the thick pink towel around her. The mirror was fogged up, reducing her face to a hazy blob. She smiled and reached out her hand and traced in the patch of moisture the outlines of an animal: four legs, sloping body, ears pricked.

She suddenly yawned uncontrollably. She really was very tired indeed; she should go to bed.

Just before leaving the bathroom, she wondered, had she locked the front door? She hesitated, trying to recall her actions after she had arrived. She couldn't remember, although . . . she probably did. Yes, no need to pad down the drafty passage and chilly staircase for nothing. Besides which, she really should guard against becoming paranoid.

She opened the bathroom door and started to walk down the passage to where the soft light of her bed lamp shone through a crack in the door left ajar.

Time for sleep, she thought. Time for dreams.

THE ANIMAL WAS INSIDE the house. He was moving on silent feet down the moonlit hallway. His paws barely brushed against the slippery linoleum and he threw no shadow against the moonwashed walls. On and on he went down that long passage with its row of smooth closed doors. On and on he went, toward that one room at the end of the passage with its door open.

He was at the threshold. He crouched down till his belly touched the ground; his senses locked on the soft breathing of the sleeping figure in the bed beneath the window. The woman stirred and sighed.

The animal delicately stretched out one paw and moved his body stealthily forward. The muscles in his massive shoulders bunched. His eyes were phosphorescent blue and glowed like coals inside his head.

She opened her eyes. The man was standing next to her bed. The moonlight in the room was strong and she could see his face. "Justine," he said. He held out his hand. "Justine," he said again.

Twenty-four

SHE WAS WATCHING HIM without blinking. The moonlight was pooling in her eyes. She hadn't lifted her head off the pillow and her hand resting lightly on the white bedsheet seemed relaxed. But as Adam said her name again and stretched out his own hand at her once more, she tensed and her fingers jerked spasmodically. And in her eyes he saw fear.

He stopped.

"Don't be afraid." His voice was no more than a whisper.

Still she said nothing. She continued to look at him with eyes wide and gleaming. Her face was at once both familiar and unknown to him. The eyes were spaced very far apart, almost disconcertingly so. Her face was broader over the cheekbones than the picture in the magazine had led him to believe. But her mouth—the full mouth with the tender but extravagant curve to the upper lip—oh yes, he recognized her mouth, and the long pale neck, the ineffably vulnerable hollow at the base of her throat . . .

He swallowed and tried to moderate his breathing. His

skin felt flushed and hc could feel sweat forming in the hollows underneath his arms. The urge to touch her was overwhelming, but he managed to push his hands deep into the pockets of his coat. Inside his mind was a refrain: *Please. Oh, please . . . Don't turn from me . . .*

Taking a deep breath, he stepped back from the bed, stopped beside the chair. "Is it OK if I sit down?"

She did not answer, but he could sense her mentally shrinking from him. She was still very much afraid. Terrified even. But what the hell had he expected? A woman alone waking up to find a stranger in her room . . . The real surprise was that she wasn't screaming the roof off.

She was now pushing herself into an upright position and he caught a devastating glimpse of the sweet curve of her breast before she pulled the bedsheet up to her shoulders. Her hand moved from underneath the bedclothes toward the lamp on the bedside table. It sprang to life, chasing the shallow glare of the moonlight, replacing it with softer shadows and deeper light.

He kept his eyes on her, but his surroundings were pushing at the edge of his awareness. This was the room in which he had spent the first years of his life. He looked at the woman in front of him and it suddenly felt as though what was past and what is yet to come had collided in a freakish twist in time.

She was watching him warily. Her face had lost its mask-like expression, but the set of her shoulders was taut. She had placed one foot on the floor, he could see her toes peeping from underneath the overhanging blanket. The tense line of her back warned of imminent flight.

He eased himself slowly onto the chair, taking care not to make any startling or abrupt gestures.

At the corner of her one eyelid was a tiny tick. She lifted her chin and he could see where her pulse was drumming in her throat. His own heart was beating like a trip-hammer. He felt suddenly clumsy: too large, too hulking. He searched desperately in his mind for the right words to reassure her, the words that would put to flight the panic in her eyes. But he could think of nothing. He was struck dumb. Words started to form inside his mind, but were unable to leave his lips.

The silence stretched out between them, as vast as a desert.

THIS WAS ALL WRONG, she thought. This was not how she had imagined it would be. She had fantasized about this moment—a man and a woman running toward each other in slow-motion, the landscape an improbable field of multicolored flowers, the sky a celestial blue. This clichéd, soft-focus fantasy felt more true than the reality in which she now found herself—the night black outside the window, an intruder in her room.

Who was this man, really?

The dark blue coat he was wearing seemed very new. The coat was just slightly too small for him, fitting tight over his chest with the sleeves an inch or so too short. His hands were exposed up to the wrists and black hair curled from underneath the white cuffs of the shirt riding up his arms. His fingers were long and calloused. He was very dark from the sun; the skin across the cheekbones seemed almost varnished. High bridged nose. Wide mouth.

And the eyes—the eyes were the same burning eyes that belonged to the boy in the painting, that stared feverishly out of the face in the newspaper photograph. His body was almost aggressively relaxed, but the restless intensity of his gaze made her mouth go dry. Even though he was several steps away from the bed, she imagined she could feel the heat coming off his body.

She had searched for this man. She had been about to fly thousands of miles into the unknown with no more than a blind irrational compulsion steering her course. And now, without any effort on her part, he was here. But it was all too much, too unexpected.

She recognized vaguely that she was in shock. Her hands were cold and her brain felt as though it had shut down. Even the fear, which had flooded her body as she woke up to find him next to her bed, was somehow blunted, like pain in a lightly anesthetized limb—benumbed but waiting to flare into awful life.

Who was he really? A murderer. She was alone in a deserted house with a murderer. She should be running from him, not sitting here calmly with the sheets primly wrapped around her shoulders. She should be running and screaming and calling the police. A wad of panic was tightening inside her chest, creeping up her throat . . .

But then he leaned forward, his elbows braced on his knees. He said simply, "Justine, don't you know me?"

Something broke inside of her. The pent-up tension and anxiety shattered like glass. She placed her hand against her mouth.

Slowly, very slowly he got to his feet, keeping his eyes fixed on her face. He eased himself onto the edge of the bed and the mattress dipped underneath his weight. She watched him, didn't move, even though his face was now so close to hers, she could see tiny red veins in his eyes, thick stubble against his jaw.

"You know who I am," he said. A statement this time, not a question.

"Yes." No hesitation. "I know who you are."

His fingers brushed the skin stretched taut over her collarbone, and his fingers were hot. He touched the swell of her breast—a butterfly touch—but she imagined she felt the tips of his fingers pulsing with the beat of her heart.

She did not pull away. She gave a kind of sob and grasped his hand in hers.

He closed his eyes briefly.

"I have been looking for someone to walk with me," he said.

She answered, "You have found her."

Twenty-five

MARK BOTHA GLANCED AT his watch and pushed his chair away from his desk. It was time for him to make his rounds. He was especially curious to see how Mrs. Brewer was doing. When she came in earlier today he was convinced he had a case of malaria on his hands. The fact that she had just returned from a trip to Outjo—malaria country—had seemed to clinch it. But something had nagged at him and he had ended up doing a spinal tap. Just as well. It turned out to be meningitis, not malaria.

As he walked down the one central corridor of the tiny hospital, his eye fell on the windowsill jutting out from underneath one of the windows. He frowned. The dust was almost an inch thick. He should talk to Nurse Roode about it. Although, to be fair, with the constant wind and only a thin sheet of glass separating the inside of the hospital from a vast ocean of billions of sand particles, it was a near impossible task to keep the desert at bay.

He was just about to enter the female ward when he heard

his name being called. He looked over his shoulder. Rita was standing at the end of the corridor. In her hand she held a letter. She was smiling.

"What is it?" He walked over to his wife and gave her a brief kiss before taking the letter from her hand.

"I hope you don't mind, but the back of the envelope told me who it's from and I opened it. I couldn't bear to wait until you came back this evening."

His heart quickened. He pulled the stiff sheet of paper from the envelope. At the top of the page was an official-looking stamp. His eyes passed quickly over the formal sentences.

"You won." Rita spoke quietly, but there was a note of triumph in her voice. "There will be no hotel on Pennington's Island."

"No." The joy and relief that gripped him was intense. "No, there won't be, will there."

"I wonder if Yuri Grachikov knows already?"

"He probably got a letter just like this one." He looked at the page in his hands and his eyes skipped through the two terse paragraphs once again as if to reassure himself that he hadn't misread it the first time around. But no. The message was unequivocal. Pennington's and its fragile marine terrace would be spared a rape by greedy men and their destructive machinery.

"I wish Adam was here to open that bottle of champagne with us." Rita smiled. "You haven't heard from him?"

"No." Every morning he woke up wondering if he was ever going to see his friend again. Eight days had passed since Adam had left. He knew Adam would not contact him while he was in England. One day he would simply walk through the door unannounced, just as he did nine years ago. That is, if he made it back.

He shook his head as though he could physically clear his mind of unpleasant thoughts. Placing his arm around his wife's shoulders, he said, "We'll open the bottle of champagne, anyway. We've won a good fight. What can go wrong now?"

Twenty-six

SHE WAS SITTING ON her heels, balancing easily, reading from the newspaper spread out on the floor in front of her. Boyish knees. Pink toes. The wintry sunshine slanting in through the window, turning her short fair hair into silver dandelion fluff. She was so tiny, he thought. The picture in the magazine had not prepared him for how small she was. The first time he had held her, it had been almost a shock; it was like having the skeleton of a bird in his hands. The delicate sculpture of her rib cage, the fragile wrists and ankles. Infinitely breakable. But the beat of her heart insistent, urgent, flooding her body with electric blood.

Sitting there like that, rocking on her heels, she looked almost a child. But then she glanced at him from the corner of her eye and the smile around her lips belonged to a woman: seductive, brightly sexual.

He wanted to hold her to him. His desire for her breaking from his skin like sweat. Desire for her body, for her mind and her clear, hard intelligence. He had to stop himself from constantly reaching for her. His hunger was too desperate, too needy. He was afraid of scaring her and voiding the miracle—the miracle of her accepting him as he was. He: scarecrow, with his split pockets, untidy smile, and damaged heart. He had entered her life like a thief in the night, but she accepted him unquestioningly.

LATER HE WOULD THINK back on those days and nights at Paradine Park and marvel at what a celebration, what an adventure, they had managed to fit within such a tiny bubble of time.

Every sensation heightened. His senses so alert, he thought he might hear the stealthy growth of the moss on the trees. The winter colors not drab at all but leaping out at him as vivid as a shout of joy.

Justine, her face alight with mischief, running away from him into the maze of hedges in a crazy game of hide and seek. Justine, listening to Brahms, her eyes as serene as the eyes of a Madonna. Justine sitting on the branch of a tree, legs dangling. "Catch me" and suddenly she's falling forward—so swiftly, so unexpectedly—he felt his heart jump into his throat. And then she was in his arms, a tangle of legs, skinny arms, and wide mouth laughing; covering his face with short, dry kisses. He was able to pull her deep, deep within his embrace until she laughed and pushed him away, struggling to find her breath.

In the desert he had drawn pictures of her in his thoughts. He would search for her image in other women: this woman's hair, that one's bright eyes, this one's way of carrying herself. He sifted through the images like someone desperately trawling for treasure, clutching to him those aspects he thought he recognized. But when he tried to combine the sorry fragments into a unified whole, they crumbled into nothingness. She was always hovering at the white edges of his dreams. Unattainable. Just out of reach.

But now he was able to study her face in every detail. The blue veins at her temples; the tender knob of her upper lip; the breath-catching way her pupils would swell under his gaze. He could feel her pulse surging underneath the tips of his fingers, hear the rhythm of her heartbeat, catch the sparks flying off her thoughts.

The smooth surface of her inner arm and the strong fold of muscle. The sweat-slicked hollow at her neck. Her damp skin bonding with his and his body sensing the crackle of electricity generated deep within her brain, running through every cell in her body, a lightning storm of muscle, tissue, mind.

"Say my name," he said to her and her lips formed the word, "*beloved*."

Her words were made of water, his of sand. When they whispered together in the night, it was water seeping into sand and a desert blooming.

SHE RESTED HER HEAD on his shoulder and listened to his voice in the darkness. He was describing to her a land thousands of miles to the south, a sterile land bordered by a bountiful ocean whose generosity ceased at the line where water met shore. A land of once prosperous diamond settlements, now abandoned, the only sounds the patter of the webbed feet of seabirds and the creaking of doors crumbling on their hinges. A land where beautiful Himba women tended sacred fires, their skins gleaming red with ocher powder, butterfat, and aromatic herbs. A place where the Welwitschia grew, living fossil plants dating from the time of Christ.

And the windwalkers—creatures made of blood and dreams. Warm-blooded animals miraculously able to roam the dunes without any water, relying solely on moisture drawn from their food. Survivors, just like every creature who dwelled in that barren land. And the sky that spanned this wilderness was a sky like no other sky in the world. At day a blistering cloudless blue. At night blacker than black, blazing with stars burning phosphorescent white: the Southern Cross and the pale swath of the Milky Way.

She moved her head. In the icy blackness outside their window there were no stars, only a murky darkness thick with clouds and long trailing fingers of mist.

"I think I will like it there," she said.

He was quiet for a moment. "You'll be sharing your life with a fugitive."

"It doesn't matter."

"Have you thought about how you will explain it? Your parents, your friends—won't they find it extraordinary that you will want to live there?"

She smiled ruefully. "I can assure you no one finds anything I do odd anymore. I've done so many off-the-wall things in my life, they would probably find it strange if I did something normal for a change. No, they'll just sigh and shake their heads and say that's Justine for you. A hopeless case."

"I love hopeless cases."

She smiled into the warm skin of his shoulder. "Of course you do. That's why we were meant to be together."

"Yes." He picked up her hand and pressed his lips against her palm. "In every life to come."

In every life to come. He said these words often and with such certainty. But the truth of it was that she did not believe they had more than one life to live. She believed passionately that they were meant for each other, yes. She had never believed in the supernatural, but the identical tattoos, the phantom animal in her pictures—these were tantalizing glimpses of something fantastic, something outside—her frame of comprehension. And she now accepted without reservation that they were signs and that she and Adam had been destined to meet. But the possibility of the two of them traveling together through all eternity—a vast cosmic ocean with no limits of time or space—was somehow too devastating to contemplate. Her brain shrank from the immensity of the thought. She believed you were given one life only. If you squandered it, there was no second time around. She and Adam were given this one chance. They had to make it work for them now, not in other lives yet to come.

But as she rested there in the crook of his arm, listening to his voice so calmly impassioned, all she said was, "You really believe it, don't you? That we have successive lives?"

"I believe we wander from death to death, yes."

She shivered. "Successive lives sounds better."

"We're travelers—vagabonds—on a journey during which we have to pass through many closed doors." She felt him shrug. "Each life, another door."

She ran her fingers down his arm, paused when she reached the soft skin between wrist and elbow. In the darkness she couldn't see the tattoos, but she knew they were there. It still took her breath away—images transferred onto her shoulder one summer afternoon many years ago had found their way onto his arm as well. But whereas she had picked the images at complete random, he had chosen with care.

"Doors. Pascaline said that's why you have the wolf on your arm."

"Yes."

"Explain it to me."

"*Wepwawet.* Opener of the ways. Also called the desert jackal. Sometimes portrayed as an animal with a man's body. In war, he opened pathways for the pharaoh to cut into the armies of the enemy. He was worshiped especially in the Egyptian city of Assiut. The Greeks called it Lycopolis: the city of wolves."

"A war god."

"You sound disapproving." She could tell from his voice he was smiling.

"Well . . ."

"He also opened the doors of the underworld for the dead. And with his adze he would break open the mouth of the deceased during the opening-of-the-mouth ceremony to ensure that the person will retain all his faculties in the afterlife."

"Good grief. What the hell is an adze?"

"Something sharp and thin with an arched blade, I believe."

"This is starting to creep me out."

"It shouldn't. Don't you find it comforting—the idea that there will be someone to open the door for you into the next life?"

"Who is going to cut my mouth open with something sharp and thin. Yes, really comforting."

"You can take it." He laughed and placed his arm across her shoulder. "Life is war, you know. And you're a warrior."

She didn't answer.

"Justine?"

"Warriors are brave," she said.

"Yes?"

She shook her head.

"What is it?" He sat up straight and clicked on the bedside light. He looked at her searchingly. "What's wrong?"

She stared into the circle of light. "You have to know this about me, Adam. I'm not brave, I'm destructive. There is something in my nature that causes me to always step wrong. I have this compulsion to sabotage everything worthwhile in my life. Where relationships are concerned, I'm a walking disaster. And I'll even make sure to trip myself up at work. For a while things will go well and then I'll start missing appointments, or quarrel with editors—just do something stupid so as to make things go sour. And Jonathan. He died not only because I was careless, but because I was petulant. Spiteful. I didn't really want that cigarette. I lit up because I knew it would irritate him."

"Shh . . ." He stroked the hair off her forehead, his fingers gentle.

"I could hear him scream. He was screaming but he was on the other side of the house and I couldn't get to him. And then the screams stopped because he was overwhelmed by smoke and suffocated. He was a good man, Adam. Not like me. He was the oak tree, I was the poison ivy."

He continued to smooth her hair. With the other arm he drew her close to his chest.

She spoke again, her voice muffled. "I've always felt like an intruder in my own life, a stranger set on wreaking havoc. And all the time, I'd be conscious of this longing inside of me. But a longing for what? I could never describe it to myself, could never give voice to what it was that I was searching for. All I knew was that once I found it, I would stop being so destructive. Once I *knew*." She gripped his hand tightly. "I've found what I was searching for. But now I'm afraid."

"What are you afraid of?"

"That this will end and never come again."

His fingers stopped smoothing her hair. Gripping her shoulders hard, he forced her to sit up straight, facing him.

"Listen to me. We are soul mates. You are my life raft and I am yours. But if I've learned only one thing during nine years in the desert, it is that there are some things you have to come to terms with yourself. I can help you. But you will have to heal yourself and the question is, can you do it?"

She looked at him, stung. "And you? Can you do it? Have you healed yourself?"

"No. It starts with self-forgiveness. I'm not there yet. But I've looked the devil in the face and I know who I am."

"And you're saying I don't."

"You haven't even begun to learn to know yourself. You see ugliness and you close your mind and you don't look any further."

"There's not a lot left besides."

"Yes, there is. You *are* a warrior. Don't you know how incredibly special you are? Steel and grit and great determination, you have all of that within you."

She held her wrists at him, pulling her palms backward so that the pink scar tissue stood out against the white of her skin. "This is not the work of a warrior. This is the work of a coward and I am ashamed. You kept fighting. I can't match that. I gave in to the despair. You didn't."

He was silent. When he spoke again, his voice sounded remote. "I did not dive for almost a year after I had killed Richard. The day I went back to the ocean and into the caves, I was filled with joy. I was home. It's such a quiet world down there, Justine. Inside the caves you're in a place where you become aware of yourself like nowhere else—the beating of your heart, the sound of your breathing, even the ebb and flow of your thoughts. Your only link to the outside world is the guideline, which snakes back toward the light. Without it you'll be lost in a labyrinth of tunnels and caverns, which all look the same. So you understand—it is essential that you keep hold of the line."

He paused. "That day I felt happier than in a long time. The dive was going well. And then, all of a sudden, I looked at the line in my hand and I wanted to let go. At my back was the sun. In front of me was darkness. It was beckoning me. I wanted to lose myself in the maze of tunnels without ever finding my way back. The urge was overwhelming. I opened my fingers and let the guideline slide from my grasp."

"But you pulled back."

"Yes, I did. I managed to step back from the brink. But there was that one moment when I gave in to despair absolutely."

He placed his hands on her wrists and lifted them up to his face. Softly he kissed first the one, then the other. "Don't ever say to me again that you're ashamed."

She could feel her eyes burning with tears.

"Let's make each other a promise, Justine."

"A promise?"

"From now on we will live life ecstatically and with a vengeance. No matter what happens."

She nodded. "No matter what happens."

"My friend Mark always accuses me of hovering on the outskirts, living life on the edges. He's right. From now on I'm going to embrace life. And so will you. Before moving on to the next life I need to redeem myself, make amends for Richard's death. And you also have a task ahead of you. You need to get to know yourself and your potential. This is the journey you have to make. Redemption and self-knowledge—we can't achieve this if we do not engage fully."

She felt suddenly immensely tired. "I would like to sleep now."

"Sleep," he said.

She closed her eyes and she felt him kiss her forehead, so gently.

"I love you," she murmured.

His lips close to her ears whispered, "I love you *forever*."

HE HAD OPENED A locked door. Memories, ideas, secret wishes—she now offered them to Adam unedited. She had never stripped herself bare like this for anyone—not for Barry, not even for Jonathan when he was still alive. Some of her confidences were valentines, tokens of love, others came from a dark and edgy place and she'd give voice to them as though she were doing penance. Time and again she'd find herself saying, "I have never told this to a soul . . ." or start the sentence with, "You're the only one who knows . . ."

Adam listened to her. He listened to her fractured thoughts and her anger and he didn't turn away. He accepted her, just as she accepted him—the man he had become, the man he used to be. Between the two of them there was no shame. If soul mates meant giving yourself to the other utterly—body and mind, in beauty and in ugliness—then yes, they were soul mates.

And they had no need of successive lives, she thought. What they were creating right here, right now: this was the miracle.

* * *

THE DAYS FOLLOWED EACH other and there were no boundaries between dark and light.

Sometimes they slept through entire days, closing their
eyes against the winter sunlight, their bodies hugging each
other. At night they lit candles throughout the house so that
every window showed a flickering flame. The downstairs
rooms sounded with the music of Chopin and Beethoven, the
bewitching notes rebounding off the high ceilings, creating
glimmering echoes in empty spaces. For such a long time
music had been largely absent from his life. He had never really thought about it. Truth be told, he hadn't missed it that
much. But now that music was suddenly within his grasp
again, Adam wanted it obsessively. Later, looking back, his
memories would always be set to music. And he'd remember
the night they danced together to the strains of a Strauss
waltz, moving deeper and deeper into the house until finally
they could no longer hear the song of violins, only the swish
of their feet and the sound of each other's breathing.

*And all her face was honey to my mouth. And all her body
pasture to mine eyes.*

His hands tracing the outline of her body, feeling the uneven, knobbly contours of her shoulders, the disks of her
hips; lingering at the hard button of bone in her ankle, cupping the fleshy heel. Smooth arms, soft small ears. The
heady scent of her sleeping breath and the glow of her skin.

The long lithe arms and hotter hands than fire.

Her mouth hunting in the darkness, her breasts and the
small of her back slippery with sweat. Her fingers slipped
into his mouth and they tasted bitter.

*The bright light feet, the splendid supple thighs, and glit-
tering eyelids of my soul's desire.*

She pulled her head back and her lips opened slightly. The
muscles in her legs strained against his weight. He buried his
face in her neck and inhaled the vanilla smell of her skin and

the fugitive scent of roses and jasmine. Bone, tissue, fragrance: her body an alchemist's vase. Her kisses red powder, her heart the philosopher's stone. If he could clasp her to him close enough, if only he could meld his body with hers seamlessly, he would be transformed: lead turning to gold.

JUSTINE LOOKED OUT THE window. The blue jay was there again.

She heard the light but sharp tapping sound of its beak. For the past three days the usually timid little bird had been pecking at his reflection in the glass pane. Every morning, when the wintry sun hit this side of the house, there he'd be, frantically pecking away.

He was a male bird. He and his mate used to be permanent inhabitants of the courtyard garden. In the summer she had listened to their chattering and had watched them build their nest, scurrying around the garden for twigs, impressively busy and active.

And then, four days ago, she had picked up the body of the female bird where it lay dead. It wasn't clear why she had died. Justine felt almost sorrow at the sight of the tiny body, so stiff in death, the feathers no longer neat and groomed but caked with dirt.

Soon after she had found the dead female, the male bird had started pecking away at his shadow. Adam believed it might be because the bird saw in his own reflection his dead mate come to life. Whatever the reason for his behavior, it must be compelling indeed for the bird to venture so close to the house.

The blue jay cocked his head and the beady eye looked at her warily. Then he started pecking again. Justine wished he would stop. A few times he had even flown straight at the closed window. She was afraid he might injure himself. The little bird looked bedraggled. The dapper tuft of feathers on his head was bushy and unkempt.

She lifted her arm and waved her hand vigorously. The

bird hesitated and then, with a flutter of wings, disappeared into a nearby tree. But as she stepped out of the room, she heard once more the despairing peck, peck of its beak against the pane of glass.

HE PREFERRED DARKNESS. NIGHTTIME was when Adam felt most at ease. She noticed that even during the day he sought the shade. It was done instinctively; she doubted he was even aware of it himself.

He was now standing in front of the window, looking out into the light, his body hugging the shadow thrown by the tall shutter. He had taken a shower and a few wet drops of water glistened on his back. His body was still, but as always she sensed in him that inner tension, as though total relaxation was not an option and his muscles needed to be held at the ready to explode at once into either fight or flight.

His thigh and calf muscles were honed by hours of walking through thick sand and swimming through deep water. The skin around his waist and buttocks was a startling creamy white against the sun-darkened skin of his torso and legs. There was a line of hair running down his stomach. His feet were slender and elegant but with calloused toes. Powerful arms and shoulders. Sunburned creases around his eyes.

She walked over to the bedside table and picked up the Leica.

He turned his head to look at her. "What are you doing?"

"I want to take your picture."

"I haven't had my picture taken in nine years. It's dangerous. I'm still a fugitive. If anyone should see it . . ."

"I'm going to develop the film myself. No one but me will see it."

"No, Justine. Besides, why do you need a picture? You have the real thing now."

She didn't answer. How to explain it to him? How to explain her irrational belief that something isn't real until you've caught it on camera? Years ago she had covered one of Somalia's famines, shooting reel after reel of skull-like faces, bodies covered in swarming flies, and sickening scenes of emaciated victims viciously fighting each other for food. She hadn't thrown up until she was back in London, developing the prints in the darkroom of her apartment. It wasn't real until you printed it. It was ridiculous, she knew, but now that she had found Adam, she felt that only by capturing a picture of him—black and white—would she be able to relax and accept that he was a tangible presence in her life. Here to stay.

She hefted the camera to her shoulder. "Come on, Adam. You can't deny me this, it's what I do. Besides, I need something better than that." She gestured at the enlarged photocopy of the newspaper picture of him still taped to the wall.

"We should get rid of it." He smiled a little grimly. "It looks exactly like a most-wanted poster."

"Please."

"No."

"Pretty please?"

He walked over to her and quite calmly wrested the camera from her grasp. She tried to resist but he was too strong.

"There." He slipped the Leica back in its leather glove and placed it on the table out of her reach.

She slapped at his wrist, irritated.

"Hey," he laughed and grasped her face with his hand.

Quickly she turned her head and bit into his palm. He swore lightly and tightened his grip on her jaw. His fingers were strong. They could probably crush the bones in her face should he so wish. She saw him smile slightly. Using the full weight of his body he pushed her up against the wall. She all at once got a breathtaking sense of how powerful he was, of the frightening strength in his arms and heavy shoulders.

"Do you want to play, Justine?" He pushed against her again. His skin was still damp from the shower.

She turned her head petulantly to one side. "No. Get off of me." But the contact of skin on skin made her breasts swell. Dead giveaway. His eyes gleamed.

Placing one arm across her body, effortlessly holding her immobile, he moved his other hand confidently over her breasts. The hand moved down to her stomach, lingered at her belly button. His fingers reached for the inside of her leg. She gasped.

He strained against her, pushing her up against the wall so tightly, she felt her shoulder blades press painfully against the plaster. He thrust his thighs inexorably against her legs. Removing his arm from across her breasts and pinning her against the wall with his body he grasped both her hands and linked his fingers through hers. Slowly he lifted her arms up and above her head. She looked into his eyes. Black. Inscrutable.

When he pressed his mouth against hers, she kept her lips stubbornly closed. He kissed her hard, so hard that she felt her lip mash against her teeth and she tasted blood in her mouth. She set her teeth, unwilling to let him in.

His mood changed. Even though he was still holding her imprisoned, his tongue licked her mouth delicately and pleadingly probed the fleshy part of her inner lip. It made her want to stretch and moan and arch her back. Her mouth opened. Releasing her arms, he placed his hands underneath her buttocks and hoisted her up.

She licked the side of his neck. He tasted of salt and musky sweat. She ran her fingers through the thick hair and traced the outline of his heavy black brows. The rhythm between them was becoming urgent again. His lips pulled away from his teeth in a grimace. He was grasping her shoulders with such force they hurt. Power. Heat. Desire. His touch now almost painful, her skin feeling unbearably tender. She tried to move away, to get some relief from the irritation, but he pressed against her more urgently and again she registered the strength of his body. So powerful. Over-whelmingly male.

He was talking to her, but she was unable to follow his words. She was only able to follow the intonation of his voice. Her thoughts were froth and the world was liquid. A dark sea, the surface boiling and turbulent, a riptide carrying her along like a piece of flotsam. The sense of something dangerous and dark sucking at her body, drawing her down. Waves crashing over her head, forcing her under. Drowning, choking, stillness.

Death.

Resurrection, with his mouth kissing the lids of her eyes, and his large hand wiping the tears and sweat from her face. His low voice still murmuring words she had difficulty grasping.

Only when they finally separated did she realize that what he had said again and again was: *Never leave me*.

LATER, TAKING A SHOWER, she looked at her swollen mouth in the bathroom mirror and saw that her lower lip was split. On her upper arms were bruises left by his fingers. Her body felt satisfyingly sated but also battered, achy.

Slowly she toweled herself dry. The bruises would fade and the lip would heal. But she had had a disconcerting glimpse of something unbridled and dangerous.

Undeniably thrilling.

She looked into the mirror again. Her eyes were under-scored by dark shadows. Her lips looked inflamed. Passion and a hint of danger. A potent mix.

When she entered the room, Adam was lying on the bed on his stomach. His head was cradled on top of his arms. His face was in profile. Next to him was an open book.

He turned his head slightly toward her and reached for her with one hand. "Hi."

"Hi." She sat down next to him. He sighed and dropped

his head back on his arms. After all that passion and heat, his face now seemed vulnerable and defenseless. She reached out and stroked her hand across his hair. He sighed again, sleepily.

Turning her head sideways, she read the title of the book, which was lying face-down next to the pillow.

"Call of the Wild?"

"Hmm. I found it downstairs in the library. It used to be my favorite book as a boy." His voice was muffled.

She picked up the book. The pages were yellowed and on the title page were red crayon marks. The spine was broken and the book fell open in her hands.

And when, on the still cold nights, he pointed his nose at a star and howled long and wolflike, it was his ancestors, dead and dust, pointing nose at star and howling down through the centuries and through him. And his cadences were their cadences, the cadences which voiced their woe and what to them was the meaning of the stillness, and the cold, and dark . . .

Adam had closed his eyes. Maybe he had fallen asleep. His breath was soft and even.

She looked back at the text in front of her. His favorite book as a boy. She wondered if he had tried to read it himself or if someone had read it to him. He had told her of his dyslexia and how it had bedeviled his childhood. But the desert had allowed him to grapple with his disability. The determination it must have cost him to sit there night after night, patiently worrying the letters until they made sense, still took her breath away.

. . . behind him were the shades of all manner of dogs, half-wolves and wild wolves, urgent and prompting, tasting the savor of the meat he ate, thirsting for the water he drank, scenting the wind with him . . .

He was definitely in the land of Nod. His one hand, resting on the pillow, twitched involuntarily. He was probably dreaming.

Very quietly she reached over for the camera bag and

drew the Leica from its protective glove. She brought the camera to her eye.

For just a moment it was as though she was looking at his face for the first time. Tight black curls, strong jaw, wide sensuous mouth. She watched him, the lens trained on his face, and wondered what dream was lurking behind his eyelids, what impulses hid deep within the neural pathways of his brain.

The Leica was quiet, it was one of the reasons she liked it so much. He wouldn't even know. Slowly she pressed the shutter.

He stirred, mumbled something. Quickly she pushed the camera into the folds of the bedclothes and picked up the book once again.

The strain of the primitive . . . remained alive and active. Faithfulness and devotion, things born of fire and roof, were his; yet he retained his wildness and wiliness . . . Deep in the forest a call was sounding . . .

Twenty-seven

THE SOUND OF THE ringing phone pierced Mark Botha's sleep-fogged brain. He opened his eyes into the darkness and the first thing he saw was the luminescent face of the bedside clock. The red digits pulsed: 1:55 A.M.

He groaned and pushed himself upright against his pillows. Beside him Rita was already answering the phone, her voice calm and friendly. She was an old hand at these late-night calls. He never answered the phone himself. Rita did the screening, deciding whether it was a real emergency or whether it was one of his patients who was simply in a chatty mood after having had a few too many at the Palace.

But the person on the other side of the line was Mrs. Dama, an eighteen-year-old single parent, and Rita gave the phone to her husband immediately. Carol Dama's husband had died only months before in a fishing accident and she had given birth to their baby a mere two days after his death. The baby had been born premature and even after eight months, his weight was still too low. And tonight, it seemed, little Michael had developed a fever. Promising that he would be there as soon as possible, Mark replaced the phone and reached for his shoes.

As he pulled on his shoes and ran a comb through his hair, Rita took his coat from the closet. Mark usually didn't even bother changing into day clothes when he was called out at night. Very often he was called out more than once during the evening, anyway, so it wasn't worth going to the trouble. Slipping into the coat Rita was holding for him, he picked up his black bag and gave his wife a peck on the cheek. "Get back into bed," he told her. "I probably won't be long."

Mark didn't take the Land Rover. The Dama house was only three streets away. As he approached the house, the front door opened and the slight figure of Carol Dama stood silhouetted against the yellow light. As he stepped into the tiny front hall, Mark looked at her with concern. She was a pretty girl, but her skin seemed blotchy and there were enormous shadows underneath her eyes. The pilled wool sweater she was wearing had a stain across the front.

"He won't stop crying," she said despairingly as she led him into the baby's room. "He never stops crying."

As Mark gently examined the tiny body underneath his hands, the woeful little face—so red and angry when he first entered the room—started to uncrumple and the screams and hiccups stopped. Mark brushed his thumb against the velvety cheek. The baby had his mother's beautiful coffee-colored skin and black eyes. But the long, long lashes belonged to his father. Trevor Dama had been a good-looking man and he had used those long lashes of his to devastating effect, effortlessly charming women wherever he went.

There was nothing wrong with the baby, Mark decided as he slipped the pacifier into the tiny mouth, but the mother was another matter. She looked malnourished, her face too bony, her arms far too thin. She was close to exhaustion and there was panic in her eyes. It was clear she wasn't coping. He would have to find someone to help. He certainly didn't have a nurse available, but maybe Rita could stop in tomorrow and give the young mother the opportunity to get a few hours of uninterrupted sleep. And he'd ask the ladies of the prayer group at church if they could also help out for the next few weeks.

Before he stepped out into the night again, Mark told Carol to visit him at his consulting room before the end of the week. He wanted to give her a thorough check-up and some vitamin shots. "And bring that handsome young man with you," he said, nodding toward the baby's room. "I'll look him over again. He has certainly inherited his father's good looks, hasn't he?"

She smiled and for the first time looked like the very young girl she really was. "Bless your heart, doctor. We'll both be there."

As he walked back to his house, Mark pulled the night air deep into his lungs. The smell of brine was sharp as a knife. The sky—the blackest black imaginable—was frosted with stars. Mark suddenly felt at peace with the world. He was doing a job he found deeply satisfying, living in a place whose stark beauty never ceased to fill him with wonder. At home Rita would be waiting for him.

His house was at the top of a hill, a steep climb. Breathing slightly faster from the exertion, he stopped and looked out over the sleeping town with its modest houses and their darkened windows. In the distance, the ocean glimmered. His eyes traveled to where he imagined he could see the dark blob of Pennington's Island. He knew that Grachikov's mechanical diggers were still stuck there. He wondered for how long. It was probably going to cost the man a lot of money to remove the heavy machinery from the island. But that was certainly not his problem. Mark turned away.

But as he placed his hand on the front gate, he thought he heard something behind him. He swung around.

Nothing. But he still had the unnerving feeling that there were eyes in the darkness, hiding behind that wall,

maybe . . . and the shadow on the other side of his neigh-
bor's house, was that a figure? He stared into the night.

Opening the gate, he started to walk swiftly toward the
front door. The breeze felt suddenly much colder. A chill
moved down his spine and he pulled his shoulders forward.

He fumbled with his keys, his fingers strangely clumsy.
When he finally found the right one, he opened the front door
hastily. Without looking over his shoulder again, he stepped
quickly inside and shut and locked the door behind him. His
heart was beating rapidly and his mouth was dry. He registered, almost with surprise, that he was afraid. But why?

A few minutes later he was removing his shoes and coat
and easing himself into bed. He was beginning to feel better.
Rita's warm sleeping body was beside him and the house
was quiet and peaceful. Everything was fine. There was no
need for alarm. But as he pulled the blanket over his shoulders and closed his eyes, he relived for one brief moment the
sense of imminent danger that had gripped him. Try as he
might to make himself believe otherwise, he knew it hadn't
been his imagination. There had been something—someone—outside. And the air had hummed with malevolence.

Twenty-eight

THE INTIMACY OF HIDING out together.

Paradine Park was their harbor, an unlikely refuge allowing them shelter. How bizarre to have found her at this place, he thought. Nine years ago he had fled the house, his brother's blood on his hands. Now he was celebrating their union within these blank walls and empty rooms.

He wandered through the house and was amazed at how detached he felt from it. In the desert he had dreamed of Paradine Park and had desperately longed to walk through its rooms again. But it was no longer the house of his imagination. Without furniture, the place seemed alien and the few memories entering his mind were pallid. The oil painting of the family hanging in the main living room could as well have depicted any other family. Even the yellowed shirts and pieces of underwear, which he had found in the closet in his old room, felt to him as though they were things that belonged to a stranger. He did not feel like wearing them, but his other clothes were still at the hotel in King's Cross. He

had called the hotel and had asked them to pack his bag for
him and keep it until further notice. He certainly did not
want them to initiate a search for a missing hotel guest, perhaps even contacting the police.

The letter *A* was carved into the doorway of his bedroom;
scratched through and replaced by the letter *R*. Richard's
handiwork. He remembered the incident well and the fight
that had ensued. But as he walked through the house, Justine
at his side, he sensed no echo of anguish or pain. Even the
mirrors throwing back his image at him in room after room
had lost the power to disturb. This was no haunted house, he
thought. It was only a shell.

Until the day he was left alone.

The big freezer was empty and the larder bare. They were
running out of food and a foray into the village was called
for. They sat together at the kitchen table, drawing up a list,
filling it with items extravagant and fanciful. Chocolate ice
cream. Champagne. Foie gras. Stilton cheese. Marshmal-
lows. "Everything you've missed having over the past nine
years," she said, "we'll get. Let's go wild." After twenty
minutes she looked at their wish list with satisfaction. "I
probably won't find half this stuff in Ainstey. I'll have to
look further afield." She picked up her bag and slipped into
her coat. "But I'll hurry back."

From inside the hallway he watched through the window
as she ran out to the car in the sifting rain, her head bowed,
her face shadowed by the brim of her hat. As the car turned
into the avenue of trees, she leaned out the window and blew
him a kiss.

He felt restless. He wandered into the library and stopped
at the desk. For a while he lingered over the pictures she had
taken of the house, his hands reverently touching the surface
of the prints. They were so amazing. The phantom animal in
the photographs looked just like Dante. He knew Justine was
still trying to make logical sense of these pictures. He accepted them unquestioningly. He had always been at ease

with things that defied rational explanation. His belief in soul mates was only one such example. But Justine persisted in describing herself as a realist. "I'm not a thoughtographer," she said. "You've seen my work. I photograph the real world, not the supernatural." But he knew better. He remembered when he had first opened that magazine and looked at the photographs that had brought her into his life. He remembered his reaction to them. The pictures had been oddly dreamlike, almost ethereal—even the photographs that depicted dreadful, graphic images of real violence. He had sensed her thoughts in those pictures; it was as though she had succeeded in capturing a snapshot of her own recollection of the horror, not merely the horror itself. And she herself admitted that the wolf pictures might be the product of longing. "A dark longing," she had said.

Sighing he turned away from the prints on the desk. He wondered how long she would be away for. He missed her already. Without her the silence in the house felt oppressive. Maybe he should take a walk outside, clear his head.

Long tendrils of mist hung in the silent air; the artificial lake seemed to drift inches above the ground. He entered the maze of hedges, his hand brushing against the prickly leaves and twigs, barely able to see two feet in front of him. But his feet still knew the way, his brain was still able to map the twists and turns.

He heard something scratch in the undergrowth—a bird? He stood quietly, moving his head slowly from side to side but he could not spot it. He placed his hands around his mouth and tried to emulate the warble of a wood pigeon, but his voice had no echo, the sound deadened by the fog and he let his arms fall to his side.

His shoes were becoming soaked with the socks clinging damply to his feet. He should return to the house.

There was one room he had avoided up till now. His mother's bedroom had the door shut tight and he had no wish to open it. But now he walked up the stairs purposefully and placed his hand on the knob. The door opened silently.

The room was empty, the light in here milky as though filtered through water. The only object in the room was an Oriental vase on the mantelpiece. He remembered it well. Vanilla porcelain tinged with paradisal blue, the curve of the vase as perfect as the curve of a woman's hip. Against the wall above the bed had hung a heavy mirror encrusted with cherubs and cornucopia overflowing. It was no longer there. He wondered what had happened to it, it used to be one of his mother's favorite pieces. In contrast to the ornateness of the mirror, the bed itself had always been dressed austerely: a simple off-white linen spread draped over its massive frame. The room had reflected that strange mixture of piety and deep sensualism, which had personified his mother. On the bedside table had stood a tiny statuette of a pot-bellied cupid; next to it a leather-bound Bible with polished buckles made of brass.

Over there, in front of the window, had been her dressing table. If he shut his eyes he could picture it. The polished mahogany surface, the tall, tilting mirror. His mother's silver-backed brushes in a neat row and next to them the veined alabaster urn holding her hairclips and pins. His mother's hands moving deftly to secure the low chignon in her neck; removing a tissue from its box to blot her lips. The tissue with its red kiss fluttering to the floor.

He had fled to Ireland that night nine years ago and it was there he had learned of his mother's suicide, standing in the shelter of the striped awning of a tiny corner shop, the rain sluicing down in fluorescent rivers, his fingers black from the newsprint of the paper gripped within his hands.

He looked around the empty room, dazed. His heart was suddenly racing. The white wall in front of him was all at once red with blood—large, extravagant splashes spattered across its entire breadth. Did she place the shotgun in her mouth? Against her head? Was she lying down? Shivers were running over his scalp. His thoughts a swarm of black bats blocking out the light.

"Adam?" Justine's lilting voice floated up the staircase as bright as a promise of salvation. "Where are you?"

"I am here," he shouted, stumbling out of the room and slamming the door shut with clumsy hands. "Wait for me, I'm coming. Wait for me."

THAT NIGHT THEY LIT long tapering candles for their feast and retrieved the paper-thin gold-rimmed plates and dishes stacked away in a dusty corner of the china closet. For the first time since his arrival, they sat down for dinner in the dining room at the formal mahogany table. Outside thick clouds were rolling across the sky and the trees swayed in the wind.

She looked across at him. The light from the candles threw dramatic shadows on his face. His eyes were fixed on the stem of the champagne glass he was turning between his fingers.

Something wasn't right. She had sensed in him a disquiet ever since her return from the shops. He hadn't said anything and had smiled at her, touching her face, her hands. They had even danced together, but she wasn't fooled.

The windowpanes behind him gleamed red in the flickering light as though a fire was burning on the other side. She shivered and got to her feet. Walking over to the window, she stood for a moment, staring out.

"What's wrong?"

She glanced at him over her shoulder. "I don't know. I keep having the feeling that there are eyes outside watching us." She rubbed her shoulders. "I'm just being ridiculous." But she unhooked the tasseled restrainers and pulled the heavy velvet curtains together.

"Something happened to you this morning while I was away," she said as she returned to the table.

He lifted his hands, looked at them as though seeing them

for the first time. "I detest my hands. Sometimes I feel as though they don't belong to me."

She looked at him steadily.

He shrugged. "Earlier today I was reminded that the past cannot be undone. No matter what, it will always seep through into the present."

"We can put the past behind us."

He smiled and she knew it was because of the ease with which the cliché had sprung from her lips. "The Himba people see time as a river," he answered. "The past is not behind you, but in front of you. You have already lived through it and therefore it is ahead and visible. The future lies behind you where you cannot see it. If it was ahead of you, you would know what will happen in the days to come and that, of course, cannot be. So it is simply not possible to look ahead—that is a peculiarly Western delusion. And you also cannot put the past behind you. If you could put the past behind you where it cannot be seen, it would be dangerous as you might forget it and the past should never be forgotten."

"Why not?" Her voice was fierce. "Why can't it be forgotten, put aside? Why can we not reinvent ourselves and start afresh? It *is* possible. We will make it so."

"We can try."

"We can fight. Warriors, remember?"

"I remember."

"Live life ecstatically. Our promise to each other."

"Yes." He smiled, the somberness leaving his face. "It's the only way we can progress, the only way the next door will open into a reality that is better than the one we're living in at present."

"Now that I've found you I'm perfectly happy with the reality we live in now, Adam. I don't need another, better life after this one."

He shook his head. "The connections between our lives are in place. Some lie in the past, some are forming now and the rest are in the future."

She was silent.

"Justine? You do believe that, don't you?"

She hesitated.

"Say you believe it." He brought his head close to hers, his eyes very dark. "Say you do."

"Adam . . ."

"If you don't believe it, it may be a long time before we meet up again. Not in the next life, or even the one after. I know it in my heart. You have to believe."

He grasped her hand so strongly, the champagne slopped over the edge of her glass and onto the white linen cloth. The intensity in his eyes made her feel afraid.

"I do," she said quickly. "I believe."

BUT OF COURSE, SHE did not—not really. It was miracle enough that they had found each other in this life and under these circumstances. To wish for more was tempting fate.

She turned her head on the pillow. Adam was sleeping. He was lying on his back, his head to one side, his one hand clutched in a loose fist. She looked intently at his face. She placed her hand on his shoulder, felt the powerful mesh of muscle and bone.

For the first time since he had stepped out of her dream and into her room, she had difficulty falling asleep. She was wearing a long-sleeved nightdress, but she couldn't seem to get warm. She lay awake, blanket clutched to her chin, watching through the thin lace curtains the ghostly shadow of a trailing bough of creeper. Maybe it was time for them to leave Paradine Park, she thought. They had talked about the new life they would have together, but only in the vaguest terms. It was like building a castle in the sky, opening windows set into airy walls, walking down passages and staircases made of glass. The idea that she would have to leave this country for good had not really sunk in at all. But at some point she would have to square up to what her new life was going to be like. Every day Adam stayed in England was a day he was in danger. They had been together for seventeen days now. Soon they would have to come to a decision. But not yet. Maybe they had a few more days of grace left.

She was just about to slide into sleep when she heard a high whimpering sound. She rolled over on her side and looked at him. He was weeping. He was asleep but there were tears rolling down his cheeks.

"Adam," she said urgently and shook his shoulder.

His eyes jerked open. "What is it?" His voice sounded perfectly normal, neither sleepy nor confused.

"You were dreaming."

He turned away from her and sighed. "I don't think so."

HE TURNED OVER AND almost immediately drifted off again. One moment Justine's hand was on his shoulder, her voice urging him into wakefulness, the next moment he had stepped back into the world of slumber. He wasn't dreaming; he wished he were. He was trapped in a no-man's land between consciousness and sleep. It was claustrophobic here, dark and confining. He could feel his eyeballs jerking as images so fleeting as to be impossible to remember raced across his retina. He was intensely conscious of his breathing. In, out, labored. His thoughts liquid and incoherent. Part of his brain still alert.

He jerked awake into full consciousness, his body suddenly flooded with adrenaline.

Something was wrong.

Against his arm he felt Justine's hand, the fingers relaxed. Her breath against his neck was warm and slow. She was sleeping peacefully. No, whatever it was that had propelled his senses into high alert, lay elsewhere.

Without moving his head, he allowed his eyes to travel slowly through the room. The outline of the chair. The dark shape of the dresser and the curve of the mirror.

The window was open a tiny crack and the wind gently lifted the white lace curtains. The pictures and newspaper clippings that were taped against the walls were stirring, as though a ghostly hand was leafing through them surreptitiously.

Click. An alien sound, this. Tiny, but it jerked his attention toward the door as though he was tethered to a leash. He forced his breathing to stay even, closed his eyes until they were mere slits.

One moment the gap between door and jamb was empty and then, there it was. A figure. Moving quickly.

The intruder was nervous. He could smell him.

The figure stopped beside the bed.

Catapulting his body into an upright position, Adam slammed his hand into the intruder's throat, his fingers stiff. The gasp of pain that met his action was loud. He pushed himself to his feet, away from the bed, and rammed his shoulder into the body in front of him. The figure collapsed as though it had been cut off at the legs. Without hesitation, Adam straddled the prone figure, putting his weight on the man's chest. Grabbing the intruder's windpipe, he squeezed hard.

He heard Justine shout in confused alarm and the next moment she had switched on the light.

The face looking up at him was contorted. The eyes were filled with tears of anger and pain. A gurgling sound came from the half-open mouth.

Adam relaxed his grip slightly. In response a strangled noise and an attempt to hit him.

"Stop that." Adam tightened his grip again. "Or I'll keep this up until you pass out."

"I know him."

He looked over his shoulder. Justine was staring at the man on the ground. "I know him," she repeated.

He looked back at the face in front of him. Sharp-chinned, pimply, a straggly mustache clinging to the upper lip.

Painfully thin. Very young. A kid, really. But in his belt was a knife, unsheathed, and it was not the kind of knife you slipped into the dishwasher after dinner. Large, with serrated edges, it was a knife with which to intimidate, a knife that could do serious damage. He pulled it out of the waistband and flung it to one said. The kid winced, breathed shallowly through his nose.

"Who is he?"

"Timmy somebody. He trespassed once before, he and his girlfriend. We had a run-in, outside in the courtyard. I should have called the police then, but there didn't seem to be much point."

"Take the belt off your robe. Use it to tie his hands."

She shook her head. "I've got something better." She reached out to the table and picked up a roll of silver duct tape. "Standard photographer's equipment," she said as she kneeled down beside him.

When she was finished taping the intruder's hands, they looked at each other, then at Timmy, who was easing himself into a sitting position, then at each other once again. In her eyes he could see the question that was forming inside his own mind. *Now what?*

And to make it worse, as they stood there suddenly speechless, he saw the weaselly face look past his shoulder and the expression first turning into puzzlement and then into dawning comprehension.

Adam turned his head and looked straight into a photograph that was ten years old. His own. The picture Justine had cut out of the newspaper and had blown up to several times the original size. *Face of a Killer.*

He looked at Justine. "He recognized me."

She nodded, her eyes stricken.

He felt as though time had become suspended. It was so quiet he could hear the trickle of water down a pipe, the soft dragging sound of leaves barely scratching the windowpane.

In some part of his brain was the realization that what happened next could determine the outcome of more than just this night. But he felt paralyzed, unable to even pick up his hand.

"Adam." Justine's face had sharpened. The expression in her eyes was one of such ice-cold determination, he could only stare. "Get him to his feet."

"Oh, shit." Timmy's voice had shot up an octave. "I won't tell, man. Don't kill me. I swear I won't tell."

"Shut up." Justine's voice was a whiplash. She walked over to the closet and opened the door. "Bring him here."

He dragged Timmy to his feet.

She prodded the boy in the shoulder. "Turn around."

"What?" Timmy was looking at her fearfully.

"I said, turn around."

He turned around slowly. His one eyelid was twitching, and he was making involuntary sucking noises with his lips.

Adam watched as Justine picked up the small bronze statuette of the cowboy on horseback from where it rested on the table. She positioned herself behind Timmy. The next moment she had swung the statuette against the boy's head. With a soft sigh he crumpled to his feet.

"What the hell—" The suddenness of the whole thing had taken Adam by complete surprise.

Justine's face was white. "Is he out?"

Adam sank to his knees and placed his fingers on the boy's pulse. Then he pulled up the eyelids.

"He's out all right. Christ, you could have killed him."

"I didn't hit him that hard. Put him in the closet and lock the door. Come on, we don't have much time."

He stared at her.

"Adam, do it. You have to go. Now. I have to call the police."

"The police? There's no way he's not going to tell them what he saw. We should just let him go."

"He's going to tell, anyway. Whether I call the police or not. He'll brag about it to his friends, his girl, whomever. I know his type. Besides, I remember now. His mother is into unsolved crimes and all that. His girlfriend told me the mother even goes to inquests." Justine smiled grimly. "She's a big fan of yours. No way he'll keep it from her. So I'm going to call the police first and tell them I found a burglar in my house and they should come over immediately."

"And then? When he tells them about me?"

"I'll say he's lying his ass off. That I don't know what the hell he's talking about. They'll think he's trying to get himself out of an incriminating situation. Who are they going to believe. Me? Or him? What was he doing in my room to begin with? And with that knife? They'll believe me. I know they will. And while I'm waiting for them I'll clean up. Just you make sure to take all your stuff with you. Oh, wait." She picked up the knife and wiped it with the corner of her nightdress. "Your prints are on this." Kneeling beside Timmy, she pressed the boy's flaccid fingers around the hilt.

He watched, dazed. "If they're going to dust for prints, they're going to find my prints, anyway."

"They won't dust for prints. Maybe the knife, but that's all."

"They're never going to believe you managed to overpower him all by yourself. They'll know you had help."

"No, they won't. That's why I knocked him over the head. I'll tell them I tied him up after I got him with the statuette. Lucky blow. Now help me get him into the closet and lock the door. *Come on.*"

SHE WAS SHAKING. SHE couldn't stop shivering.

He was scribbling a telephone number on a piece of paper. "Here. This number belongs to my friend Mark, the one I told you about. He knows about you. Don't call him from the UK—I don't want to expose him to any risk. But when you get to Namibia, call him. He'll get in touch with me."

She took the paper from him. The number danced before her eyes. "I won't come to you for at least another month, she said, pushing the piece of paper into the pocket of her robe. "Maybe longer. Just in case the police do decide to watch me. I'll give notice. No one is going to think it odd that I'd like to get away from this place after a break-in. But I'll do it properly, take my time so as not to arouse any suspicions. I won't contact you at all during this time—no calls, no letters—and you shouldn't call me, either."

He shook his head emphatically. "How will I know you're all right? That you're not in trouble with the police?"

"If it comes to that I'll have my solicitor call your friend. That way it will remain privileged communication and the police won't know about it. But if you don't hear from me, everything is OK."

Adam's face was hard and set. He brushed the hair from her forehead, then cupped her face in his palms.

"I love you, Justine."

She didn't trust herself to speak. She closed her eyes and forced back the tears.

"Don't be sad." He kissed her eyelids, his lips barely brushing her skin. "Warriors, remember?"

She nodded, tried to smile. She clasped her hands to her arms to try and stop the shivering, which was now gripping her entire body.

"You're cold." He pulled her into his arms and draped the sides of his coat around her so that she was cocooned in his warmth. She stood without moving, trying to breathe in his essence. The scent of his skin. The sound of his beating heart.

He stepped back. "I should go. Are you sure you'll be all right with that guy upstairs? He's probably awake by now."

She tried to keep her voice light. "He'd better behave if he doesn't want to be knocked over the head again."

He gave her a strange little half-smile. "You're quite a woman, Justine Callaway." He touched his hand to his head in an abbreviated salute. The next moment he had turned around and was running swiftly down the stairs.

She stood in the open doorway, watching him as he hurried down the avenue of trees. There was a break in the clouds and a moon peeped through the ragged edges. She could see his shadow following his hasty footsteps. But as he moved farther and farther away from her, she had the strangest sensation. It was as if she could not see the dark shape of his figure anymore, only his moon shadow.

Twenty-nine

SERGEANT PAUL GOODWIN LOWERED his notebook and placed the pen in his pocket. With difficulty he stifled a yawn. He was tired. The new baby was not yet in a routine and he and Lucy were getting precious little sleep. He had just drifted off after another pajama drill when the phone had rung. It was the station telling him to get over to Paradine Park and to make it snappish. There had been a break-in and the intruder was still on the premises. PC Evans was on his way over there already, but they needed him to take charge. Robeson should have handled it, but he had been called out to take care of a domestic disturbance: Mr. Castle knocking his wife about again.

He yawned again and looked across to where the girl was sitting. She certainly looked knackered as well, poor thing. She had her robe clutched around her so tightly her knuckles showed white, and even from where he was sitting he could see she was shaking. Well, no wonder. If it had been Lucy, she'd have been in hysterics good and proper.

"Miss Callaway . . ."

She did not answer. She was looking into space. "Miss Callaway," he said again, louder, and with a start she transferred her gaze to his face.

"I'm sorry, did you say something?"

"We'll put him in the lock-up tonight. Do you think you could stop by at the station tomorrow? To formalize your statement."

"Of course."

She bit her lip and her face was suddenly so white, he wondered if she was going to pass out.

"Can I call someone for you? Family, a friend?"

She seemed to consider. Then she said, "Maybe I'll call my mother. She's in London."

He looked around him. They were sitting in the library, it looked like. He glanced at the florid murals and moved his shoulders uncomfortably. What a spooky place. He wouldn't be happy staying here on his own and that's the truth.

He looked back at her. "We discovered how he got in. He broke a window in the kitchen."

"I didn't hear it."

"Well, it is a big house."

"Thirty rooms." She nodded.

"A lot of places to hide."

"I suppose so. I've never thought of it that way before, but after this I don't think I'll be staying on. I'll probably give my notice tomorrow."

"I'm sure I can't blame you."

He looked down at his notebook again. Her statement had been straightforward, but he hadn't managed to get much sense out of Tim March. The creep was babbling about Adam Buchanan returning to the house, which was certainly the biggest load of rubbish he had ever heard.

The murder at Paradine Park was before his time, but he knew about it. The present chief constable had worked the case initially and still talked about it every now and then. But

March was simply trying to get off a sticky wicket by fabri-
cating such a feeble lie. He had probably gotten the idea
from all the newspaper clippings lying around. Miss Callaway had already explained that she was a photojournalist
and was thinking about doing an article on the house and its
history. That was one of the reasons she had taken the job,
she said.

He wasn't exactly surprised to find Tim March in a situation like this. He had been caught shoplifting and there was
the joyriding incident. Also, he always had his suspicions
about the mugging of that architect who rented from Mrs.
McEvoy—nice enough chap but no denying there's a limp
wrist there. He was sure it was a hate crime and that March
had been involved. They could never find any evidence to
pin it on him, more's the pity. Vicious little bugger. Miss
Callaway was bloody lucky she managed to hit him over the
head otherwise who knows what might have happened. Especially with her being so tiny.

He got to his feet. "Well, that's it for now. I'll be seeing
you at the station tomorrow then."

"I'll be there."

He took the hand she held out at him. It was small and
cold.

"Are you sure you're all right, miss?"

She gave him a tired smile. "No, I'm not. Not just this
minute. But don't worry about me." She paused. "I know I'll
be fine."

SHE SHUT THE FRONT door firmly behind the two police officers.
For a moment she leaned against it with her back, listening
to the car outside revving up, the wheels crunching on the
gravel and then the noise of the engine dying away.

The two police officers had seemed to believe her story,
but if Tim March stuck to his version of events with enough

conviction, who knows? They may start to investigate more thoroughly. She had only the haziest idea of what such an investigation might entail: phone taps, opening her mail? It was a good thing she had made Adam promise not to get in touch with her until she arrived in Namibia herself.

It was then that it really hit her.

He was gone.

The realization took the very breath from her body. For a moment she actually placed her hands against her stomach.

Feeling like an old woman, she walked slowly across the hall. Earlier tonight, she and Adam had danced here, lost in each other. It felt like a million years ago. Now there was no music. And everything seemed over-bright. She reached for the light switch and the hall sank back into shadow.

As she placed her hand on the banister of the staircase she paused. A slit of yellow showed underneath the swinging door leading to the kitchen. The light was still on in there. She'd better go turn it off.

She walked over and placed her hand on the door. Before she could put her weight against it, the swinging door opened into her face with the force of a freight train. Her head snapped back on her shoulders and the world went black.

You will be looking at me with your night eyes.

The similarities between a camera and the human eye are remarkable. Both are designed to catch and manipulate light. The Watcher wondered if Justine had ever given a thought as to how much the two mechanisms resembled each other.

He tentatively touched her face. There was no response. She was out cold. Legs sprawling. Head tilted to the side. Her eyes were closed, the lashes black spikes against the soft skin of her lower lid.

You will be looking at me with your night eyes.

The retina is the camera film of the eye. Covering the

back of the eye, it consists of millions of photoreceptor cells, which convert light into electrical signals that are channeled through the optic nerve and into the brain.

Just like a camera, the retina needs light. It cannot function without it. Light is life.

But too much light is darkness.

The Watcher knew the time had come to act decisively. During his enforced absence he had given a great deal of thought as to what his next course of action should be. He was now clear in his mind what had to be done.

His emotions had always been secondhand emotions. Every sensation filtered. He would experience feelings about a feeling rather than the feeling itself. His fantasies and sensations were the fantasies and sensations of the other players in the game. Justine had changed all that. What he felt for her was immediate and intense.

But if the game were to continue indefinitely, there were two problems he needed to solve. One: Adam Buchanan. Two: his own weakness.

Was it at all a surprise to find that Buchanan had made his way over here? For a moment he recalled the shock—the sickening lurch of his heart—as he had looked through the frost-rimmed window. His fingers frozen, his breath a bloom of white in the chilly night air. Unaware of the cold. His mind stunned by the beauty of the scene he was watching.

They were dancing. The man and the woman were gliding together to the music of a silent melody. The woman smiling with delight. The man touching her face with such tenderness it had made the Watcher's heart ache. He had recognized the inevitability of that moment.

Nine years ago he had let Adam Buchanan go. It had been his choice. This time, his choice would be different.

Buchanan had become an obstacle. But not for much longer. The Watcher was reminded of that old Persian proverb: *When its time has come, the prey goes to the hunter.*

The time had come.

Fortunately, Buchanan was now on the run again. The whole episode with Tim March was a bonus. And come morning the Watcher would see to it that the police were fully informed as to where Adam Buchanan was heading. An anonymous tip should do it.

First problem taken care of. The second problem was more intractable.

He had to face facts. It was only a matter of time before he would give in to temptation and force Justine to look at him, really look at him. The compulsion to have her recognize him for who he is was growing. But if he gave in, the game would be over. He didn't want that. So he had come up with a plan that would protect him against his own weakness and still allow the game to continue. He had spent the past three weeks putting the plan together. It had required a lot of research.

The Watcher touched his face. He was wearing a pair of goggles. The goggles were very large and covered his face all the way past his cheekbones.

After making sure the goggles fit to his satisfaction, he opened his bag and extracted a piece of equipment that had the appearance of a very large laptop computer with its keyboard missing. Attached to the box was a long thin tube, which ended in a pen-shaped object. He plugged the box into the power outlet in the wall and the screen lit up.

It was amazing how easy it had been to obtain this surgical diode laser. He hadn't even had to buy it. The number of Web sites on the Internet actually renting out laser systems was quite astonishing. What had attracted him to this particular model was the fact that it was compact, lightweight, and portable. Even more important, it was able to operate from a standard electrical outlet.

Although only suitable for soft tissue work, this little laser packed a big punch. It came in a 20-watt configuration with 810 nanometers diodes equipped with a flexible fiber deliv-

ery system. Once he beamed the light into her eyes, the focusing effect of the cornea and lens would increase the irra-
diance on the retina by up to 100,000 times. The light
absorbed by the retinal tissue would be converted to heat by
the melanin granules in the pigmented epithelium or by pho-
tochemical action to the photoreceptors. The light entering
her eye would be such a concentrated force, it would burn
right through the retinal cells and destroy them without any
hope of repair.

She probably wouldn't even blink. The aversion reflex
was absent in the presence of light of 700 to 144 nanometers—near infrared intensity.

Of course, he was no surgeon. And in order to perform
true precision work a split lamp was needed, which would be
completely impractical in this situation. So he was taking a
calculated risk. But even if complete blindness did not result, he was betting that the macula would be severely damaged. She would be unable to view fine details. She would
not be able to read. Or type. Or work a camera.

Or recognize faces.

For a moment the enormity of what he was about to do
made him pause. But he had no choice. And there would be
no pain. He wasn't a madman. No hacking at her eyes with a
sharp object or splattering her face with acid. Just the purest
light.

And he was not planning on abandoning her in her disabled state. He would be there for her, a hero on a white
horse coming to her aid in her darkest hour. Just like Rock
Hudson with Jane Wyman. It would be a big step for him.
From Watcher to participant . . .

She was starting to come to. Her mouth moved and her
lips made a light smacking sound. Her eyes rolled restlessly
underneath the smooth lids. He should do this now before
she regained full consciousness.

Leaning forward, he placed the palm of his hand across

her eyes. But then, within the embrace of his fingers, he felt her eyelashes open and close like a butterfly's wings.

PAIN. THE ONE SIDE of her cheek hurt fiercely.

She opened her eyes, but there seemed to be something resting on her face. A hand. Not her own.

The realization shocked her into full consciousness. She tried to heave herself into a sitting position, but a strong arm kept her down. At the same time the hand moved away from her eyes.

She screamed. She couldn't help herself, the grotesque goggled head was so unexpected, for a moment she didn't know what it was she was looking at. He appeared not quite human. The effect of some kind of monstrous being towering over her was heightened by the fact that he had rubbed his face and neck with black pigment. Coal? He was sweating and the drops of sweat streaked palely through the dirt.

He brought a finger to his lips. A shushing gesture. He wanted her quiet. And indeed, she thought despairingly, who would hear? She could scream her head off and no one would come.

Her hands were useless. He had tied them together. So she still had her legs free, didn't she? *Come on, Justine! Kick him where he lives!* She drew back her leg and kicked wildly. It didn't connect. She tried to roll out from underneath him, but he easily restrained her. He said something but he was whispering and in her panicked state her mind refused to make sense of the words.

"Stop it."

This time the whispered words were clear. "Stop it, Justine."

The use of her name made her heart miss a beat.

"I don't want to hurt you." Still that creepy, whispery voice, but every word uttered carefully and with emphasis.

"But I will if you don't stop fussing. I can easily knock you out again. Would you like that? No? So stop it. I just want to show you something."

She ceased struggling, but her body was tight with tension. She wished she could see his face more clearly, without all the black stuff. And the visor was unnerving. If she could see him without the mask she would be able to anticipate his moves more easily. She tried to make out the flattened features behind the goggles. Had she ever seen this man before? He knew her name and maybe the whispering meant she could recognize his voice. But his face—what she could see of it— did not remind her of anyone she had ever met. Or did it?

He was now sitting spread-eagled over her. The smell of his skin made her nauseous. Her tied hands felt awkward. But the rope was not that tight. Would she be able to work one of her hands free?

He was reaching behind him. For a moment she thought he had a knife in his hand. But it wasn't a knife, it was merely a long penlike object attached to a tube of some kind. The pen had a delicate hook at the top.

"I just need you to look at me. That's all. Look at this."

He slowly brought the thing in his hand close to her face. "Don't be afraid."

She stared at the object unblinkingly. He was holding it delicately and his hand was trembling. There was something mesmerizing about the smooth elegant shape.

Again he turned around, reaching with one hand for something on the floor next to them. She couldn't see clearly, it was on the periphery of her vision, but it appeared to be some kind of lit box.

He coughed—a nervous sound. It snapped her out of her stupor.

With a massive effort she brought her bound hands from her side, swinging them violently upward, knocking the object from his fist. He shouted something and lunged for it.

He was scrabbling sideways and his weight on her body

eased somewhat. She brought her knee up with as much venom as she could muster and caught him squarely in the crotch. There wasn't much momentum behind the swing, but she had hurt him nevertheless. He made a noise at once surprised, pain-filled, and angry. She immediately jerked her upper body straight up and head-butted him with all the desperation inside of her. She connected with the goggles and pain flooded through her head. But again, he grunted. She was doing damage. Rolling madly to one side, she managed to get her upper body free from his hand. His one leg was still pinning her down, but she swung her elbow into his midriff. Even with her hands tied, there was still enough force in the movement to halt him. His body slackened.

She was free. She could feel him reach for her legs as she crawled away and she screamed again. Long and uncontrollably. Fear clotting her brain. No one to hear, but the horror taking over. And then she was running up the staircase; stumbling, righting herself, taking the steps two at a time. Her tied hands made balancing a problem, but she was moving her wrists vigorously and she could feel her right hand starting to work itself free.

He was following her. She sensed him behind her. Terror ripped through her body. Thoughts no longer coherent ricocheted through her mind like bullets hitting steel. Her mouth was moving and she knew she was constantly repeating the same words. *Adam. Adam. Please. Please.*

He was gaining on her. Oh, God. Her limbs felt sluggish, her brain stupid. If only she could get to her room. If only she could get her hands free to lock the door. Get to the phone . . .

She would never make it. As she reached the landing, he flung himself at her like a rugby player, and she catapulted forward. *No. Get up! Get up! Don't let him trap you on the floor again.* But her hand was finally free. She grasped the railing and managed to pull herself upward. He rammed his body into hers and she felt the edge of the balustrade cut into her back.

"Why? What do you think you're doing?" He was no longer whispering. He was shouting at her and his breath was ragged. The eyes behind the goggles were crazed. "I've been watching you tonight. You and Adam Buchanan."

He knows about Adam? She stared at him, shocked. He must have seen the surprise in her eyes because he laughed. "Oh yes. I know about the two of you. I'm part of your story now, you know. You'll never know how much." The knowing intimacy of his tone made her shiver.

"What do you want?"

"It is not a question of want. It's a question of what is right. Buchanan killed his brother. I don't think he should be rewarded for his act, do you?" He cocked an eye at her as though expecting her to answer.

When she simply stared at him, he continued. "No. He should not. No happily ever after with the woman he loves. That would go against the laws of nature and justice."

"What are you going to do?" Her voice sounded hoarse.

"I'll be letting the police know about Adam Buchanan, you can count on that."

Anger flooded through her body. Lunging out she pulled the goggles straight down his face. The strap snagged on one ear but she tugged viciously and it came loose.

The scream that left his lips was frightful. His mouth stretched wide and she could see his glistening tongue. His eyebrows arched high against his forehead. His eyes were rimmed with white.

"What have you done?" He lifted his hand and hit her across the face. Pain shot through her jaw with such intensity that her breath exploded from her body in a sob. "I didn't want this. Now you know me. Now you know who I am."

Through the haze of pain the black smeared features of the face in front of her struck no chord of memory. For a moment she felt like laughing hysterically. All this, and she didn't even recognize the guy.

But then it hit her.

The church. A man who looked like a jolly little bear. A jolly little bear with fangs.

He drew in his breath with a hissing sound and grabbed her face. His thumb and forefinger cut into the hollow between her cheekbones and her teeth.

"You wanted to look at me. So look at me then. Look at me."

She stared at him, eyes watering with pain and fear. His face was so close to hers it seemed out of proportion, huge. She tried to look away, but his grip was iron. She wasn't even able to move her head. They stood motionless, staring at each other.

But then he made an odd moaning sound and brought his hands to his face in a strangely defensive gesture. He stepped back.

This was her chance. Her eyes darted to the passage leading to her room. Go for the telephone. *Now*.

But he saw her move. He stepped forward, blocking her way. She expected him to pull her toward him again but instead he was pushing her. His fist jabbed at her chest. He was pushing her backward toward the stairs. Jab. Jab. She tried to get out of his reach, but his march on her was relentless. Jab. Jab. She was moving backward fast. Her foot rested on the edge of the top step of the staircase.

He was coming for her again, pushing hard against her. Jab. Jab. He was trying to push her down the stairs. He was succeeding, she felt her foot slip. At the very last moment she grabbed his arm. *I go down! You go down!* She felt him resist but then she was falling, falling and he was falling with her.

How many steps? She let go of him, tried to break her fall with her hands but still she went tumbling. Stairs. Ceiling. Wall. Rolling over and over. A rag doll. Her head slammed into the marble floor at the bottom of the staircase. He was already there, waiting. He was lying on his stomach, staring at her.

Her vision was blurring. Flashes at the edges of her consciousness. She struggled to her feet, swaying on rubbery legs. The table lamp on the console table was made of heavy brass. She pulled it down. He was still lying prone, watching her.

No happily ever after with the woman he loves . . . I'll be letting the police know about Adam Buchanan, you can count on that.

She brought the lamp down on his head with all the strength she had in her body. It smashed into his skull with a moist, mind-shuddering smack.

Her legs gave way and she sank to the floor. Just before she lost consciousness, she wondered with a strange feeling of detachment why the darkness she was entering was colored white.

Thirty

JUSTINE. JUSTINE.

Someone was calling her. Over and over again. Insistent. Tiring. She wished the voice would stop.

A faint red glow on the other side of her eyelids. The color of the sun falling through a colored glass window. Pretty. She tried to open her eyes to see better, but someone must have glued them together because they wouldn't open.

Justine. Open your eyes, Justine.

Well, she would if she could, now wouldn't she? She tried again. No go. Her eyes were pieces of rock. Dead.

Fear. It was replacing the irritation in her mind. Why couldn't she see?

Justine. Come on, Justine.

The voice again. Her insistent cheerleader.

The fear was growing. What if she tried and tried and her eyes never opened? Maybe it would be easier not to try, to simply fall back again into the soft darkness . . .

Something she needed to do. Someone she needed to find.

Try again. So hard. Like struggling to get out of quicksand.

The red glow growing in strength. Someone she needed to see . . .

Adam.

Her eyes opened into a room bright with sunshine.

Her mother's voice. "Thank God."

THE NEXT TWO DAYS brought increasing clarity and coherence.

She was in the hospital. She had sustained head trauma. Two of her ribs were cracked, her jaw had suffered damage and the cut above her lip had required stitches. But all in all, the nurse assured her cheerfully, it could have been much worse.

At that moment, it was difficult to see how. Despite the drugs, every time she moved her head, a steel skewer rotated its way up her neck. It hurt to breathe.

"I was so worried about you." Her mother's voice was the shaky voice of an old woman. "When they called me and told me you were in hospital . . ."

"Who found me?"

"You called 999 yourself. Don't you remember?"

She shook her head, winced. Moving her head was not a clever thing to do. "A phone call? I don't remember anything about that. All I remember is passing out."

Another memory, this one horribly fresh and stamped with fear. She pushed herself upright. "What happened to—"

"It's all right, darling. He's gone."

"Gone?"

Her mother hesitated. "He's dead."

"Yes." Justine leaned back against the pillows and closed her eyes. In her mind the memory of a lamp heavy in her hands. The sickening feel of metal hitting flesh.

"He can never hurt you again."

He can never hurt Adam.

"He broke his neck."

Her eyes flew open. "What?"

"When he fell down the stairs. That's what the police say. Justine . . . What's the matter?"

But she couldn't speak. She was laughing, laughing even though the tears were running down her cheeks.

THE POLICE CAME LATER and filled in the rest of the blank pieces. But they were unable to answer the one question that occupied her mind.

"Why me? I met the guy once. That's all. Once."

DI Donald Josephs shrugged. He was a tall, almost impossibly handsome man. And she noticed he had really expensive taste in clothes. The cut of his suit was impeccable. His tie whispered Hermès. Not at all her idea of a policeman.

"It's impossible to know why Wyatt fixated on you. It could have been anything. If it's any consolation, you were not his only victim. We've searched his place and he had entire filing cabinets filled with notes on people he stalked."

"Did he hurt them?"

Josephs hesitated. "One—we think. A woman, three years ago. Drowned in her own bathtub after sustaining a head injury. From what we managed to glean from his notes on her, we're pretty sure he was responsible. So, I'd say you can count yourself lucky."

"He had this—" She hesitated, how to describe it? "—penlike thing attached to a tube, which he wanted me to look at. Do you know what that was?"

Josephs threw a look at his partner. DI George Ackroyd fitted her profile of a police officer a whole lot better. Grizzled, beer tummy, weary-looking. He spoke with a voice coated in cigarette tar. "He wanted you to look at it?"

"Yes. He said it wouldn't hurt."

Ackroyd sighed. "Depends on what you call 'hurt.' That thing was a laser. It could have fried your eyeballs." He sighed again. "Pretty sick."

Pretty sick. No kidding. She swallowed hard.

"You certainly had an eventful night." Josephs again. "Knocking out two men in one evening."

For a moment she didn't understand. "Two men?"

"Tim March."

An icicle of caution slid down her spine. She looked at him warily. "Oh . . . yes. Yes, of course."

"We still need to talk to you about exactly what happened, Ms. Callaway. March gave the police a rather . . . imaginative . . . version of events. We'll need to go through your statement again." He got to his feet. "We realize, of course, that you're not well. There's no rush. But as soon as you feel up to it, we'll have a talk."

Josephs had shrewd eyes. She had only just noticed. Her breathing felt shallow. Careful. Be careful. She had toyed with the idea of calling Adam from one of the hospital phones, but that was definitely out. Not while this well-dressed shark was circling.

She wondered if he had sensed the sudden tension within her. Her heart was beating triple-time. But she managed to smile warmly. "Certainly. Let's talk later."

Thirty-one

THE DAY WAS VERY hot. The spire of Kepler Bay's only church floated in the haze of heat. As Adam walked into the town he narrowed his eyes against the glare of a wrinkled sky.

He hadn't seen this place in almost a month, but it felt as though he had never been away. After his midnight flight from Paradine Park, the rest of the journey back home had been completely uneventful. There were no news flashes on the radio or TV. No uniformed men pulled him from his airplane seat at the very last minute. He had prepared for the worst and in the end the trip had been almost anticlimactic.

It was hellishly difficult to stop himself from calling Justine. He ached to hear her voice and to make sure she was OK. He supposed she was right, though; at this point self-discipline was needed. They would be together soon enough. Until then, extreme caution was the name of the game.

It was noon and he could see no one on the streets. There was also little sign of life in the tiny houses with their deep verandas. It was difficult to believe that anyone actually lived behind those old-fashioned lace curtains. He passed by a front door that stood open and caught a brief glimpse of a dark sunless interior. The swing chair on the porch of the neighboring house was moving slowly back and forth as though someone had just vacated it. But the rest of the town seemed deserted.

Mark's house was an old colonial building that had once been used by the Germans as the town's administrative offices and later as a girls' boarding school. As he approached the front door, he noticed new scaffolding at the side of the house. Restoring this white elephant of a place was an ongoing project of Mark's. But out here it was mostly all do-it-yourself, and unfortunately Mark was not handy—a clumsiness strange in someone whose hands could wield a surgeon's knife with breathtaking skill.

He lowered the knocker to the door and waited. This time of day he was sure to find Mark at home. He always had lunch with Rita between twelve and one.

The door opened. It was Rita. He only had time to register her distraught expression before she threw her arms around his neck, squeezing so tight he gasped for breath. "Oh, Adam." Her voice was a sob. "Oh, thank God. Thank God you're back."

THE CURTAINS INSIDE THE house were drawn against the heat. The passage leading to Mark's bedroom was gloomy. Against the shadowy walls were photographs of Mark and Rita's boy, Simon—an entire gallery recording every milestone in Simon's short life: birth, first steps, first day of school, a photo of Simon in the company of fellow rugby players, all of them looking disheveled but proudly holding aloft a gleaming trophy.

He had just reached the door to Mark's room when it opened and Kobus Vos, Mark's partner, stepped out. In his hand he had his black doctor's bag.

"Kobus."

"Adam." They shook hands.

"How is he?"

Vos sighed. "He'll be fine. But someone roughed him up really badly. He was kicked in the head. One of his ears was almost torn off. His body is very bruised but there are no bones broken—a miracle if you ask me."

"Rita says Grachikov did it."

"There's no proof, Adam. Grachikov has an alibi. Says he was playing cards with his friends. Who knows if that's true. But the person who did this was clever. And Mark said there was more than one. Unfortunately he wasn't able to see properly because it was dark—he had been called out to see a patient—and also because they had thrown a sheet over his head before getting down to business."

"What about his hands."

Vos looked tired. "They took off the little finger."

"Oh God. Will he be able to operate again?"

"Maybe. I don't know. It's his right hand."

Adam closed his eyes and rubbed his fingers across his face. "Can I go in?"

"Sure. He'll be glad to see you. But he may not be awake for long. I just gave him his pills." Vos nodded at Adam and started to walk back down the passage.

Adam knocked softly and received a muffled reply. He gently pushed open the door.

The curtains in this room were only partly drawn. On the bedside table stood three plastic capsule bottles and next to them a glass and a pitcher of water. There were several arrangements of dried flowers in the room; fresh flowers weren't really an option in this part of the world. Adam guessed they were from some of Mark's patients.

"Hey." He walked closer, his eyes on the figure in the bed. He could feel his face growing stiff with shock.

From where he lay propped up against a mountain of pillows, Mark smiled at him. The smile was grotesque. Mark's upper lip was badly torn and he had lost several teeth. His face seemed to be twice its normal size, the cheeks swollen and gleaming with some kind of ointment. One side of his head was bandaged as was his one hand. His eyes stared at Adam from purple sockets.

"Don't look so shocked. I'll live. Weeds don't wither."

Adam cleared his throat. "I knew I couldn't trust you to look after yourself. I go away and look what happens."

Mark gave the ghost of a laugh. "So next time, don't go away."

For a while the two men merely looked at each other. Then Adam leaned over and gripped Mark's healthy hand in his. "Mark, I'm so sorry."

"Oh." That dreadful lopsided grin again. "What must be must be."

"Tell me about it," Adam said. "I want to know everything."

"I will, but first . . . did you find her?"

"Yes." Adam smiled. "Yes, I did."

HE LEFT THE ROOM half an hour later. Mark's words had become progressively slurred and by the time Adam pulled the door quietly shut behind him, Mark was asleep, his head turned from the neck, his body set in a stiff unnatural angle.

As he walked down the passage toward the kitchen to find Rita, Adam was aware of a headache that was settling just behind his eyes. He recognized it for what it was: a deep, slow-burning anger. It had been building up inside of him as he had sat there watching his friend's battered face. This was a good man. A man whose life made a difference to others. Not many people left a mark. Most people when they die leave behind little of value. But if Mark were to fall away, the lives of many people would be affected for the worse. This windswept little town, hundreds of miles away from civilization, desperately needed men like Mark for its survival.

He paused outside the door to the kitchen. Rita was sitting at the kitchen table. In front of her were two white ceramic bowls. She was shelling peas. She did not notice him at first and he was able to observe her. Her long black hair, flecked with gray, was braided and pinned to her head. The soft heavy breasts sagged underneath the flowered dress she was wearing. On her face was a great weariness.

She looked up and saw him standing there.

"Adam. How is he?"

"He's sleeping." He sat down in the chair opposite her.

She nodded and picked up another pod from one of the bowls. She was looking down at her hands, her expression calm, but from the corner of one eye a tiny, pinched tear was rolling down her cheek.

"Rita." He placed his hand on hers.

"I'm so scared, Adam."

"Don't be. He's going to be OK. Kobus told me so."

"But what if they come back?"

"Come back? No, sweetheart. I don't think they will. These guys are cowards."

"They told him they would."

"What?" He stared at her. "Mark didn't tell me this."

She nodded. The tears were flowing easily now. "They told him they weren't finished with him. That they're coming back for the other hand."

He continued staring at her, but he wasn't seeing her face. The anger that gripped him was now a black thing that blotted out thought.

"Adam?"

The apprehensive note in her voice got through to him. He blinked. She was looking at him with alarm. The tears had stopped but her eyes were wide.

"I have to go." He squeezed her hand, got to his feet carefully. "Tell Mark I'll be back."

It wouldn't take him long to track the man down.

Grachikov was usually in one of two places: his office at the canning factory, or the Purple Palace. As the sun was still high in the sky, he was probably in his office.

And so it proved to be. Even before he pushed open the office door, Adam could hear Grachikov's voice on the other side. The man was talking in Russian, the rapid stream of words and thick consonants sounding like a round of machine-gun fire. He turned the handle and placed his shoulder against the door.

Grachikov was in a swivel chair facing the window, the telephone to his ear. As Adam burst into the room, he spun the chair around. The expression on his face changed from annoyance to caution. He mumbled something into the phone and replaced it slowly on its stand.

"Mr. Williams . . . you're back. I thought maybe you leave us forever."

Adam walked to the desk and gripped the edge with both hands. "I only need to know one thing from you. Did you do it?"

Grachikov leaned back in his chair. His face was expressionless. His eyes were cold and calculating. He didn't answer.

"You fucking coward. You don't even have the guts to own up to what you've done. What a man."

Grachikov flushed brick red. In a quiet voice, he said, "As I told your friend. You look for trouble, you find it."

Without hesitation, Adam launched himself across the desk. His hands gripped the sides of Grachikov's collar. Grachikov was a very big man indeed, but his anger was so great that he pulled the man right out of his chair and threw him across the desk. Grachikov crashed to the floor. He shouted. Adam pulled back his arm and smacked his fist straight into Grachikov's face. He felt the nose break underneath his hand.

His mind had shut down. He was hitting the face in front of him again and again. Blood. So brightly red he felt some surprise. The flesh underneath his fist soft, pulpy. Grachikov's head lolling on his shoulders. Again and again. The muscles in his arm bunching painfully as he smashed his fist downward. Grachikov's mouth moving wetly. He was saying something but he made no sound. His eyes rolled whitely inside his head and again he said something.

Please.

A trivial word. It stopped him like a bullet.

He looked down at his hands. The one hand was smeared with blood and what looked like snot. He slowly wiped it against his shirt and stared, stupefied, at the red streak his fingers left behind.

He got to his feet. His ears were buzzing as though they heard the roar of a thousand oceans. He felt lightheaded and inside his head was a black hole, a vortex sucking in all sensations, all rational thought.

He stumbled out the door and down the steps, past two men who had come running. As he walked away, his legs buckling, he heard them shout after him.

He stopped and bent forward. The sunlight beat down on him, but his skin was cold as ice. The next moment he was throwing up, his stomach muscles jerking violently, a stream of thin, sour liquid leaving his mouth.

Oh God. He closed his eyes. Oh God.

Thirty-two

SHE COULD HARDLY BELIEVE she was almost there. Journey's end was in sight.

Justine shifted in her seat and tried to stretch her cramped legs. Twelve hours in an airplane cabin did wicked things to your body. And since her fall down the staircase at Paradine Park, her back acted up under the slightest provocation. Whenever she stayed in one position for too long, a red-hot poker would replace her spine. She couldn't wait to get out of this chair.

The plane had left Heathrow last night, crossing the continent of Africa in darkness. They had encountered bad weather and for the first part of the journey she had seen blue flashes of lightning just beyond the wing of the plane. Thousands of miles below her, cloaked in black, were forests, crystal rivers, teeming cities, and barren plains imprinted with the fossilized footprints of giant lizards. But she saw nothing: not a light, not even the glow of a fire. She had gone to sleep with a vast continent drifting by silently and invisibly beneath her feet.

But now, long fingers of molten light were burning into the inky blackness of the sky. Red and orange streaks stabbed the horizon. And as she looked down with sleep-dazed eyes, she had her first glimpse of the desert.

It looked old. That was her first thought. How old, how ancient the corrugated mountain ranges and vast open plains. The chain of mountains looked like the spine of an immensely old animal; the dry riverbeds and their tributaries streaked across the cracked earth like shallow veins. And there, in the distance, coated in apricot light, the dunes, long ribbons of shimmering summits. The enormous ripples of sand stretched ahead as far as the eye could see.

She placed her forehead against the window and stared down unblinkingly at the terrible beauty of the landscape below her.

THE BLAND MODERNITY OF the city of Windhoek was a shock. As she looked out the dust streaked window of the taxicab, the scene that met her eyes seemed deeply strange. Independence Avenue, which appeared to be the main thoroughfare, was lined with pavement cafes, shops, even fountains. From her research she knew that Windhoek was the country's capital city and seat of government, as well as home to a significant number of Namibia's population of one and a half million people. But the sheer ordinariness of the place was mind-bending after her glimpse of the vast primordial landscape that slumbered just outside the town's borders.

Her hotel was nondescript and the room with its bed, TV, and speckled carpet looked like a million other hotel rooms anywhere else on the planet. She lowered her suitcase and collapsed on the bed. For a few minutes she simply lay quietly, her eyes closed.

She had made it. Finally. She still couldn't believe she was actually here. It had taken so much longer than she had thought it would.

In the end the police were not the problem. They had pretty much accepted her story of the night's events. Tim March would be spending the next two months in jail. Even though she continued to be supremely cautious, things seemed to be going better than she had any right to expect.

But then, one day before she was due to leave the hospital, she came down with nosocomial pneumonia. How the hell one manages to contract pneumonia lying in a well-heated hospital room was still beyond her, but there it was. For two weeks her chest filled with fluid and on top of it a virulent infection settled in her ear. Not good. She had never felt as sick before in her entire life. When she finally left her hospital room, she was so weak, her only choice was to move in with her mother. But her sojourn in the house in St. John's Wood had been unexpectedly calm. To say that she and her mother had found each other during this time would be a gross exaggeration, but they had managed to discourse like civilized people, even finding some small pleasure in each other's company. Her mother had even accepted without comment or reproach her explanation that she would be traveling to Africa on assignment as soon as she felt better and that she did not know how long she would be away for. And her mother hadn't mentioned Barry's name once.

Last night she was finally well enough to board the plane that would take her south. And now, here she was. Tomorrow she would take yet another plane—prop this time—which would deposit her deep within the southwestern Namib.

She glanced at her watch. It was difficult to believe that although she had traveled for twelve hours by air, the time difference between the UK and Namibia was minimal.

She opened her handbag and took out her wallet. Tucked in between her credit cards was the slip of paper with the telephone number Adam had scribbled down in such haste.

She had been very tempted to call the number after she had moved into her mother's house. One time she had even found herself with her hand on the telephone pad, the receiver against her ear. But her paranoia had stopped her going through with it. What if she was wrong? What if the police were suspicious after all and were simply waiting for her to make a wrong move? What if they were unobtrusively monitoring her? Even the slightest risk at this stage of the game was unacceptable. She also didn't call from the airport last night. She was almost there, anyway.

Well, here goes. She was suddenly nervous; her mouth felt dry. Picking up the receiver she asked the operator to connect her to a phone number in the town of Kepler's Bay.

As she waited for the connection to go through, she glanced out the window. The sun was so *bright*.

Thirty-three

THE SUN WAS BRIGHT. The morning mist had already burned away and the sky above them was an unbroken blue. The air was filled with the screeches of seabirds and the bass-baritone honking of seals.

The two men stood side by side, their hands quick, their movements neat as they went through the checklist of diving equipment: line reels, waterproof lamps, cylinders, harnesses, compasses, regulators, gauges, knives . . .

Mark placed his hand on a green diving cylinder. On the side was stenciled in white lettering: OXYGEN. Mark was using his right hand, clutching the bottle in a four-fingered grip. Adam looked away quickly.

This morning they were planning a three and a half martini dive, going down the caves at Giant's Castle to a depth of a 170 feet. They had considered using "trimix," a combination of helium, oxygen, and air, which would lessen the effects of narcosis and help them maintain better mental clarity down there, but in the end they had decided against it.

Apart from the fact that trimix was expensive and had to be carefully prepared, it would require them to carry even more bottles, including a separate bottle of argon to inflate their dry suits. Both men had done dives to 170 feet before on air alone, so it made sense to keep it simple.

Mark was whistling under his breath. *If you were the only girl in the world, and I was the only boy . . .* Adam knew that Mark usually whistled when he was feeling tense. He looked at his friend with concern. Mark was a good diver, but he was suddenly worried that Mark wasn't up to the dive today. Mark looked OK; the bruises he had sustained in the mugging were mostly all gone, except for the scar at the top of one eyebrow, the result of a fourteen-stitch wound. Still, a dive like this was stressful and Mark's body as well as his mind had had only seven weeks to recover from the trauma they had been subjected to. But Mark had insisted on this dive. "If I do it, maybe Rita will stop treating me like an invalid." Adam guessed it was also Mark's way of trying to establish control over his life again. He knew nothing he said was going to change Mark's mind. Besides which, he didn't feel he had the right. The ocean was a great healer. When things had gone badly for him in his own life, he had always turned to deep water. In the cool embrace of water, most everyday problems seemed manageable.

As he checked the five-foot-long hose of the octopus regulator, Adam's eye fell on the thin scar that ran across his own knuckles. The scar was the result of Grachikov's teeth slicing into the skin as he had tightened his hand into a fist. It looked as though the scar would be permanent. For a moment a memory of hard teeth and soft bloodied lips sprang to his mind. He winced.

Grachikov had ended up in the hospital with a concussion but he hadn't pressed charges and for that Adam was grateful. If he had, the police might have started to probe into his own background. Grachikov had probably refrained from making trouble for him because he did not want his movements on the night of Mark's attack to be scrutinized in greater detail. So the police were out of it, but everyone in town knew what had happened.

Adam had no illusions: the war between him and Grachikov was not over. Retaliation was inevitable. But this was not what troubled Adam.

Lying on his bed at night, eyes wide open, he would remember the moment he had succumbed to violence once again, as though for one instant a curtain of rotten fabric had given way, exposing a yawning black hole in which rage swirled like something dark and viscous. He could have killed the man. He almost did. And he'd lie there, filled with self-loathing and fear.

At these times his longing for Justine was fierce. Hold me, he thought. Place your hands on my lips. Close my eyes. Rescue me.

But where was she? Fifty-one days had passed since he had left her on the steps of Paradine Park. The memory of that cold night—Justine shivering, her eyes frightened, her shoulders set with such determination—was starting to fade into the heat and wind of the desert. A few days after they had said goodbye, he had been able to recall every gesture, every word. But now his memory was softening, as though hollow pockets were developing inside his mind.

Two nights ago he couldn't stand it any more and had called the number of Paradine Park from the post office, only to be informed that the number he was trying to reach had been disconnected. He had stood with the receiver to his ear, suddenly—irrationally—terrified. *Justine, where are you?*

"Did you hear that?"

He looked up. Mark was standing with his head to one side, listening.

"What?"

"I thought I heard the sound of a motorboat."

Adam concentrated but all he heard was a massive stir of echoes boomeranging around the cliff face, hundreds of birds, all of them screeching at once. But it was not inconceivable that a motorboat might be approaching. It was probably only a fisherman emptying his lobster pots.

He shook his head. "I don't hear anything."

Mark shrugged, unconcerned. "It was just for a second there. Probably my imagination." He brought his hand to his eyes. "The sea looks toxic this morning."

Adam straightened and his gaze followed Mark's. In the distance, past the still waters of the lagoon in front of them, the ocean was stained a strange electric-colored turquoise. Adam did not need the turquoise bloom of the sea to tell him what was happening. His nose had already picked up the rotten-egg odor, which warned that they were in for a bad period. For the next few days fish and rock lobsters were going to die by the hundreds. This happened every now and then. The southerly winds, assisted by the earth's rotation, was transporting surface water in an offshore direction. The surface water was being replaced by cold deep-lying water, which sometimes contained very low oxygen levels because of the rapid degradation of the organic-rich material of the bottom sediment that was welling upward. This process of sulfate reduction by anoxic bacteria produced poisonous hydrogen sulphide and the gas was bad news to marine life. They would be finding beached, dead fish for days to come. The wind that was blowing today was truly an ill wind.

With a last look at the deadly water sparkling blue-green in the distance, Adam turned his back on the ocean. He stretched out his hand toward his harness. "So, shall we get going?"

The two men donned their dive gear slowly, methodically, each attaching to himself equipment weighing almost 200 pounds. On came the diving harnesses with tanks and a myriad of hoses leading to gauges, inflators, and mouthpieces. Neatly stowed around their bodies were knives, backup lights, and line reels—everything duplicated in case of loss or failure. On their arms they carried dive computers, compasses, depth gauges, and watches. The number of items they were taking with them was stupendous, but nothing was carried that was not needed. The process of kitting-up took some time, but they each had their own routine that never varied, a self-imposed discipline that was a vital part of the mental preparation for the dive and which prevented them from inadvertently leaving behind something important.

They were just about to start moving in the direction of the water when Mark's radio crackled ominously from where he had left it underneath his canvas pants.

"Shit." Mark staggered toward the pile of clothes.

Adam continued moving backward toward the water. Maybe he was going to make the dive alone, after all. This call could only be from Rita or Kobus informing Mark of an emergency.

He stopped at the water's edge. Mark was standing with his back to him and Adam could not see past the bulky tanks. From this distance the static crackle of the radio didn't make much sense either.

After listening for a few more moments, Mark slowly lowered the radio and replaced it underneath the clothes. Adam watched as his friend waddled awkwardly toward him.

"What is it? Bad news?"

Mark's face split into a grin. "No, good, buddy, good news, the best. And it's for you."

"For me?" Adam frowned.

"That was Rita. She has just had a call from, and I quote: 'A friend of Adam's who was very anxious that he should get this message at once.'"

Adam stared at Mark, his mind suddenly touched by hope. "Is it . . . ?"

"Yes, it's Justine. She's just arrived in Windhoek and will be taking the flight into Kepler's Bay tomorrow. She should be here by ten at the latest."

For a moment Adam was stunned. Then he gave an enormous whoop of joy. "Justine," he called and laughed. "Justine, Justine." His voice sailed into the air, echoed off the rock face, mingled with the cries of the birds who were joining in. "Justine, Justine."

FROM WHERE HE WAS watching, hidden behind an outcrop of rock, Grachikov could clearly see the figures of Mark Botha and Adam Williams within the sights of his binoculars. He watched uncomprehendingly as the two men clasped each other by the arms and started to do a supremely clumsy ring-around-a-rosy dance, laughing all the while. He was too far away to hear what they were saying, but this was clearly a celebration.

He lowered the binoculars. He had no idea what had given rise to the bizarre behavior of the two men and he didn't care. All he cared about was whether they were going to do the dive.

He brought the binoculars to his eyes again. Good. It looked as though they were going to go ahead with it. Adam Williams was hobbling backward toward the water, his swim fins turning his feet sideways. Botha was following. Both men were wearing a staggering array of tanks and bottles clipped to their harnesses and dangling from underneath their arms. So this was going to be a long dive. Grachikov smiled.

He himself didn't plan on going that deep or staying that long. Only long enough to do what he had come for and he would make it quick. He wanted to keep his decompression time to a minimum and get out of here and away as soon as possible. That's why he had taken a chance using the noisy motorboat. A rowing boat simply would not have been an option.

He blinked and tightened his grip on the binoculars. The two men had turned and were splashing into the water. One moment they were still within his sights—lumbering into the water with their cumbersome loads and looking like visitors from an alien world—the next moment they had vanished as though they had never been.

GLIDING SLIGHTLY ABOVE AND behind Adam, Mark watched as Adam carefully checked the line belay around the solid branch of a gnarled tree that had fallen—who knows how many years ago—into the cave's entrance. The tree looked like a giant figure that had drowned, its arms yearningly outstretched toward the water's surface. Light from the sun still penetrated the water at this level, but on the other side of the tree, beyond the slitted mouth of the cave system, the color of the water deepened into black.

As Mark waited for Adam to sort out his rig, he thought back to the radio call and Rita's placid voice conveying such an explosive message. He was truly happy for his friend. To be truthful, he had nursed all kinds of treacherous thoughts. Although Mark would never have dared utter these thoughts aloud, he hadn't been able to shake the feeling that Justine had gotten cold feet about coming out here. Thankfully, he was proven wrong. He couldn't wait to meet this woman; she had certainly arrived at just the right time.

Mark would never forget the bleakness on Adam's face the day after the incident with Grachikov. Adam had looked bereft, as though he had lost something of value.

"I thought in the nine years I've been out here, that I had changed—that I had put the beast to the sword. I was wrong. I might have killed that man."

"But you didn't. You stopped and you stopped of your own accord."

Adam's face retained its stunned look. "If only I could talk to Justine."

She was here now, Mark thought. May his friend find peace.

He watched as Adam swept his light in a slow deliberate

circle. It was the signal that it was OK for Mark to follow
him through the entrance. Mark returned the signal, and the
two men dropped weightlessly through the narrow entrance
and into deeper darkness. Almost simultaneously their powerful diving lights shot out bright beams of white. The blackness of the water gave way to a green glow, retreating from
the wash of light as if in panic. But as always, it felt to Mark
as though he could sense the weight of the darkness where it
lurked just outside the edges of his vision.

They were in the "Waiting Room," the large submerged
cavern acting as an entrance portal to the continuing cave
system. He and Adam would do their ten- and twenty-foot
decompression stops in this chamber on the way out and this
was where they would leave behind their oxygen bottles.
Breathing oxygen at depth was a big no-no because the resulting oxygen poisoning could push the diver into convul-
sions, causing him to drown. But he and Adam would only
be using the oxygen at these shallow decompression stops.
At this depth the oxygen would work wonders in helping
their bodies eliminate the excess nitrogen that builds up during a dive and significantly reduce their decompression time.

Pitching forward, they started to drop down swiftly.

YURI GHACHIKOV WAS SEARCHING for the entrance to the cave system. Cave diving held little appeal to him. He preferred
wreck diving where you could gather artifacts during your
dive to hold as souvenirs and exhibit to your brother divers
once you were back on the surface. Trophies: that was the
way to earn respect and admiration.

The bottom of the lagoon was soft and muddy. Right below him was a burrowing hagfish. The creature looked blind,
its reduced eyes covered with skin. He had a brief glimpse
of fleshy barbels encircling a jawless mouth before the
snake-like body disappeared in a swirl of brown water.

A few feet in front of him, a black shadow was taking on shape. The tree. He had found the entrance to the caves.

He swam closer, his eye caught by a gleam of white. Tied to one of the branches was a nylon guideline. Ah yes, Ariadne's thread. If it weren't for the regulator stuck between his lips, he would have smiled widely.

ADAM WAS CONTINUING TO follow the guideline with a practiced hand. Mark admired the skill with which Adam had laid and belayed the line. Guidelines were not easy to use. When they're set poorly, they could pull into every nook and crevice and lead the diver beneath an impossibly low undercut to the side of the passage. Adam had laid the line perfectly, making good use of natural and artificial belays to keep them on a central course. Mark knew exactly the kind of patience it required to attach the line firmly and securely at regular intervals, it was an exercise which he, himself, never relished doing. Suitable projections never seemed to exist when he was looking for them. Adam, on the other hand, operated as if he'd been born with line reel in hand.

Adam was now rounding a bend, his shadow in the beam of light expanding and retreating sinuously as it wrapped itself around the curve of the cave wall. The slow-moving water in these tunnels had created fantastic sculptures in its wake. In the wash of light Mark noticed a rock formation that looked for all the world like a weeping woman: the face weirdly elongated, the brows lowered in despair, the mouth open in anguish. A portrait of grief sculpted in darkness over millions of years.

He brought the dive computer up to eye-level. Still a long way to go.

GRACHIKOV ENTERED THE FIRST chamber of the system, leaving the light from the sun behind. He did not switch on his diving lights. For a few moments he hovered, trying to see if he could spot the diving lights of the two men who had entered the caves before him. But around him was only blackness.

Good. They were out of immediate range. He clicked on his lights and the water lit up.

Snaking downward in front and to the side of him was the white guideline of the two men and clipped to it the oxygen bottles the men would be using at their shallow twenty- and ten-feet decompression stops. He had plans for this line, but not yet. He needed it to guide him in the direction of the two divers: without it he would never find them in this maze where tunnels branched off, twisting and turning unpredictably.

He glanced at his watch. If he could keep his time down to ten minutes only, he may not even have to decompress on the way up.

With a powerful kick of the leg he started his descent.

ADAM EXAMINED THE PRESSURE gauges attached to his side-mounted tanks and consulted his dive computer. The readings indicated that it was time to unburden themselves of the stage tanks containing the air they'd need for exit and decompression. They would clip the stage tanks to the guideline and from here on proceed relatively unencumbered.

Up till now the tunnels had been roomy and the water quite clear with good visibility. There was a current here, and Adam was convinced there were other entrances and exits to this system, as yet undiscovered by them. The water was slow moving but the constant movement did help to disperse disturbed silt particles. As they penetrated deeper, however, they would encounter tight openings and try as they might, their movements would dislodge clouds of silt. Visibility would become a real problem.

Nothing they couldn't handle. So far the dive was going well. And why shouldn't it? From now on everything would work out well. It felt to him as though his blood was fizzing with joy; as though joy was pumping his heart—as life-giving a substance as the air he was sucking in through his regulator. Justine: tomorrow he would see her, draw her into his arms, feel her breath against his cheek. They would start their life together.

The magnitude of the idea suddenly gripped him.

A life together.

Mark had taken out his knife and was now scratching a large *Z* in the surface of the rock. The lines—a deep, mustard color—stood out against the dun-colored cave wall. The lines were not permanent; on their next dive they would probably already have vanished because of the movement of the water.

Adam swam toward his friend and scribbled on Mark's slate: *The Mark of Zorro?*

Mark was nodding vigorously; his eyes behind the mask crinkling with mirth.

Yes, a good dive. A good day.

GRACHIKOV HAD FOUND WHAT he was looking for. There, in the beam of his light, neatly clipped to the guideline, were the tanks containing the air the two men would need to finish their staged decompression and surface safely on their way back. Grachikov ran his hand over one of the bottles with satisfaction.

Up till now he had been following the guideline of the two men. Now he tied his own shorter search reel to a knobbly projection of rock. Clipping the men's decompression tanks to his harness, he swam away, following a tunnel, which was twisting off to the left. He wouldn't need to go far. He could park these tanks only a few yards beyond the curve in the cave wall here and the odds of the two men finding them would still be stupendous. There were several tunnels branching off and they wouldn't even know where to start looking. And with what he had in mind for their guideline, they may never even reach the original spot anyway.

He turned around and started to swim back, carelessly stirring up the muddy floor behind him. Now all that was left was to take care of the guideline.

Using his knife, he cut through the men's line and, line in hand, headed in the opposite direction. After swimming for a minute, randomly selecting tunnels and chambers, he found a suitable outcrop of rock and tied the line off. The men would be following this line, thinking it was going to lead them to their decompression tanks and eventually to the outside. But they would end up stranded here. And even if they managed to find their way back, by this time there would not be enough air for them to reach the surface. Their death-bloated bodies would hang suspended until someone—who knows when—found them.

Using his own guideline, Grachikov swam back to the original chamber. Giving a last look around him, he prepared to start his ascent.

MARK CHECKED HIS PRESSURE gauge and dive computer. What it showed him made him feel concerned. He seemed to be consuming air at a faster rate than he usually did. This was irritating. If his air supply was used too quickly, they would have to turn the dive early and they wouldn't be able to go as far as they had hoped. They had already passed the spot, which marked the limit of Adam's previous exploration and was now entering unchartered territory, the most exciting part of the dive. He certainly did not want to head for the exit now.

Mark wondered if the beating his body had received seven weeks ago was somehow responsible. His fitness level was probably not what it should be. Of course, he had never been able to match Adam's low level of air consumption. His friend's lungs had always been able to draw methodical breaths of air with incredible breathing efficiency. Still, in the past he had managed to hold his own. Today, though, the gauge was dropping far too quickly.

The shaft suddenly narrowed sharply, but Mark could see that it widened again after a few yards. For a moment he wondered if they'd have to remove their tanks, push the tanks through ahead of them and reattach them. They occasionally had to do that during a dive such as this.

But as they inched forward, it turned out not to be necessary after all. They just managed to squeeze through, their tanks giving a hollow clunk as they tapped the cave roof. But their movements and their exhalation bubbles had stirred up a vicious swirl of opaque silt.

Suddenly his diving lights were of no use. In front of him was only a green haze. He couldn't see Adam at all. He knew they were both holding the same line—he could feel the twitches down the fine cord transmitted from his friend—but his senses seemed to be shutting down. He couldn't see, sounds were muted, his hands were numb. For a few moments he felt unwelcome and surprising pangs of alarm.

His heart was starting to beat faster—he could feel it—and that, of course, was causing his breathing to increase and his air consumption to rise. Not good, he chided himself. Get it together. But controlled fear continued to lurk at the edges of his consciousness. As he swam forward unable to see, his eyes stretched open in an unblinking stare, he remembered Adam once saying that in a silt-out the best way forward was to close your eyes.

Close his eyes. How could he do that? Some part of his brain registered that Adam was right. If you kept your eyes open, you started imagining things, became even more disoriented. And as it was, his light was simply reflecting off a madly swirling curtain of silt and sand. He was effectively blind anyway. But the idea of going forward with his eyes shut seemed utterly unacceptable. It took several moments before he managed to force the lids together.

Darkness. Better, but the unknown forces were still there. His hand was on the guideline, following it inch by inch. It felt like an eternity before he felt something grasp his arm.

He opened his eyes. Adam was looking at him, making a hand gesture. The meaning was obvious: Adam wanted to know if he was all right. Mark brought his thumb and fore finger together to form a circle. Yes, he was OK.

But was he really? As he continued to follow Adam, he thought back on those moments of rising fear. What the hell had happened to him back there? This was certainly not the first blackout he had experienced. Had his run-in with Grachikov somehow affected him at some deeper level? Was he losing his nerve? Or maybe the martini effect was to blame as nitrogen continued to travel from his lungs to his blood, and from the blood into the tissues of his brain. Maybe his brain was getting fogged up from the narcosis, causing him to become slightly paranoid.

He glanced at his gauges once more and was alarmed. He had almost finished the first third of his air supply and would soon be on his second third. But this air was not to be used on the way in. That was the golden rule: one-third of your air supply for entering, one-third for leaving and one-third for emergencies. He should signal to Adam that it was time for him to turn the dive and head for the entrance.

But he held back. There was still a small margin remaining and he didn't want to let Adam down after such a poor show back there of his own making. He also didn't want his friend to think he was slurping up air at unacceptable levels—always bad form in a diving buddy.

No, he was going to hold off. He knew it was risky, pushing his air margins, but they would probably use less air on the exit. The guideline was already laid. They need only follow it back. Besides, the slight current would be in their favor on the way out. Just a few more minutes . . .

* * *

THEY HAD REACHED A depth of 170 feet and had been down below
for forty-five minutes. It was time to head back. Adam
touched Mark's shoulder and made the sharp thumbs-up
"back-to-entrance" signal. He had emptied his line reel,
which now hung motionless in the water, tied off at the fur-
thermost belay—a record of their deepest penetration so far.

Following the guideline, Adam started swimming back in
the direction they had come from, picking up the pace significantly. Each additional minute they stayed down here
would require additional decompression time and they were
looking at a good hour and a half of stops already.

The first order of business would be to retrieve their tanks
with the compressed air they would need for their ascent.
The guideline stretched ahead of them, a white thread spool-
ing in the direction of home, tracing its route through chambers, restrictions, along twisting tunnels . . .

Something was wrong.

Adam stopped swimming. He peered into the gloom.
Surely they should have reached the tanks by now? But
Mark was already pushing impatiently against his arm, sig-
naling that they should go forward.

He started swimming again, but a question mark was
starting to form in his mind. He didn't recognize this passage. Still, there was the line, their guide leading to safety.
Probably he was simply getting tired from the mental concentration required to overcome the effects of depth.

He rounded the curve of the cave wall and stopped, his
mind suddenly shouting with alarm.

Neatly tied off to an outcrop of rock was the guideline. It
led to nowhere.

WHAT WERE HIS LIMITS? How far was he prepared to go?

It was a question he—Yuri Konstantin Grachikov—had

asked of himself before, and now he knew the answer.

He had always considered himself a pragmatic man, but ever since he was a boy he had also believed in the concept of revenge. Humiliation called for retaliation, otherwise you could not call yourself a man. If he had let Adam Williams get away with what he had done, he—Grachikov—would have slowly sickened. Over the years the knowledge that another man had bested him so utterly would have eaten away at him like cancer, sucking from him his energy. Even had he continued to live his life elsewhere, where no one knew anything about his past, the memory of the contempt in Williams's voice, the dismissal in his eyes, the terrifying blows of his hands would have forever shadowed his thoughts, causing him to hesitate at crucial moments. What he had done today had been absolutely necessary in order for him to wrest back his self-respect.

It was sheer good fortune that he had found out about the two men's diving plans. Talking to his friend Jukka on the phone this morning, the man casually mentioned that the doctor and his friend had just left his shop and were on their way to Giant's Castle.

Good fortune, yes. But also fate. What was meant to be, was meant to be. Another man might not have had the guts to grasp the opportunity suddenly presented to him. People often misjudged him initially, fooled by his accent and his smile. But they always left the final losers in any confrontation.

Namibia had turned out to be a bad card for him. After the Pennington's Island fiasco, he was facing financial disaster. He had now finally faced up to the fact that there was no way he would ever be able to pay his creditors. So he was simply going to skip out. It was time he got going, anyway, the diamond trade was far too regulated in this country. Which was why he would be leaving for Angola tomorrow. He had already arranged for passage on a fishing trawler that was sailing up the coast to the Cote d'Ivoire. Even though he had business contacts in Angola, he had never visited the country before. He knew the trade in diamonds up there was rough and dirty and without rules. Such a place would suit him perfectly.

But although he was now anxious to leave, he was heartsick at the knowledge that his beautiful hotel would never become reality. The careful architect's drawing—an artwork in itself—was destined to be relegated to a dusty shelf in the planner's office. The thought gave him almost physical pain.

A gull suddenly plummeted from the sky and skimmed past the boat, causing him to look up, and he saw that the sun was climbing in the sky.

For a moment he looked in the direction of the far end of the lagoon. He could not see the cave entrance from here, but in his mind's eye he saw murky water and a black tree with an outstretched branch like the arm of a man reaching toward the light.

Feel: his pulse was calm. See: his mind was clear. He had done what he had set out to do smoothly, efficiently, with a minimum of fuss.

He fired up the engine and turned the wheel in the direction of the open sea.

THEY WERE LOST.

Mark's mind had stalled, but this one thought was stuck in his brain like a sharp-edged pebble lodged in a groove.

They were lost.

They were now swimming without using their legs, holding on to the side of the cave and dragging themselves forward with a pull-and-glide motion to conserve air. Arm muscles required less fuel than leg muscles. By not kicking, their air consumption would be lower.

Mark's head was throbbing, his mind filled with the repetitive sound of drumming: his beating heart. But he also felt strangely detached. He had stopped looking at his pressure gauge. What was the point? Whatever air he had left was all there was.

He was tiring. The sound of his heart so deafening, it made his skull feel soft. Was he going to die? Was he going to die here within this world where the color had bled out of everything, where one waterfilled cavern followed the other with numbing similarity? He did not want to die. He wanted to sce his son again. He wanted the chance to kiss his wife.

He was aware of his breathing, every breath inhaled, every breath exhaled. From the corner of his eyes he saw hands winking at him from the shadows. A disembodied face floated up from the cave mud. Come to me . . .

No. Stop it. This was the narcosis taking over. Get a grip. Concentrate. But he was so tired . . .

In front of him Adam had stopped. He was signaling something, but he was only able to stare at his friend stupidly, his mind slow to work.

"Mark!" Adam's grunt shook him into awareness. He blinked, his mind snapping into some sort of focus. He looked to where Adam was pointing.

In the side of the cave wall a sign. A giant Z.

At the same time that his heart leaped with relief, his mind exploded with a new fear.

Where were the tanks?

MARK WAS LOSING IT. Adam reached out and placed a calming hand on his friend's shoulder. The eyes behind the mask remained dilated. And Mark's movements showed how close to exhaustion he was.

But fear had entered Adam's own mind as well. It was coating his every thought like a sticky substance, slowing him down mentally, killing him physically. The adrenaline that flooded his body was causing his heart to beat too fast, his breathing to accelerate too quickly, his consumption of air to speed up horribly.

Stay calm. Adam closed his eyes and forced himself to breathe slowly, normally.

He opened his eyes and looked carefully around him. There was the Z. It was at this spot that they had tied the decompression tanks to the guideline. He had hoped that whoever was responsible for tampering with the line would simply have dropped the tanks right here. But no such luck. The scuba tanks were nowhere to be seen. Someone had wanted to make very sure indeed that they would not get out of here alive.

He checked the stop time remaining on his computer and the pressure left in his tanks. Bad but not awful. Not hopeless. He might just have enough compressed air to finish his decompression; that is if he juggled around with the oxygen tanks waiting for them at their twenty-foot decompression stop. It was a big if—the oxygen bottles may no longer be there, either.

He turned to Mark and checked his friend's pressure gauges. He felt his mind contract.

The readings were frightening. Unlike the pressure in his own tanks, Mark had little compressed air left.

For a long moment Adam stared at the readings, trying to force his mind not to implode with the significance of what he was looking at.

They had been down here far, far longer than they had planned. They needed to decompress. But between the two of them, they did not have enough air left for a staged ascent.

If they simply shot up to the surface, their bodies would collapse utterly under the onslaught of nitrogen bubbles. For a moment he remembered his long-ago diving buddy—blind, deaf, crippled by the bends—dying in agony after insufficient decompression. But if they stayed down below, they would drown.

Think. Don't panic. Think. But his heart was slack.

Think. No time. Act.

His movements methodical, Adam unclipped the tank from his harness. Taking a deep, deep breath from the tank, he affixed it to the shoulder ring of Mark's harness, taking care to affix it to his friend's hip ring as well. There was not enough air for two divers to ascend. There might be enough for one.

"What are you doing?"

Mark was shouting through his mouthpiece. The speech was disjointed, but the panic came through loud and clear.

Adam kept his eyes locked with Mark's. He signaled emphatically with his hand. Go!

Mark screamed. He flailed his arms wildly in denial.

Without hesitation, Adam grabbed his friend's face mask. Mark grunted in surprise. With one cut of his knife, Adam sliced through the strap. Mark, blinded, turned away and reached instinctively for his spare mask.

Kicking strongly, Adam finned away, back into the maze of tunnels. By the time Mark had his vision restored, he would be gone.

THE COLD. HE WAS feeling so cold. Adam looked at his hands, they appeared deathly white.

His diving light lit up the wall of the cave, which looked like melted wax. Against the wall, the outline of his shadow—a companion, keeping watch.

So cold. The seconds ticking by in strange slow motion. His chest hurting. His mind starting to shut down. The last thought at the moment of death determines the character of the next life. He remembered that from the Bardo, the Tibetan Book of the Dead. The last thought . . .

Justine—she was leaning over him, her arms encircling his head. As he looked up at her, her eyebrows were the wings of a bird and the curve of her lip looked like a kiss.

He is sitting on the wide windowsill, watching her as she bends from the hips. She is adjusting the volume of the music and her sweater is riding up against her back, exposing a glimpse of perfect skin. The high-ceilinged room filling up with sound, drowning them in melody. "You need to listen to the pauses, as well as the notes," she said, smiling at him over her shoulder. And he had thought back to the only time he had seen rain in the desert. Purple clouds against a green-tinted sky and a feeling that every single living thing was holding its breath. In the cities rain seemed noisy, the drops spattering against the black tarred roads, drumming against the windows, dripping from open gutters. In the desert, he had learned that rain had no sound.

When had he first known of Justine? How had the idea of her first entered his consciousness? He could not remember anymore. It was as if he had been walking in the desert, his eyes blinded by sand and then a tiny piece of grit had lodged itself in his heart, chafing the surrounding tissue, and from the dirt and the blood had bloomed a pearl, a thing of beauty.

How wide was a man's longing, how deep his dreams? For nine years he had tried to answer that question by writing to her, hundreds of pages of his thoughts, his doubts, his desires. How sad that she never got to read them.

He took out his diving knife and pressed the tip against the surface of the rock. The rock face here was crumbly. If you put enough pressure on the outer layer, it started to give way.

He increased the pressure on the knife and it released a shower of flakes. As he started to carve, the water around his hand became cloudy and he had difficulty seeing through the particles of dirt. But he continued to carve the string of words into the wall, the letters angular and spiky and of different sizes: the *J* of *Justine* out of proportion large to the rest.

So cold. His chest on fire. So tired.

He tilted his head back and the rocks above him soared upward like the vaulted ceiling of a cathedral. He let his arms fall to his side, his mind at peace.

His life, his different selves.

A small boy throwing into the air a model airplane made of wood and his mother laughing.

A killer fleeing the scene of his crime, the edges of his shoes wet with dew.

A man taking a book in his hands and reading words that seemed maimed and garbled, but persevering until the letters slipped into order and worlds opened inside his mind.

A woman parting her gown for him, her thighs cream in the darkness. His head on her stomach and her hand resting on the nape of his neck.

A wolf watching him and a closed door reflected in the moist arc of the animal's eye.

Adam turned his head to look at the door behind him. It was open.

Thirty-four

A STIFF SOUTHWESTERLY WIND was blowing and the tiny prop plane swerved from side to side. As it came in to land, it looked as though it might overshoot the runway, but then, with a clumsy three-pointed touchdown it landed and moved swiftly down the tarmac, its propellers slowly winding down.

The door of the small aircraft opened. A fat man in a Hawaiian shirt and a camera around his neck descended the rickety stairs. Behind him followed a woman in a yellow dress. Her face was hidden by a wide hat and Mark stared, his heart suddenly beating faster. But then she lifted her head and he saw that she was elderly.

The doorway remained blank. The plane looked like an outsized toy where it squatted on the runway. The wind blew. The sunlight was harsh. Nothing seemed to move inside the plane.

And then, there she was. She stood framed in the door-

way, looking in the direction of the small, tin-roofed building from where he was watching her through a smeared
plateglass window.

   She was wearing a long floating skirt and the wind tugged
at the hem. The enormous black sunglasses obscured most
of her face. But as she walked down the stairs and started to
cross the tarmac toward the entrance of the building, he
knew it could only be her. "Tiny," Adam had said, "but with
steel in her every movement. The way she carries herself is
one of the things I love about her the most. You'll see; it's
this extraordinary mixture of defiance and vulnerability."

   His palms were moist. His eyes were burning inside his
head.

   "Justine?"

   She turned toward him. "Yes?" There was a question mark
in her voice.

   "My name is Mark Botha."

   "Oh . . ." She smiled. She took off her glasses and he saw
that her eyes were blue.

   "Where's Adam?" she asked.

THE STRENGTH OF THE wind had increased. The sea was churn-
ing. From where she sat, she could see thick flecks of foam
blowing across the watery surface that gleamed like a mirror
caught in sunlight.

   "More tea?"

   Justine looked away from the window. Rita was hovering
with a teapot in her hand.

   She shook her head and pushed to one side the old-
fashioned teacup with its pattern of pink roses.

   Rita sat down again, perching awkwardly on the edge of
her seat. "Mark should be ready any minute."

   Justine nodded. She knew she should at least try to say
something to this woman who was looking at her with com-

passion, but her mind felt incapable of forming even the simplest of words.

On the laundry line outside two shirts and a pair of pants flapped wildly in the wind. The outside awning above the window was creaking.

The wind. She had been here for only three hours and already her brain felt tired from its constant presence.

"Does it ever stop?" The sound of her voice produced a slight shock in herself and she saw Rita start.

"The wind?"

"Yes. Is there ever an end to it?"

Rita sighed. "We have a few calm weeks in June. But the wind is always there. You become so used to it, you know." She glanced out the window. "I don't think it's going to continue at this strength all day, though. It should quiet down somewhat."

Silence again. They were now avoiding each other's eyes. They sat there, two women caught in a situation of having too much to say to each other, but also too little.

Then she saw Rita look past her shoulder, her face showing relief.

"Are you ready?" Mark was standing in the doorway, a bunch of keys clutched in his hand.

"Yes." Justine got up from her chair. For a moment the kitchen with its white painted cupboards and yellow check curtains was spinning about her. She took a deep breath and placed a steadying hand on the surface of the table.

"Yes, I'm ready."

THEY DID NOT SPEAK on the way. The roar of the wind and the sound of the Land Rover's engine would have made conversation difficult in any event.

For the first twenty minutes they stuck to the road, the ocean on their left, but then, without warning, Mark turned the Land Rover's nose inland. For the next few minutes Justine clutched the dashboard as the vehicle bumped and swayed, the wheels skidding in the thick folds of sand. She found herself instinctively pressing down on an imaginary brake pedal, but Mark seemed to be increasing their speed, pushing the revs way up so that the vehicle produced a high-pitched labored whine.

Suddenly—sticking up from behind a dune—the gaunt outline of a pitched roof. High against the stone wall a window staring at them like a damaged cyc.

She brought her hand to her throat.

THERE WAS NO LOCK on the door. As they entered, they had to step around the bulky shape of a motorcycle. The wheels were caked with dust.

On the windowsill, a gas lamp and a box of matches. Hanging from a peg on the wall, a bone-colored canvas coat and a hat, the suede band stained with the sweat of a man's head.

She walked slowly into the large room. It was quite bare. An armchair, table and stool, and an antique apothecary chest were the only pieces of furniture. On top of the desk was an old-fashioned nibbed pen and a pot of ink. Against one wall ran several shelves propped up by wooden brackets hammered into the wall. The shelves dipped in the middle from the weight of the many books.

Next to the single battered armchair, she paused.

The room still felt alive, she thought, as though it still expected to hear the footsteps of the man who once called this place home, who rested his head against the back of this chair, who read through these books, the oils from his fingers working into the pages.

She turned around. A passage led off the room. To the left, at the end of the passage was a doorframe—the hinges still attached, but no door. Through the opening she could see that it was the kitchen. She glimpsed a wooden crate filled with bottles of water, a large enamel bowl, a red and white tea towel, a plate, and an upside-down mug. To the right, the passage ended in a long narrow staircase. She started to climb the wooden steps, vaguely aware that Mark was following her.

It was much lighter on this floor. The rooms were large and empty with sun streaming through the windows, some of them without panes, completely open to the outside. There was sand on the floorboards.

She leaned against a wide wooden windowsill and looked out. From this vantage point she had a view of the other desolate houses that formed a straggling line, their pitched roofs tilted toward the horizon as if stoically challenging the constant onslaught of burning sun and wind-driven sand. And all around her the desert, so vast it took her breath away. Later this week she would release Adam's ashes into that wilderness. The thought seemed utterly surreal.

"His bedroom is over here."

Mark spoke behind her and she turned away from the window, blinking her eyes after the brightness outside.

A metal framed hospital bed with a thin mattress stood in the middle of the room. The sheets were white and the blanket navy blue. On an upturned crate, which served as a makeshift table, yet another gas lamp and next to it a book spread open and turned face down. Against one wall a metal rod from which hung wire hangers supporting two jackets, a few shirts, and three pairs of pants. A pair of walking boots with thick laces rested next to an open, woven basket holding underwear and pairs of socks. She picked up the book, taking care to keep her finger in the fold at which it was open. These would be some of the last words he had ever read.

I stayed, not minding me;
my forehead on the lover I reclined.
Earth ending, I went free,
left all my care behind
among the lilies falling out of mind.

She sat down on the edge of the bed, suddenly so exhausted she couldn't lift her hand.

"Justine."

She looked into Mark's face and the anguish she saw made her mind flinch. She wasn't up to dealing with anyone's pain right now, not even her own. Her heart was numb. Her eyes felt dusty as though no tears would ever flow from them again.

"He saved my life."

She waited.

"I don't know what to say to you. I feel responsible." Tears were rolling soundlessly down his cheeks.

The next moment he had crossed the room and was sitting on his knees in front of her, his arms clutching her legs tightly. He wept as though his heart was breaking. She placed her hand on his head. She could feel the wet tears seeping through the fabric of her skirt.

He was slowly calming down. His shoulders heaved once more and a shuddering breath left his body. He looked up at her, his eyes still blurred. "I'm so sorry."

For a moment she was silent, feeling eerily remote from his grief. But then she felt ashamed of herself. Adam had loved this man. And Mark must have gone through hell. She couldn't even imagine the torment he must have faced as he floated in the water for hours during his decompression, all the while knowing that Adam had already died somewhere in the tunnels below him.

Making an effort to keep her eyes fixed on his, she spoke slowly. "Adam had such respect for you, Mark, for what you were doing with your life. And you were a good friend—without you he would not have survived here, he told me that. He called you his brother, did you know that?"

"His brother?" Mark shook his head, his face still crumpled. He pulled out a handkerchief from his coat and blew his nose sharply.

"You say they found this man, Grachikov."

Mark nodded, his voice calmer. "Just in time. He was about to leave the country. He hadn't planned on my surviving, otherwise he probably would have made tracks immediately."

Silence. Then he said, "It's time to go. Rita will be waiting."

"No. I want you to leave me here. Come back for me tomorrow."

For a moment it looked as though he was going to argue with her. But then he simply said, "I'll leave the radio for you. Call if you need me."

As they walked outside, she heard—very faintly—the sound of church bells. Of course, it was Sunday. The sound drifted with the wind into the dunes from the direction of the sea.

When they reached the Land Rover, she placed her hand on his arm.

"When Adam was at Paradine Park I wanted to take his photograph. The only photograph I had of him was that dreadful one all the newspapers ran and in that picture, he is not the Adam I knew. But he wouldn't let me. So when he was asleep I sneaked a picture of him without his knowing about it."

She paused. "I developed the film after he had left for Namibia again. But he wasn't on it."

"I don't understand."

"It was as though he had never been there. There was the bed with the sheets rumpled and the pillow had a dent, just as you would expect if someone had rested his head on it. But the bed was empty. He wasn't there. No Adam, no wolf even."

"Wolf?" He frowned.

She shook her head impatiently, made a dismissive gesture with her hand. "What I mean is, it feels as though it was all in my imagination. As though I was so lonely and so desperate that I had created this image in my mind—perishable, not real—of the man I was yearning for. And I suddenly wondered if the seventeen days we spent together was only a waking dream."

She looked him in the eyes. "Adam had this idea of soul mates, you know."

"Yes."

"What a sad illusion that was. We have one life only and this is it. And somehow Adam and I have managed to cheat ourselves out of our chance together."

Mark hesitated. "I wanted to wait before giving these to you, but . . ." He opened the door of the Land Rover. Leaning into the interior of the vehicle, he opened the cubby hole. From inside he took a manila envelope.

"What is it?" she asked.

"Adam's watch. I thought you might like to have it. And a photograph."

"A photograph? Of Adam?"

He shook his head. "Adam left you a written message, Justine."

"He told me he had destroyed all the letters he wrote me."

"It's not a letter. Well, not in the conventional sense. When the rescue team went down to the caves yesterday, they found that Adam had carved some words into the cave wall before he . . . he . . ." Mark swallowed, continued swiftly. "Because I had told them that someone had tampered with our guideline and the tanks, they treated it as a crime scene and brought an underwater camera with them. So they took a picture. It's in there. The message was addressed to you."

She took the envelope from him with trembling fingers.

"You'll probably want to read it by yourself," he said. "I'll be back for you tomorrow first thing."

He got behind the wheel and turned the key in the ignition. The Land Rover growled into action. A spray of sand kicked up from underneath the back wheels.

She could hear the noise of the Land Rover long after she had lost sight of it and was left standing alone in front of the empty house, the envelope clutched in her shaking hand.

SHE WAS WALKING IN the direction of the ocean.

Water had been his solace. He had told her that this was where he had headed that night after he had casually opened a photography magazine, discovering a miracle inside. And so she was following in his footsteps.

As she walked past the desolate houses, she wondered wearily how Adam had managed to stand living among these derelict ghosts. The houses were decayed but their design was ornate; some even had tiered balconies and pillared entrances. They told of careful craftsmanship and the wealth to pay for it. The richest place in the world, Adam had told her, for a few months, anyway, in 1917, when the diamond rush was at its height. As she ghosted past the empty shells, the entire idea that these houses had once echoed to the sound of laughter and the voices of the living seemed absurd.

High in the bright blue sky was a gossamer thin moon. The sun was beating down on her. The wind blew sharp particles of sand against her skin.

She could hear the roar of the ocean drawing closer and then she crested a sleek white dune and the beach stretched out in front of her, miles and miles of pale sand and turquoise water. It was high tide and the driving wind was whipping the waves deep onto dry land. When the water pulled back, it left a thin film of slimy foam in its wake.

In the distance she could just make out the wreck of a stranded ship, the masts still tall and proud, the hull broken. It was pushed so high up dry land, it looked as though the crew had sailed the ship there on purpose, as though they had become confused, unable to distinguish between an ocean of water and an ocean of sand.

She sat down and crossed her legs, tucking her fluttering

skirt underneath her ankles. The envelope was not sealed and she lifted the flap and placed her hand inside.

She took out the watch first. He had been wearing this watch at Paradine Park and her heart jerked in recognition. The chunky knobs, the black Roman numerals—the watch was exactly as she remembered it. She fastened the watch around the wrist of her right arm where it dangled loosely. She was surprised at its weight.

She slid her hand back into the envelope and her fingers closed around the edges of the picture.

The quality of the photograph was surprisingly good. Even though the water was murky, she was able to read the words without any trouble. The size of the various letters were uneven and the words were strung together in a lopsided sentence:

Justine I will find you again

She placed her hand against her mouth but it was no use. She could not force back the sobs. Her entire body was shaking and the strangled sounds that forced their way past her fingers hurt her chest. She let her hand fall away and tipped back her head. And now she was howling, her mouth wide open. She shrieked his name, screamed into the roar of the ocean. The wind lashed her face and dried the tears immediately as they left her eyes. She placed both hands against her breast. Such terrible pain. Her heart would collapse under the burden of so much pain.

She did not know for how long she wept, but her body grew exhausted, the muscles in her shoulders tight and sore, her ribs aching. Her face felt swollen and a great tiredness made her lie down on her side and draw her legs up against her body. And there, in the hot sand with the repetitive, hallucinatory sound of crashing waves all around her, she went to sleep.

When she woke up, the first thing she noticed was that the wind had died down. The merest breath of a breeze lifted tendrils of hair off her forehead. The sand underneath her cheek was cool.

Dusk was at hand. The sea was calm, the waves broke quietly. The wet sand gleamed pink with the light of the setting sun. The first stars were out.

She was not alone. She knew that even before she turned her head. She was not alone.

The animal was barely eight feet away. He was watching her, body turned sideways, head lifted. The thick collar of hair around his neck was almost blond and the flanks were hazed with silver. But the long hair growing down the strong legs and sloping back was spotted with darker flecks, deepening into black. His shadow was an uncertain shape on the white sand turned dusky in the twilight.

Windwalker.

The ears were pricked, alert. The nose was black and moist. The eyes gleamed.

Her breath caught in her throat. The animal had lowered its head. One paw was poised hesitantly. She thought: he will come to me.

For a long, long moment they stared at each other. She sensed an ancient communion pass between them and the hairs on her arms lifted. She stretched out her hand yearningly, but the animal had turned away.

The strandwolf's gait was unhurried. The strong shoulders moved easily, gracefully. It rounded the hump of the dune and she could no longer see it.

Epilogue

The thick curtains were drawn tight against the windows, shutting out the blackness of the night. A table lamp with a scarf thrown over it to cut out the glare, and the flames from the gas fire at the far end of the room provided the only light. It was quiet outside except for the faint scream of a car alarm in the distance. The hands of the old-fashioned clock on the mantelpiece stood at four.

The man in the deep armchair stretched his legs and massaged his arthritic hands. He got to his feet, wincing at the dull ache, which had settled in his lumbar region.

Quietly he moved over to the bed. He brought his head close to that of the sleeping woman. She was lying on her back, her face half-turned, her mouth slightly open. Her long white hair was caught loosely in a bun that had started to unravel.

Satisfying himself that she was not in distress, the man returned to his chair. He tilted back his head against the headrest and allowed his tired eyes to wander through the room.

They came to rest on the writing table pushed up against one wall. On top of the gleaming surface were books neatly stacked on top of each other and photographs in silver-plated frames. He felt himself smile as his gaze moved from one to the other.

Justine standing in front of the poster announcing her first New York exhibition. Justine swinging Thomas in the air, his chubby little face alive with glee, his dumpy legs flailing. Justine adjusting Chloe's veil: mother and bride caught in the framework of an oblong mirror. The photograph he had taken of her on their silver anniversary: one of his favorite pictures. She was sitting at a candlelit table decked in white, a glass of champagne in her hand. By some trick of light the candles had reflected in her eyes, so that tiny flames danced in their depths. She was smiling at him as if in secret.

A soft groan made him glance quickly at the bed. She was moving her head restlessly back and forth.

"Barry . . ." Her voice was whisper thin. "Water."

He poured water from the carafe into the glass and helped her into a sitting position. As he slid his arm around her back, he could feel the ribs. She had lost so much weight. Her neck was thin and her head with the thick hair seemed out of proportion large.

"What time is it?"

"It's just after four."

She nodded and sank back into the pillows. Her hand, veined with blue, stretched out toward his. Her grip was still surprisingly strong.

"You look tired, old man." She smiled at him.

"I'll still be able to dance you off your feet."

"That will be the day." She smiled again, but her eyelids were already drooping and a spasm of pain flitted across her face.

Her courage was remarkable. It was twelve months since he had sat with her in the consultant's office, listening to a prognosis that had stunned him. His immediate reaction was denial—there were other specialists, other doctors—they would find someone who could help. She, in contrast, accepted the diagnosis stoically but she also refused to follow doctor's orders to slow down. "Live life ecstatically and with a vengeance" she said, "you know that's my motto."

And so they had traveled, camera in hand, to all her favorite places: the Blue Mosque; the Alhambra Palace; Florence; Salzburg and its music. And for three weeks the entire family—their two children and their partners, as well as their four grandchildren—had rented a house in the Lake District.

A month ago she had told him she wanted to come home.

There was only one photograph on her bedside table: a picture of a house with a pitched roof and scarred walls. The one window was without glass and the picture was taken from an angle so that the viewer looked straight through the peeling timber frame, the eye carrying onward through yet another broken window on the other side of the house and beyond it to the desert and a translucent horizon.

He had long since made peace with this photograph and with the memory of the man who had once lived within those walls. It was not always easy—sharing her with a ghost. He knew he would never be first in her heart. He knew his was not the face she saw in her dreams. He now accepted it, but when he was younger he had found himself jealous of a dead man. It had taken several years of marriage before he had reached a place in his life where he could simply be grateful for what he had.

And he did have so much. Justine had given him two wonderful children and she was indeed the joy of his life. Who would have thought the angry tortured woman with whom he had first fallen in love would develop into a supportive loving partner? He was aware she did not tell him her deepest doubts and most fervid desires. And she wasn't always happy—of course not—but she never flinched. She attacked life head-on. And she rarely talked about Adam Buchanan.

As a matter of fact, he could recall her mentioning Adam Buchanan only once. "He and I were meant to be," she had said simply. "But our journeys followed different routes. His journey was one of redemption. Mine was one of self-knowledge. The two did not overlap. The time line was off."

Her fingers twitched slightly and he looked down at her hand clasped in his. Until a month ago, she had worn watches on both her wrists. On the left wrist her own petite watch; on the right a man's watch with a thick chrome strap, its bulky shape making her wrist look even more fragile than it was. The watches were set at different times: the one an hour ahead of the other. But she didn't wear them any-more. Her skin was too sensitive now and her bones hurt.

She sighed deeply and he looked at her with concern. She was breathing so slowly all of a sudden. Surely no one could breathe this slowly. He leaned forward in alarm.

"Barry."

Her eyes were wide open and a tentative smile hovered at the corners of her mouth.

"What is it darling?" He placed his hand on her wrist. Her pulse was fluttering like the wings of a tired bird.

"Listen," she said. "Do you hear it?"

THE ROAR OF THE ocean was immense. She was running down a beach of sparkling sand and the pale dunes seemed ghostly in the light of the moon. The darkness was velvet. She was running freely, feeling none of the aches and pains of old age. She looked down at her hands and the skin was smooth, a young woman's skin. She laughed out loud and whispered a name into the wind.

The animal was beside her now. She sensed his presence. She couldn't see him, but his shadow was keeping pace. He was moving across the sand effortlessly and the strong loping gait was unmistakable. It was the powerful stride of a Windwalker.

The joy that swept through her was unlike anything she had ever known. Her mind soared, her heart ached with anticipation.

Adam, Adam. Wait for me. I'm coming.

Do You Believe?

by Ann Lawrence

0-765-34888-8 $6.99 ($9.99 CAN)

"I'll take my bag, please." She held out her hand. "I need to find my sister."

Vic pursed his lips. Her skin was pale, her freckles like scattered gold dust on white silk. How could he delay her?

He took a grip of a budding lust.

"Just because your sister hasn't returned a few e-mails doesn't mean she's missing. Maybe she met the man of her dreams."

"Don't." She shook her head. "Don't patronize me. I didn't fly over here because my sister failed to keep me informed of her social plans."

"Sorry, mate." He felt a compulsive desire to touch her. She had been his first thought when hunger had struck at dawn. And it hadn't been an English breakfast kind of hunger at that.

"Don't do it again," she said. "Now, good-bye."

"We were going to have tea."

"You can have tea. I want a cup of coffee. Black. Stand-your-hair-on-end black."

Her bum looked great as she stalked away.

"I have a coffee pot," he called.

She wheeled around. Her eyes were bright. She took a deep breath. "Mr. Drummond," she said. "If you can make a cup of coffee as well as you write about fornicating corpses, I'll follow you anywhere."

. . . coming in May 2005 from Tor Romance

Warprize

by Elizabeth Vaughan

0-765-35264-8 $6.99 ($9.99 CAN)

"Xylara, the Warlord has named his terms for peace." Xymund did not turn. He made his announcement as he stood looking out the window. His hands tightened around one another. I looked over at General Warren, who grimaced, and looked down at the floor.

"That is good to hear, Your Majesty." I swallowed, sensing a problem. "Are they acceptable?"

Xymund still did not turn. "I and my nobles are to swear fealty to him. The kingdom will remain under my control and the taxes and tithes that are to be paid are reasonable. All prisoners and wounded, if there are any, will be exchanged." There was a bitterness in his tone. Maybe because they had more of our men then we had of theirs. Xymund continued. "But he has claimed tribute."

My brother's gaze remained fixed on the horizon. My fears for a peace grew. If the Warlord claimed something of Xymund's his pride would forbid acceptance of the terms.

"What does he claim?" I took a step toward Xymund. Still, he did not turn. I looked around, but no one would meet my eyes.

At last, General Warren drew a breath. "You," he cleared his throat. "He claims you as tribute."

. . . coming in June 2005 from Tor Romance

The Dare

by Susan Kearney

0-765-35192-7 $6.99 ($7.99 CAN)

Inhaling the scent of his tangy breath, Dora savored the fact that Zical was coming to her in his own rough-hewn fashion. Ah, this was one of the reasons she'd so much wanted to be human, to experience the senses that fed the emotions that—

His lips caressed hers. He took his time, and the warmth of his mouth raked hers, heat slipping and sliding into her core, raising her temperature until a fever raged and erotic shivers trembled down her spine.

She parted her lips, welcoming his tongue and the taste of full-bodied masculine heat. Until now she hadn't understood how she could feel fire and ice together, in the same moment. She hadn't believed that every last sizzling cell in her body could be electrified by such a kiss, or how that energy could wrap her in a sensual cocoon of crisp and tangy desire. She hadn't understood that one kiss would make her want so much more.

Kissing Zical was like all the stars in the universe shining on her at once. Dora glowed from the inside out with a happy, uncontainable thrill that she would never forget. She wound her hands around his head, threaded her fingers into his thick dark hair, pressed her chest against his and reveled in the richly-textured sensations of humanity.

She, who had spent her life in a parched desert of circuitry, was drowning in lustrous, gleaming, torrid . . . life.

. . . coming in July 2005 from Tor Romance